Queen's Reprisal

By J.A. Peter

This book is a work of fiction. Any references to historical events, real people, or real places are used fictitiously. Other names, characters, places, events are products of the author's imagination and any resemblance to any person, place, name or event is entirely coincidental.

Copyright © 2024 by J.A. Peter

All rights reserved. No part of this book may be reproduced in any form or by electronic or mechanical means, including information storage and retrieval systems, without written permission from the author, except for the use of brief quotations in a book review.

Cover design J.A. Peter

A heartfelt and special thanks to my team for bringing this work to life.
Aaron Rakuu - Map artist
Belle Manuel - Copy editor
Belle Manuel - Line editor
Mia Hedgie - Cover artist
Xann Smith - Critique partner
Emma Morgan - Beta reader
Gina Wright - Beta reader
Blessing Mavin - Beta reader

I dedicate this work in loving memory of Laurana L. Hamlin-Shaw and to all those who supported me through this amazing opportunity and experience.

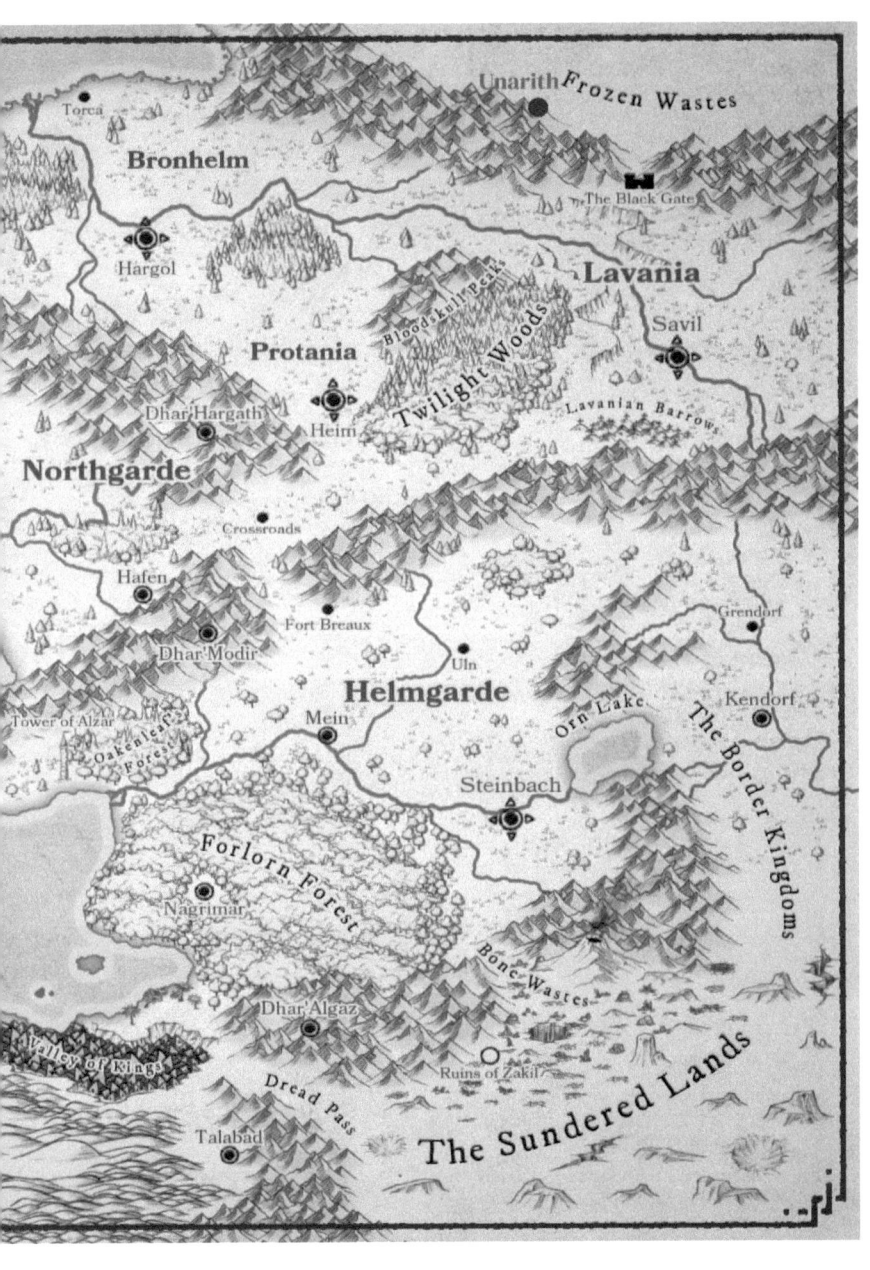

Chapter 1
The Cries of the Mourning

The town crier's solemn voice rang through the streets; however, Queen Darlana could barely hear him. Clutching her husband's pillow and daughter's stuffy, she curled inward, her body wracked with sobs. The scent of Velnir still clung to the fabric, a cruel reminder of what she had lost. Outside, the wailing of her people echoed through the palace walls. The queen's council sat in quiet contemplation patiently waiting for her to attend their scheduled meeting in the dimly lit council's chambers.

Queen Darlana clutched her husband's pillow and daughter's Ismi poppet, her grip trembling as the town crier's solemn voice echoed outside. His words pierced her soul, unleashing a torrent of tears. Her beloved daughter lost but never forgotten; her husband trapped in a heavy sleep despite her healing efforts. The assassin's blade, meant for her, shattered her world. The pillow's familiar scent wafted up, a heartbreaking reminder of her husband's absence. His fragrance still lingered. A bittersweet agony. Darlana's heart plummeted, crashing beneath guilt's oppressive weight. Sobs wracked her body, echoing through her chambers.

"By the celestials, why must I be alone?" she thought as she cried while gripping their things as tightly as she could.

Her servant gently knocked on her chamber door and did not say a word. Everyone was attempting to be as sensitive as possible but understood that she was queen, and she had her duty. Darlana was not pleased.

"Must I be queen on this day of days?" she yelled at her servant.

Outside the door, stood a petite elven woman who was herself crying. Everyone had grown to like Paeris and Velnir even though he was of Tanimaran birth. She had no desire to bother her queen today but knew it was her duty to remind the queen to meet with the council regardless of tragedy. Such is the responsibility of royalty.

She thought for a moment before speaking through the door. "My queen, I do apologize for the interruption, but your council awaits you."

Darlana had laid down and turned over in her bed facing away from the door. She had her nose buried in Velnir's pillow and took one more sniff before gently placing it back next to hers and putting Paeris's stuffy between them. It was soaked in her tears and snot. She sat up and threw on a silk gown and slippers. She didn't bother standing in front of the mirror, nor did she bathe first. She opened the door right as the servant was about to knock again. Startled, the servant stepped back.

"My queen, I…" she began.

"Do not wash his pillow," was all Darlana said before walking past her servant who hastily nodded and without another word, went into the queen's chambers to clean it up.

The queen's bard was still playing sad music and did not even notice that she had left. The room smelled of body odor and was a complete mess.

There were several tubs of what once was frozen cream with the utensils left in them all over the place and face tissues in piles all around the bed. Plates of half-eaten or *not-*eaten food were scattered about and on every conceivable surface possible.

The mage that was using cryomancy to freeze the queen's treats stepped out of the en suite with another tub of the frozen treat also not realizing that Darlana was gone. She turned her attention to the bard who sat down and closed his eyes, clearly exhausted. The mage moved over to him and also sat down. She nudged the bard to gain his attention and gave him a spoon. They began to share the treat as they welcomed a break.

***

"She has been in her chambers for a week," stated Magris.

"Understandable, considering the circumstances, General," said Meric.

Rizim didn't say anything but was observing the two younger dragons, Yzat and Nythint. It was clear that they were deeply hurt but chose not to say anything. They wore their emotions on their elven visages which was intriguing to Rizim.

Darlana entered the council chambers and had attempted to mask her overpowering scent with an elven perfume, but her pungent odor proved to be much stronger. The council observed her walking around the table and over to the drawer which was stocked with several boxes of facial tissue. She grabbed one and made her way to her seat. She sat down and opened the tissues while the others simply observed. She wiped her tears and blew hard. Her ears drooped, which was a sign that an elf was in a terrible mental state.

No one dared to say anything right away. It was up to Darlana to break the ice, and she took her time. She sat there with her arms folded and stared out the window observing griffins and hippogriffs. It was a comfortable sunny day and yet, it was somber.

A bell rang, indicating the beginning of the next hour. This snapped Darlana out of her moment. She sniffled before speaking.

"What news from your spies, Meric?" she asked.

Meric presented a letter with the seal of Madir. He turned his attention and grinned smugly at Darlana. "Thanks to the efforts of my esteemed colleagues, word of the assassination of Paeris and the attempt on Velnir has reached Tanimara. Many of the regions grew discontent but Atlantin, Caphry and Madir were openly speaking of rebellion as they viewed Velnir as a hero of Tanimara. Consequently, this forced the High Magister to bring the regions of Atlantin, Caphry and

Madir under his direct leadership and threatened military intervention and declared himself Emperor of Tanimara. He began having Magistrates, lords and ladies who he deems as a threat arrested and executed with the intent of replacing them with some that are sympathetic to his cause without elections. Atlantin, Caphry and Madir have seceded and are building up their armies seemingly preparing for civil war. This letter came from Madir and is signed by all the lords of Caphry, Madir and Atlantin to name Velnir High Magistrate of eastern Tanimara should he survive and be willing to aid their cause. It would seem that Raften's intentions are no longer a secret, and the republic has failed."

A glimmer of pleasure seemed to reveal itself through her darkened eyes. "Excellent work, Meric. The time to strike may yet sooner come." She then turned her attention to Magris. "What do you have for me, General?" she asked before grabbing another tissue.

"I have issued several contests to develop the next generation of weapons and armor that we could use to compete with Tanimaran weaponry and their overwhelming numbers. The criteria is simple—something to increase stealth, stronger armor, some type of rapid firing handheld device that is quickly reloadable among many other things. I have also increased the production of enchants and imports of spell components to keep up with the pyromancers and production of new armaments," said Magris.

She nodded and mustered a small smile to express her gratitude. "Thank you, General." She then turned her attention toward the dragons.

Yzat spoke up and stated, "I have taken an interest in metallurgy and am assisting in the production of armor with the smiths in the smelting district."

The other dragons did not say anything, so Darlana looked at Dravon.

"My queen, the people are not ready for another war. They are mourning the princess and may possibly as well for the king soon and will resume their protests after. I fear that there are not enough centaurs to keep the peace. Furthermore, Warlord Skroatug has not been seen but the orcs that retreated from the Sundered lands have made their way to the orcish lands farther to the eastern coast of Agia and assimilated into other clans. Rumors have spread that the clans are creating another mighty force and are planning a war of unimaginable magnitude. We must be ready if they intend to attack the Forlorn Forest," he said.

Darlana sat there and looked at him with daggers in her eyes. Her sadness had turned into anger for the moment, and it appeared she was going to take it out on the centaur general. Her facial expression changed from anger to understanding as his words settled in. She took a deep breath. Dravon had grown used to this by now. He tended to be the only one brave enough to tell her what she did not want to hear.

"My heart cannot handle this right now. I desire nothing more than to hug his pillow and relive our short memories," she thought.

She had not been married to Velnir for long and most of the time they were married, they were separated because of the war against the orcs and Maphisian transgression.

"Many Nagrimarans are fleeing to other elven kingdoms," said Meric.

"The elven king of the twilight woods... oh, what is his name," asked Magris.

"Glade-King Eldar," answered Meric.

"Right, thank you. Glade-King Eldar is welcoming them with open arms. He sent his condolences." Magris smirked.

Darlana shot a glare at Magris. "Eldar is most noble. He is a good king, and I could think of nowhere better for my people to be if they cannot be here with me."

"My queen, while noble, it is not helping our cause. We need to ramp up recruitment, increase morale and begin training. The Tanimarans are aware that the assassin failed to kill you but instead killed your daughter and wounded Velnir. It is only a matter of time before they try again," said Magris.

Tears began flowing down Darlana's cheeks. Meric shot a glare toward Magris. He looked at Meric and shrugged. Darlana was trying not to let it bother her.

"We sent out ambassadors to our allies and others who may be interested in the fall of Tanimara. What have we heard?" she asked.

"Most of the Araban city states are already at war with Tanimara. Over the last year, Raften has sent armies all over the world to capture and colonize areas rich in resources. Queen Sabreen has accepted your request and is mustering her forces now. Bronhelm, Lavainia, Northgarde, Helmgarde and the border kingdoms have denied your request fearing reprisal by the Tanimarans which have already broken their trade agreement with Nemis for acting against Tanimaran interest. Nemis offered to supply our forces with goods, allow the use of ports and are willing to give us a substantial loan along with Thebe, Talabad and Nartec of Araba so the only one willing to give us military support is Maphis. The dwarves of Dhar'Algaz are willing to assist if the Tanimarans come back to our continent but Dhar'Modir and Dhar'Hargath have not responded. The Magister of Madir has discreetly asked for our assistance to restore the republic."

"Even with all our gold, we do not have the forces to take on Tanimara," said Magris.

"We may not need to do it alone. Tanimara has stretched their forces very thin in an attempt to maintain their grasp on their territories across the world. The fear of Raften's desire to tighten his power over Tanimara has Madir, Atlan and Caphry in open rebellion. It is rumored that any who disagrees with him while the magistrate is in session simply disappears. If my source is truthful and correct, we can count on her support and with her help, I may be able to convince the other lords to help us," said Meric.

"Help us? If we were to march our armies to Tanimara, we would be helping them. We are not interested in the restoration of the Tanimaran republic. Discreetly write back to her. We will march our armies to Tarvana, and we will conquer it. After all, Tarvana is my birthright! They can help us if they are so inclined though I would not trust a Tanimaran. I would think they are more likely to take it for themselves if they could or they would not be asking us for help. Dragons make all the difference," said Darlana.

Magris and Meric donned an offended expression. Darlana did not notice or seem to care. Dravon spoke up. "I agree that it could prove valuable to attack while they are divided and spread thin, though an enemy on two fronts is not ideal."

Meric nodded and added, "it has also been reported that Tarvana is amassing a large fleet with supreme commander Vulas at the helm and rumor has it, Raften plans to deploy him and sail around the world and bring the rebellious colonies to heel. This is supported by the other rumor that he has called to arms all the houses loyal to Tarvana. At least, according to this letter."

"We would make quick work of ships. After all, we are dragons," said Rizim.

Darlana had her face buried in her hands while the other council members were speaking.

"Velnir remains in deep slumber at the Tower of Alzar and If the orcs are still a threat, then perhaps war with Tanimara is not in our best interest right now," she suggested.

The council chamber fell silent, Magris and Meric exchanged a weighted glance. Their eyes then swept the room, meeting others. The dragons, however, seemed apathetic, their expressions unreadable. Dravon, on the other hand, looked visibly relieved.

Meric's face darkened, his discontent evident. Magris's expression mirrored his, their shared desire for revenge still simmering. The memories of Paeris's brutal murder and Velnir's near-fatal attack remained raw, fueling their unrest.

"My queen," began Meric before he was interrupted by Darlana.

"I have a lot to consider, and I will do it alone and in my chambers. In the meantime, Dravon is right. We need to calm the nerves of the Nagrimarans. We must hold off on our talks of war for now," she said. She began to think of how they could bring happiness back to Nagrimar then an idea came to her. She looked around and forgot for the moment that her council was made up of all males. She sighed.

"I will plan a costume ball a week after the funeral procession of my daughter which is to be held in the palace. The nobles and military leadership are to be invited, and the denizens can participate in the courtyard. We will need food, desert and entertainment. Everyone is to wear an elegant costume and enjoy themselves. We have all suffered so much loss," said Darlana.

Magris and Meric were discontented but remained quiet. Dravon straightened up and told Darlana that they would keep the peace. Darlana got up and excused herself. She walked past Paeris' chambers and the memories of Velnir playing with her flooded her mind. She began to cry and hurried to her chambers. Her bed was made but Velnir's pillow and Paeris' stuffy were not moved. This warmed her heart as she crawled into her bed and began squeezing them tightly.

"Begin," she said.

The bard understood and began playing more sad music. The mage began using cryomancy to freeze more cream for Darlana.

Meric and Magris walked together out of the council chambers while the dragons, and Dravon went their own way.

"Why did you not tell her that we had several promising ideas for the contest," asked Meric.

"I did not want to burden her with it. For all we know, his invention may not work. We will test the weapons tomorrow. I will select a winner and award the contract," said Magris.

"In the meantime, she wants to throw a party after the procession of her daughter. I do not know why she did not give me the reins on this matter. I throw marvelous parties," said Meric with a confident tone. Magris scolded Meric and walked away without a word. "Perhaps that was in poor taste." He put the wine down with regret and was glad his queen was not present.

The twentieth day of Aean had arrived casting a somber shadow over the city, but none felt its weight more heavily than Darlana. Sleepless and held hostage by anguish, she dreaded the awful tradition that awaited her. The painful ritual of observing her infant daughter's funeral procession, bearing her beloved child to the pyre and watching as flames consumed her tender flesh, threatened to consume Darlana's own soul with grief.

For the second time in her life, she had lost an infant child to murder, both either by the hand or the order of her own father. She closed her eyes and said nothing. Her mind thought of nothing else but revenge. She would never again find peace so long as Raften lived but this was not enough. All Tanimarans and the land itself must be annihilated for her to find peace again or so she began to think.

Her council stood behind her and simply observed in silence. They too loved Paeris but to see their queen in such a state only served to strengthen their resolve. Revenge was on their minds, and it went without saying. All who gathered mourned the loss of the only Princess of Nagrimara they have ever had.

The week of mourning had withered away and while everyone else was moving along with their daily routine, Darlana could not and remained in her chambers.

The palace was decorated with lavish flowers. The pillars were wrapped in beautiful purple and gold ribbons. The floor was completely clear of everything, and the space was enormous. From the vaulted ceilings hung beautiful multi-colored chandeliers. The musicians began to play light music, and people began to enjoy themselves. Meric and Magris were standing over by the drink dispenser when a masked but decorated Nagrimaran elf approached them.

"Who may you be?" asked Magris.

"General Magris, General Meric," acknowledged the masked elf.

"Glad you could make it. The mourning has been very taxing. I am sure everyone is ready to get back to the way things were," said Meric with a smile.

"You are telling me, General," said the elf as he lifted his mask and took a drink of fine Nagrimaran wine. "I will enjoy this night one way or another. I need a lady," he said while looking around.

"Ah, Folwin," said Magris as he took a sip of his beverage. "There are plenty to go around that would love a decorated soldier such as you."

"You are decorated, Magris yet you do not get many ladies," said Meric as he eyed Magris's eye patch, scarred face and peg leg.

"You would be surprised," replied Magris confidently.

Folwin locked eyes with a beautifully masked lady not too far from where they were. He finished his wine and set the glass on the table.

"Gentlemen, it's been nice. I think I will go introduce myself," he said before taking his leave and making his way toward the masked patron.

Magris and Meric began talking among themselves while Folwin approached the elven lady. Without a word, he motioned her to dance, and she accepted.

So elegant was their movement that others began to watch. He looked at her trying to see if he could recognize any of her features without making it obvious but it was in vain.

Elven masked parties were taken very seriously and when they craft the masks to wear, they make sure they do not reveal any recognizable feature. For all he knew, they have crossed paths before. She did not seem interested in knowing who he was.

After the first dance, she placed her hand on his epaulets indicating she was impressed with his rank. Not a word was spoken but confidence swelled in him. They began to move again to a second dance, only this time it was more intense.

Folwin enjoyed elegant dancing and for years, took classes in the academy. He was impressed and it seemed she was too. Her fragrance was of an elegant perfume which reminded Folwin of the Thalnor mists.

After the dance was over, she kissed him. She then grabbed his hand and began to gently guide him through the crowd, up the stairs and into a room specifically for this type of private encounter. She began removing her clothes as she kissed him, and he responded in kind. It wasn't uncommon for noble elven ladies to have a single night of pleasure with military commanders. They are revered by the Nagrimarans nowadays.

Dravon and the centaurs were patrolling the streets. It seemed that things were calmer tonight. Centaurs did not have any interest in elven parties. The denizens were having a good time in the courtyard. Many had too much wine and were falling over themselves while the other patrons were laughing and helping them back up. The community was together again and enjoying their time together.

Folwin and the mysterious elven lady had finished and walked out of the room. He took her hand and pressed it to his masked lips one last time before escorting her back down to the first floor where they went their separate ways. Meric and Magris were still standing by the table discussing something to themselves. It looked very serious and Folwin decided not to intervene but as he was walking past them, Meric motioned him over.

"Have you seen the queen?" he asked.

"I have not, I was... occupied," said Folwin with a smug smile.

Meric smiled at him and began to speak when Magris interrupted. "She isn't here. She chose to remain in her chambers instead of coming to her own masquerade."

"I do not blame her. However, I am alarmed. During our last council meeting, she was speaking against her plans to go to war. I fear her emotional state is clouding her judgment," said Meric.

Folwin grabbed another glass of wine from a passing wine courier. "Well, Velnir is still in a state of deep slumber and is not even in Nagrimar. Perhaps she does not want to go to war without him. After All, the war will be fought in Velnir's home region of Atlantin most likely," he said as he took a sip of wine.

Both Meric and Magris's facial expressions indicated that they had not thought of that.

"What then, if he were to die?" asked Meric.

"Rest assured, if Velnir dies, Darlana will deliver vengeance the likes of which no Tanimaran has ever seen," said Folwin.

"The weapon tests went well, Folwin. The prize for the weapon was awarded to a professor of the academy of engineering and science. A team of mages created an invisibility cloak and divided their prize among themselves, though the spell components required to create the enchant are scarce. Many of them grow in the wild and cannot be farmed. Unfortunately, this means the cloak will be very rare," said Magris.

Folwin looked pleased; however, before he could speak, Magris started again. It was clear he was very excited.

"This is truly remarkable, gentlemen. The weapon is a type of bow horizontally laid across a stock. It has a folding mechanism that reloads by pulling a small arrow through a spring loaded magazine while drawing the bowstring back and allows for rapid fire. The concept is great and now we are in the process to fine tune the prototype into a weapon worthy of mass production," said Magris.

"How does the invisibility cloak work? Does one simply place it over them like a cloak and turn invisible?" asked Meric.

"Precisely, it is necessary for it to function with as minimal effort as possible as not to distract from the mission or lower one's awareness," said Folwin.

"Ah, so you too are familiar with these cloaks. It would seem things are moving along quite nicely so that just leaves the queen… What should we do about her?" asked Meric.

"Nothing, she is the queen, and she has spoken," said Magris.

Folwin agreed and Meric stood there looking between them both. "Perhaps we can launch an aid mission into the friendly region of Tanimara. I know Madir would be an excellent target for they are most likely not to resist. My spies tell me that the military forces of all three regions are amassing on their southern border, Madir having the fewest and I know the Magister there would greatly appreciate it. We can say we come on behalf of Velnir. We can also slowly and carefully introduce Darlana into the negotiations. Now before you start talking about how Darlana said what, understand that this is all simply a suggestion to you know… show support or what have you. Nothing more," stated Meric.

Folwin decided he had enough and excused himself. Magris shook his head at Meric.

"You are not making any sense, Meric. You clearly had too much wine, but I think I understand what you mean. I will see what I can come up with," said Magris.

Chapter 2
Unexpected

Darlana had made numerous journeys to the Tower of Alzar in what seemed like vain efforts to help the wizards with Velnir's recovery. A knock at her chamber door stole her thoughts. She frustratingly got up and began calming herself down.

"*It's not their fault,*" she kept thinking. She opened the door to a messenger and Nythint who was standing guard.

"My queen, a letter of urgency from the wizards tower," he said.

Darlana's heart began to pound. The worst thoughts plagued her mind. Her fingers trembled as she tore open the letter. Her breath hitching, she read the letter out loud. "Darlana, your presence is requested immediately. Make haste!"

"Nythint, we must go now," she said. They rushed to the chambers of her squire and woke her. They rushed to the armory, and she helped Darlana don her armor.

"My queen, is everything all right?" asked the squire.

"I do not yet know, Mardi. I must go to the Tower of Alzar and see for myself."

"Would you like me to come with you," Mardi asked, concern flickering in her eye.

Darlana shook her head "No, no, that is quite all right. Nythint will accompany me." Darlana then grabbed her daggers and twirled them in between her fingers and palms before expertly sheathing them. "You have been as efficient as always. For this, I am pleased." She tossed her a gold coin.

"Many thanks, my queen."

Darlana and Nythint hurried through the palace as quietly as they could. She did not want to raise any alarm. Once they got to Magris's chambers, she simply opened the door and walked in. She gently shut the door behind her and went to go wake him.

"General… General," she whispered as she nudged him.

"My queen, the hour is late, are you all right?" he asked with concern. He looked her up and down and noticed she was in her full armor, had her hair up and then it dawned on him, she was leaving, and he knew why. "I see, I will let the council know in the morning."

Darlana smiled as she placed her hand on her general's shoulder. "Thank you," she said before hastily making her exit. They rushed to the platform where Nythint morphed into his natural majestic form. She vaulted onto his back and with a powerful beat of his wings, took to the sky. The twin moons Canis and Majoris hung low and full, casting an ethereal glow over the landscape. Their luminescent light danced across Nythint's scales as he climbed higher into the night sky.

"I am growing accustomed to this. I think this sets the record for the most speedy of take offs," remarked Nythint.

"Last time I was there, the infection had not receded. I fear…" she began but she could not say it out loud. Nythint knew and chose to remain silent. He did begin to fly a little faster for her sake. A full-size dragon could fly at a steady speed of just over one hundred kilometers per hour.

Just shy of five hours, they landed on the platform of the tower.

"I won't be long, Nythint. Wait for me here," she said before making her way into the tower. By now, she knew her way through the confusing corridors and maze-like hallways to the room where her husband was receiving the best treatment possible. As she got closer, anxiety began to grip her. To her, he seemed as though every time things were getting better, they would then fall apart in the most tragic of ways and for the most part, she was right to feel this way. Her life had been fraught with tragedy and loss.

"Master Alzar, Queen Darlana has arrived," said a tower servant. Just then, the door was opened and Darlana made her way in toward Velnir. He was laying still and covered up to his chest in a blanket. His arms were exposed and Darlana immediately noticed that the color had returned to his skin as she approached. She turned her attention toward Velnir's face and to her surprise, his eyes were open just barely and he was looking at her. He mustered a smile.

"At long last, my love. Your slumber is over," she said as tears began to well in her eyes. She made her way to him and gently hugged then kissed his cheek.

"He is still very weak and unable to move much. We have been giving him everything he needs but now, it is time to set aside magic and let nature do the healing," said Alzar.

Darlana kept her attention on her husband. She was filled with joy, and he could see it in her face.

"At long last indeed," whispered Velnir. It was clear it was difficult for him to even speak at this point.

As they were sharing their moment, Alzar approached and interrupted. "It is important that we let him rest, Darlana. You are welcome to stay here by his side if you wish. I would like to speak with you outside for a moment if we could."

Darlana looked up at Alzar grinning ear to ear and wiped the tears from her cheeks. "All right, one moment." She turned her attention back to her husband. "I won't be long, my king consort."

He simply nodded.

She grabbed his hand and squeezed tightly, and he attempted to reciprocate. She did not want to leave his side, and what felt like only a moment turned out to be several minutes and Alzar was getting visibly irritated.

Alzar cleared his throat. "Let us go outside the room and into the hall for a moment… please."

Darlana came out of her moment and apologized. She got up and made her way out of Velnir's chambers but not before looking back several times. She still could not contain her excitement.

Outside the room, Alzar did not share the same expression of excitement as Darlana did and she noticed immediately.. "What is wrong, Alzar?

"Fortunately the worst of it has come to pass; however, I am no longer confident that even through rehabilitation, he will be able to use his right leg to its fullest extent. He may need a cane or a mobile chair."

"A cane? That is it? That is all the bad news?" she asked.

"I'm afraid so." Alzar nodded.

"We almost lost him. I could not save him despite my knowledge in healing. Your magic was his best chance of saving him and you succeeded where I could not. A sorrowful smile trembled across her lips. For once, I am spared the pain of another loss and for that, I am eternally grateful. I will hold this favor close, cherishing the gift you have given him and me."

This struck Alzar right in his feelings and that bothered him greatly. He quietly cursed the human side of his paleolithic emotions. "Right, I must be off to rest. The hour grows late. Of course you are welcome to stay."

Darlana returned to Velnir's side, her heart heavy with unshed tears. As he struggled to sit up, she gently eased him back down, a reminder he needed to rest. "Velnir…my love," her voice cracked. You have been in that dark slumber for so long. His eyes, filled with sorrow and regret, met hers.

"I am sorry, Darlana," he whispered, coughing, his face contorting in pain. "I am so sorry for all of this. I am alive and that is all that matters right now. We can still move forward." Darlana's fingers intertwined with his as she grasped his hand. She remained silent and combed her fingers through his long white hair. "Paeris?" he asked, his voice laced with longing.

For months, she had dreadfully contemplated how she would bear the terrible news to him. She had tried to prepare herself but every time, she would break down in tears. Nevertheless, she knew this day would come. She looked him in the eye and tried to say something but the words failed to escape. She met his gaze as her lips began to quiver. Velnir's concern deepened. "How is our little Paeris?" He pressed, unaware of the anguish his question brought.

Her composure shattered. "They killed her." She sobbed, the words tearing from her soul.

Velnir's expression transformed from concern to shock, then to crushing guilt. He was unable to protect her. He covered his face with his hands and began to sob as anguish overcame him. He wept as his body was shaking and Darlana's sorrow poured out beside him. In this moment, the weight of his failure to protect his daughter nearly destroyed him.

Over the next few days, Darlana and Nythint helped Velnir around the tower with everything from using the latrine to going for walks in the effort to build his strength. Elves were hearty and able to heal quickly though in Velnir's case, it was not so. The news of his daughter's murder weighed heavily on him. The time it took was much longer than any had expected however, it did seem that he was regaining his strength much faster.

After only a few days more, Velnir was strong enough to ride the dragon back to Nagrimar and their return was met with cheers of joy and triumph. The denizens, both Nagrimaran and Tanimaran, expressed their joy in seeing the King Regent return alive. Not wanting to waste any time, Darlana, Velnir and Nythint made their way to the council's chambers.

"I have had a hard time trying to convince the people to go to war again but now that you have returned, perhaps you will have better luck convincing them," Darlana said to Velnir as they arrived. It was clear that Velnir was not fully recovered. He walked in with a cane and was helped to his seat. The council became aware that Velnir had only recently been made aware of Paeris murder so it came as no surprise to see him in such a somber state. He remained quiet. Darlana looked over to Meric. "Have you heard anything from your source in Tanimara?

"Unfortunately, I have not. These things are difficult to manage and execute."

"Very well," she said, sighing. "I am tired and think I will retire to my chambers." She looked over to Velnir. We can continue tomorrow." She moved her hand over his on the table and looked into his eyes.

Velnir was tired as well. His eyes were flushed, and he wanted nothing more than to go with her; however, he felt that time was of the essence and things needed to get moving immediately. "I will meet you in the chambers, my queen. I must come up to date with my cousin and general." His voice was a little cracked and tired. She understood and exited the council's chambers but not before stopping and looking at him one more time. She could hardly believe he was sitting there again. A sense of joy filled her heart.

"My queen, it would be an honor to escort you to your chambers," said Nythint with Dravon.

Darlana looked at them and smiled. "Of course." As they were taking their leave, Meric and Magris were watching discreetly through the door to make sure they were around the corner before speaking.

"We do not have time to sit around and wait. Our scouts report the Tanimarans are amassing an enormous fleet and expeditionary force," said Meric.

"Nagrimar is not ready, Meric."

"Darlana is not ready. Now is the time to act before Vulas is marching his army through the Forlorn Forest and could surround Nagrimar!" Magris did not say anything.

Velnir interrupted, "Why did you not inform Darlana of this when she was just here?" His tone exasperated.

"It has been more and more of the same, my king. We come to these meetings and nothing gets done. She has been very distracted with you gone and everything else that has happened," said Magris.

"It seems to me that she clearly understands what is going on. Before we came in here, she admitted she was having a hard time convincing the people to go to war and suggested that I do it," he said as he began to think. "We cannot allow the Tanimarans to march an army through the forlorn forest. We must attack first!"

Meric was thinking for a moment before speaking up again. "Leave it to me. Statecraft is my specialty."

The other two did not disagree.

Chapter 3
Discovery

Rizim and Yzat had become quite close. They would spend hours together flying around and hunting. They brought food back for the dragons only, the rest of the denizens of Nagrimar had their own way of gathering. It was not uncommon for the dragons to walk among the people of Nagrimar. It was quite easy for them to blend in while in their visage form. They seemed to grow accustomed to the lifestyle in Nagrimar and were less introverted and uncaring.

Yzat was working in the foundry moving huge vats of molten metal. While in his visage form, he appeared to have the same level of strength as the other elves but when it came time, it was obvious he was no ordinary denizen of Nagrimar.

Strength was not forfeit while maintaining their visage form. Nythint had requested that he forge a sword for him to use in his training and even though Yzat thought it was strange, he wanted to prove to his brother that he could not only do it but exceed his expectations. Rizim had come to visit Yzat while working.

"Of all the mortal blades, I have never seen one look like this," said Rizim while observing Yzat's craftsmanship.

"It is for no mortal, it is for Nythint. He requested that I forge for him a sword to use while he practices the elven fighting style," responded Yzat without taking his eyes off the masterpiece.

"You would indulge his behavior? It is not natural for a dragon to behave like an elf."

"I have forged many swords. I have mastered the craft. It would take a mortal a lifetime to achieve what I have done and I have not been doing it for very long. We were both raised by elves," he said before making eye contact with Rizim. "I understand why he wants to train like them. It is to simply understand them better so that he may serve Darlana to the fullest extent. For that, I have crafted him this blade. Not just any blade though, this blade was forged with dragonsfire. The properties are of magical origin."

"Mmhm, and other than slashing his enemies, what else will it be able to do?" inquired Rizim.

"It will increase in size as he morphs into his dragon form and decrease in size as he transmorphs into his elven visage. No matter what visage form he takes on, the sword will always be comfortable and useful," said Yzat with a confident and eager tone.

Rizim has asked for the details only because he saw how much forging this weapon meant to Yzat. In reality, he cared little for its purpose.

"These people seem amazed by you. Do they know you are a dragon?" asked Rizim.

"I suppose they suspect something because few ever

choose to converse with me. I hear whispers that they fear I will rob them of their employment. I do not wish to do that."

"Dragons are creatures of pure magic, Yzat. The first of us were created by Ata herself. There have been only a few times where the celestials have ever come to Abrion and intervened so that makes you quite special," said Rizim.

Yzat looked at Rizim and smiled. "Perhaps I will not work so tirelessly. I do not want to be asked to leave."

Yzat began looking around the foundry. It was enormous and had huge columns of track where giant vats of molten metal were hung from. It was how the elves moved them around. They would be heated in the furnaces over on the south side of the foundry and then moved over to the west side to be poured into another vat that had its bottom coned to funnel molten metal into molds for armor and weapons. It was precise and quite fascinating to Yzat.

"I love the heat, the smell and the production. The color of molten metal is mesmerizing," he said.

"Dragons naturally love flame. Our magic is celestial and pyro…" He paused.

Yzat noticed his expression had changed. "What is bothering you," he inquired.

Rizim turned his attention to Yzat. "I must tell you the truth. We came to Velnir to aid against the orcs. They had specialized in hunting dragons and even seemed to make a sport of it. They were thinning our numbers quickly, and no matter how many we burned, they did not cease. We need the elves as much as they need us. Our strength while great and powerful does not make us all powerful. We must be cautious, and it seems Nythint understands that. I am old and set in my ways, you whelps are our future, and I have faith that…"

Suddenly, an explosion occurred, and the alarm bell began ringing. Everyone was rushing to the south end of the foundry. The furnaces were destroyed and many were killed. Among the dead appeared to be Tanimarans. Yzat was alarmed.

"Saboteurs," he said quietly before making a quick dash out of the foundry and toward the palace. Rizim was not far behind. Meanwhile, a hooded figure met with Meric.

"I have done as you asked, now for the reward," said the hooded figure.

Meric handed him a pouch of gold and nodded, dismissing him. Two other hooded figures came out of the shadows and followed the first one. A moment later, they began to attack him. They beat him down, slit his throat then took the gold. The two slipped away momentarily. When the coast was clear, they appeared next to Meric.

"Your gold, my lord," said the shaded figure as he handed the pouch back to Meric who took it without a word and made his way to the palace where he would surely be expected in the council chambers.

***

By the time they got there, the council had been convening. Magris was there first, then followed by Rizim, Yzat, Nythint then Darlana, Velnir and of course, Meric showed up last.

"Where is Dravon?" she asked.

"The people are frightened. The explosion sent a shockwave through the whole city. I believe he is keeping the peace," said Meric.

"Very well, what do we know?" she asked. Rizim looked at Yzat and nodded.

"Rizim and I were in the foundry when the explosion happened. When we got to the south end, the furnaces were destroyed and among the dead were what we think are Tanimarans," said Yzat.

"We must strike back," demanded Meric.

"I will address the people in an hour. All of you, see what you can do to help," ordered Darlana.

Yzat returned to the foundry where he saw many of the workers distraught. Fear gripped the workers and Yzat could feel it in them. He morphed into his dragon form and could quite easily make his way to the south end of the foundry since none of the vats were in the way.

Seeing a full-grown dragon moving through a foundry was not an everyday occurrence in Nagrimar and the workers were awestruck. Yzat began picking up the raw materials and placing them in the vats. Inspired by the forging of Nythint's sword, he decided to no longer keep his abilities secret. He took a deep breath and unleashed his fire.

The materials melted a lot more quickly than the furnace could get them too. Rizim was also inspired and began helping Yzat. Soon other dragons heard about it and made their way to the foundry. Many dragons came and grabbing picking up raw materials and smelting them with dragon fire. Production not only ramped back up but began to move much faster than before. Armor and weapons were being forged quickly and when cooled, emitted a bluish hue.

"Why are the armor pieces blue?" asked one of the workers.

Another who was familiar with magic was wide eyed with wonder. "Dragonsfire," he said before grabbing several pieces of armor and motioning for the other worker to help.

"We need to figure out what kind of magic it is and what its properties are."

***

Magris was in his chambers when Meric and Velnir began knocking. "Let me in, Magris. We have much to discuss."

A moment later, a naked Magris opened the door. Meric flashed his brow when he saw Magris like this, tall, scarred, long black hair, eye patch and peg leg was not at all what he thought to be grotesque. He actually found his scars to be befitting of one such as Magris as he believed they complimented his masculinity. He was a handsome elf regardless.

"Oh, please, General. Put some clothes on," demanded Velnir.

Meric didn't seem to mind looking at Magris as he did so with what appeared to be envy. He gently bit his lower lip while staring at him until he noticed Velnir looking at him awkwardly. Meric then noticed the two women were in his bed grinning from ear to ear as if eager for Magris to return. Frowning, Meric kept his mouth shut and cleared his throat. Magris caught on and immediately began to dress much to the disappointment of the two in his bed. They waited outside the chamber door until Magris came out.

"They insisted on waiting for me to return so I told them to help themselves to my pantry and library," said Magris with a smirk.

The trio made their way to a lobby and took a seat. A server brought to them each a glass of Nagrimaran wine.

"Wish they had honey mead," said Magris.

Ignoring the comment, Velnir began, "What news of the weapon, Meric was telling me about?" he said quite eagerly.

Magris took a sip of the wine before setting it down. "The prototype was successful and exceeded our expectations. It does not hinder the visibility of the soldier. It rests against the shoulder to improve the aim and the accuracy of it. I assure you, it is absolutely outstanding, Meric. We have several iterations as we try to improve the design of the…..wait for it," Magris said, attempting to build up excitement. Meric and Velnir were sitting on the edge of the chair in anticipation. "Repeater crossbow," said Magris.

Meric still was not quite sure what to think, however, Velnir was very excited.

"Oh… I do wish to see this in action. It sounds magnificent. I do not care for the name 'repeater crossbow', but I suppose you know what you are doing, Magris. So, what is to be done with it," asked Velnir.

"We will be spending several weeks experimenting with new strategies and tactics. Our army is small and we have selected one thousand soldiers who have all taken oaths of secrecy to master these weapons. We have also taken into account the invisibility cloaks." Magris took another sip of his wine noting how delicious it is. "Oh yes, you will be pleased to hear that our alchemists have come up with an item they call an Arcane stone. Somehow, and I do not know how, they figured out how to trap arcane magic in a type of brittle stone which when broken over an enchanted object, replenishes its magical properties," said Magris.

Meric's demeanor changed to awe. He grabbed Magris' arm. "You understand what this means, Magris?"

"I do indeed, Meric, I do indeed."

Velnir was also surprised. "The elves have been in a technological stagnation for so long. In such a small amount of time, you two have managed such feats in advancements."

"We will need to train day and night until the skill is perfected. We must also plan a retaliation strike to demonstrate our strength if we wish to convince our allies to join us. The Tanimarans cannot be allowed to destroy our foundry with impunity," said Meric with conviction.

"Has our queen said anything about…" began Velnir.

Meric interrupted him, "she has not had much success trying to convince the people of war." He looked to Velnir. It is up to you to convince them," said Meric. Velnir thought about it for a moment.

"I will see what I can do," said Velnir.

Meric nodded and got up to leave. He made his way to his own chambers where an elven woman was waiting for him. She wore a black cloak that hid her face well, only revealing that she had one dead eye with a gnarly scar over her brow and down to her cheek. Meric was startled.

"Do not be alarmed, master Meric, I bring news from Tanimara," she whispered. To his relief, she was one of his spies though he did not recognize her. She handed him a scroll with a black wax seal. He broke it and it read

"Tanimara is under martial law. It is difficult to reach you hence why it has been some time since we have last spoken. I apologize for the delay but as you know, discretion is paramount. The weakest fortified city is Madir. I made certain the Magistrate only saw it fit to garrison one thousand soldiers and auxiliary. The Tanimaran army as a whole is stretched thin with conflicts erupting in several of its colonies. Orcs, Dwarves, Men and Umbramari do not take kindly to Tanimaran aggression. Raften is struggling to keep his power after declaring the republic no more and declaring himself emperor. Now would be the time to strike since its armies are dealing with the rebellious colonies. Best regards, you know who."

Once Meric stopped reading, the scroll ignited itself and burnt to ash. The cloaked elven woman bowed and then jumped out his window without making a sound. He ran over and looked out to see where she landed however she was nowhere around. An uneasy feeling crept up his spine.

***

A few months after the attack on the foundry and after several council meetings, things were going seemingly well at least out in the open and as far as the council was concerned. The foundry was producing armor, not only for the Nagrimarans but also the centaur, dragons, griffins and hippogriffs. Anything that could wear armor somewhat comfortably was fitted for it. They were calling it dragon steel. It was discovered that the blue hue that coated the metal was caused by the dragon's fire and the properties of the metal during the smelting process. The magic in their breath was absorbed by the molten metal and remained even after cooling and hardening. It was also discovered that it added fire protection.

Once formed, it had to be smelted again to be destroyed. Fire itself could not heat it up. This proved to be a wonderful accidental discovery. In their recorded history, dragons never had a reason to smelt metal and if it ever happened, there was no record of it. It surprised everyone.

Magris and Velnir decided to call the elite troops training with the repeater crossbows and invisibility cloaks, Shades. Considering their particular skill, this was most appropriate. His Shades were progressing well with the weapons and production of them was nearly complete.

The industrial might of Nagrimar has increased exponentially in only a few months. Now it was time to do something about Tanimara but Darlana was still apprehensive. She believed the people did not want to go to war and she had assured them that she was pursuing alternative means. Then the foundry attack occurred and some people wanted blood and vengeance. They were the Tanimarans that Velnir had brought with him to Nagrimar and assimilated into the culture. The native Nagrimarans were still afraid and that was enough for Darlana to avoid taking action.

Enough time had passed for her to calm down and start thinking in the best interest of her people.

She looked around the council chambers at all the members. The dragons simply looked content. Dravon looked weary. She began to think of how much she asked of him and his people. They had not complained even one time. Their loyalty was not a question. Centaurs powered through every challenge that they faced, but even they had their limits.

"General Dravon, I would like for you to have a sabbatical. You have kept the peace and maintained stability for so long, it is making you weary. Please take your people and run through the forest to your heart's content," she said while smiling at him.

"You are good to us my queen, but who will keep the peace if not us?" he asked.

"We will," said Nythint, surprising everyone. Rizim and Yzat agreed with a nod. "There are fifteen adult dragons and a few hatchlings in Nagrimar. It is now in our best interest to protect the kingdom. Nobody is going to challenge a dragon, my queen," said Nythint.

Darlana nodded and Dravon seemed content. Meanwhile on the other side of the table, Velnir, Meric and Magris were discussing the issues of the military.

Darlana appreciated their commitment and trusted them. They are native Tanimarans but now they serve her. She did not really understand a lot of what they were saying and neither did the rest of the members of the council besides Nythint who remained silent.

Dragons simply seemed disinterested but when called upon are incredibly dependable. Darlana came to love the dragons, especially Nythint. He was one of her most dependable council members and even a friend.

No matter what form he took, elven or dragon, she could always count on his loyalty and determination to learn as much as he could from the Elven warriors around him. He would stand guard outside her door every night while her and Velnir slept. Having Nythint outside and Velnir next to her gave her a sense of safety and ease. She had been sleeping much better of late.

"My council, you have all been incredibly supportive. I'd like to allow all of you a sabbatical."

Velnir, Meric and Magris looked disgusted. Dravon was pleased and the dragons didn't care.

"My beloved, we are only getting started," stated Velnir. The other two agreed.

"We can discuss the plans in a moment," she said, smiling at him. She got up and offered to escort Dravon out, which he happily accepted. Together, they walked out of the council chambers and down the hall.

"Thank you for allowing us to go on a sabbatical," said Dravon.

"Between you and I, Dravon, I cannot see us going toe to toe with Tanimara. We simply do not have the support. We do not have enough soldiers in the army to invade Tanimara and defend the Forlorn Forest from a possible Orcish attack and I cannot bring myself to conscript anyone for this. It is personal for me and I want to avenge my daughter, but I have to listen to them. Why should I demand them to go to war for my grief which time can heal. I may need to overcome this another way."

"Darlana, the attempted murder of the king consort and the murder of Princess Paeris hurt us all. It was not just an attack on you, and we understand that nations cannot allow other nations to commit war crimes with impunity.

In short time, my queen, we will be ready for war. I cannot imagine the Tanimarans will be able to quickly quash all the rebellions they are forced to deal with. They are stretched thin. I would suggest allowing the King Consort and his generals to plan our counter offensive. After all, Velnir overcame many odds and is now hailed a hero by many people," stated Dravon.

Darlana smiled. "I know everything you say to be true, General. I just wanted to hear it from you. I appreciate your unwavering support and wisdom."

Now they had made their way down the stairs, through the throne hall and out to the courtyard. "Enjoy your time off, General."

"How long are we allowed out?" asked Dravon.

"As long as you like. If you decide that it is best for your people to come back, then do so, if not then do not. I will not force you or your people to serve me."

"You never have, Darlana. We chose you, remember?"

She smiled, "I certainly do."

Dravon trotted away and Darlana turned around and went back into the council's chambers. Velnir, Magris and Meric were patiently waiting for her to return.

"Darlana, we have some suggestions if you would hear them," said Velnir.

"Very well," replied Darlana. She sat down and placed her hands on the table and laced her fingers. She gave him her undivided attention.

"I believe that Meric's spies have revealed an excellent opportunity for us to strike. Madir is the weakest coastal city and all we would need to do is send in a small elite force to secure it. I believe that we can rally the Tanimarans to our side if I am there," said Velnir. Magris and Meric exchanged glances and then turned their attention to Darlana. She took a deep breath and looked down before speaking.

"Velnir, I want to strike at Tanimara and deliver a blow that will send shockwaves throughout the land. I support this expedition…" she began while the other three could barely contain their excitement. "However, it would bring me great pain again," she began while she looked up to lock eyes with him, "to watch you leave me to go on a dangerous mission like this. How could you even suggest going?" Tears began running down her cheeks.

Velnir realized that he had made a mistake again. "*Why am I so naive?*" Velnir collected his thoughts and proceeded in the most loving manner he could.

"They nearly killed me, they killed our daughter. They killed my uncle. I too have lost so much. We all have. An opportunity to be part of the force that strikes first would be most glorious and start to satisfy our revenge. If I am there, Atlan will rally to me. When they do, Caphry will also," he said, trying to convince her.

Her emotions were clear, but elves did not normally let their emotions cloud their judgment. Besides revenge, it would be far better for the hero of Tanimara that defeated the orcs in their own land, who was wronged by the magistrate and spurred much of this rebellion in the first place to go and be the beacon of resistance and revolution than the apostate or one of her generals.

"You have made mistakes before, Velnir. I am forbidding you to go. You swore allegiance to me. You married me." She got up and made her way over to him. He stood up and held her. "I forbid you to go, If I have to get on my knees and beg you not to, I will," she said looking up to him with teary eyes.

Velnir looked away. Everyone was quiet and an eternity seemed to pass by. While still holding on to her husband, she looked toward the rest of the council but did not make eye contact with any of them.

"Send Commander Folwin to lead the attack. I need Velnir and Magris to stay here and lead with me for the time being. The Nemisians are ready to begin shipping supplies," she said as she sniffled. "Have Folwin make contact with them through the dragons. He will know what to do from there. I have already spoken to him." Velnir was disappointed.

"You already made the decision without consulting us first?" he asked as he tried to make eye contact with her.

"I figured you would try to leave so I took it upon myself to set it up." She looked at him with authoritative but teary eyes. "I am the queen."

Velnir was clearly upset. Magris and Meric were silent.

"I think it is best if you and I stay in separate chambers for the next few nights," she said as she let go of him and wiped her tears away. "I will see you here when we next convene." She decided it was time to retire for the evening and without another word, made her way to her chambers. Nythint was there and at attention as always.

"I have never asked you to stand here all night like you have been for the last…" he interrupted her.

"Since Paeris was murdered by those elves and Velnir was almost killed." He paused… "I choose to be here because I feel like I have failed them."

She caressed his cheek. Even though he was a full-grown dragon, he was only a few years old. Compared to her, he was still so young.

"I had no idea, Nythint. I want you to know, I will never think you could have done more to save them. You couldn't possibly have known."

He looked at her with no expression from his visage. A tear formed and rolled down his cheek. Darlana knew that it is not that Dragons do not feel, they simply cannot show it through facial expression however, they can through their actions. She pulled him in for a hug and held him tightly for a long moment.

"You do what you feel is best, Nythint. I appreciate you no matter what."

He simply nodded and stood there facing the wall across the hall. She entered her chamber and crawled into bed. For the first time, she left Paeris's stuffy alone and as long as it was next to her, she would be fine.

Her mind began to race about Nagrimar, the dragons, Velnir, Nythint, Magris, Meric, Tanimara and much more.

"*How could a creature as young as Nythint feel so responsible? Why do Magris and Meric tirelessly work as hard as they do to boost the economy, strengthen the military and try to increase the morale of the people. How is it that Velnir can be so determined and keep going? Why do Dravon and all of his people serve me without complaint? Why am I so worthy of all of them,*" she thought to herself.

She certainly did not feel like she was worthy, but then the thought came to her.

"*Velnir is a hero, a Prince and now a King. He understands his duty and what it means to the people Nythint is a dragon, not a child,* not a human or elf but a Dragon! Magris is a master pyromancer and swordmaster. He was a noble of Tanimara and sacrifice is in his nature, all one must do is look upon him to know this. Meric was a Tanimaran Lord and wanted to feel validated. Dravon is a centaur and centaur are naturally devoted herd people. I am a queen and for months I have locked myself in my chambers and cried myself to sleep. I am the apostate of Tarvana, a pariah of Tanimara but I built a kingdom from the ground up and saved thousands of refugees. I am Darlana and I know that none alive could dance with blades better than I can," she told herself.

"It was devastating to lose my family not once but twice, however, it is time I lead again. They all sacrificed for me and for Nagrimar. I must also," she thought.

Her confidence came back for the first time since that fateful day. She was beginning to feel like herself again and then she fell asleep.

"Darlana," said an ominous voice. She was dreaming and looked around only to see darkness. "Darlana," it said again but she could see nothing. Fear began to consume her. "Darlana," it said again, only it was right next to her, and she could still not see it. "Queen Darlana," said the sweet voice of her elven servant. It was morning and time for breakfast. Darlana had awakened and was sweating profusely. The memory of her dream began to fade as she sat there trying in vain to recall it.

"Queen Darlana," said her servant once again and very patiently waiting outside her door.

"Please, come in. I am sorry, I have…" She scratched her head trying to remember. "No matter."

"I have brought you breakfast, my queen. I was standing out there for quite some time so if it has lost its warmth and freshness, I can have it remade for you of course," said her servant.

Darlana looked at her for a moment before speaking, "You have been my personal servant for several months now and I had just realized, I do not even remember your name."

"Elza, my queen," she said.

"Elza, thank you for always coming in a timely fashion." She sighed as she looked around and noticed Velnir was gone. Her thoughts shifted to the mess she had left and the many messes she had created over the last several months. She threw her hands in her lap and took a deep breath. "My chambers. Celestials, this had to be a nightmare for you."

"It was not, Queen Darlana. It is my pleasure to serve. My family has served you for hundreds of years and I am the first in my family to be your personal servant. It is an honor, and I have made my parents proud."

Darlana smiled at Elza and looked at all the delicious food she brought for her. "Join me, Elza. Let us have breakfast together. It seems my husband has gone, and I would hate for this wonderful meal to be wasted."

Elza's expression was that of shock and her demeanor of reluctance. "This is a meal fit for…" Darlana interrupted. "For both of us dear." Elza sat down and they began to banter and laugh.

***

Earlier that day, Commander Folwin had cut his hair short and tucked his ears. His mother was curious, but Folwin was ordered not to say anything. She understood that his job had secretive aspects and did not press him. His sister, Lina, was staying with them, and it was breakfast time. She began to banter with her mother while her brother was eating.

"So, you remember when Queen Darlana held that masquerade that she didn't even go to?"

Her mother nodded and inquired, "Yes, why?"

Folwin was enjoying his breakfast and decided not to mention anything.

"I met a commander there. We danced together and he was amazing. Just about as amazing as you, Folwin."

Folwin began to choke. "*There was no damned way,*" he thought. No no no no, this is not so," he thought again to himself.

"We danced, we kissed and then we went and shared some bliss," said Lina lost in her lustful thoughts.

Folwin spit out his food. Sweat began to bead down his face. He was going to be sick.

"I have to go! Breakfast was great, Mother, Thank you kindly." He then turned to his sister. He began to look ill but could not raise suspicion. "Lina," he acknowledged before he took his leave. He could not hurry fast enough.

***

Velnir, Magris, Meric, Rizim and his dragons including Yzat and Nythint met at the barracks in the military district.

"I received a missive from one of my spies in Tanimara. The Tanimarans are stretched thin trying to secure their influence globally. There was no mention of supreme commander Vulas however, I think it should be a priority to locate his forces before we act."

"Everything is ready, five hundred of the Shades will deploy tonight on griffins. A few dragons will accompany the Shades to Madir under the cover of night. The Shades will donne invisibility cloaks and be armed with repeater crossbows and tripod mounted repeater crossbows that have a five hundred bolts magazine. The dragons are equipped with dragon steel armor covering all their vitals in the event they face resistance from the Madirans with bolt throwers. The Shades will jump from the backs of the griffins and into the city of Madir. The dragons will give them air support if needed. They will rendezvous with the Magister in the keep and secure it to begin the occupation of the region. Chance of success is high if we can count on your contact to be truthful. If not, we have dragons" said Magris with a smile.

"We still do not know where Vulas is. We need to look for him first or we risk failure.

"I understand what has to be done and if it is a success, you get the credit you deserve," said Velnir to the other two.

The hour was late. The dragons came in their visage form and stood in the courtyard of the barracks side by side with enough space for them to morph into their natural form when it was time.

Five hundred heavily equipped Shades were painting black streaks across their faces. Many shaved their heads and pinned their ears down. They were ready and began to quietly form ranks. This was done with remarkable haste as was expected of the elven leadership. Magris and Meric showed up for inspection. Velnir stood in between the Shades and the dragons to address them all.

"You are Nagrimar's finest soldiers. The elite of the elite, best of the best. You all volunteered to undertake this extremely dangerous mission and for that, I cannot express my gratitude enough. Your bravery and commitment to Nagrimar and our queen will never be forgotten. That said, we will be joining you," said Velnir much to Magris' shock.

"What? Just a few hours ago, Darlana forbade you from going, my king!" stated Magris.

"He is king, he can do as he pleases," said Meric, clearly pleased with Velnirs decision.

Velnir turned to them and smiled. "I am aware of Darlana's feelings. Once we take Madir and rally the Tanimarans to our side, she will calm down and forgive me. Meric, I trust that you will do everything you can to console her. Besides, who am I to ask of these elves to do something that I would not do myself? What kind of king would that make me? One who only gives orders?"

Magris had no words; however, Meric was inspired and proud.

"Commander Folwin, pack it up, it is time to fly," said Velnir.

"Yes, sir," said Folwin somewhat disappointed. He felt he had been robbed of his opportunity to make a name for himself however, having Velnir and Magris come made everyone feel much better about the mission and he could not argue it was for the better.

Truly, he wanted to be as far from Nagrimar as he could get. This was a great opportunity either way and he would not be too unhappy to lose his life in combat at this point. Magris grabbed his staff and sword and led the Shades to the dragons who began to morph into their natural forms.

The armor that the dragons wore and anything attached to them was enchanted to morph with them whether they are in their visage form or natural form. This was necessary so that they could switch back and forth without issues.

They all took to the sky as if it were routine. No one but them knew that this was an actual operation.

***

Nythint was standing on the balcony overlooking the city when the dragons had taken to the sky. It pleased him to know that something was finally being done. Yzat had come up behind him.

"Brother," he said in a calming tone so as to not startle. He then remembered that he was a dragon and dragons do not startle. For a moment, the thought that they are becoming too elvish crossed his mind. When Nythint turned to him and saw what Yzat was carrying, excitement began to fill his heart.

"Ah, the sword I had commissioned several months ago. I thought that there were higher priorities," said Nythint with a smile.

"The Tanimarans will never get between you and I, brother. Credit ought to be given to Rizim and his brood for if they had not helped us, we would still be behind on armor production. We are however far ahead and have a surplus freeing up an allotment of time to finish your order and then some." Yzat presented Nythint with the sword. Nythint took it with bewilderment.

"I have never seen such a blade, brother," he said with excitement.

"There is no other blade like this one. It was forged and crafted specifically for you, Nythint."

"I am pleased. It is blue and constantly hot. The edges are thick and serrated. The hilt is thick and bulky. Not even the strongest of mortals could wield this sword in battle," observed Nythint.

"Even though we appear as elves in our visage form, our strength is not forfeit. No mortal will be able to pick up such a heavy blade. For you, it is light and comfortable so long as it is in your hand. When you morph back into your dragon form, the blade will expand to fit your size," Yzat said with a bit of pride in his voice.

Nythint grew wide eyed with excitement and was about to morph into his dragon form when Yzat stopped him.

"Wait, there is more," he said before removing the wooden crate he had strapped to his back and setting before Nythint. He pulled the lid off to reveal a set of armor. Nythint peered into the crate and furrowed his brow.

"You forged a set of armor for my visage form as well?"

"No, I forged a set of armor for your visage and natural form. It, too, will expand with you and it will change shape based on whatever form you choose. Allow me to help you put it on."

Nythint wasted no time. Yzat began helping him put it on and it was stunning. In his elven form, it gave off a purple, black and blue hue unlike his sword which was blue and red hot at the edges. Nythint morphed into his natural size and form. They were both massive dragons by now as they were full grown and Nythint towered over most of the buildings in Nagrimar. The armor and sword had indeed grown in size along with him. Nythint stood up on two legs and brought his sword up to get a good look.

Many of the denizens were startled; they had never seen a dragon stand on two legs and use their front legs like arms and hands before. On two legs, Nythint was several stories tall. The sword added weight to his already colossal size which began to crack the foundation of the balcony. He quickly took to the sky in his armor and wielding the sword. It was surprisingly easy. The armor did not get in the way and allowed for his wings to move as if he was not wearing anything at all.

"Superb craftsmanship, Yzat," he said.

Yzat smiled as he too morphed into his natural form and met his brother in the sky. "Not in recorded history has a dragon ever wielded a sword or armor. You may go down in history as the first."

"Never has a dragon been raised by elves, brother. We will both go down in history."

They carefully landed and transmorphed back into their visages. "Thank you for these gifts," said Nythint.

"It was my pleasure. You know, the mortals tend to name their blades. What will you call yours?"

Nythint looked at it closely and thought for a moment before meeting the gaze of his brother. "I will call it Razorheart."

Chapter 4
Swift retribution

The dragons were flying above the clouds as were the griffins. The armor of the dragon was designed in such a way to allow one of an elf size to sit fixed without falling off. The repeater crossbows were mounted on a swivel which was fixed to the armor of the dragon as well.

The dragons had been practicing flying in the combat crate formation. The formation protected the dragons and their riders from aerial attacks, created an organized drop pattern for soldiers, and prevented friendly fire. Bolts would likely not kill a dragon, but they could pierce a wing and cause severe injury. With the rapid fire of repeater crossbows, it was unlikely a dragon would be brought down—but no one desired to find out.

The dragons were over the great sea by now. The moons, Canis and Majoris were illuminating the night sky. The dragons and griffins were moving very fast and maintaining formation. The clanking of the dragon's armor was almost rhythmic and in some cases was supported by the sound of the flapping wings to create a metronomic tune.

Magris and Folwin were both riding together on the back of the largest of Rizim's brood, Vysol. She was enormous and old even by dragon standards. Her scales were a dark red and black. Her horns were jagged and swept back and her eyes were reminiscent of citrine. No one was speaking, Folwin seemed bothered by something and Magris noticed.

"It will not be that bad, Commander. You have been through worse, I promise," said Magris with a smile.

"I am not worried about the mission, General. I know exactly what we are up against."

"Then what is it? We cannot have you distracted when we need precision focus, Commander."

"That night, at the masquerade… the woman," Folwin began.

"Ah yes, the one you made love to. She was a sight for a wounded eye," said Magris. He would often make puns at his own expense.

"Indeed… well, she is…" he had trouble finding the right words, "I would come to find that… she…" Folwin was trying to muster the courage to tell his senior officer the truth, but Magris interrupted him.

"She is pregnant," he said while covering his face with his hand and slowly bringing it down revealing his good eye and a half smile.

Folwin looked at him in complete disgust. "What… no, absolutely not! She is my sister."

Magris's smile quickly faded. He was at a loss for words. The silence was awkward and the sound of the armor clanking and wings flapping was all that could be heard before Vysol spoke up.

"You know," she said quietly. "Dragons mate with their siblings all the time. In fact, generations of dragons are from the same blood line. I have laid eggs from all my brothers multiple times. I do not see why you are so uncomfortable, Folwin," she said nonchalantly.

Magris was uncomfortable but Folwin was reeling with regret for saying anything.

"Are we there yet," he asked Magris.

Not long after the awkward silence, something came to the mind of Magris.

"Meric's spies reported the Tarvanan fleet to be somewhere in these waters? I see no ships, did you?

Folwin had a quick glance around and confirmed that he too did not see any ships. This left Magris feeling uneasy. The few dragons who came along would have been enough to deal a significant blow to the Tanimaran ships should they have encountered them like they expected.

"Where are they?" asked Folwin.

"I cannot say, we did not take this into account, though I would count our blessings. We will have the complete element of surprise when we attack Madir," said Magris, attempting to ease Folwin. Folwin was no fool. The Tanimaran ships from Tarvana not being where they expected to be was alarming. If they are not here, then they are somewhere out there lurking in the open ocean and led by the legendary supreme Commander Vulas.

Several hours later and late into the night, the dark silhouette of the coast of Tanimara came into view. The majestic peaks, city lights and towering structures of

Madir. Magris looked down toward the city and memories of home began to flood his mind. He longed to be back in Tanimara.

They were approaching the dropping point. The elves were unstrapping their harnesses and getting ready to jump. Everyone was making sure that their parachutes were correctly packed and that they all had their gear ready. Their faces were painted, their ears were tucked. The time was now.

Velnir gave the signal, the Shades mounted on the dragons jumped first, followed by everyone else from the griffins. Soon the sky was littered with parachutes but the Tanimarans, not expecting an attack to come from the air, were none the wiser. Most of the five hundred landed in their designated location. Only a few were off but made it to the location with the rest of the Shades. The invisibility cloaks already proved invaluable. The parachutes were ditched and left wherever the Shades left them. A city guard was bound to come across one and perhaps the alarms would be raised.

"*Come on, Vysol,*" thought Magris encouragingly. She agreed to lead the air attack if it was far enough away from the palace which is where they were hiding.

A moment later, the screeching of dragons could be heard, followed by alarm bells and screaming. Vysol had feigned an attack against the barracks and the siege works. The dragons began strafing but were careful not to destroy anything. Velnir gave the order to storm the palace. Several groups of Shades led by Commander Folwin while wearing their invisibility cloaks made their way up the stairs leading to the grand door of the palace.

They came upon two guards and disengaged them without a fight. Velnir and Magris made sure not to kill anyone they did not have to. Several more Shades threw grappling hooks up the sides of the palace and began to scale it. When everything was in place, the Shades stormed the palace. The sound of the repeater crossbows was muffled. The sounds of bodies slumping on the ground was the only thing that could be heard. They were not only very silent but also deadly accurate. A few minutes later, the grand door opened and Folwin motioned Velnir to enter.

By now, the garrison of soldiers and auxiliary were trying to handle the armored dragons. The arrows simply bounced off their armor but the bolts from the wall mounted bolt throwers had to be dodged. Once fired, three blades sprung out from their shaft and began to spin with haste. This motion helped to not only propel the bolt farther, it also expanded the area of effect and could shred a dragon's wings which were not protected by any armor.

Velnir, Magris and the rest of the Shades entered the palace. They removed their hoods revealing their faces. Some of the other Shades did as well. They began to barricade themselves in the palace in case the Madiran defenses came but so far they were occupied by the dragons.

"The Magister has surrendered and is being held in the council chambers of the keep, my king," said Folwin.

The three made their way up the staircase and into the

council's chambers where the Magister was being held. Magris was the first to enter and immediately recognized her.

"Imra? You are Meric's contact?" he asked to be sure.

"Magris, you are leading this assault?" she asked in an amused tone.

"I am," said Velnir as he stepped around Magris to face her. Her demeanor changed quickly. She could not believe it.

"Forgive me, Velnir. I simply had not expected this. I did not receive a reply from Meric."

"Where is Commander Vulas' fleet?"

"They left over a week ago. They started to sail northeast. I do not know their destination," said Imra.

"Northeast is toward the human kingdom of Northgarde. Why would the Tanimarans be…" Then the thought came to him. He pulled out a map and examined all possibilities.

"Did Vulas have an army?" asked Magris.

"Of course, Magris. You ought to know that no Tanimaran fleet leaves without an army," said Imra.

"How many ships and soldiers?" demanded Velnir.

"I am an elected Magister of Tanimara and put so much on the line. What assurance do I get in return?"

"You have been honest and forthcoming so far. I will, of course, spare your life and protect you, but we are not done yet. Now tell me," he demanded.

She was reluctant until Magris placed his staff under her chin. "Tell him, Imra, how many ships and soldiers were in Commander Vulas' fleet?"

"I do not know exactly, there were a lot though. Much more than a simple expeditionary force and given the fact that we are experiencing rebellions in most of our colonies, it would have to be for something colossal to send that many troops leaving us so vulnerable as I stated in the letter I gave Meric."

"You mean the letter that did not mention anything of Vulas' fleet?" said Velnir.

He was frustrated. Vulas was either going to invade the continent through Northgarde and make his way through the mountains, down through Helmgarde and attack the Forlorn Forest, or he was going to attack Nemis for assisting the Elves of Nagrimar and then attack the Forlorn Forest.

"Magris, over here." Magris quickly made his way to Velnir who was now speaking quietly. "We were wrong," he said in a frustrated tone.

"We have no choice but to trust her, my king. I believe her. She did take an enormous risk," said Magris.

"We did not see any ships where they were supposed to be. Vulas must have caught on to our plans and escaped leaving Madir to us."

"Either way, he will find out we are here soon enough. We chose to attack even though we did not locate him."

"If his ships appear off the coast, the dragons will make quick work of them. If not… we need to find his fleet. Send word to the queen."

Magris looked over to Imra. "What of her?"

"Keep her locked down here. We need to secure the city," said Velnir.

Folwin and his Shades moved through the streets and began to secure the city. The Shades were yelling at the Tanimarans to lay down their arms and said that the magistrate had surrendered.

Most of the Tanimarans surrendered but some of them were confused and clearly unsure what to do. They decided to ignore the warning and initiate fighting. The Shades would take up safe positions behind cover and mount their repeater crossbows. One group would give cover fire, another group would move up and this was repeated which gained the Shades more ground. The rapid fire of the repeater crossbows terrified the auxiliary which retreated in droves.

Folwin was hiding behind an overturned wagon when the supply courier brought him three magazines. The elf began re-supplying everyone to give the next group cover fire. The elves that were in the back were setting up a defense to keep the section of the city that they had captured by mounting a larger repeater crossbow on a swivel and tripod that was fired by a crank. These nests were equipped with several five hundred round bolt magazines and were able to fire three bolts a second. Hour after hour, the city sections fell to Magris' small force and by the time the sun had risen, most of the city was taken.

The defenders that had survived the attack began to flee the city. The dragons landed and morphed into their visage form. Velnir and Magris approached Vysol.

"Excellent work, Vysol. It was most impressive. You gave us enough of a distraction to secure the keep and take the streets," said Velnir with a smile.

"We took initiative to not destroy the buildings themselves, but the stores of weapons were not spared our flame. Bolt throwers, and whatever else are destroyed so they cannot be used by any insurgency," she said.

"Excellent. I have a date with the Magister so Folwin, make sure all the defenders are well equipped. Vysol, make sure that the supplies from Nemis are air dropped daily and if you could keep your eyes peeled for Vulas' fleet. Destroy it if you spot it. Protect the Nemisian ships that bring supplies as well," said Velnir.

Vysol got her dragons and pack griffins together and took to the sky and were well on their way to Bali, the capital of Nemis.

Velnir and Magris made their way down to the dungeon where Imra was being held.

"The city has fallen, Madir is ours," said Magris though with an informative tone rather than a gloating one.

"I see." She nodded. "Very well, I am your prisoner. Should I expect to receive lawful and fair treatment in accordance with Tanimaran law?" she asked with a quivery lip.

"This war is not with you, Imra, it is with Raften. We did not destroy Madir, or kill many Tanimarans. We are seeking to liberate Tanimara from a Tyrant."

She let out a sigh in relief. "Raften would never afford you such mercy," she said.

"Though Queen Darlana is of Raften's stock, she is not Raften."

"Darlana? You are doing this for the apostate? Meric never mentioned…" She paused and an expression of displeasure displayed on her face.

Magris looked at Velnir who looked surprised. "Meric was supposed to send you a discreet letter. Did you not receive it?"

Imra looked as though she had no idea. "I sent him a missive inviting the Tanimarans who left to return and in exchange for their service, they would be granted immunity if we were to succeed in restoring the republic."

Magris also looked as though he had no idea.

"I can say with certainty that we never received that missive. We are here to exact revenge and overthrow Raften. We will decide what to do with the republic if and when we succeed."

Imra's face turned pale. "Nagrimar…" she said quietly to herself before taking a seat and covering her face with her hands. Her ears began to droop and Magris took notice.

"Imra, Darlana is not at all what we were taught. Please do not worry, I have faith in her and Velnir to succeed."

"Succeed in what exactly? Restoring the republic or replacing one tyrant with another."

Magris remained silent. Velnir knew he would have to address the Madirans of their intentions and he feared they would not receive it well.

Imra stood up and collected herself. "Velnir, you are a national hero. When we heard of your accomplishments in the Sundered lands, we had a statue of you made and placed over the fountain in the courtyard. Never to our knowledge has an elven army made it to the Sundered lands and lived to tell of it nor has any single elf killed a dragon let alone the deceiver." Imra looked over to him. "I am truly and terribly sorry for your loss, Velnir. I cannot imagine burying a child."

Velnir sighed but was unsure if her sympathy was genuine. "I could have never imagined what it would feel like," he said.

She moved closer to him. "Atlantins were always the enforcers of Tanimara. It was no surprise that Raften immediately seized the region. To tell you the truth," she sighed, "he is taking over the whole continent. As you know, we are no longer a republic. Magisters are mysteriously disappearing and he is replacing them without elections. Madir, Caphry and Atlantin were the first. Did Meric at least tell that or did he leave it out as well?" She was clearly angry but it was obvious she was trying to not let it get to her. "I was allowed to stay because I feigned fealty. Lord Baefric and I were more than just friends."

"I had heard rumors but never paid any heed," said Velnir. Magris smirked.

"Anyway, It is likely that the Magistrate thinks you killed me and will send an army. I would also see Raften deposed. I assume Meric has spoken to you in that regard?"

"Meric said that he had contacts in Tanimara. I had not realized that he had such prestigious contacts. I am aware that some Tanimaran lords are talking of rebellion. If this is the case, we need to act fast and secure alliances."

"How many soldiers do you have, Velnir? I am sure, I can convince some of the other lords to help?"

Velnir was not quick to trust her. Yes she knew a lot and was seemingly giving him valuable information but he had to validate it first.

"Not so fast, Imra. You do not want to know anything or tell me more in case Madir is recaptured by the Tanimarans and you are also."

"That is more than fair, Velnir. I understand." She walked away from the bars and sat on her cot. Velnir took his leave and after thinking about it, decided it could benefit him to treat her well in case he is also captured, however unlikely.

He ordered her to be placed under house arrest and removed from the rat infested dungeon.

Once the city was secure, the town crier decreed that Prince Velnir of Atlan, King Consort of Nagrimar would be speaking in the town square. Hundreds of Madirans would attend. As they walked past the Shades, an uneasy tension began to grow. All that could be heard was their footsteps. No one was saying anything. Elves unlike humans rarely spoke their mind in times such as these for they had much more to lose.

Magris appeared on the balcony overlooking the town square from the magister's chambers within the Palace of Madir. The Madirans did not recognize him at first. He wore an eye patch, and had a peg leg. Injuries he sustained from the battle of Atlan when the Orcs had attacked. His armor was not the smooth silvery Tanimaran armor typically worn by one of his stature but had a bluish hue and was ornamented in a way that would suggest dragon homage. The Madirans did not seem to be comfortable. They were intimidated by him. His long black hair waved in the wind as he stared down at all of them with his one eye. Velnir then walked out from behind him. The people of Madir immediately recognized him and began to speak amongst themselves. He looked over at Magris and winked.

"Madir sent Nagrimar a request for assistance. It has come to my attention that Madir did not receive our response and correspondence had ceased entirely. Queen Darlana and I are committed to overthrow High Magister Raften. All we require in return is your allegiance."

An elven commoner decided to speak up. "Will you help to restore the republic?

Velnir could not afford to lose the support of the Madirans but on the other hand, the truth was still more important. "We have not yet discussed what we will do with the republic," said Velnir.

Another elf in the crowd decided to speak up. "And if we refuse?"

Velnir took a moment to think about his answer. The people watched him eagerly awaiting his reply. "Nagrimar is coming to Tanimara. It is in your best interest to support us in our efforts to overthrow Raften rather than work against us. After all, we have dragons." Just then, Vysol and her companions morphed into their natural forms. Their roars echoed around the city. The crowd cowered for a moment before returning to a standing position. They began talking amongst themselves.

Velnir was not a statesman. He was a soldier and felt that a straightforward answer was always preferred over one that is not. As far as he was concerned, he was done here and retired into the chambers. The crowd had more questions but he would not afford them the opportunity today. They were visibly uneasy and would reluctantly return to their daily duties. The Shades watched but did not provoke them. The denizens refused to make eye contact.

Chapter 5
Truth

The council had convened. Darlana was the first one there. Dravon had not returned from his sabbatical and Velnir nor Magris were nowhere to be found.

"Where is Velnir?" Darlana demanded, panic rising in her voice.

The dragons kept quiet. They knew as their kin had gone with Velnir and Magris to Madir and would not have without the permission of their brood patriarch. It was up to Meric to answer and he was very reluctant. Sweat began to bead down his forehead and cheek. It would appear that perhaps he regretted his involvement now that it was time to answer for it.

"My queen…" he started. He locked eyes with her with his mouth still open though the words could not escape.

"Meric, where is my husband? Where is Magris, Oh and did I mention, we are missing several of your brood, Rizim?" she stated.

"My brood are accounted for, Queen Darlana. I appreciate your concern..." he said before she interrupted him and asked Meric.

"Where are they?"

"He is...well...they are likely now destroying Vulas's fleet and attacking Madir in Tanimara."

Darlana's breath hitched. Her hands clenched, nails biting into her palms. Rage simmered beneath her grief, consuming the rest. Her purple eyes glaring at Meric. Her hands turned into fists, and she bared her teeth. Never had any of them ever seen her like this. It was almost animalistic. She leapt up onto the table and ran over to Meric. She grabbed him by the collar and with surprising strength, lifted him up as if he weighed nothing. Meric eeped. "You did this. You planned this. Your spies gave your information and you acted without validating it. You fool! What if they fail? This is TANIMARA!" she yelled in his face.

Meric was terrified. Darlana was exceptionally strong and fast. He was dangling from her grip and felt vulnerable and powerless.

He pointed at Rizim. "The dragons took them to attack Madir. We had been practicing for months for this operation." He had begun to calm down and collect his thoughts. "Many of your people demand retribution for the foundries and Paeris. Velnir is doing what he thinks is best."

The mentioning of her daughter robbed her of her anger. She began to calm down and put Meric back in his seat but remained on the table though crouched staring at him. Her arms resting on her knees with her hands hanging freely in front of her. While Darlana was chewing Meric out, Nythint was observing her in this position and was rather enjoying it. Yzat was observing and began to suspect that Nythint was becoming physically attracted to Darlana.

"She is the queen and an elf. Our kind do not mate with hers. I do not even think it is possible to produce offspring," said Yzat quietly. They both looked at Rizim who raised a brow inquisitively.

"It is not unheard of, Yzat. Dragons are creatures of celestial magic. We can transmorph into any species. Our… reproductive appendages work just the same as theirs. Have you heard of the Drakonids?"

"Drakonids?" inquired both the young dragons.

"Indeed, they are the offspring of humans and dragons, hence their almond shaped eyes," said Rizim.

"I have never…" began Yzat before Darlana looked at them and began grilling.

"Dragons," she started. "Rizim, why would you think not to tell me of this plan?" She looked at Nythint. "You as well? You knew and did not tell me?" Her expression was that of disappointment and Nythint began to slouch in his seat. Yzat looked at him with disgust.

"Stop acting like a mortal," he whispered before nudging him.

Darlana made her way back to her seat. "I am without words. You all went behind me, issued orders to my soldiers and did not tell me. This is treason… betrayal. After I took you in, Meric… you were a refugee!"

Until this moment, Meric was not sure who she was talking to. His face turned pale. He gulped. "Treason? Wait, please. We... I meant no harm. We were only trying to..." Darlana interrupted him.

"They listened to your nonsense. He looked up to you and trusted you, and you would allow him to go on this dangerous mission without telling me?"

Meric began to speak when again, Darlana interrupted him once more and turned to face the dragons.

"You would send your dragons to their deaths?" She was looking at Rizim. He glanced at her and cocked his head to the side. "Oh. Darlana... do not underestimate the power we possess. I would never send my family to do something that would significantly reduce their survivability unless it was more dire."

"You give my people a false sense of security, Rizim," she stated accusingly. "You came to us for aid because the orcs had killed many of your brood."

"Yzat shot a glare toward Nythint who slouched in his seat, however, Rizim sat there and looked at her. His glistening slitted eyes locked with hers. He could tell she was very angry and no longer trusted him. He felt ashamed and lowered his head. This surprised Yzat and Nythint.

Darlana looked at Meric. "And you," she scolded him. "You are to stay in the dungeon until I figure out what to do with you or until my husband returns." She rested her forehead on her hand.

"What if he does not return?" he naturally inquired.

She slammed her hand on the table and glared at him. "You would convince him to do something that could cost him his life. That is very selfish, and you strike me as the kind of elf who would sacrifice others before doing anything yourself. You are to stay in the dungeon. If he never returns, you may never get out so start praying to the celestials!" She then motioned for the guards to arrest Meric. Meric understood and somewhat expected this to happen. He did not resist but instead bowed to his queen before being taken away. Darlana sat there and placed her head in her hands.

"Get the hell out of my city, you and all your dragons, Rizim" she demanded. The three dragons got up and were about to leave. "Yzat, Nythint, if you wish to go with him then I understand. If not, then you two are of course welcomed to stay. I do not fault you for his... antics and you are the closest thing to a family I have left."

Yzat and Nythint looked at each other and then to Rizim. "We will stay with Darlana," said Yzat. Rizim nodded in understanding but did not bother to try and hide his disappointment. Being raised by elves, he could not expect anything less.

Rizim and his dragons took to the sky and headed northwest toward Nemis. Yzat stood at the balcony and watched. He was genuinely sad to see his father go. He had enjoyed his time with him and was glad to get to know him. However, he believed that he would see him again soon however and, rather than despair, looked forward to seeing him return.

"She is right, you know. Dragons do give the Nagrimarans a false sense of security," said Nythint who was walking up to Yzat.

"Yes, she is. Most dragons do not care for these mortals like you and I do, brother."

"Let us vow to protect her with our lives, Yzat. We give ourselves to her and serve her until her death or ours. What say you?"

Yzat was thinking. He turned toward the direction that Rizim and his brood flew in and then back to Nythint and sighed. "I do care about her and these mortals." Nythint could sense frustration in his brother's voice. "I also care about Rizim and long to join the brood. You are free to take that vow, brother. As for me, I will serve until I no longer wish to."

Nythint nodded and Yzat walked past him leaving him on the balcony alone. Nythint turned toward the now setting sun for a moment. He donned an expression of frustration. After a few moments, he turned and made his way back into the palace.

Chapter 6
Close Call

Word reached Tarvana of the fall of Madir. Raften was enraged. He sent out a call to arms and ordered the closest army to recapture it. Armies from Linia and Starland answered the call and were on their way. Most of the population of Madir were now willing to rebel against Tarvanan rule and had taken up arms against Raften. Several thousand people ended up swearing allegiance to Velnir and surprisingly Darlana. The defense of Madir was paramount and very strong. When the Tanimarans arrived, they wasted no time placing the city under siege but it did not matter.

Vysol and her dragons were escorting ships from Nemis daily to deliver supplies to Madir. The Shades were soldiers but they were also liberators and began passing out supplies and food to the Tanimarans of Madir. This increased morale and support. Word got out to the other Tanimaran lords of what happened in Madir. They were hesitant to act for either side though many would bet against the Nagrimarans. For now, Tarvana was alone yet Vulas was still nowhere to be found.

Magris and Commander Folwin had confiscated several scrying orbs, scrying crystals and griffins.

"Go to Nagrimar. Tell the queen of our victory and get us some reinforcements. If we are fortunate enough to keep receiving supplies from Nemis and the protection of the dragons, we will be able to hold out indefinitely. If for some reason it stops, we can hold out for two years and by the looks of things, the Tanimarans are dug in," said Velnir.

"Yes, my king," said Folwin. "What we have done here will go down in history."

"Only if we win, Folwin. Now go," he ordered.

Folwin took to the sky and flew in the direction of the forlorn forest.

***

Meric was in his cell thinking about how he was going to get out. He paced back and forth periodically calling out to the guards and begging them to get the queen. Hours of this had annoyed the guards who, when had enough of his antics, decided to hang Meric upside down against the wall.

Meric had learned his lesson.

This did not deter the guards who now thought it was fun to torment Meric. Every day, they would hang him upside down for an hour. It was humiliating. The other prisoners began to laugh and haze Meric for being so stupid as to upset the queen.

"Oh, come now, please do not do this to me again," he pleaded.

The guards pretended not to hear him.

"I have to urinate. Please take me down."

Again, his plea fell on deaf ears.

Meric could no longer hold it and began to urinate while upside down. It ran up his torso and up his neck until it moved up his chin and into his mouth. He began to move his head to try and avoid more but it kept coming. It eventually made its way into his eyes. He cried out as it caused severe discomfort, embarrassment and irritation. The other prisoners and guards began to laugh.

***

Folwin was making his way across the ocean with considerable speed. He had his repeater crossbow but that was it. He would periodically scan the horizon to see what was out there but most of the time, it was the curvature of Abrion.

The flapping of the griffin's wings and its steady breathing were enough to soothe him into a sleepy state. He decided to rest on the back of the griffin but not before making sure he was strapped in. Several hours later, he had awakened to the rising sun. He had been flying for just over a day and in the distance, he could see the coast of the forlorn forest. This pleased him.

"I am almost home," he thought, though not too eager.

Anxiety immediately gripped him. The battle had taken his mind off the reason why he was so eager to leave in the first place. He wondered if his sister knew yet.

In the distance, he could see several hundred wakes behind several hundred vessels. Folwin was alarmed. He would not dare swoop in for a closer look for he saw squadrons of griffin riders mounted by pyromancers. As of now, it appeared that they had not spotted him so he decided to ascend above the clouds.

"That has to be the missing fleet of Vulas," he thought.

He veered to direct east which was slightly away from the fleet. Just then, a fire bolt nearly hit his griffin. Three pyromancers mounted on griffins had spotted him and gave chase. Folwin was startled but knew how to fly very well. He made sure his parachute was nice and tight and that his repeater crossbow was loaded. He then made a hard left and went down. The pyromancers followed him.

Folwin was moving toward the water at a high rate of speed while dodging fire bolts. Right before he was about to hit the water, his griffin pulled up and flew toward the sun. The fire bolts stopped. The pyromancers could not see Folwin as he climbed to a higher altitude.

Folwin could see them however and he knew he was banking at a higher angle than they were and took the opportunity to roll in behind them. He descended right above and behind the pyromancers before pulling up his repeater crossbow and taking aim. He aimed a little farther ahead and began to fire. He fired the bolts at a high rate of speed.

The sound of the cocking and firing were muffled by the sound of air rushing past them. They were silent killers. The first pyromancer's griffin was hit in the wing, head and rump. The pyromancer fell from its back as the griffin reeled.

By this time, Folwin had exhausted his magazine. He pulled up and darted toward the coast. The other pyromancers caught on and gave chase. Folwin had a hard time reloading as the griffin was not equipped for a mounted repeater crossbow. This was very frustrating. He was trying to reload, and dodge firebolts while his griffin was all over the place.

Finally, he was ready. He turned and pointed the repeater crossbow at the pyromancers and released a volley. The pyromancers broke off in opposite directions and were missed. Folwin kept firing and hit the pyromancer who went left; however it did not kill him. He was out of bolts and went to reload again when his griffin was hit in the left wing with a firebolt. The griffin screeched and began to descend. It could not move its wing and was howling in pain.

Folwin deployed his parachute and held on to the griffin as tight as he could. They were very heavy but Folwin was very strong. He used all his strength to break the descent once his chute deployed. The griffin squawked. It had obviously not expected to slow down so quickly but it began to panic. Folwin tried to calm it down. The pyromancer was gaining on him and about to fire another firebolt.

Folwin was almost to the ground by this point and could hold onto the griffin no longer. The griffin broke free of Folwin and fell through the canopy of the forest. It had just donned on Folwin that his parachute would not make it through the canopy right as he slammed into it. He fell through several branches and received many cuts all over the exposed parts of his body.

Then he came to a complete stop and realized it was suspended halfway between the canopy of the forest and the ground. Not a good place for him to be for sure. He looked around and saw fireballs impacting trees around him. It was clear that the pyromancer did not see him and would not dare attempt to chase him here. This bought Folwin a moment of respite and time to figure out what to do next. The griffin was alive and walking on the forest floor just below him. Its wing was severely damaged and it could not fly even though it spared no effort.

Once it had realized it was no longer going to fly, it had stopped trying. It saw Folwin suspended and got under him. Folwin called out to it.

"Hey, hey, hey," he said while whistling to it. "Hold still, I need to cut myself down and I need you to break my fall."

"*This was ridiculous. Griffins were animals and barely understood commands let alone complete complicated sentences,*" he thought, but to Folwin's amazement, the griffin seemed to understand and did exactly what it was told.

"Ha ha," he said with excitement.

He grabbed his knife and placed it between his teeth while attempting to untangle the ropes holding the chute. He began to cut them, and one by one they snapped, and he inched a bit closer until—

SNAP!

Unexpectedly, he began to fall. The griffin turned its attention up and was right under him. Folwin attempted to position himself to land on the griffin, and just as he was about to land, the griffin backed up and out of the way. Folwin hit the ground hard and broke both his legs.

He was unconscious for several hours. The griffin grunted and woke him up. He began to grunt more as if offended he even tried to land on him or perhaps it was upset that Folwin got it in this predicament in the first place. Who knew, but Folwin did not care at the moment. Agony pulsed through his broken legs, each heartbeat a fresh wave of torment and the griffin knew that.

Folwin pulled himself up against a tree. He looked around to see if he could recognize where he was through the dense trees. The smell of garrigue was unique to the Forlorn Forest. He was relieved to know he was at the very least near Nagrimar.

His legs throbbed, sweat began to bead down his forehead. He searched for something sturdy and crawled over to a thick branch. He wrestled it out of the ground and jostled his left leg.

He let out a bellowing howl. "Son of an ogre, ugh… Celestials damn it to the nether!" he screamed.

Folwin brought the branch with him over to where his repeater crossbow was and broke the stock off. He searched around and found some cord that had snapped from his parachute which fell to the ground to tie the stock and branch to his broken legs.

Unfortunately for Folwin, the bone on his left leg had broken through the skin and he could not get it back in place. He knew if he did not get help fast, infection would set in and he would die.

He was enthralled by the agony. Folwin looked over to the griffin. "I am sorry, griffin. I am sorry I got you into this. I tried to guide you the best I could," he said while reeling.

The griffin cocked its head to the side. Its eyes blinked and its beak closed. Folwin was sure that it could not understand him but he kept talking to it. The griffin got closer to Folwin and looked at his wound. It squawked at him.

"I am injured and I cannot walk. It is likely that I will die here so go. Save yourself," he said half expecting it to perform a miracle and pick him up or drag him back to Nagrimar.

It would seem that the griffin understood because it galloped off and left Folwin there to die but not before pooping right in front of the imobile elf.

"Damn you to the nether, beast," Folwin said defiantly.

The griffin was squawking as it was running away. The movement combined with the sound of its squawk sounded like laughter. Folwin could not believe it. He began to crawl but the pain was too much. Nightfall was approaching and he had to find shelter.

Fortunately for him, some of the parachute had fallen through and made it to the forest floor. Thank the wind. He retrieved what was left of it and tucked himself in as best as he could. He could not sleep. He felt himself getting cold so he looked around and gathered the closest sticks he could find. He put them in a nice little pile but not without exerting a lot of energy.

From his field kit, he pulled out a firestick. These sticks were enchanted to combust when broken. They were very useful in times such as these. He broke it and it ignited the sticks much to his relief. Folwin then kept trying to feed it as much wood and sticks as he could find.

When the fire was large enough, he placed the extra sticks in a pile next to him so he could casually toss more in if he needed to. He began to grow hungry. He searched his field kit for dried rations and found that he did not have much but it will have to do. He fell asleep.

"Wake up, Commander," said a familiar voice.

Folwin was too weak to open his eyes. Infection had set in and all he could do was lay there but he could hear. A moment later, whoever it was picked him up with ease and tossed him on the back of a horse. Folwin's broken leg kept bouncing off the side of the horse and caused immense pain. He began to cry before he passed out from extreme pain.

Hours later, he awoke.

It seemed that he was getting his strength back. He looked down and noticed the stint was off and that his leg, while still obviously broken, looked as though the bone had found its place and his wound was sewed and dressed with a waxy substance. He looked around and saw centaur.

"General Dravon," he cried out.

Dravon appeared in front of the commander.

Folwin looked up at him and smiled. "I am so pleased to see you. I did not expect anyone to find me."

"A wounded griffin came to us while we were hunting and led us to you."

This surprised Folwin. He opened his eyes and looked at Dravon. "A griffin? Sounds like *my* griffin."

"It most certainly was. He led us to you," said Dravon and upon mentioning it, the griffin's attention turned toward Folwin and it squawked.

"It would seem the griffin cares deeply for you, Commander. It even left its scat for you to eat should you go hungry." Dravon scooped some up with his hand and placed it in his mouth. "Very nutritious for us. It is rich in antioxidants and vitamins that are not useful to the griffin."

Folwin was disgusted. Some of it was around Dravon's lips and he licked it up and began licking his fingers. "This is very rich. Mmmmm," said Dravon.

"Enjoy it then," said Folwin while he turned to grab one of his rations.

"You would think that even you Tanimarans would understand the benefits of griffin scat. It is a superfood," said Dravon.

"I am not Tanimaran, I am Nagrimaran. You know that I serve Queen Darlana."

"I do, my apologies, I did not mean to offend," said Dravon.

Folwin remembered, he had an urgent message for Queen Darlana. "I must get her a message. Please take me to her, General.

Dravon's eyes widened in concern. "What's wrong?" he asked, his voice tinged with alarm.

"Magris has taken Madir in Tanimara. We need reinforcements and support. The dragons have committed to airdrop supplies but for who knows how long."

"I was not privy to this information. We have been on sabbatical."

Folwin looked at Dravon. "It is my understanding that Meric and Magris kept the operation to themselves."

Dravon's face darkened, his eyes flashing with frustration and disappointment. "They should know better," he growled, his voice low and menacing. "I fear the Queen will be... displeased when she learns of this betrayal." His gaze turned glacial as he reached for his spear, "Perhaps I should spare her the trouble and deal with you myself.

Folwin began to panic. "Wait… wait, General. I just followed orders. Magris is my senior officer. What was I to do?"

Dravon hesitated and thought for a moment. "You knew and yet you said nothing. I will never understand elves." He sighed. "Fortunately for you, it is not my place to be the judge and executioner. It is the queen's. I will take you to her," said Dravon but not before he feigned accidentally kicking Folwin in his wounded leg. Folwin howled but was grateful that he was at least spared.

"Many, many thanks," said Folwin.

They made their way to Nagrimar and were welcomed with cheers. Darlana herself came out to greet Dravon and the centaur. "I hope you enjoyed your sabbatical, General," she said genuinely.

"We did and enjoyed many good hunts. We are ready to come back to Nagrimar and," he said before motioning to Folwin on the back of the griffin, "we brought with us a messenger. It would seem that General Magris attacked Tanimara."

"I am aware of the antics of Magris and Meric. Come, let us have a meeting. Commander Folwin will give his report and then be taken to the medical ward for treatment. I do not wish to speak to him more than I must."

Folwin was ashamed but complied without question. The council convened. Dravon noticed that Meric was not there but did not inquire.

"Report, Commander," demanded Darlana.

"Magris and the dragons have successfully captured Madir. The defenses are strong and the dragons are escorting supply shipments from Nemis daily." Darlana looked surprised. Yzat and Nythint did not. "Magris asks that you send reinforcements. The people of Madir have declared rebellion against Tarvana. They have joined you, my queen."

Darlana was not expecting such good news. Five hundred Nagrimarans were able to capture and hold a major Tanimaran city. The weapons have exceeded her expectations. She was frustrated, however.

"The Tanimaran fleet has blockaded the coast of the Forlorn Forest, my queen. I was attacked by several griffin riders mounted by pyromancers. Tanimarans do not send fleets without sending an army; however, I noticed several ships only had the crew needed to sail and the griffin riders to protect them."

"I imagine that is because they need their army to recapture Madir," said Darlana.

"We can take care of those ships," said Yzat, speaking on behalf of his brother too.

"Very well, Folwin, retire to the medical ward. I must visit the dungeon."

She thought about it long and hard and decided against her better judgment to go and release Meric since Magris was able to capture Madir and was alive. The council was dismissed, and she went to the dungeon. As she walked down the stairs and opened the door, she saw the guards leaving Meric's cell and they were laughing. Darlana walked past them while they stood at attention and bowed to her.

She approached Meric's cell and as she looked in and saw him, she could not help but smile.

"Are you comfortable," she taunted him.

He was chained upside down, and by now he was used to it.

He simply looked at her and said, "I have stayed in better. What took you so long?"

Darlana frowned. "You are in no place to be cynical. You are getting what you deserve. Do not speak to me in this way."

He did not need to be reminded she was his queen. "I meant no disrespect to my queen, I apologize."

Darlana looked at him. She did not pity him. She thought of him as a snake. She had used him to get information on Tanimara and he proved to be very accurate but she wondered if information was returned about her and how much. She knew he would never admit it. She did not trust him and did not want him on her council but he had been right so far. "I do not want to let you out. I would love nothing more than to simply leave you here for the rats." She could not bring herself to tell him he was right.

"Yet here you are because…Magris successfully captured Madir perhaps?" he inquired, truly unsure.

Darlana smirked and folded her arms before walking away.

"Wait… wait… wait. I am sorry. I'll keep my mouth shut. Please Darlana… I mean my queen." He closed his eyes and lowered his head. "Please, he said quietly one last time." The door opened. It was the guards who kept chaining him up upside down. They approached him and opened the restraints allowing him to fall and hit the ground.

"Ooof," he said as he completed his fall. They walked out of his cell but left the gate up. Meric couldn't believe it. She let him out. He stood up and dusted himself off. He walked out of his cell and down past the guard station. He turned and gave them a smile, "It has been real and it has been nice. In fact, it has been really nice but I have to go council the queen now."

They knew not to be fooled by his polite demeanor. If they had known that the queen would have let him go, they might have been nicer to him. Now they were scared.

Meric made his way to the council chambers after getting cleaned up.

"Glad to see you have returned, General Dravon."

Dravon grunted.

"Shut up and listen, Meric," demanded Darlana. "Velnir has successfully taken five hundred soldiers and captured a Tanimaran city with the help of a few dragons. The king Consort has requested aid. Nythint, I am giving you command of the army. March through the Araban desert and to the city of Maphis. Queen Sabreen has agreed to allow us to use her ships to sail to Madir. I trust that you will let no harm come to my soldiers."

"I will burn every Tanimaran ship that I can see, Your Grace."

Meric raised his hand, "If I may, Your Grace. Have you addressed the people over this?"

She shot him a glare. "Of course not. If they found out, I fear I will lose what little support I have. This kind of move is not only dangerous for the soldiers but it is also dangerous to the monarchy. Without the support of the people, we cannot go to war."

"Perhaps tell them of Velnir's success. They are wary, yes but if they know that Tanimara is not invincible and there is hope of revenge, perhaps you will gain more support than you had," suggested Meric.

As much as Dravon did not like Meric, he had to agree and Darlana trusted Dravon.

"Very well, I will address the people tomorrow.

Meric let out a sigh of relief. He looked at the dragons and smiled. They got up and were leaving but Dravon did not move. He was staring down and glaring at Meric and he only now realized it. It made him uncomfortable, so he decided not to say anything and simply left. The next morning, Darlana went to her balcony and began to address the people. She was nervous and chose her words carefully.

"Nagrimarans, it has come to my attention that The King Consort and one of our generals led an attack against Tanimara."

The people all started to gasp and talk amongst themselves.

"The force that went to Tanimara consisted of five hundred elite soldiers and some of Rizim's dragons. All of whom volunteered for this dangerous mission completely unbeknownst to myself and some of my council. While the perpetrators of this treasonist act have been punished…" she lied. "I am here to be transparent with you." Darlana was getting nervous, the people seemed nervous but no riots had broken out, so she decided to keep going. "King Velnir and his elite Shades have successfully captured…"

Before she could finish, the Nagrimarans began to cheer. Darlana was stunned. The denizens of Nagrimar began chanting, "War on Tanimara! War on Tanimara!"

Darlana thought that they would resist war, but it was not clear that she had misunderstood all along. For a snake, Meric was invaluable and he knew it as he stood there with that smug sense of self-importance. Darlana was irritated with him but pleased at the same time. She waved at the people of Nagrimar who were now no doubt ready to dispense some Nagrimaran justice.

The people were ecstatic even more than Meric had expected. Tens of thousands of Nagrimarans were flooding into the city from all over the Forlorn Forest and signing up to go to war. It became obvious to Darlana that they wanted revenge. They did not want to feel so vulnerable and now believed they had a chance. They trusted her and she loved them.

Messages were sent to Madir informing Magris that Nythint would be bringing reinforcements. Nythint took command of the army and left Nagrimar. He made his way southwest toward the Araban desert. All that remained in Nagrimar was a small force and twenty thousand centaur to defend the city in the event that either the Tanimarans or Orcs attack. Darlana needed to act.

Chapter 7
Old Friends

Darlana was sitting in the council chambers alone and lost in her thoughts. Folwin and Dravon came in and set their scrolls on the table.

"My queen, production is in full swing. We have an accord with the dwarves to keep exporting electhril. There is also good news. The Thunderforge clan of Dhar'Modir have doubled their shipments at no extra charge. They cited their hatred for the elves of Tanimara and would gladly give their electhril freely to whoever would see to it that Tanimara was destroyed," said Folwin with an uncomfortable tone.

"Our coffers grow empty, my queen," Dravon warned. Darlana was well aware the kingdom was slipping deeper into debt.

"Yes, I am aware. I will need to take a loan but first, I must seek out more alliances. We are well equipped and now are training a large army. Nythint is well on his way to Maphis and the scrying orbs indicate that they are doing fine. As for Meric and I," she said, peaking the interest of Meric, "We will go to the tower of Alzar and seek his help. I am aware that he is likely not going to be interested in fighting Tanimara with us but I'm sure he has a trinket or sword that will help us like he helped Velnir."

"With respect, my queen. Velnir stole Illuminar from Alzar and he was quite unhappy about it if you recall the battle of the Sundered lands," stated Dravon.

"I remember, General, but I have known Alzar for hundreds of years and I am sure there is something he can do to help."

Darlana and Meric donned their armor and packed their things on the backs of their hippogriffs. The two took to the sky and made their way to the tower of Alzar in Nemis.

***

Magris spoke very highly of his queen. She was now aware that he had attacked Madir and sent word that she placed Meric in command of the army and sent him to Maphis to board ships and reinforce him. She also said she would send him everything he needed as often as she could. Imra was surprised that Darlana was merciful and showed it toward Magris despite what he had done. This went against everything she was taught about Darlana, and she began to believe Magris and have faith in her as well.

"I thought that she would be vengeful and wrathful," said Imra.

Magris was displeased to hear these rumors about his queen. "She is a noble elven lady and created a kingdom from the ground up when her father exiled her. She has helped so many people and refugees find a place in this life. The rumors you heard are lies from the Magistrate, Imra. Darlana fell in love with Prince Sampsin of the Araban Empire and fell pregnant. Raften killed Prince Sampsin and that child, sparking the war that ultimately fractured the Arabans into the city states they are today."

"I am aware of how we reminded the humans of our superiority and aware of her relations with the human. I just thought she did not care what she let inside her. Human or centaur, does not make a difference. They are inferior."

"You would do well to change the way you think. Such close mindedness is what caused this mess in the first place," said Magris.

Imra decided not to speak of it further. She was having dinner with her capture and for now, he was treating her a lot nicer than he had to.

***

Several weeks have passed. Now, the Tanimarans are attacking Madir by launching boulders indiscriminately over the walls and into the city. Nothing they threw at the city could reach the keep and any time they brought ships around to bombard the city from the sea, the dragons ignited them. Right now, they are trying to cause terror.

Velnir was not comfortable eating when the people of Madir were under siege. He felt compelled to do something. "I am tired of this." He threw his utensils down and got up.

"Where are you going?" Imra asked, concern in her voice.

He turned to look at her and Magris. They want to hurt Madirans, Imra. I'm going to send them a message and show them what will come to pass… with dragons!"

Magris protested but Velnir continued to make his way through the city with his sword.

"If you are going to do this, then I am coming with you," stated Magris.

"Together then," said Velnir. Madir was a major city in Tanimara and was enormous. The bombarding was far enough away but he could still hear the smashing of buildings. By now all the Madirans living in that district have been relocated. The Tanimarans were not interested in hitting the walls just yet. They thought they were softening up the Nagrimaran army but little did they know.

Velnir and Magris went to the courtyard where Vysol and the other dragons were.

"Will you permit us to mount two of you and together, we can ignite some Tanimarans?" inquired Velnir.

"I thought you would never ask," replied Vysol.

Magris smashed an arcane stone onto his staff. He had several more in his satchel. It was obvious he planned to be up there for a while. His robes were enchanted to resist fire and he had learned from Alzar how to enchant a trinket to activate a shield around him from which nothing could enter at a high rate of speed but things could exit at high speeds. He smashed an arcane stone on the trinket as well. He mounted Vysol and Velnir mounted a dragon called Zira then they took to the sky.

Zira climbed to gain altitude and made her way along the coast while Magris and Vysol went in the opposite direction. She intended to get to the side of the army to inflict as much damage as possible. She began her ascent. She took a deep breath and unleashed hellish fire. Her flames quickly smashed the ranks of the Tanimarans and at the speed she was going, it ignited scores.

Magris and Vysol came around their other flank. Magris held up his staff and began conjuring firestorms in the ranks of the Tanimarans. The heat was intense and the screams-deafening. The smell of burning flesh and foliage began to permeate the air.

The Tanimarans were caught off guard and were powerless against the dragon. Velnir's intention of being there with her was to let the Tanimarans know who was in command. He was hoping they would see him and flee. Magris was one of the most powerful pyromancers alive so surely they would recognize him and this would also serve to incentivise them to flee however this was not the case.

Firestorm after firestorm, Magris would cast. The Tanimarans would send griffins to attempt to attack but Magris' aim was true even with one eye. His fireballs were accurate and he made quick work of anyone who would attempt to stop them. The Tanimaran army began to strategically fall back from their dug in position. Vysol did not pursue it because she knew what was awaiting if she did. Zira was excited and made her way toward the enemy.

"No, Zira, it's a trap!" cried Vysol.

"Turn around, Zira, Vysol said it was a trap," ordered Velnir.

"I can handle it," snapped Zira as two bolts came flying past them. Zira dodged them with ease which only served to build her confidence. The Tanimarans had hundreds of bolt throwers waiting just out of range of the city. They would tear her apart. Just then, hundreds of bolts made their way toward Zira.

"Lookout," warned Velnir. She meant to fly through several of them but just as she was about to pass in between, blades that were embedded within the massive wooden shafts of the bolts sprang out and began to cause the bolt to spin. Zira panicked and halted mid air completely exposing her wings. The bolts shredded her wings and pierced her body.

"GO TO THEM," demanded Magris to Vysol. She did not turn around.

"They are gone, it would be foolish to fly into that," she said somberly. Magris could not deny that to be true. His heart raced and anxiety struck him hard as he watched Zira with Velnir on her back fall to the ground.

"NOOOOOOOOO," he cried.

Zira hit the ground hard and was seemingly killed on impact. Luck would spare Velnir as he was on top of her when she landed and softened the impact though this did not come without consequence. It was clear his leg was broken.

He unstrapped himself from the saddle on Zira's back and fell from her. The pain was immense. He could hear the footsteps of Tanimaran soldiers closing in on his position. He grabbed a fallen branch and used it as a walking stick. He began to hobble as fast as he could but it was no use. The Tanimarans gained on him. This was it, now it's really over. He was captured and began to lose hope.

"I could not believe it when I saw two dragons strafing our ranks that Prince Velnir was mounted on one of them. I thought my scrying orb was deceiving me but here you are. Battered and broken, defeated and humiliated." That voice was familiar to Velnir. He closed his eyes and stopped moving. He turned to realize his fear. It was General Revan. He bowed his head in shame. Revan was known for his ruthlessness. "I will receive quite the rewards… perhaps even a promotion for your capture," he taunted as he leaned his elbows onto the saddle of his griffin facing Velnir.

Velnir's throat tightened. His pulse hammered as Revan loomed closer. "All I would ask is that you bury my body in Atlan in accordance with Tanimaran law," said Velnir.

"Tanimaran law is whatever Emperor Raften and his magistrate say it is." He turned to face the dead dragon. "What to do about that… Surely, we cannot haul the whole thing. Far too large and heavy. What to do, what to do," he said as he began tapping his lip in thought. "Ah, remove its head. It is just the right size to fit on a cart. Guards, take the prisoner and the head of the dragon over to the grove."

The guards grabbed Velnir without care for his wounds and dragged him to the grove. They got to work on the dragon's head and once it was removed, they carted it over next to Velnir. Revan and an entourage of guards approached. It seemed to Velnir that this was it. He closed his eyes. Thoughts of Darlana flooded his mind. He saw her smiling back at him. He remembered his only daughter who these people he once called his brothers murdered and stole from him. His father, Ruvyn and how disappointed he would be.

"*It will take days to get to Tarvana. By the Celestials, send someone to intercept them, send someone to rescue me and I will never do something so reckless again,*" he thought to himself.

In a desperate attempt to try and secure his freedom, sat up and began saying, "Many more dragons, my army and the Nagrimaran army along with many others are coming to the shores of Tanimara. Consider what you are about to do, Revan. Spare me and join…" he was interrupted as the bottom of Revan's boot met his face. Velnir fell to the ground. It was hopeless.

"Anyone know how this thing works? I have never used one and am not adept in any sort of magic," asked Revan with a chipper and polite tone. Velnir was surprised and looked up to see that Revan was not holding the sword to which he thought was to pierce his heart or sever his head. Instead, he was holding a rune of teleportation.

Magris and Vysol landed on top of one of the wall towers. He scrambled to try and deploy a scrying orb. Once it was in the air, it moved toward the position where Velnir was being held. He grabbed his scrying crystal and desperately observed as the orb got closer and closer. He knew that there was a small chance it would actually get close enough before being destroyed but it seemed to be easily making its way through and that is when Magris realized, it was intentional. They were letting it go through.

As it got closer to Velnir, Magris' heart swelled to see that he was alive but it was clear he was badly hurt. The head of the dragon was grotesque and off putting but what intrigued him most was the elf standing in front of Velnir. The elf stepped in between the head of the dragon and Velnir and a moment later, they were pulled through a portal right before the scrying orb. Magris was horrified. He observed an unfamiliar elf was moving toward the scrying orb. Magris moved it closer.

"General Magris, it is remarkably hard to believe that the hero of Tanimara, the one who defeated the orcs in the Sundered lands and brought us so much glory, was so easily trapped and captured. You are next," said Revan revealing his maniacal smile.

"Where are you taking him, where is…" he began before Revan clobbered the scrying orb into bits. Magris knew how this would look. He had a pretty good idea where Revan was taking Velnir.

"How will I break this to Darlana," he asked Vysol.

Hundreds of Tanimarans were killed. Their charred corpses littered the battlefield and the stench of death permeated the air. Magris and Vysol remaining dragons had the sky to themselves for now but it came at a great and reckless cost. They landed on the field that was occupied by the Tanimarans and began destroying their shelters, the supplies they left behind and violently tearing apart the corpses of the elves who had perished in the flame. All this for the Tanimarans to see from afar. This was now no man's land. All that stood between Madir and the Tanimarans was death and destruction. The land had blackened and even still, this was far from over.

"Come on, we've done enough for one evening." Vysol said. She took to the sky with him on her back and made their way back to Madir. When they landed, Vysol morphed into her visage form and Magris had a somber expression. Imra saw them land and quickly made her way down to them.

"Where is Velnir?" she said with panic in her voice. Magris looked up at her.

"They shot down Zira and captured him."

Imra was without words. She stood there for a moment longer before retreating back into the palace. *"This was for no other reason than to get the Tanimarans far enough away from Madir so they could no longer bombard it,"* Magris thought.

***

Darlana and Meric were on their way to the Tower of Alzar to meet with the stewards of Abrion. The wizards were the most powerful practitioners of magic on Abrion and believe that they were charged by the celestials themselves to maintain balance. Darlana knew that the chances of convincing any of them to join her cause was highly unlikely.

Meric had never been to the tower of Alzar. This was something he was very much looking forward to doing. The pair had to stop and make camp for the evening. Darlana insisted that they land just outside the forest of the trebors. Meric was confused but remained quiet. She was delighted. Once they noticed where the land appeared to be extremely well taken care of, she motioned for him to land.

"Are we prepared for staying the night here," complained Meric.

"Look," she pulled the bush aside revealing the magnificence of Oakenleaf's forest. "The tree trebors that assisted us in the battle for the Sundered lands maintain this forest. Isn't it marvelous?" Meric was intrigued. "*How could land this vast be so well maintained,*" he thought.

Darlana dared to not disturb the land. She remembered the story Velnir had told her when they went to the tower of Alzar. Oakenleaf was very unhappy. Darlana and Meric were sitting back and enjoying a fire that he had prepared.

Darlana had caught two small rabbits, dressed them and put them on a makeshift spit to cook. Meric was embarrassed and felt useless. He had no idea how to hunt and dress anything let alone a small animal. Most queens had servants and an entourage of people to go with them whenever they traveled. Not Darlana. She did enjoy servants while in Nagrimar but definitely knew how to take care of herself. She pulled the rabbits off the spits and started breaking pieces off with her bare hands. She began to eat and handed some of the pieces to Meric.

"Thank you," he said as he took the meat and began to eat."

Darlana looked at him with a furrowed brow but chose not to say anything. "*Silly elf,*" she thought.

Meric did not bother asking for more. He was really embarrassed. He was not sure how to politely refuse. She kept offering and was amused by his demeanor.

"What is the matter, Meric? Have you never been served by a King or Queen? Tell me, have you ever had a king wash your feet?"

"I uh… well, Your Grace. No, I cannot say that I have. Typically, I would be the one washing their feet."

"You can call me Darlana out here. It is just you and I. Nobody has to know," she said while smiling and taking another bite. Meric forced a smile and laughed. This whole trip was awkward. He had a feeling she brought him because she did not trust him. It served to make him more uncomfortable since it appeared that Darlana was loving it.

Meric had no idea what they were going to be doing at the tower of Alzar and he didn't know why they had to stop for the night. They could have easily made it to the tower had they kept going.

All of a sudden, there was movement next to them. The creaking of wood could be heard. Meric leapt to his feet and produced a small knife. He stood in between Darlana and whatever was to come, determined to protect his queen.

"Stay back, or I'll cut your throat!" he said menacingly.

Darlana was surprised. Meric was no warrior, he was a statesman. If she were in any real danger, she would have leapt up and taken care of it herself. The fact that Meric thought there was something coming to bring harm to her and without hesitation, moved to defend her, flattered her.

Nonetheless, she smiled, got up and moved toward what was coming. He was quickly right behind her. Meric squinted as the sun was going down. The firelight didn't illuminate the whole area very well and it was hard to see but it looked like a tree was moving toward them. Meric let his guard down and was embarrassed.

"Who goes there? Who nearly disturbed this sacred ground and why on Abrion is there a fire. Oh no, I hate fire," said a familiar voice.

"Oakenleaf," said Darlana.

"What? Wait...Who and what are you doing here? Queen of Nagrimar?" said Oakenleaf.

"We are on our way to the tower of Alzar and thought we would stop here and say hello. It is considered rude to not visit friends if they are on the way," she said.

"I see, well, gratitude then. I would prefer not to go near the fire. I hope you understand."

"I do and of course I would not expect you to. Oakenleaf, this is Meric," she said before motioning Meric to step forward.

"Pleased to meet you, Oakenleaf," said Meric.

Oakenleaf was not interested in Meric. "Where is Velnir? I have not seen him since the battle against the orcs."

"He is in Madir, Tanimara," said Darlana angrily and without hesitation. She hated being reminded of his recklessness but maintained her composure.

"I do not understand elves; so much like humans." Oakenleaf smirked.

Meric was offended. "Now wait just a moment. I'll have you know that..." Darlana interrupted him.

"Indeed, not much of a difference in the way our species think, unfortunately."

Meric decided to keep his mouth shut.

Oakenleaf looked at Meric. "Let me tell you a couple of... four things. Velnir was a hero. I was going to smash a little guy, and he took his place. Willing to sacrifice himself for others, that one. While I was escorting him and his companions to the tower border, we were attacked by orcs. He protected me from their fire. He and the wizard defeated that awful black dragon. Oh, I fear that this world is a lot less safe without him."

Darlana was bowing her head and agreeing. Meric did not know that Velnir had crossed paths with the trebors. It was intriguing. He decided to tuck in for the night while Darlana and Oakenleaf spoke.

After Oakenleaf had left, Darlana had begun to tuck in for the night as well. She looked at the stars through the clear sky and then over to what looked like a blue river against the blackness of the cosmos. It was the lifestream and it is believed that all those who perish are carried by it to the Phatra, the great citadel of the cosmos where souls go to celebrate their lives.

As she fell asleep, an ominous voice whispered "Darlaaaaana." She was in a run down castle devoid of all life. The stench of sulfur permeated the air. "Darlaaaaana," it said again.

She looked all around and saw nothing. She could not tell where the voice was coming from. A cold tendril gently caressed her shoulder. Fear gripped her. Just as she turned to look at it, she was shaken awake by Meric. She jolted up and accidentally headbutted her unsuspecting companion.

"Oh, my, I am sorry," she said while rubbing her head in confusion.

"By the celestials, were you having a nightmare? My nose... I think you broke it."

"I... I am not sure," said Darlana, still confused. She did not even pay him any heed. She began to pack their things and got ready to leave.

When they took to the sky, Meric looked down and noticed that the entire forest was moving. He realized it was all of the trebors tending to the forest keeping it pristine.

Meric had never seen it before. As they approached, he noticed the maze that surrounded the tower. Several people were dismantling it and he wondered why.

Soon they were landing on the steps leading up to the entrance. A beautiful statue of a blue dragon decorated the courtyard just below the staircase.

Darlana looked at it and sighed. "We have all lost so much."

Meric understood. He recognized the statue to be that of Ismi and was quite impressed with its detail.

"Greetings and salutations," said a little man with a long white beard, a pipe from which he was smoking and a hat that appeared to look like a little home atop his head.

"Greetings to you as well, Lemmi," said Darlana.

"Alzar is expecting you. Please, follow me." The little wizard pushed a crate over under the knocker. He jumped up but did not quite make it; however, he was determined to overcome this challenge. He kicked his right leg up several times, trying to get it to land on the top of the crate.

Finally when it got there, he pulled himself up and pounded on the door with the knocker. The door then opened and holding the door from the inside was yet another wizard only this time, he was an enormous and jolly fellow.

"*Perhaps a giant*," Meric thought.

"Rubus, a pleasure to see you again," said Darlana.

"Queen Darlana, it is indeed. Please come in and make yourselves comfortable. Alzar will be down soon."

The pair walked in the tower. Darlana had been here many times and didn't seem super interested but Meric was absolutely dumbfounded. The ceilings looked as though they were not there and entered the cosmos. There was another world moving above them.

"Perhaps a massive telescope of some sort," thought Meric.

The tower seemed a lot taller inside than it did outside. This confused Meric. The ambiance was dim and comfortable. The staircases going up the side of the tower were going every which way. It was physically impossible to traverse them yet there were people doing it before his very eyes. Somehow, books were flapping their covers and floating around to a perceived destination. Students would grab them and shut them, making them inactive. There were cleaning utensils operating without a handler. They were moving themselves and Meric had never seen anything like it save for a scrying orb.

The pair walked up the grand staircase and down a majestic hall. The architecture was that of someone for whom the laws of physics did not apply and Meric became very interested in this type of magic. They approached a room and within was in fact a large telescope. The tower resembled a structure undergoing a makeover.

"Darlana," said the man in the room who Meric did not notice at first. "I heard and I am terribly sorry again for your loss. You are just unable to catch a break, are you?" He then moved in and embraced her in a hug. She seemed to be really comfortable with this man who was now looking at Meric.

"I am Alzar, steward of Abrion, charged with maintaining balance across the world… and by the celestials themselves, mind you," he said as he reached to shake Meric's hand.

Meric was unsure what to do. This must be a human thing but he caught on and shook the wizard's hand. Meric looked into Alzar's eyes and noticed they were not normal. It was at that moment he realized that Alzar was in fact, not human or at least not entirely.

"What brings you to the Tower of Alzar and the Academy of Higher Arts?"

"As you are likely aware, we cannot allow this transgression against Nagrimar to go unpunished," started Darlana before being interrupted.

"I have heard that before and not that long ago," said Alzar, seemingly realizing where this was going. Nonetheless, he let her finish.

"I lack the strength to take on the Tanimarans myself and need help," said Darlana.

"You know, I do not get involved in the affairs of mortals very often. I am not supposed to get involved at all. Specific instructions were given, Darlana. No allegiances, no kingdoms and no sides."

"I understand that and I would not ask you to directly get involved. We have pyromancers and weapons. We do not have the numbers to compete. I have maybe one hundred thousand soldiers, twenty thousand centaur and two dragons."

"Ah yes, You told Rizim and his brood to leave Nagrimar. They are here now, working with me. It is too bad you let your anger cloud your judgment for the security they provided Nagrimar was not false. You do not understand dragons, do you?"

"I was angry and it is complicated," replied Darlana.

"Of course it is," he said while rolling his eyes. "Now what exactly do you want from me then?"

"Velnir had used Illuminar to defeat the orcs in the Sundered lands and Necrosith in the bone wastes. You had a trinket that summoned a meteor, and I was wondering…"

Alzar interrupted her. "Absolutely not. These are trinkets of mass destruction. They are to be used by me and only me to maintain balance. The orcs got too big for the world to handle so I thinned the herd. You and Velnir did the rest with the help of the dragons and even then, millions of orcs remain. You would do well to secure your border, Darlana. I digress. Necrosith was massive and powerful, undefeatable by any mortal army, so I was forced to act. Since Velnir stole Illuminar, he was obligated to make it right by helping me. We saved the world and it made him a hero. There are no songs sung about Alzar. No statues erected of Alzar. No one is grateful for what I do. But Velnir… you should be grateful."

"Velnir would have not succeeded without the help of my people, the dwarves, you or the dragons. Please do not misunderstand me. I am simply looking for a way to defeat the Tanimarans without taking heavy losses."

"You should not have sent a small force to capture Madir then. What was your plan after the capture of Madir, Darlana?"

She looked at Meric. "It was his idea, ask him."

"It is your kingdom, it should have been by your order, not his," Alzar retorted, completely ignoring Meric. "You will face heavy losses if you invade Tanimara with the force you have. The best I can do is give you some advice. Pull Velnir and Magris out of Madir and bring them all home or they are going to die. I can…. teleport them out, I suppose. I see no harm to balance there."

This was not what Darlana was looking for but it was a very very kind gesture from Alzar. Truly, their relationship is hundreds of years old. She showed him a lot of respect and he reciprocated. Meric was having trouble keeping up with their conversation.

Alzar had offered to keep them overnight and invited them to dinner. Darlana was unhappy about not receiving help from the wizard in any form outside of teleporting her soldiers back but she made sure to enjoy the company of the wizard. Alzar talked about Velnir and Paeris a lot and Darlana would often allow tears to escape. It was clearly moving Alzar as he left a case of tissue near her. Meric asked if he could be excused and they ignored him. He simply got up and left to explore the tower.

Meric found himself wandering down a hall that appeared to have classrooms lining it. He went up several flights of stairs that he thought were impossible to traverse and found great joy in it. Some of them made him walk upside down or sideways, completely defying physics. Magic was awesome and Meric loved every moment of it.

Students were coming in and out of the rooms on the side, going up the same stairs and to their destinations. They were not just human. There were orcs, halflings, giants, strange cat and fox people just to name a few. Meric thought he saw a group of tiny mushroom people wandering around the hall as well. The most intriguing species he saw here was a flower in a pot that greeted him as he walked by.

Meric came to a hall that had an opening large enough for a man to walk through but once he walked in, it was a massive room big enough for a dragon complete with a balcony for one to leap off of. There was dust everywhere as if this place had not been used in ages. Something about this area of the tower made Meric uneasy and so he left. Going down a different hall, he came across rooms guarded by two guards each with gates that required a key to get into.

"Excuse me, what is in there that you would need two soldiers to protect," Meric asked one of the guards.

"The master's treasures and trinkets," said the more expressional guard. He stroked his chin in thought. "Could be a number of things ranging from weapons to trinkets, scrolls or whatever. Either way, we are not permitted to let any guests in. Especially not after that elf stole Illuminar. Nope, since then, security has been increased," he said with a confident tone.

"That is right," said the other guard.

"I see," said Meric, understanding they were talking about Velnir. *"Cunning cousin. How did he manage to steal that sword from this place even without all this security,"* he thought.

"Very well gentlemen. I will take my leave." Meric kept going in the direction he intended to go and would look in each room to see what was in there. He saw swords, bows, staves and trinkets. He kept going and there was another that intrigued him. It was an orb that looked as though it had within it, the cosmos itself. It was not a scrying orb or anything he had ever seen before.

"What is that," he decided to ask a guard.

"That is the orb of falling stars," answered the guard.

"What does it do?"

"It pulls rocks from the cosmos and places them wherever the wielder wills it."

Meric remembered Darlana asking Alzar to use such a trinket. This must have been the trinket, and he was fascinated by it. Right then, Darlana had approached and startled him. When he turned to look at her, she was smiling at him.

"It is time to tuck in, Meric. Our time here is for one night only and then we must return to Nagrimar.

Chapter 8
Tragedy

A flickering light glowed from the cabin of the Tanimaran flagship. Through the window, a figure could be seen, writing on a scroll. Supreme Commander Vulas was writing to High Magister Raften and informing him of what was to come. He placed the scroll in a scrying orb and sent it off. He walked out onto the deck of the ship and had a careful look around.

For as far as the eye could see there were ships manned by their crews. Several of these ships had griffins stabled on them. The pyromancers were coming out of the hull and mounting them. Quickly they all took to the sky. The wind was blowing east.

"*Perfect*," thought Vulas.

At once, hundreds of griffins made their way toward the Forlorn Forest but stopped short of flying over it. All of them were flying stationary and side by side.

Vulas was pleased to see the line of griffins in the sky as the sun was setting. He reached into his satchel and pulled out a scrying crystal. It was the shape of a flat crystal but the images from scrying orbs could appear on them. He could also give commands from it and the pyromancers would hear it because they too had enchanted scrying crystals. From his post on his ship, he pulled the scrying crystal up.

"Ignite it," he ordered.

All at once, the pyromancers began to conjure firestorms within the forest. They kept conjuring them. The heat generated sucked air from all around. The coast of the forest became a raging inferno, a hellish landscape. The wind caught the fire and pushed it east toward Nagrimar.

"It is only a matter of time," said Vulas while grinning wickedly and petting the cat he keeps with him at all times. He began to cackle maniacally.

***

Nagrimar was bustling. Traders were coming and going daily, the economy was doing quite well and the people were pleased. Dravon was in charge while the queen was gone. He stood there proud that everything was in order. A messenger came rushing up to him which was typical though this one was urgent.

"General, I bring grave news. A fire has broken out and started on the coast. We think the Tanimarans are responsible. We saw mages conjuring firestorms from griffins, sir."

"Pyromancers…" Dravon muttered, testing the wind with his finger. It blew east. His stomach tightened. "If we don't stop it now, it'll reach the city."

"General, I am afraid that the fire is already out of control and headed here. We must evacuate while there is still time. It is moving too fast."

Dravon was clearly stressed. "Very well, sound the alarm."

The alarm bells began to ring. It was not long before all the alarms throughout the whole city were ringing. There were thousands of people in and around Nagrimar. The centaur began going door to door.

People grabbed what they could and began exiting the city from the north exit. The army stayed behind to keep order. They were encouraging denizens by giving them water, blankets and medical treatment. It was paramount that they stay in line and keep it going.

Smoke could be seen in the distance. The fire was moving unnaturally fast and two thirds of the people were still in the city.

***

Darlana could not sleep. She knocked on Meric's door.

"Yes, come in," said Meric.

Darlana opened the door and stepped in to his surprise.

"I do not wish to be alone. May I stay with you for a few hours?" she asked.

Meric could not believe it. He could not say no. "Of course, Darlana."

He was sitting in the chair going over some scrolls and she made her way over to his bed where she sat down. It was clear something was bothering her but Meric did not want to ignite any more of her trauma.

When it was clear to her that he had no interest in talking, she decided to lay down. It was not long before she turned over and fell fast asleep. Meric was extremely uncomfortable and thought it was very strange for a queen to act like Darlana was. This was not at all how royals acted in Tanimara.

He thought he would be better off sleeping on the floor so he sat up and began to prepare what little bedding he could find. He crawled in and looked at the ceiling and then over to his queen sleeping in his bed in a strange magical tower, unable to protect her even if he tried with all his wisdom, not to mention she just let him out of the dungeon not that long ago.

Meric would remain awake and could not stop thinking about the orb of falling stars. He in his mischievous ways stopped thinking about it and began to plan. He looked over and observed Darlana fast asleep. He slipped out as slick as an elf could and snuck out of the room. He breathed a sigh of relief. He was not sure if he should be out this late at night and decided that it was in their best interest if he did not get caught so he donned an invisibility cloak and began to roam freely looking for those interesting rooms.

Meric edged toward the chamber, heart pounding. The guards were still there, oblivious to the invisible intruder creeping past them. He had no interest in eavesdropping and started to come up with a plan to get in there. Another guard came and told the two guards there would be a shift change soon.

"What do you say about stepping out a little early. Think anyone will notice?" said the guard on the left.

"Only the next shift," said the guard on the right.

"They owe us one. For the last three nights, they left early when we had to come in. Block three, four, five and six have all been leaving early too," said the guard on the left.

"Agreed, let's leave them a note." The two wrote the note and then tucked it around the key ring before they left.

Meric could not believe it. What dumb luck. He made his way over to the door and unlocked it. It was that simple. He brought the keys with him inside the room and shut the gate behind him but did not lock it.

"I have some time before the new shift shows up," he thought. *"Let's have a looksee."*

He peered into the orb and was fascinated. Never in his life had he seen something so amazing. It was like it had an entire galaxy within it. He went to touch it. Suddenly, he could hear the new shift of guards coming. He panicked and made his way to the other side of the pedestal holding the orb.

The guards had arrived and were blocking the door. Meric became nervous and began to panic even more. He turned to get a better look and gently bumped a broom leaning against the pedestal causing it to fall. The noise alerted the guards who opened the gate and came to investigate. Meric took the opportunity to sneak out but stopped. He almost forgot about the orb of falling stars. He thought about it for a moment longer, then he snuck back in while the two guards were confused and arguing over how it fell on its own. Meric reached up, grabbed the orb and made a hasty escape.

On his way down the hall, he began to think about it when guilt began to overcome him. He stopped and cursed himself for the thievery. He turned around and looked back down the hall. *"What was I thinking? I could not do this to Alzar, especially since my queen is here. No, I must put it back."* Cursing himself, he carefully walked back to the cell that contained the orb while still under the cover of the invisibility cloak. The guards were panicking.

"I do not know, I did not see it when we came in here," said the blonde guard.

"You were the first here, Rytan. This is on you. It is your fault," said the red-haired guard.

"My fault? You were right behind me. We came in here together. If anything, we will both be turned into something… unnatural as punishment," said Rytan.

"Oh no, I have no desire to become a frog. You know, the only way to break that spell is to be kissed by a beautiful woman. I have never ever heard of a beautiful woman kissing frogs. We cannot allow this. What are we going to do, Rytan, what are we going to do?"

Meric began to panic. *"A frog,"* he thought. *"That could be me as well."*

"Calm yourself, Dastan. This isn't my first loss on my watch. The wizards have not discovered many other missing trinkets because of my quick thinking," he said while tapping his head and grinning. All we have to do is search his stash for something that looks similar and replace it with that one. He will not even notice."

Meric sighed in relief. He would simply wait for them to go search for whatever they were going to get and return the items, but they did not go anywhere. Instead, the one called Rytan pulled out his knapsack and opened it.

"Wait here Dastan, I will be right back."

Rytan climbed into the sack and disappeared. Meric was astonished. He could not believe his eyes. Dastan was keeping his eyes peeled and sweating profusely. Meric thought these humans were very strange but was impressed that they must know some magic to be able to perform a trick like that.

Soon Rytan was climbing out of the sack with the help of Dastan. He pulled from his satchel something that looked closely identical to the orb of falling stars and hastily put it in the place that the original one was in.

"There, it is like it never happened. Do not worry, Dastan. Let us return to our post and stay calm." Rytan and Dastan returned to their post.

Dastan was looking for their keys. He thought he had left them in the room so once again they went in there and looked for them. Meric took this opportunity to quietly and carefully stick them back into the gate. Once Rytan came out, he noticed.

"You fool! They were in the door."

Dastan began to nervously laugh.

The two began to banter and Meric could not bear it. He had no way of returning what he had taken. He was disgusted with himself. He made his way back to his chambers and quietly snuck back in. Darlana was fast asleep. She looked peaceful and content. There was no need for him to disturb her. Meric's knapsack was on the ground next to a desk. He placed the orb within it.

Meric slipped back into his makeshift bed, careful not to wake her. She would expect him there in the morning.

"*Uhg, what have I done,*" he asked himself over and over. His mind was racing. "I have to put it back. I cannot keep it… ohh why why why," he whispered.

As he continued to dwell on it, his thoughts reminded him that the whole reason Darlana was here was to possibly collect that trinket. He wanted her to have it because he knew that a weapon with such power was their only chance against Tanimara. Now he was conflicted even more. Betray the wizard and see that his queen receives what she was looking for and win the war or risk possibly losing the war and their lives. After all, she was content simply leaving without it.

As she slept, her dreams began to stir. She was watching herself walk with what seemed like a parade though she looked miserable. The group made their way around the street, she could see herself turn back and look at a tiny casket.

Darlana's heart plummeted as she realized she was witnessing Paeris's funeral procession all over again. The pain was suffocating, like a physical weight crushing her chest.

She tried to flee, her legs pumping furiously as she sprinted away from the haunting scene. But no matter how fast she ran, Paeris's casket seemed to be everywhere, taunting her around every corner. Her screams echoed through the air as she desperately tried to escape.

Suddenly, the ground gave way beneath her feet, and she tumbled through a hole that had opened up in the road. The fall was disorienting, and everything went dark.

Darlana jolted awake, her body drenched in sweat, her breathing ragged. She sat up with a start, her hand flying to her forehead as if to ward off the lingering horror. Her gaze fell upon Meric, who had fallen asleep on the floor, his presence a comforting reminder of reality. A pang of guilt struck her for taking his bed, but it was quickly overshadowed by the residual fear and sadness from her dream. With a quiet sigh, Darlana lay back down, turning away from the darkness that still lingered in her mind.

***

Alzar had on his mind something that had been eating at him for months. Even though Darlana and Meric were staying in the tower, tonight was the night he mustered up the courage to do what he had thought about for months. He made sure that the tower was quiet as he did not want anyone to know he was leaving and so he waited until the middle of the night. He snuck out and made his way to the portal room. It was his tower so the guards paid him their respects as he walked through it not thinking anything was out of the ordinary. It was not unusual for Alzar to leave from time to time in all hours of the day and they were used to it.

He made his way into the portal room and pulled one of his teleportation runes from its chest. It glowed a deep blue and had a nice swirl etched into the stone in the shape of a portal. He tossed it on the ground and from it spawned a portal which had the view of sand dunes on the other side. He stepped through and found himself right where he intended to be. The valley of kings in Araba. This ancient site is littered with pyramid tombs of the kings of Araba from a time long since passed. The moons provided excellent light even through the shadows of the tall pyramids.

The wind was blowing the sand as Alzar trekked his way through the valley to a specific tomb. Once he arrived, he wasted no time muttering the words to unseal the giant ancient stone structure. The stone vault door seal cracked and shifted. It began moving back toward Alzar by his will. No mortal man could move such a heavy piece of stone by themselves but Alzar made it look effortless with his magic.

Once he moved it gently off to the side, he summoned a miniature orb which followed him around and provided him light with fire. Piles and piles of neatly stacked golden ornaments, statues and coins littered the inside but Alzar was not here to rob the tomb of its riches. This tomb was of a different significance to Alzar.

Millenia ago, when he first captured and imprisoned Necrosith, he confiscated a tome from him. It was called the Liber Necrom and as far as Alzar knew, it was one of a kind. Bound with the face of a dead man and created by the dragon to bring back the dead, Alzar knew that this tome was far too dangerous to even keep at his tower so he sealed it where he thought no one would look; in the Sarcophagus of a particular Araban king.

Alzar searched through a maze of halls until he finally came upon the chamber containing it. The orb glowed brighter as he got closer. Alzar was relieved to see that the sarcophagus had been undisturbed for all this time. He blew the sandy dust off the inscription and remembered who lay here now.

The first emperor of Araba, King Akenatu the Immortal.

Alzar was taken back with the memory of this man. Akenatu had mustered his forces to help Alzar capture Necrosith and imprison him within his tower. The king was mortally wounded in the battle but did not pass into the Phatra until much later. Alzar confiscated the Liber Necrom from Necrosith and when he discovered its purpose, he began to think that it was not safe to even keep in his tower considering how often things go missing. Akenatu told Alzar to bury it with him and he would guard it for eternity and so it was.

Alzar hesitated to open it. He and the king had developed a good relationship during his life. He began to feel that disturbing this site would lead to making Akenatu's spirit restless. Shame befell him as he thought more about it. The memory of Ismi and his love for her was too powerful. He muttered an incantation to gently remove the lid covering the king and moved it off to the side revealing the remains of King Akenatu wrapped up in ancient linens.

The king's arms were crossed and over the tome that Alzar sought. He lifted the king's remains out of the sarcophagus and began gently unwrapping him. The wrapping began to simply break apart revealing the mummified remains. Alzar gently pulled the Liber Necrom out from the grip of the dead king. The skin began to crack and break. The sound in such a silent place was eerie. Finally, he had what he came for. He had forgotten that he had sewn the eyes and mouth of the tomes cover shut.

Once again, he began to question what he was doing. The memory of how dangerous this tome is came back and he paused to contemplate once again. The desire to have Ismi return won again and he cursed himself. He could now clean up the mess he made and put Akenatu back in his resting place.

Alzar carefully placed Akenatu back into his sarcophagus and then using his magic, levitated it back into the stone container from where it came. He was carefully laying the lid back onto the container when the tome jostled. Startled, Alzar dropped the lid creating a deafeningly loud thud. A moment later, silence returned to the tomb.

Alzar turned his attention to the Liber Necrom. The binding still sickened him. The poor unknown individual whose face was torn from their body and wrapped around this awful tome now looked old and withered. The stitching around the eyes and mouth looked like it could break at any moment if he were not careful.

The tome jostled again. It became clear to Alzar that it was self-aware and was trying to open its eyes and mouth. He knew he had to return to his tower and get to work quickly. He got up too fast to notice the knocking within the sarcophagus and ran out of the pyramid. Alzar used his magic to replace the heavy stone door to recover the entrance and then stuffed the Liber Necrom into a satchel. He reached into his other satchel and grabbed a teleportation rune only this time, it had an etching of his tower.

From it a portal spawned and on the other side, appeared the room from which he left. Not realizing that he had forgotten to seal the pyramid, he stepped through. Back within the safety of his tower, he set to work on the tome. He stitched over the previous stitches and resealed it the best he could. Tonight was too much for him. The thought of resurrecting his companion and the thought of the possible consequences of using a tome of necromancy began to take their toll.

He fell to his knees holding the Liber Necrom. His hands trembled, his breath hitched, tears began to flow down his cheek as he felt so conflicted. He began to wonder what to do with the Liber Necrom. He thought about all the mortal races including elves. Their resolve was too weak to allow something so powerful to exist. He was certain that if someone got a hold of it, they would bring about the end of life on Abrion.

Such power, such authority could never get into the hands of a mortal and yet the thought of Ismi returned. The years they had spent together, the adventures they had. He looked at the tome and knew nothing was more of a burden than something like the Liber Necrom and thought that it could even tempt elves who were in most cases able to muster the strength to withstand that kind of temptation, the Liber Necrom needed to be hidden in a place where only he knew of and no one else. Deep within the catacombs and caves under the tower.

He would first go to his private study high in the top of the tower. He would enter and casually toss the amulet on the desk. He would then walk over to a pillar and hug it. The thoughts of Ismi overwhelmed him and he began to sob.

"Ismi, how I miss you. My heart aches so much and I know not what to do. I have the power to bring you back yet I know such a sacrilege would betray my charge…" he began when a small spark ignited out on the foyer where he and Ismi spent quality time discussing everything regarding Abrion.

He moved down the steps and stepped into the foyer overlooking the rest of the walled tower outside. The place was windowless to allow Ismi to take to the sky if she needed to. As he turned around to go back up the step, a dragon made of fire stood before him. He immediately recognized her.

"Do my eyes deceive me? Is it really you," his voice desperate with his inquiry.

"My dear Alzar, for millennia we stood side by side and did the celestials' work. It pains me so great to see you in such despair. Ata saw you enter King Atenaku's tomb and allowed something that Thalamon himself would never. She allowed me to leave the Phatra and come to you and confront you," said Ismi.

Alzar was taken back. Here she was but made of flame and in her natural form though only partially in his plane of existence. It did not matter, however. He would relish this moment with his dearest companion and friend. It was not that long ago that she had passed but to him, it felt like an eternity. At long last, he could tell her.

"We did indeed, Ismi. I miss you so much. I have a hard time going day to day and when I remember that you are gone, it clouds my judgment and I lose my bearings. I did go to the tomb and retrieved the tome we took from Necrosith millennia ago. I did this to bring you back to me yet I understand the consequences." He wiped his tears from his cheeks and took a deep breath. "I am so conflicted," he said.

Ismi gently raised her talon and caressed his cheek. The fire did not burn him for it was not actually fire but the manifestation of light. Ismi was a being of light like all who have entered the Phatra. "Alzar, I do not wish to come back, and I do not mean to bring you more pain by stating this. One day, you will understand. The moment I passed, my soul ascended into the cosmos and entered the life stream. Ledros was kind to make it so gentle. I gently flowed through the gates of the majestic Phatra. Alzar, I have a new calling. I am to remain there and protect the holy citadel from an even greater cosmic threat. Surely you understand."

Alzar did understand but he still felt the way he felt. "I despise being in this, this human form. I despise these human emotions and sometimes, what I desire most is to die," he said painfully.

She morphed into her visage form. She desired that he see her expressions. Alzar looked so hurt and Ismi wanted to help.

"My dear Alzar," she began to say as she reached into his heart. Her body now made of light allowed her hand to pass through him. "Your burden is great, this I know. Everyone knows. You do have celestial power and being human allows you to relate to all those you are charged to protect. Oh, how I wish you did not despise it so much, but Ata made the right choice when it came to your father. I will take the despair from your heart but you must keep the Liber Necrom secret and hidden away safely for eternity."

With tender fingers, Ismi reached into the depths of Alzar's being enveloping his heart. Though her grasp was gentle, Alzar felt the weight of her celestial magic. Yet, there was no pain, only a soothing sense of release. As she drew out the despair that had been suffocating him, Alzar felt his sorrow ebb away, like a dark tide receding from the shore. When Ismi finally withdrew her hand, Alzar's chest felt lighter, his heart freed from the burden of grief.

He met Ismi's gaze, his eyes locking onto hers in a silent expression of gratitude. With a subtle nod, he acknowledged the solace she had brought him. "The Liber Necrom," he began, his voice low and measured, "proves too powerful even for my abilities. I fear I am unable to destroy it." He paused, his eyes searching Ismi's for a glimmer of hope. "Perhaps, however, you might—"

Ismi's interruption cut off his words, "No, such a thing can never enter the realm of the afterlife. Its taint is too great. It comes from the very bowels of the cosmic consumer of souls. Remember. Necrosith along with all the evil in the cosmos is meant to remain in that putrid ever expanding bile for eternity, their souls never able to fully dissolve but also never be numb to the pain. Somehow, Necrosith crafted this tome to pull souls from the Phatra and even the bowels of the consumer to return to their corpses but not with their free will attached. They would be slaves to the necromancer, Alzar. If you use it on me, I would be stolen from the Phatra and brought back a slave to do your bidding."

Alzar knew the Liber Necrom was a tome of death to be used to bring back the dead but he never knew how it worked and to what extent it would have to go. "Very well, Ismi. I will keep it secret, and I will never allow another to know where it is."

"There will always be a place in my heart for you, dearest Alzar," said Ismi before petering out and returning to the Phatra. Alzar knew what he must do and wasted no time. He walked out of his private study and went to retrieve the Liber Necrom. As he grabbed it and walked out of the room, he felt a presence behind him. He turned to find no one there and thought it could be coming from the tome.

Lurking in the shadows was an eavesdropping looky-loo however unbeknownst to Alzar. He walked with haste further and further down into the tower until he was at the very bottom. This is where the tower and the catacomb caves intersect. He unlocked the gate and continued further down all the while watched by the unknown intruder who stopped short of following him down there not wanting to risk being discovered. The intruder decided to retreat back into the shadows of the tower.

***

Meric woke up and realized that his knapsack was open, and the orb was in plain sight. He looked over at Darlana who was also just waking up and quickly scooted over to his knapsack and closed it.

"Eager to leave so hastily," she said halfway through a yawn.

"We need to return to Nagrimar, my queen. I have another plan we should discuss with the council," he said while getting his things together.

"Very well, I will say goodbye to Alzar and…" she began before he interrupted her

"No… I mean. My queen, we have not a moment to lose. War looms and we cannot afford time. This was not a wasted venture, I assure you. Let us return to Nagrimar as soon as possible."

"We can leave now, Meric but I will say goodbye and thank him for his hospitality." Her voice resonated with scorn. Wisely, he did not argue. Soon, they were off.

Chapter 9
Forsaken but Not Forgotten

The fire was getting ever closer to Nagrimar. Embers were floating down coating the buildings with ash. Tens of thousands have escaped Nagrimar but tens of thousands more were trapped in the city. Yzat and Nythint were trying to help by carrying people outside of the city. The army was trying to get as many out as they could. By now, panic had stricken the streets of Nagrimar and the army lost control. They made their way out of the city and continued to try and help the denizens of Nagrimar.

After what seemed like ages of awkward flying, Darlana and Meric were almost home. In the distance, Darlana could see smoke. "Nagrimar! Meric, there is a fire. We must hurry."

Meric was alarmed. He attempted to make his hippogriff fly faster but he could not. It seemed like forever before they could reach it. The flames had reached the city and quickly began engulfing the buildings. The dry season only made things worse. They landed about five hundred meters from the north gate. The army was desperately trying to get as many out as possible. The fire had reached the gate before Darlana could get to them. Flames separated the people who were outside the city from the ones on the inside. These flames were not natural. Fire does not burn like this. The cries of the people of Nagrimar who were left inside began to echo through the forest. They were burning and there was nothing anyone but the dragons could do about it.

They could not be damaged by fire so flying in was not an issue for them but to the horror of Darlana and everyone else who escaped, the dragons were flying out of the city seemingly covered in fire. It was realized as soon as they started falling off the dragon that they were the people trying to escape engulfed in flames.

Darlana was on her knees, trembling and in disbelief. One million refugees, immigrants looking for a better life or people who simply wanted to live in her kingdom were perishing in unnatural flames before her eyes. Tears flooded her cheeks. She was screaming in vain and looked as if she could feel all their pain. It was a hellish sight to behold.

Dravon grabbed Darlana and began to run with the people out of the forest. They had a long way to go and had to do so quickly. They marched for several days, barely making time to rest. The fire was not moving as fast and indicated that it was intended for Nagrimar.

"The magic used to conjure such a fire had to come from several pyromancers," thought Meric. When they finally got out of the Forlorn Forest and made it across the river, they were in Nemis right outside of Oakenleaf's forest. Tired and in need of much rest, Many collapsed.

***

Velnir never liked being teleported. It always made him feel somewhat nauseated after. He looked around and noticed he was in Tarvana. He was teleported to somewhere close to the entrance of the city.

The elf who brought him wasted no time throwing him in a makeshift dungeon. The dragon's head was so large, they needed to use cranes to hoist it onto a cart. It was a dreadful sight for Velnir.

Another ornamented cart was being brought out. It had the standards of Tarvana on each corner and a pole erected in the middle. Two guards came and grabbed Velnir.

"I demand council," he shouted but nobody cared to listen. He protested as they hoisted him onto the ornamented cart and tied him to the pole.

Velnir now understood what was happening as he saw the cart with the dragon head in front of the cart he was on. He was to be paraded through the streets of Tarvana as a trophy of victory for the High Magister before his trial. Velnir became angry but kept his mouth shut. He did not want anything he said to be used against him in court.

The Tarvanan soldiers began to form columns in front of and behind the carts. Once everything was in place, the parade had begun. Triumphant music could be heard blaring from the elven battle horns.

Parading the defeated had not been seen since Tanimara's golden age, when Velnir's ancestors carved an empire beyond its borders. Now, most of the colonies have gained their independence and over the centuries, the practice of parading the defeated enemy had faded.

Personally, Velnir had never witnessed it but heard stories from his father, Ruvyn and his grandfather's epic battles. Velnir had hopes to keep the legacy of the Melfarin name alive by taking the fight to the orcs in their own land like the elves did in the days of old. He had been naive and so eager to prove himself that he ignored the danger he left behind when he went to war. He should have listened to his uncle.

The parade was now in full swing. Velnir had a rope tied around his body and neck. His hands were bound behind his back and around the pole. It was a very unpleasant experience. Crowds gathered and hurled insults and rotten fruit at Velnir much to his surprise.

"I defeated the orcs in the Sundered lands, I brought justice to our people, why do you do this to me? Why do you…" he began to yell out toward the crowd before the elf standing behind him pulled the rope around his neck causing him to choke. After the painful attack, the elf behind him released his grip loosening the rope around his neck. Velnir got the message.

His hands and neck were being rubbed raw by the bindings due to the jostling of the cart being driven down the road. It was clear that these were not designed to be comfortable. Velnir wondered why in this day and age would anyone tolerate such torture of their own kind in Tanimara. It was a travesty to say the least.

Finally, the parade came to a stop. The cart Velnir was bound to was turned towards the balcony from which the

High Magister and his Magisters were sitting. He was wearing an elegant purple robe and carrying a scepter that Velnir was unfamiliar with.

Velnir did however recognize the crown he was wearing to be the ancient crown of the elven emperors before the republic was formed. It came as no surprise that all along, Raften was plotting and scheming behind the backs of the Melfarins.

When his opportunity came, he took it and so the Melfarins were no more. No one would stand in his way and now there he stood with that smug look Velnir came to immediately hate. He could not wait for the opportunity to tell his side of what happened during his trial.

"Soon when the people hear of what you have done, I will be released and it will be you on this cart," yelled Velnir.

The crowd cheered and Velnir was confused. Was this not the crowd that just threw insults and rotten food at him? Could he win them over that easily?

Excitement filled Velnir's heart. He was determined.

Two elven guards made their way to the cart. He could hardly wait for them to untie him so that he may face Raften in court but they did not untie him. They stood behind him, each grabbing a piece of rope that was threaded through the pole and wrapped around Velnir's neck. Velnir's heart sank. It was at this moment that he realized there would be no trial.

Raften nodded and the two elves pulled on the rope tightly and began to strangle Velnir. He was not immediately expecting it and was exhaling the moment they pulled. It was so painful. Velnir opened his mouth in vain in an attempt to get some air into his lungs. His body began to convulse and he began to lose consciousness.

As he faded, his life passed before his eyes. Quality time with his father, growing up in Atlan and getting married to Darlana. How he missed her. The day his daughter was born was the best day of his life. He pictured their faces during their happy times together.

Thoughts of Magris and Arlen in their youth filled him with regret just before he felt himself losing the last bit of his strength and losing consciousness.

Once it was clear that Velnir was dead, one of the two guards pulled out his sword and decapitated him. The other grabbed a box and placed his head into it and brought it to Raften. The people were left outside to look at the head of the dragon that was brought with Velnir. They were relieved to see it as it meant that Dragons were defeatable with their technology. This spurred recruitment.

Raften smiled as he received the box containing the head of Velnir. He opened it and saw Velnirs eyes looking at him. "It appears it has become a new family tradition for the Melfarins to lose their heads and be delivered to loved ones," he said before closing the box and handing it to a servant.

***

Once everyone that could cross the river did, the Nagrimarans felt fortunate that the army had made it. Many of the people did not. Both of the dragons were accounted for. The army was on the west end and the civilians were on the east.

From the north, volleys of arrows rained down and many bolts found their way to the exhausted Nagrimaran ranks. It was a surprise attack by the Tanimarans from the north.

Darlana realized that the ships sent by Tanimara dropped the soldiers off first in Northgarde and came back around to the coast of the Forlorn Forest to cause the fire and burn them out. They were looking to end the war quickly.

The Nagrimarans began firing at the Tanimarans unleashing devastating amounts of carnage upon them. The denizens began to panic. They had nowhere else to go so they fled toward Nemis. The Nagrimarans were advancing on the Tanimarans but were exhausted.

They stopped short of their spear line and set up the repeater crossbows on tripods and loaded them with the five hundred round magazines. When the Nagrimarans began to fire, the bolts tore through the Tanimaran shields and killed scores of them.

Hundreds after hundreds fell. The fighting was fierce. The Nagrimarans used the trees to their advantage and were picking Tanimarans off left and right.

The Tanimarans formed ranks in open ground and this left them at a severe disadvantage. They were completely caught off guard by the Nagrimaran technology. They began to panic. The Nagrimarans were able to establish a line which was to the west and the Tanimarans have crossed the river into the east and into Helmgarde. This would not suffice. Centaurs led by Darlana who was mounted on Dravon, charged the flanks of the Tanimarans, leaving a wave of carnage in their wake.

Darlana dismounted and began cutting throats, shoving her daggers under the chins of her enemies and disemboweling them. She was angry and full of hatred. She screamed as she made her way through the ranks, tears still running down her cheeks.

Soon the noise left and Darlana could not hear anything. Her emotions were out of control. Anger, resentment, hatred and regret all flooded her heart at once. Then there was only rage which had overcome her.

Not a moment later, She held her daggers out and screamed at the Tanimarans. With all the speed and agility she could muster, she leapt into the air and descended upon them.

It was a small victory for Nagrimar but one that was bitter.

Darlana snapped out of it and witnessed scores of dead Tanimarans that she seemingly had killed. She stood there and contemplated how she was capable of this. She remembered every moment but had zero control. Something else took control of her because she let it… she would not do it again.

The army began to recover and set up defenses. The Tanimarans remained on the other side of the river. The Nagrimarans were trapped because they could not break through the Tanimaran line. As far as Darlana knew, the coast of the Forlorn Forest was still under blockade.

Darlana called for her council to meet over by her. Dirty, battered and beaten, they all came except for the dragons. Nobody knew where they were. Dravon's hairs were singed and he was covered in the blood of Tanimarans as was Meric to Darlana's surprise.

Darlana came in looking rough. She was also covered in blood and recovering from her blood lust. She looked at all who were present and realized just how battered the army and denizens were. She looked around and saw the injured and dying, most of which had soot on their faces from the fire. She turned back to her council and took a deep breath.

"The strategy used by the Tanimarans should not come as a surprise to anyone," said Darlana in a very stressed tone.

"We should run them down," said Dravon angrily. Darlana shook her head.

"We cannot compete with the Tanimarans right now. Everyone is weary from trying to get out of the forest. We must retreat and find shelter somewhere else." She sighed.

The sound of a dragon's roar could be heard from the direction of Nagrimar. It was Nythint and Yzat. They swooped down from the cloud cover and pummeled the Tanimaran camp with fire. The Nagrimarans began to cheer. They made pass after pass. The Tanimarans began to flee and the dragons pursued.

Once the Tanimarans were too spread out, they returned to the Nagrimaran camp. Darlana was relieved and so was Meric but Dravon wanted blood. The time for fighting was over for now though and the people needed rest.

"Yzat, they attacked us while we were trying to escape. They knew we would be here," said Darlana.

"Only Vulas would be so cruel," said Meric.

"Who is Vulas?" asked Dravon. Everyone else was interested as well.

"He is the Supreme Commander of the Tanimaran army and is known to be very cruel. His strategy relies on surprise and fear. He was promoted after Velnir's father, Lord Ruvyn, was killed in battle," said Meric.

Commander Folwin had approached the council.

"Now we know where the Tanimaran army went. They must have landed in Northgarde and made their way through the crossroads and down through Helmgarde to here. This is not a large Tanimaran force though. We were able to beat them too easily after days of weary marching out of the Forlorn Forest," said Meric.

"Nonsense, they were on the other side of the river when we came and scattered them," said Yzat.

"It does not matter. We have almost one million people to manage and most of them are in the surrounding woods," stated Dravon.

"Nagrimar is a ruin. All those who remained have perished in the flames. Nagrimar was the only city in the Forlorn Forest. The surrounding settlements were used by centaur and are primitive," said Rizim. Dravon was displeased with his comment about primitive centauren settlements.

"If they are here now, Madir must have been taken back by the Tanimarans and Magris was either captured or killed. We must make our way to the Tower of Alzar. We will figure out where to go from there but as it stands. I feel the war is lost," said Meric.

"Silence," demanded Darlana. She was extremely stressed out. The council obeyed her and waited for her to speak. "Velnir and Magris are still in Madir. We will figure it out and Nagrimar is not a ruin. We can rebuild! The city is made of stone and last I observed, stone does not BURN," snapped Darlana.

"What now, my queen?" asked Dravon.

"Alzar has expressed no desire to assist us. We are on our own unless I can negotiate an alliance with other elvish or human or even dwarven kingdoms," said Darlana.

"Where do we…" Meric started before Darlana interrupted him.

"Silence, please. I am trying to think," said Darlana. She was on her knees with both of her hands, palms down in the blood-soaked dirt. "Where are we currently?" she asked.

"We are where the river Haran forks between the border of Nemis where we currently are and Helmgarde," answered Dravon.

"Camp here. Send an emissary to the Nemisians so they know that we have not invaded but sought shelter for nearly a million of my people. Dravon, Yzat and Nythint, take the centaur and follow the Tanimarans. Kill them all. Meric, you and I are going to go to the twilight wood and speak with Glade-King Eldar."

"Darlana, are you all right?" asked Dravon.

"I do not know. Too much happened too fast."

"I will take Yzat, Nythint and the centaur to find the Tanimarans. Dravon, we will alert you when we find them," said Yzat.

Dravon began to rally the centaur as the dragons took to the sky to begin their search. Darlana swayed on her feet, blinking rapidly as her vision blurred. She looked down at her side and noticed she was bleeding. She had been stabbed during the battle.

"Meric, I need you to speak to them. I am in no condition right now. Tell them… whatever you need to to calm them down and make sure they do not lose their hope. It might be all they have left." Darlana then crawled over to a tree and curled up in the fetal position.

Meric was confident in his ability to do as she asked. He made his way to the top of a hill overlooking the riverside where all of the elves started building their camp. It would seem they are ahead of his message to camp here and he was pleased to see that. He was giving a powerful speech about the fighting spirit, the will of a Nagrimaran and how they have always overcome things like this.

Darlana smiled. Hearing Meric speak was soothing. He was not a fighter but he was an excellent statesman and of that, she had no doubt. Thoughts of Meric had to wait however. She was worried about the amount of blood she was losing and unsure what to do. They had brought no medical supplies in their hasty escape from Nagrimar.

By the time Meric had returned, she was sitting upright and cross legged.

"You did better than I could have, Meric. Thank you," she said.

"Darlana, are you all right?" he asked her genuinely.

"I will not deceive you," she said before looking up at him with genuine worry on her face. "I am losing a lot of blood. I think I was stabbed in the battle, and I need to see Alzar." She removed her hand which she was covering her wound with and showed Meric.

"Very well, I will arrange for it immediately. They decided to spend the night in the camp. Her people did not forget to serve her, and she was humbled. They built her a tent and brought her whatever they could. Several soldiers were posted right outside.

Darlana began to think quickly and ordered people to forage for herbs that she could create a healing salve with. She felt compelled to allow several of the injured and burned elves to stay in the tent with her.

She applied a healing salve to her wound which seemed to slow the infection immediately. She worked long into the night applying healing salves and bandages to the wounded. She had not slept but had to leave. She left Commander Folwin in charge until she returned.

The smoke was thick and people were getting sick but there was nothing they could do. Darlana saw how distraught her people were and they looked up to her for leadership. She wondered if it was truly right to leave them now but she was concerned that infection might take hold in her wound and felt she had to do something so she and Meric made their way to the Tower of Alzar. They had about a five day walk in her condition but the road was on the outskirts of Oakenleaf's forest. Perhaps they could hitch a ride.

They met with Oakenleaf who was more than happy to give them a lift. For two days, he walked them through his forest and when they got to the edge, he bid them farewell. Unbeknownst to both Meric and Darlana, this was the same route that Velnir and his companions took when they first set out on their quest to meet the wizard.

Meric noticed that this part of the forest was different from the rest. It seemed more alive and he felt as though something or many things were watching them.

Darlana showed no interest. Her skin had turned pale and her veins turned black. She was sweating and feeling very weak. The infection was manifesting but she still kept walking. Meric felt for her. They stepped off the path and decided to rest against a tree. Darlana slumped over and Meric began to panic.

"Darlana, Darlana… my queen."

Darlana had found herself in complete darkness.

"Darlana," said an ominous voice. She had heard this voice before.

"I am dying," Darlana said desperately.

"You are indeed but I can help you, for a price," it said.

Darlana was unable to speak now. She slipped out of consciousness once again.

***

Several little green eyes began to appear in the shadow cast by the trees. Meric stopped speaking and looked around. He grabbed his knife and stood guard over Darlana but the eyes simply sat there and blinked.

After a while, Meric assumed that they were curious wildlife critters and let his guard down. Something poked its head out but appeared to be under a mushroom. Meric did not want to step away from Darlana. He was curious, nonetheless.

Whatever it was was now moving toward them. Meric got up and was ready to stomp it when it lifted its head and looked at him. It was not under the mushroom, it was the mushroom…

"What sort of sorcery is this?" demanded Meric.

"No sorcery. I come in peace as do my companions. We see you have a companion who is not doing so well," said the mushroom person as he pointed to Darlana. Meric looked at Darlana and then back to the mushroom.

"Yes, she is sick and needs to see the wizard, Alzar. What are you?"

"I am a myconid. So are they." The little mushroom revealed the rest of his companions who were all now coming out of the shadows. "I am Sporepod. Perhaps we can help."

Meric was about to answer when all of a sudden, all of the mushrooms scurried back to their hiding holes. He heard something approaching from the path. As it got closer, Meric recognized it to be Lemmi.

Lemmi was smoking a pipe as he always does and leisurely making his way through the forest. The tiny door on the brim of his hat had opened up and from it came an arm which tapped the brim of his hat and held out its hand. Lemmi then reached into his satchel and pulled out what appeared to be food and handed it to the creature. It quickly grabbed it and shut the door. This intrigued Meric as he was not sure what was living in Lemmi's hat.

"Hey, hey, hey," said Meric, attempting to get his attention. Lemmi turned to face Meric, his lips still wrapped around the pipe.

"Ohhh, the elves who recently paid us a visit. What, may I ask, are you doing here?

"We were on our way back to Nagrimar and a fire was engulfing the city. We evacuated all that we could and crossed the river into Nemis when we were attacked by a Tanimaran army without warning. Our army quickly pushed them on the other side of the river in Helmgarde. The dragons came and scattered the Tanimarans and gave us a much needed respite. Around one million Nagrimarans are camped on the border of the Forlorn Forest and Nemis. Darlana is very sick and we need to see Alzar."

Lemmi approached Darlana. He moved in for a closer look. The halfling puffed his pipe and stepped back.

"Yeah, she is indeed in need of Alzar's attention. We must make haste." Lemmi smirked, pleased with his rhyme. He then turned and summoned a portal to the Tower of Alzar using a rune of teleportation. Meric was amazed but wasted no time picking up his queen and taking her through.

Alzar was surprised to see them. "What ails her?"

"She was stabbed and has lost a lot of blood," said Meric.

Alzar wasted no time. He said an incantation and Darlana levitated. She moved wherever he moved and he was moving fast. Meric had to keep up. "Stabbed," he inquired.

"The Tanimarans, they burnt the Forlorn Forest and the fire made it to Nagrimar. When we returned, people were evacuating. She tried to lead the people of Nagrimar out of the Forlorn and to hear but Commander Vulas was waiting for us. She was injured during the battle."

Alzar was surprised. "I had no idea the Tanimarans were on the continent. How did they slip past my scrying orbs," he said before beginning his examination of Darlana. He moved in for a closer look. "Receiving a stab wound certainly led to a loss of a considerable amount of blood; however, that is clearly not only the case in regards to her ailment." He turned to Meric and motioned him to look at her. "Her veins are black, and I imagine…" he said before lifting her eyelid. "And there you have it. Eyes as black as the abyss," said Alzar.

Meric shook his head as he was genuinely unsure. "Poison dagger?" he inquired.

Darlana was awake and coherent but could not speak. She was too weak to do anything.

"It is likely poison, yes," he said, his tone worrying.

Meric gasped. "Will she be all right? Can you cure her?"

"Darlana tried to say something but lost consciousness.

"I will need your assistance, Lemmi retrieve my medical kit and find Rubus. Meric, I need you as well," said Alzar.

They grabbed a stretcher and carried her to what Meric assumed would be a medical ward. Rubus arrived and picked Darlana up off the stretcher and placed her on a bed.

Alzar held out what looked to be a shriveled kiwi hanging from a chain and then he raised his staff. Lemmi and Rubus backed off toward Meric and they observed Alzar chanting in a language that Meric did not understand. The runes on his staff began to light up with a green hue.

Darlana's eyes shot open. She opened her mouth as wide as she could and tried to gasp for air. She could not otherwise move. Meric's instincts urged him to go to her but Rubus simply placed his hand on Meric's shoulder and the force was enough to stop him in his tracks.

Offended, Meric looked back and when he realized it was Rubus, he relaxed and smiled. Rubus was a giant jolly wizard with a pleasant calming smile and charm who possessed remarkable physical strength for a wizard.

"No hard feelings, little elf. Just cannot have you interrupt my brother at the moment. It would be best if you stayed back here with us and just let him do his thing. This is not his first time," said Rubus in a surprisingly charming tone.

Rubus did not have to ask to get the message across. It was clear to Meric that he was simply being polite. It seemed it was his nature.

"It requires an excessive amount of effort and is by no means easy; however, confidence based on one's experience is taken into…" Lemmi began to explain before being interrupted.

"I am hungry, are you two hungry?" asked Rubus.

"Not at all. How can anyone think of eating at a time like this? Our capitol city was just evacuated, hundreds of thousands likely perished in the flames. We were ambushed by our own kin and they killed tens of thousands more. My queen is critically injured." Meric placed his hands over his face and sat down.

Guilt began to overcome him. He remembered the day the forges were sabotaged and cursed the day quietly to himself. All of this had gone so far out of control and he was beginning to feel responsible.

"Suit yourself, but, uh," began Rubus as he leaned in closer to Meric while he sat there covering his face. "Be sure not to go in there… it is… well, it is a gruesome business. A pretty little pointy ear like yourself probably gets a bit squeamish around such things, I'd imagine."

Smiling, Rubus patted Meric on the shoulder. Meric gave him a glaring look before covering his face once more. It was true, Meric had no desire to watch Alzar remove the poison from Darlana.

Rubus and Lemmi left to find some food. Meric started thinking about the orb of falling stars which was still in his knapsack. He looked down at it, glad it was not captured by the Tanimarans.

The thought of that shuddered Meric's mind. He thought about turning it back over to Alzar and explaining what he did. On the other hand, he wanted revenge for his queen. They have wasted valuable time and were not sure what state the Nagrimarans were currently in.

Everything seemed to be falling apart and spiraling out of control.

Chapter 10
The Abyss of the Soul

Commander Folwin was looking through one of the few scrying crystals and fewer scrying orbs they had and had noticed that the fire was still burning and showed no indication that it would end anytime soon. He tucked the crystal into his satchel and sighed.

Horns blared in alarm. Folwin looked and on the horizon from the west was an even larger Tanimaran army marching toward them.

The dragons and centaur were still out looking for them. *"How did they miss an army this massive?"* he thought. "FORM RANKS, FORM RANKS," he yelled.

The outnumbered Nagrimarans formed ranks and began to open fire with their repeater crossbows befalling several Tanimarans. The panicked Nagrimaran denizens retreated behind the army which was now taking up defenses in the tree line.

The Tanimarans stopped and formed ranks as well. They had crossed the river somewhere upstream and made it down here undetected. Their shields were up and over them.

Tanimarans knew how to make a good defense but were clearly unprepared to go up against repeater crossbows as their bolts pierced the shields and brought the bearer down. The Tanimarans fired volley after volley of arrows and fortunately for the Nagrimarans, most hit the trees.

It looked like the Tanimarans were digging in under heavy fire from the Nagrimarans. Folwin could not believe his eyes.

By now, the Nagrimaran army had taken position along the whole tree line. There he was with his pyromancers on griffins. Supreme commander Vulas flew over his army and began conjuring firestorms and hurling firebolts into the Nagrimaran ranks.

They pulled their swords and shields out in an effort to protect themselves. It was then that the Tanimarans began an organized rush toward the Nagrimarans. Folwin braced for heavy melee combat but heard a ruckus to his flanks. More Tanimarans had ambushed them and now they were becoming surrounded.

"Where are those damned dragons," he thought. Folwin understood the Tanimaran tactics very well; however, the Nagrimaran army was trained to attack and defend with the help of dragons. They had no idea how to defend without them and Folwin became worried.

The Tanimaran army was at least five times larger than the one they engaged earlier and sent the dragons and centaur after. Folwin realized it was a ruse and bowed his head in shame. He could hear the Tanimarans slaughtering all the denizens as they began to flee farther west into Nemis. He was fighting with the fury of a hardened warrior. He hoped that the army could hold the Tanimarans off long enough for the people to make it to safety.

A moment later, an arrow pierced his eye and went through his skull, killing him instantly.

***

"We have been chasing them for hours and it seems like we are going in circles, General," observed Dravon's lieutenant.

Yzat and Nythint were soaring high above and hollering at the centaur where the Tanimarans were going but most of them were scattered and going every which way. The dragons were too big to go into the trees and the Centaur were slogged down by the natural roots and foliage.

"This does not seem right," agreed Dravon. "There are not that many of them anyway. We will go back to the camp and keep it safe." Dravon whistled at the dragons and got the dragon's attention. He motioned them down and they came and landed in front of him.

Dravon trotted up to them. "Something is not right."

"We are having trouble ourselves. It's confusing seeing all the little elves running every which way. This would be much easier if they were standing still," said Nythint.

"This is no longer worth our trouble. Let us return to the camp," suggested Dravon.

"Yes, General," agreed the dragons.

Yzat took to the sky and Dravon ordered the centaur to gallop back to camp. Several hours later, they noticed smoke as they came up on the camp. They hurried and landed.

To their horror, the Nagrimaran army was annihilated and the denizens slaughtered. The river was running red with their blood and the stench of death was growing in the air.

Dravon's heart sank as he realized that he fell for a ruse. The Tanimarans they were chasing were a distraction for the dragons while the larger Tanimaran army snuck around and attacked.

Women, children and even the animals were not spared. This was not a battle nor was it any longer a war. It was an eradication and Dravon now understood that. He took off his feathered headdress and held it to his chest in quiet contemplation. There were far too many for them to bury so they had no choice but to leave them there.

Dravon and the dragons knew that Darlana and Meric were supposed to be at the Tower of Alzar. Perhaps the Nagrimaran survivors, if there were any, headed that way. The centaur began their somber march. Above them, Yzat flew in slow circles, keeping watch. Unlike griffins, dragons struggled with distant sight.

***

Meric had returned with Lemmi and Rubus to the room that Alzar and Darlana were in. By this time, Darlana was sitting up and had a blanket over her.

Alzar was giving her some sort of warm drink and they were having a conversation. Meric approached his queen and noticed right away that her color had come back to her face. Her eyes were bluish purple again and he could not see her veins. Her wounds were also dressed and seemed to be done properly. She looked at him, her face distressed.

"I am all right, Meric. Alzar was able to help."

Meric had several questions to ask but decided to wait for another time. Alzar had recommended that they stay with him for a few days until he could make sure that she was fine.

The next morning, alarm bells could be heard and woke Meric. Alzar came banging on his door. Meric quickly sat up and opened the door to see people running around panicked. Alzar was on his way back so Meric went into Darlana's chambers.

"My queen, wake up. The wizard is here," he gently said while nudging her awake.

She got up and Alzar had also entered.

"Come with me, immediately and make haste," he said angrily.

Darlana and Meric did not bother dressing down the night before and therefore were already dressed. They followed Alzar to the balcony that Meric immediately recognized as the one he had visited during his last stay. They made their way across the platform and to the edge.

Outside of the wall surrounding the tower were thousands of Nagrimarans desperately pouring in through the gate. Darlana could see a massive Tanimaran army marching not far behind but could not see Yzat or the centaur. She threw a scrying orb into the air. It made its way toward the Tanimaran army so that she could get a better look through her scrying crystal.

At the head of it stood a tall elf with short black hair and broken pointed ears.

"Vulas," said Meric.

What is the meaning of this? Why in the nether is a Tanimaran army outside my walls?

Darlana looked at him with scorn. "Is it not obvious, Alzar. They have come for me!"

Darlana turned and angrily walked off. She pulled her daggers out and disappeared.

"Oh no, no no no…" said Meric.

Alzar caught up to Darlana. "Let me handle Vulas, Darlana. This is my tower."

Darlana was pleased to hear it and happy to oblige. Seeing firsthand what Alzar is capable of, she knew he had it under control.

Alzar pulled the brim of his pointed hat down, pulled up his robes and began to walk briskly toward the gate. It was a long walk, and it took him a while to get there. With the wave of his hand, the gate slammed open.

"Greetings, Wizard. I am Supreme Commander Vulas of Tanimara. I am here to…" started Vulas before being interrupted by Alzar.

"I have no quarrel with you, elf. Turn around and leave immediately or you shall bear witness to my power and despair!"

Vulas did not like being interrupted as was evident by his facial expression. "Under normal circumstances, harboring an enemy would be an act of war but given who you are and your connection to the emperor, I will make an exception if Darlana and Meric come with us, Wizard. I have orders to bring them back to Tarvana to face judgment, alive."

Darlana was standing behind Alzar at this point. He had not realized she followed him.

"This is long overdue, apostate. Your father wishes to end this war now," said Vulas. He then had one of his soldiers bring her a box. "A gift from the Emperor of Tanimara."

Darlana opened the box. She put her hand over her mouth and her eyes welled with tears. Alzar took it from her and closed it.

Darlana screamed in agony as her heart shattered. The cries bothered even the Tanimaran soldiers. Meric took the box from Alzar and brought it away from them. He opened it and to his horror, it contained the badly decomposed head of his cousin, Velnir. He was sickened by this and quickly closed the box and set it on the ground.

Darlana fell to the ground in agony. She was breathing heavily and her despair turned into anger and then into seething rage. She unsheathed a dagger and quickly threw it at Vulas which buried itself between his eyes. He fell off his griffin and died. The other Tanimarans were not sure what to do at first but someone ordered shields and spears. Their army braced for combat but remained in place.

"I will not tell you again, elves of Tanimara. Your leader is dead, now leave or I will…" Alzar was interrupted by several bursts of fire breath from the dragons including Rizim and some of his brood.

For the moment, Darlana had forgotten they were now staying with Alzar. The Centaur led by Dravon smashed into the heavily defended flank of the Tanimarans. Alzar was completely caught off guard.

Darlana wasted no time retrieving her dagger from the corpse of Vulas and leapt into the Tanimaran ranks. Meric was stunned. Alzar put his hands together and conjured two balls of lightning. He then combined them and from his hands lept a stream of lightning which he weaved through the Tanimarans causing thousands to explode with thundering violence. The look on his face terrified Meric.

Yzat showed up and landed next to Meric, startling him.

"Get on, let us destroy them," he said, motioning Meric to mount him.

Meric climbed up to Yzat's back and loaded a repeater crossbow with a five hundred round magazine. They took to the sky and began strafing maneuvers. Meric and Yzat were blowing fire and shooting at the Tanimarans in a zigzag pattern. The centaur were ferociously but slowly cutting down the Tanimaran flank but taking heavy losses themselves. Meric could not see Darlana or Alzar but began firing into the Tanimaran ranks. He emptied magazine after magazine.

Nythint landed in the middle of the Tanimaran army and unsheathed Razorheart. He buffeted the Tanimarans with his wings and knocked scores down. He then tail swiped several others before unleashing a terrible fire breath. He swung Razorheart around and cleaved scores more and nothing could quite prepare the Tanimarans for this. To see a full sized armored dragon standing on two legs and swinging a sword around was something they never thought they would see.

Darlana was shredding her way through the Tanimaran line. For the first time in a long time, she felt exhilarated. She hated them all. Without care for their well being and with deadly precision, she cut many throats, stabbed many in the eye and brutally eviscerated many Tanimaran soldiers with such haste, it was likely they did not even see her coming.

Darlana wrapped her legs around the torso of a Tanimaran from behind, pulled his head back and buried her dagger into his neck. This did not go unnoticed. Many of the Tanimarans turned their spears toward her.

Now they realized she was there and began to focus on her. Darlana screamed as if inviting their attention. She skillfully lept up and plunged her daggers through tens of them with unnatural speed and accuracy, piercing the heart perfectly. She landed on the shoulders of a burly Tanimaran and pulled his helmet off. She then sunk her teeth into his neck and viciously chewed it into a bloody mess.

The Tanimaran fell and began to flail in agony but Darlana's bite was too much. He succumbed but not before gurgling his intangible last words. The Tanimarans were terrified and began to retreat.

Darlana watched as the dragons and centaur began to give chase. Alzar was using some sort of gravity magic bubble to suspend thousands of Tanimarans in the air. They were kicking and pulling but unable to get anywhere. He then started conjuring thousands of small molten bolts which appeared just above the suspended Tanimarans.

Each bolt fell and found its target. They began piercing the Tanimarans and soon all of them were dead. It was then that he released the bubble and it began to rain dead elves. It was a terrifying spectacle as Alzar executed it with such ease.

She saw Meric on the back of Yzat firing at the retreating Tanimarans. Meric just fired his last bolt.

Yzat was wasting no energy. He was unleashing harsh breath attacks on the retreating Tanimarans.

They had broken and were running for the coast, undoubtedly for their ships. They ended the chase and returned to the Tower of Alzar as they were getting tired and lacked the strength in numbers to pursue.

Yzat landed on the corpses of the fallen Tanimarans with a loud squishy crunch. The other dragons joined them. The centaur began to strip the corpses of their armor and weapons and the dragons began swallowing the dead Tanimarans whole. They were hungry and needed to replenish their energy after last week.

Meric dismounted and made his way over to Alzar, Darlana, Nythint and Dravon who was informing her of what happened at the fork of the river Haran. Never has any of them seen her look so defeated.

"My husband, my people," was all she said before lowering her head and beginning her walk back to Alzar's tower.

Meric, Alzar and Dravon stood there and watched her.

"Celestials, she has been through the nether and back," said Alzar.

"Indeed," said Dravon. "The forest burns, our homes are ash. Our kingdom is in ruin. Velnir is dead. I do not see how we can rebuild. The last time she did it, it took four hundred or so years. I will not be alive long enough for her to gain back what she has lost nor will I live long enough to see her happy again."

Meric looked angry but defeated as well. He chose to remain silent. Several days had passed, the dead were cleaned up and consumed or burned. The denizens that survived were recovering despite their losses. The tower and its people had been working tirelessly to help them and for that, Darlana was grateful.

Days blurred together as Darlana isolated herself in her chambers within the tower, surrendering to the suffocating grief that pierced her heart when she saw the head of her husband in the box. The memory of her first family and the loss of her second left her in the abyss.

Numbness crept in, a hollow echo of her former self. She found herself lost in conversations with the dark side of herself for which she found temporary solace. The desire for vengeance only grew as did her hatred for Tanimarans. Time began to lose its meaning as she neglected the basic necessities of life.

Meals slipped under her door went uneaten, her body unwashed, her spirit unmoored. The darkness that long lurked within her began to seep out of every pore, revitalizing the familiar ache and depression brought on by loneliness she was all too familiar with.

Several days had passed before she stepped out of her chambers. When she did, she was surprised to see Nythint standing outside her door. Her heart swelled ever so slightly with the knowledge that he remained there the whole time and respected her privacy. She hugged and smiled at him before she made her way to Meric's chambers. He was eager to see her.

Finally, they could get back to business. His guilt left him impatient and antsy.

Meric hesitated. "My queen…"

His voice softened, unsure of the right words. She did not say anything. Her ears drooped and so did Meric's. She trudged over and sat on his bed next to him. She wrapped her arms around him and buried her face into his shoulder and began to sob quietly.

Meric felt her pain and wrapped his arms around her and held her tight. They were sharing a moment mourning the ones they loved. Meric was more levelheaded than Darlana at the moment and she was looking to him for comfort.

"We must get you something to eat. You are losing your strength," he said calmly.

"I know," she said, still sobbing and sniffling. Meric pulled a tissue out and gave it to her which she used to wipe her eyes. He got her up and walked her out and into the dining hall of the tower. She could not eat much and did not say anything. Everyone was looking at her and sympathized.

Meric knew that now was no time to bring in what was left of the council and discuss what they needed to do next. As long as Alzar was willing to allow them too, they would stay at the tower.

***

Alzar was discussing the Nagrimaran situation with Rubus and Lemmi when he was interrupted by a messenger.

"Master, I bring terrible news. Bali was razed and a dwarven army sent to counter the Tanimarans was all but massacred."

Bali had a special place in Alzar's heart. It was where he was born and raised all those millenia ago. It was the ancient Nemisian capital and if razed, would plunge Nemis into a state of Chaos. Alzar knew this was in retaliation for many things. He was aware that the Dwarves agreed to attack the Tanimarans if they set foot on the continent.

"*What a terrible price they paid,*" he thought.

He could no longer intervene himself. He got up and searched for Meric who was himself chatting with others about their unfortunate situation. He was not hard to find.

"Meric, I need your assistance. Please come with me," interrupted Alzar.

Darlana looked up at Alzar and then to Meric.

"It is all right, my queen. I will be right back," he promised her. Nythint elected to stay with her while Meric followed Alzar into a room where he met with Yzat, Rizim and several other dragons he did not know personally.

"Bali is the city of my birth. It is the capital of Nemis, and it has been razed and a Dwarven army was massacred by the Tanimarans. No doubt because of the agreements between them and the Nagrimarans or perhaps because of my involvement in the recent battle."

"I thought they were going to their ships," stated Meric.

"Obviously, they diverted," remarked Rizim. Meric was irritated by the sarcasm and disrespectful tone but remained silent.

"We must force them out of there and either send them back to Tanimara or kill them. Tanimara will not be allowed to impose its will across the globe anymore. I implore you all to go and route them out of this continent. My staff and I will make our way to the ruins of Bali and help the displaced people rebuild. I have plans for Nemis that I think will be globally beneficial."

Meric and the dragons wasted no time. They took off toward Bali as fast as they could.

The retreating Tanimarans were only an hour ahead of Meric and the dragons by now. They soon caught up to them and halted mid air. The Tanimarans had made it to the coast and were attempting to hastily board their ships but there were way too many of them crowded and clumped together.

From up here, they looked like a colony of tiny armored ants scurrying to get out of the way of something much much bigger and something bigger was coming for the Tanimarans. Thousands of Tanimarans were clumped together and Meric could not be more delighted. The dragons swooped down. Meric cocked his mounted repeater crossbow.

Fire erupted from the mouths of the dragons as they flew over. Time and time again, the dragons strafed and there was nowhere to run or hide. Once the numbers were thinned enough to no longer be worth the effort, the dragons flew away from the coast and toward the Tanimaran ships.

They all began trying to turn away in a desperate but feeble attempt to flee. "Now is the time. Light them up!" said Rizim.

The dragons swooped down and began picking the ships off one by one and with relative ease. These ships were transport ships ill equipped for combating dragons.

Scores and scores of them were destroyed before the dragons were getting tired. They had to turn back but on this day, they dealt Tanimara an equally devastating blow, or at least that was the hope.

Meric knew that Tanimara could muster another force of the same size if they felt the need. He understood that Nagrimar was no more. To him, at least. The Tanimarans had won the war.

Chapter 11
Never Give Up

Darlana was sitting with Alzar and Nythint in the library when Meric and the dragons had returned. She was eager to hear their report.

"The Tanimaran expeditionary force is no more," stated Meric.

"Nor are most of the Tanimaran ships," said Rizim.

Darlana was pleased to hear this.

"How did you do it," she asked in a rather macabre manner.

"We ignited their ranks with our fire," said Rizim.

"Did they suffer?"

Everyone looked among themselves and seemed confused. "The ones that were caught directly with the initial breath are usually incinerated instantly and likely only felt it for a moment. The ones on the outer area simply ignite once our fire reaches them. The flames are mixed with our flammable saliva and it sticks to their armor quite well."

"Heh, good," she said with a quivery yet teary eye and a half smile.

Meric felt terrible. He was no longer proud to call himself Tanimaran after witnessing what his own people did to his queen and her people all because she loved a human prince.

"They will not have died in vain," said Darlana.

"What do you mean?" asked Alzar. Meric furrowed his brow, also curious.

"Glade-King Eldar of the Twilight Wood was once one of the Nagrimarans." He felt a calling to live in the woods. Not in a city like Nagrimar. The Forlorn Forest was a great place for him for a while, but he had a following and they wanted to break away from Nagrimar. He humbly asked me for permission and said that it was not at all personal. At the time, I was angry and sent him and his followers off. Since then, we have renewed our friendship and rekindled our alliance." Darlana looked up at them from where she was sitting. "I will go to him and ask him for help. Then I will go to the dwarves and perhaps the humans again… and again," she said.

"We will stand with you, my queen," said Dravon.

"I know you will, General. The centaur and what is left of the Nagrimaran army aren't going to be enough to invade Tanimara. We will need to recruit other elves or anyone who wishes to see Tanimara fall."

Meric was shocked. How could she still be thinking of invading Tanimara after all this?

"My queen, with respect of course. You really should focus on rebuilding Nagrimar. The war is lost, and we should abandon any hope of…" started Meric before Darlana slapped him.

"They are taunting me!" Her lip quivering, she glared at him. "They kill everything I love. They burned down my kingdom and murdered countless numbers of my people." Meric closed his mouth and turned his attention away from her. "Now they are here, behind the walls of this tower, homeless and terrified." Her breath hitched. "I was supposed to protect them." Tears began streaming down her cheeks. "I am responsible for them. I am responsible. Hundreds of thousands of people," she whispered.

"You can rebuild," said Alzar.

"I do not wish to rebuild Nagrimar. I will allow all those who perished there to rest in peace. Nagrimar is now their grave. Instead, we will conquer Tanimara and make our home there. They cannot be allowed to get away with this and must be punished."

"But how," asked Dravon.

"Thousands of centaurs. Two full grown dragons. Eldar could muster a sizable force. I am sure now that the Tanimarans made an example of Bali, the other human kingdoms may be interested in assisting us. The rebellious houses of Tanimara and whoever else is willing. I will not stop until I get revenge for my people."

Dravon looked uncomfortable. "We will follow you, of course."

"Many of the whelps are coming of age, Darlana. My brood has doubled since I have met you and that is because we had a safe place to raise them. You allowed us to hunt in the forest far away from the orcs who would enslave or kill us. You have shown us hospitality and we will repay that by going to Tanimara with you, if you will forgive me and allow it of us," said Rizim.

Meric looked between them all.

Darlana looked up at Rizim and nodded without a word. She then turned to Meric with a humble expression. She grabbed his hand.

"What about you, Meric?" Darlana's voice softened as she met his gaze. "Will you follow your queen?"

Meric brushed away the lone tear tracing her cheek, his fingers lingering for just a heartbeat before he pulled away. He was opposed to trying to conquer Tanimara but if Darlana could muster a large enough force with the dragons, then perhaps it could be done. He admired her. She faced loss after loss, tragedy after tragedy and yet her will to fight remained strong. He knew no one who could have gone through what she had and keep the will to fight. He also had nowhere to go if he said no. "I will, my queen. There are many things we must discuss if we are going to continue.

Alzar had welcomed all of them to stay at the tower while he and his staff made their way to the ruins of Bali to help the denizens there. The centaur preferred to stay outside, and the dragons slept in the same chambers as Ismi while in their visage form. Meric entered his room and threw his knapsack on the ground. He kicked off his winklepickers and relaxed on his bed. His mind swam with ideas and questions on what they were going to do next. His eyes were closed when he was startled by the pulling of the door latch and opening of his door. It was Darlana and she let herself in. She stood in the doorway, wrapped in a flowing nightgown, her sorrow written in the slight tremble of her lips.

"I do not wish to sleep alone tonight but I will not force you to allow me but instead, I will ask you if I can sleep next to you," she asked almost desperately.

Meric could hardly understand her emotional state right now. She was the most skilled blademaster and most dangerous elf he knew. Four hundred years to hone her skill and yet she stood before him like a child asking to sleep with her parents because she had a bad dream. He genuinely felt bad for her and nodded. She gently crawled in next to him and pulled the covers up. She turned away from him and tucked in.

"Thank you, Meric," she said.

"It is all right, my queen."

***

Magris was observing the Tanimaran line from the balcony of the Madiran palatial estate. He was menacing standing up there overlooking the city. He had his hands behind his back, his eyepatch on and his peg leg. Imra was watching. She was no longer intimidated by him but felt quite safe based on his treatment of her.

The Tanimarans have not moved any closer for several weeks. It seemed they were waiting. Magris's spies informed him that Velnir was paraded through the streets along with the head of his dragon and publicly garroted. His head was sent to Darlana. The news struck Magris in the core. He grabbed his stomach and closed his eyes. Imra got up and came to him.

"Are you all right?" she asked. She knew that Velnir had been captured and that he had finally received the news he had been waiting for. He passed the message to her. "The other lords no doubt know of this. Some will cower at the emperor's feet, but others will resist," she said, trying to comfort him.

It was not all bad news however, Tarvana was not interested in attacking Madir for some time. They believed his army was much larger than it was considering a major city had fallen. They had become aware that the dragons were escorting ships bringing them supplies from Nemis and ordered the destruction of the kingdom yet the Nagrimarans were still receiving supplies. The setback was leading to the siege failing and the Tanimarans began to feel it. This amused Magris.

Magris had not heard from Darlana in some time and understood that after receiving such a missive would have long-lasting implications.

"Where are your allies," inquired Imra.

"I do not know. I have not heard from them in ages however, I expect to hear from them soon. We have held out this long and my orders were to take the city which I have. I will remain here until the Tanimarans attack. Then it's on.

"What about the civilians? Their homes are ruined, and many have perished near the walls."

They have been relocated further back into the city. Families have taken in several other families during these hard times." He turned to Imra. "This was Tarvanan's doing. I am not responsible for their plight."

"You attacked and captured the city. They will look to you for protection and leadership. You should consider providing something."

"Like what?"

"We need fresh water since the Tanimarans destroyed the aqueduct. Better food for a change. I am sure they are sick of the grain from the stores every day. If you do not do something, they may rebel against you and you will lose the city."

Magris knew she was right. He called for a meeting with the dragons and arranged for some of them to pick up some of the finer things.

"Very well, dragons will provide protection for the fishery as well. Send them out to fish and we will rebuild the aqueducts. Madir will not be able to sustain its population with the current stocks of fresh water."

The dragons that made their way back from Nemis were empty handed.

"The Nemisians have withdrawn their support. They say Tanimaran forces have razed Bali to the ground and its people are now displaced and suffering. Queen Darlana is in the tower of Alzar with Meric and my patriarch," said Vysol.

Magris' demeanor was as if he had seen a ghost. As far as he was concerned, the war was over. No more supplies from Nemis meant that he had maybe two years to hold out. That was long enough but he knew the Tanimarans would not wait that long. He relied on the fact that Darlana and her army would invade Tanimara and relieve him. The city was his for now though and he would keep it until he could come up with a plan. He did not share this information with Imra.

Chapter 12
Hope

Darlana and Meric were packing up and getting ready to head to the twilight woods to meet with Glade-King Eldar. Dravon and the centaur would stay with all but one of the dragons at Alzar's tower and await their return.

She made her way to where the dragons were staying in search of Nythint but he found her first.

"We are about to make our way to the twilight wood, Nythint. I would be honored if you came with us," she said while offering a smile.

Nythint had thought she would ask him. His previous conversation with Yzat back in Nagrimar has been on his mind. "My queen, may I recommend inviting Yzat to go with you in my stead. I feel that you both could really benefit by bonding while on this journey."

She looked at him with a surprised expression. "Very well, Nythint. I will ask Yzat instead," she said while looking at him suspiciously. She decided to keep her questions to herself and trust his instincts. She valued his opinion and knew he would not ask that if he didnt think it could benefit them. She left in search of Yzat and found him with Rizim. As she approached, Yzat noticed and spoke first.

"My queen, If I may, I would like to join you on your journey," said Yzat.

"Ah yes, it would be good to have a full sized dragon accompany you, if for no other reason than to display power. One as loyal as Yzat would be very useful," said Rizim.

Darlana looked between them both. She did not expect that any of them would want to go with her. Secretly, she felt this was a fool's errand. Doubt had been plaguing her and she thought that they would feel the same. If they did, they hid it well. Their faith in her was flattering to say the least but she wondered if continuing on this journey would lead to more loss, more death.

"Darlana?" inquired Meric.

Darlana snapped out of her train of thought. "Yes, Yzat, I would be honored if you joined us on our journey." She tried to genuinely smile.

Before they left and while Darlana was getting things in order, Alzar approached Meric.

"Take this, in case things do not go as planned or…or if she gets too, well, you do understand right?" asked Alzar.

Meric nodded, though he wasn't sure what Alzar had handed him. "What is this?"

"It is a teleportation rune, so only use it in the most dire of circumstances. I would give you more if I had more but I… needed them for another emergency. Simply toss it on the ground. Anything that is connected to the ground will work as well, for example. The second floor of a dwelling which is built on the ground. Do this and a portal will appear.

"What is an example of something not built on the ground," inquired Meric with genuine curiosity.

"A levitating chariot or tower, or city or anything that does not touch the ground," answered Alzar as if Meric was being silly.

"Say I am on top of a mountain made of stone…" began Meric before Alzar interrupted him.

"A mountain and the stone in it are attached to the ground, Meric. I cannot understand this for you or make it any more clear. Throw the damned thing on the ground anywhere you are in and the portal will bring you here," said Alzar who offered Meric a warm smile.

"Ah, I understand now," he said before clearing his throat. "Thank you, Alzar. You know, you have been quite helpful after all. Thank you."

Alzar was flattered to receive gratitude for once. "It is my pleasure though I cannot intervene any more in the conflict. I may be reprimanded for getting involved at all."

Meric said his farewells and met with Darlana. They mounted Yzat with their supplies. Yzat took to the sky, and they began their journey.

Darlana was lost in thought. She knew the shadow could hear her thoughts and by now the shadow knew Darlana's feelings toward her. The memories of her family were haunting her.

Once again, she felt alone in this world. The shadow thought this to be atrocious but unlike her, Darlana was unable to hear the thoughts the shadow had. She could plot and scheme without the intervention of her host and it pleased her but only if she survived. The shadow knew that Darlana no longer cared about her own life and would take enormous risks to achieve her goals. This worried her.

Meric didn't much like traveling through the sky but it was much faster than on the ground. It was cold and he did not like putting his hair up in a queue or bian. It made him look far more feminine than he already did which made him insecure his whole life.

He was observing Darlana, and she was acting strange. She had a look of intensity as if she were listening to someone and would often portray facial expressions as if she were speaking but she did not use words save for the occasional swear word. He was curious at just what she was swearing at and began wondering what Darlana was thinking. She had not spoken to him all morning and her gratitude to Yzat for volunteering to come seemed disingenuous.

"So…" he said awkwardly. "Are you all right?"

Darlana pulled her hair behind her ear and held herself tight. They were sitting on dragon steel chairs strapped to Yzat's scales. The wind was ferocious and they could not hear each other very well.

"I am," she said.

Meric was not sure where to start. He hardly understood her as it was and was struggling to figure out what could possibly be going through her mind.

The truth was, it was guilt. She could not stop thinking about Nagrimar and all those people and her family. It was a staggering amount of life lost and she blamed herself. She began to doubt like the others. Perhaps the war was over. Perhaps she should have given up.

She lost her entire family and asked them to go to war for her and they did. Now they are all dead and her home, their home is a graveyard made of the rubble from a once mighty city brought down by her enemies. She struggled with the idea of revenge and giving up.

When she still lived in Tanimara, she was a princess. She was taught that her word was law. Soldiers were fodder and expendable but Darlana never felt that way.

Soldiers had mothers and fathers that loved them too. They were fathers and mothers themselves. She remembered how her mother saved her life and sent her into exile against her fathers will. She could only imagine how her father punished her mother for letting their daughter live after committing the sacrilege of having a child with a human.

When she met Velnir, she intended to use him and his titles to secure a place back in Tanimara and plot her revenge against her father. She fell in love with him instead and followed him to the edge of Abrion to do the unthinkable and won. If only she knew what would befall Velnir and where she would be only a few years after they met, she would have done things a lot differently.

She thought of Paeris who was just a baby. Barely alive long enough to understand anything that had happened. Her life was taken from her by order of her father and Darlana developed a seething hatred for him. She thought of Sampsin and what it cost his empire to be with her.

The Araban Empire was destroyed because of her. Sampsin and her first son Alnas were murdered because of her. She built a prosperous kingdom, fell in love and it was all destroyed because of her. She felt the weight of the responsibility for the countless elves and Araban lives lost because of her. All of these thoughts finally reached a tipping point. She began to cry.

Meric unstrapped himself and carefully moved over next to her and simply held her. She buried her head in his chest and began to sob hard.

Yzat could hear her and was himself beginning to understand emotional pain. He was having trouble processing it and instead would bury it deep. He felt Meric move over next to her and thought it would be best if he cared for her now. Yzat understood the way elves thought and the weight of her responsibility and could not imagine what she was going through.

Meric remained quiet and held onto her. For several minutes she cried and soaked his robes. She held onto him tight, and he was about to say something when she spoke first.

"I am so sorry. I am so sorry, Meric." She sniffled. "I am sorry for Prince Sampsin, my son Alnas and Araba, I am sorry for Velnir, Paeris and Nagrimar. I am sorry for hurting you. I have taken advantage of Alzar. I hurt you all. Now I am going to go ask an elf that I consider a friend to fight and die for me. They will all die. I cannot defeat Tanimara. What is wrong with me? Why can't I just give up?"

Meric did not know what to say. He abandoned Tanimara and came to her as a refugee. She took him in because Velnir insisted and swore on his own name to vouch for me. She allowed him to keep his noble title in her kingdom. She let him out of prison when he deserved to be there. She still did not know what he did, and he felt compelled to tell her.

"I am sorry too, Darlana. I am sorry that I set up the Tanimarans by hiring saboteurs to destroy the foundries in Nagrimar. I am sorry I killed them afterward so they would not tell anyone. I am sorry I used you to get us into this war. I did it so I could get Caphry back. I had heard that Tarvana sent a fleet out but did not know where. I talked Velnir and Magris into finding the fleet and destroying it and then taking Madir. I severely underestimated Tanimara and if anyone is to blame for those lost lives, It is me."

Darlana looked up at him. She angrily began punching his chest. "It was you," she yelled. "You destroyed the foundries? You killed the saboteurs? What else have you done that I do not know about? Did you have my daughter assassinated too or plot with Tarvana to kill Velnir," she screamed with tears streaming down her cheeks. She pulled her hair out of her mouth ready to retort after he spoke his peace.

"No, Velnir was my cousin, he was my family," Meric said, terrified. My uncle and I were the only Tanimaran lords that came to his aid and we lost everything because of it. My uncle Baefric was murdered by Velnir's best friend before my own eyes. You are not the only one who made mistakes, Darlana and you are not the only one who lost everything as a result."

Darlana relaxed her grip and allowed herself to calm down. All this time, she had been focusing on how this affected her.

"Yes, I used you as a means to win back Caphry. I regret that but I do not regret aiding Velnir. The orcs have never reached the shores of Tanimara. Our people were terrified and no one cared but us and you. I knew like he did that we had to make an example out of the orcs for the rest of the world to see. I did not count on your father sending an army into Atlan to kill my uncle and I. I was fortunate to escape with my life and went to the only person who made me feel safe and that was Velnir. I would never kill him."

"You murdered those who worked for you. I would never do that and could never condone that even if they did destroy my foundries," said Darlana, her eyes were red and so were her cheeks. She had the sniffles and her ears were drooping. Meric's ears were drooping as well. They were both feeling really low.

Darlana made her way across Yzat's back and sat alone. She could not look at Meric. Besides, she had so much on her mind as it was. She was unsure what to think anymore.

They were now over the mountains of Dhar'Modir. Meric recognized it as he was present when Ruvyn defeated the Thunderforge clan and Dwoldrumin Brightbelt. He observed the city of Dhar'Modir. It was a massive fortress built into the mountain. He remembered how hard it was to penetrate the walls of the city but remembered the tunnelers blowing out the section near the gate. From there, it was easy for Ruvyn to conquer. Meric wondered if they have made any improvements over the last one hundred years.

Several hours had passed and they were just now approaching the neutral hub of Crossroads which sat at the oddly flat center where three mountain ranges, Nemesian mountains, Helmgarde peaks and Northgardian peaks met. There was no other place on Abrion like it. Not only because of its geographical location but also because of the diversity. Yes there was a place for a dragon or dragons to land along with many other types of flying creatures.

Yzat landed and the elves dismounted him. They gathered their things and made their way into the town. Darlana was not talking to Meric. Yzat was not either and was unhappy to find out that Meric was responsible for destroying the foundries but also understood that if he had not, they would not have discovered dragon steel. He would let Meric stew on it anyway.

There were all types of travelers and merchants here ranging from strange cat and fox people to orcs, minotaurs, ogres, trolls, giants, myconids, people with snake heads but human-like scaly bodies with tails and many more. The trio walked past three stoic Ratkin, no more taller than a house rodent, wearing scholar's robes and spectacles reading from a tiny book and bantering of stars and sciences. Soon, the trio were getting the attention of many people. This did not serve them well. They were recognized to the astonishment of Meric.

They made their way to an inn to collect supplies. Darlana threw a sack of gold on the table and gave the merchant a list.

"Your gold is no good here, leave at once," said the merchant. Darlana was confused but grabbed her sack of gold and led them to another merchant who put up a closed sign as they approached. Yzat turned to Meric. "Why are they avoiding us?"

"Tanimaran influence is global. They are afraid of reprisal if they help the enemy of Tanimara. There is no way Darlana is so naive."

"Give her a rest, Meric. She has been through much, some of which you are responsible for," said Yzat before walking away from Meric and toward Darlana.

It would seem Yzat had informed her and she would abandon trying to get anything from these people. They headed to a clearing where Yzat morphed back into a dragon. They mounted him and Yzat took to the sky. They would have to go without until they got to their destination, the Twilight Woods.

Chapter 13
Wasted Venture

Yzat descended from the clouds revealing a dense forest below much like the Forlorn Forest though this one did not have any visible cities or settlements. They had to be careful. The human kingdoms of Protania and Lavania, bitter rivals, bordered the Twilight Woods, making this land perilous.

There did not look to be a clearing large enough for Yzat to land until he got very far into the forest itself. For what seemed like hundreds of kilometers, it was simply dense forest. Finally Yzat was able to land. The clearing did not look natural.

When they landed, they were greeted by elves which Darlana expected. Darlana, and Meric dismounted Yzat and he morphed into his visage form. A tall-looking elf with what Meric thought was a staff at first, but was currently being used as a walking stick, approached Darlana slowly.

"Queen Darlana of Nagrimar. What a pleasant surprise," said the old elf. Darlana looked at him and did not express the same sentiment. "Darlana, I thought we had put the past behind us," said the old elf.

"It is not you, Eldar, I apologize. I come bearing grave news and to ask something of you that I am afraid I cannot repay you for," said Darlana.

"I see, come then. Let us speak over tea." He guided the three to a city of trees in which appeared to have their homes in or built on. Meric was impressed to see the architecture look elvish but natural. It was a form of art to him and he had only heard of it. To see it was magnificent to say the least.

Eldar brought them to one of these trees and entered it through the stump. These trees were very thick and large enough to be hallowed out in some cases and lived in. All of the furniture was elegantly carved out of the wood the tree provided. Nothing was wasted. The windows had glass in them and the hearth was made of stones. It was small compared to what Meric normally lived in but Darlana seemed to know her way around.

Eldar offered them all a seat and a woman came out wearing a crown of twine. She brought cups and a kettle of hot tea.

"Thank you, dear," said Eldar to the woman. He then turned his attention to the three of them. "To what do I owe this visit?"

"Tanimara…" Darlana began. Eldar brought his cup up to take a drink until he heard her mention Tanimaran. His demeanor changed from pleasant to serious. He set his cup down and gave her his full attention.

"I married a Tanimaran prince, and for that they killed him and our daughter. I declared war," said Darlana.

"Naturally, I understand why you would feel compelled to declare war. But to actually declare war against Tanimara. I mean no offense when I say this Darlana but that would be like a rabbit up against a pack of hungry wolves," stated Eldar.

Darlana gave him the look that she understood the decision.

"They burned the Forlorn Forest and completely destroyed Nagrimar. Hundreds of thousands perished in the flames. We evacuated roughly over or under a million people only to be ambushed, deceived and attacked again. This time they would kill everyone else. They killed all of the women and children. They killed my husband and daughter." Darlana began to tear up.

She had a hard time reliving this over and over. It was constantly on her mind and Eldar looked at her, seeing her wear the guilt.

"Such a hefty burden that no one should ever bear. I am terribly sorry for your loss." He looked at Yzat and at Meric. "All of your loss." He then looked at Darlana. "Of course, you are welcome to live here with us. You are like a local hero, Darlana. You saved our people."

Darlana looked at Eldar with confusion. "Live here? No, please do not misunderstand me. I came here to ask you to fight for me. I am not going to abandon this war and accept defeat to Tanimara."

Eldar looked genuinely stunned. It was several moments before he spoke. He seemed to take his time thinking about what to say. "You cannot be serious! Tanimara is the most supreme superpower this world has ever seen. High Magister Raften's reputation precedes him. Do not misunderstand me either. I have heard of your deeds with the Tanimaran prince and how you invaded the Sundered lands and lived to tell the tale. That is a worthy achievement, Darlana but those were orcs. Tanimarans…" he said before rethinking what he was going to say. "I suppose that I am likely misunderstanding you so please allow me to ask clarifying questions. You mean to tell me that despite your perfectly understandable reasons for declaring war on Tanimara that you, in fact, did? Lost the only army you have in a single battle, saw your people eradicated and your home completely destroyed, and you would like us to join you in your fight against them?"

Darlana nodded expectantly and looked hopeful.

"I know you are not used to people telling you no, Darlana but no. The elves of the Twilight Wood only number around one hundred thousand and we would not be able to make a difference. Besides, Protania and Lavania have declared a truce and joined forces against a far greater threat than each other," said Eldar, attempting to change the subject.

Darlana's demeanor changed to disappointment and hopelessness.

Eldar continued. "The Umbramari broke through the black gate. They are attacking Lavanian villages and enslaving the people. We need all the able-bodied elves available to help defend the wood from them. I would invite you to stay here… since you have nowhere else to really go."

"Umbramari?" asked Meric. "We helped construct the black gate. It was designed to keep them out. How did they break through it?"

"A warlord by the name of Ralnor would declare war on each tribe one by one and offer to resolve the conflict with single combat. Him versus their leader. In Umbramari culture, when one does this and wins, they assimilate the losing tribe into the victorious one just like the orcs do.

"For the first time in several hundred years, a warlord has defeated enough other warlords to grow into a mighty force to be reckoned with. Ralnor is wise and cruel. He built a city in the frozen wastes and created an economy mostly dependent on slave labor. Many other tribes joined him and for the first time in recorded history, Ralnor was declared emperor of the Umbramari.

"Of course, there are tribes that did not swear allegiance to him and there is infighting but for the most part, several cities have been erected. Ralnor needed more slaves so he built a massive army, one so large that it was easily able to overwhelm the defense of the black gate. Now millions of Umbramari have infiltrated Lavania and Protania. They will dare to enter the wood as well but the trees typically grab them. We also have an accord with the Lavanians to assist them."

"I understand. We will take no more of your time. Come along Yzat, Meric," said Darlana abruptly ending the conversation. Eldar looked disappointed.

"Stubborn as always, Darlana. There is no shame in quitting," said Eldar in a futile attempt to retain her. She did not even grace him with a glare. The three returned to where Yzat landed. He morphed back into his natural dragon form. Darlana was still not speaking to Meric. She sat on the opposite end of where Meric sat. She whispered something to Yzat before he took to the sky. Meric was not privileged to the information and wondered where they were going, so he got up and carefully moved across Yzat's back, which was large enough to carry several full-grown elves, and sat next to her. She would not even look at him.

"Can we talk about it please," asked Meric.

"No," snapped Darlana.

Meric sat next to her and looked up at the clear blue sky while he thought about what to say anyway. "Take Dravon and the centaur, the dragons and the few surviving elves and let us all go to an island to rebuild. The war is lost, Darlana. We need to focus on our future," said Meric.

"I am thinking about the future, Meric. I have been thinking about it my whole life. There will be a future. Of course I will lead the centaur, they have been nothing but loyal and I love them all. Of course I will invite the dragons. The only good thing to come out of your mouth of late is going to an Island. That is a great idea, Meric. It is too bad that you will not be around to enjoy it with the rest of us," she said before scowling at him in a challenging manner.

"If you wish to execute me, Darlana, I understand and will accept that. I know I deserve it. I have committed murder, deception and indulgence. My sins are mine to bear but please know this. It was never my intent to hurt you or bring harm to Nagrimar. I will pay the price."

"Execute? I cannot bring myself to execute you, Meric."

Meric looked at her with a look of gratitude. "You are kind to a fault," he said.

"Do not mistake my niceties for weakness. You will be exiled the moment we get back to the tower of Alzar and if I do see you again, I will kill you with my bare hands. What you have done is unforgivable."

Meric looked at Darlana and was about to say something but decided not to. He looked away from her, closed his eyes and nodded. He had connections in Tel'Aled with the humans that Caphry had many trade agreements and accords with. They were directed by him before his exile from Tanimara so he was confident they would help or at least assist him.

Chapter 14
Further than the Abyss

Yzat suddenly jolted to the left howling in pain. They began to fall from the sky and neither Darlana nor Meric could see what had happened.

"I have been hit with something, I am…. I'm," said Yzat before going unconscious. A moment later, they hit the ground hard. Meric and Darlana were strapped into a seat embedded into the armor Yzat was wearing. Once the dust cleared, Meric unbuckled himself and went to check on Darlana who was unbuckling herself as well. They dismounted Yzat and saw a massive hole in his body. He had been shot with something. It hit him right under his wing where no armor was present. Yzat was bleeding profusely. He looked at Darlana.

"I am sorry," he said before his eyes rolled back into his head and he slipped away. Darlana stood there and looked at him.

To Meric's surprise, he noticed they were nowhere near the Twilight Woods.

"My queen," said Meric in an attempt to get her attention. "Darlana." She could not hear Meric. Her mind was fixated on Yzat. She was in shock. "Darlana," said Meric one more time before they heard the shouts of marauders headed their way. "Darlana, we have to get out of here, now. Darlana," he said before grabbing her arm. She pulled away.

"I am not your queen. Leave me!" she said. Meric was beginning to panic.

He began to run as fast as he could. In the distance, he saw marauders coming and he noticed they were not human nor were they orc. They had pale skin, long ears, shaved the sides of their heads and wore their black or white hair in long braids. Their eyes were blackened and the color purple. They were mounted on talonasaurs.

A two-legged, scaly beast with sharp teeth and a long tail and massive claws attached to small arms. Their snouts had a horn at the end and they had forked tongues. Meric recognized them to be Umbramari though he had rarely seen one on land. He had mostly seen them at sea. Umbramari would raid Tanimaran ships and foreign ports and the Tanimarans were used to fighting them.

"Oh no no no no," he said.

He jumped behind a bush and observed as they surrounded the Yzat and Darlana. He could see them approach her. She was still standing there staring at Yzat's corpse. The talonasaurs began to feast on the dead dragon. Meric felt helpless. They bound Darlana by the feat and hands. They threw her over the back of one of the talonasaurs and began to go back toward where they came from.

Meric was conflicted. "Most of this is my fault… ohhhhh."

Ultimately he decided to follow them. For several days they trotted through the land and Meric was able to track them. Every time they stopped and camped, Meric caught up.

Darlana was unresponsive. Her eyes were open and she seemed conscious but the Umbramari were unsure what was wrong with her.

"She sure is pretty. I think I'll have a go at her," said the skinny one with the sides of his head shaved and a long black braid. The other Umbramari with long wavy hair and who was heavily armored got up and confronted him.

"You most certainly will not. The pretty ones are put up for sale unmolested. You know the rules, Ogron."

"They will not know. Besides, it does not look like she is going to be telling anyone," said Ogron.

"I command this war party, and I said no."

"Come on, Dartan. I'll take her backside," he said with a wicked grin. "Slavers do not ever check the rear," said Ogron.

"Go anywhere near her backside… In fact, go anywhere near her, and I'll pluck your eyes out," threatened Dartan.

Ogron pulled out two daggers and challenged Dartan. Dartan grabbed Ogron and introduced a knee to his face. He then pulled a dagger from his boot and stuck it in Ogron's eye. Ogron howled in pain and clawed at Dartan as he ground it up and scooped it out. He moved on to the other eye and did the same thing. When he was finished, he pushed Ogron down and began to laugh at him along with the rest of the war party.

"The new ones, always so lustful and arrogant," said Dartan.

Ogron was whimpering and trying to crawl away. Blood was dripping from his empty eye sockets. One of the other war party members walked over to him and put his boot on Ogron's back. He then pressed him against the ground and looked back at Dartan who simply nodded. He then brought his spear up and plunged it into his back. Ogron began to choke and gurgle before he took his final breath.

Meric was observing this from afar. He saw the big Umbramari stop the other one from hurting Darlana. He determined that she would be sold into slavery. He had to act fast if he was going to save her. He pulled out his knapsack and began to dig through it. He still had the orb of falling stars and among other things, a teleportation stone that Alzar had given him during his stay in the tower.

For a moment he contemplated using it for himself. Realistically, he could not leave Darlana behind, not after all he had done to her and Nagrimar and not after all she had done for him and his cousin.

Meric waited until the war party fell asleep. None of them slept in tents but he still could not tell how many were there. Ten possibly fifteen minus the one they killed of course.

Meric grabbed the teleportation stone and knapsack then quietly made his way to the camp. He counted thirteen in the war party, all seemingly fast asleep. Dartan was sleeping next to Darlana. The talonasaurs were also asleep much to the respite of Meric. He got closer and closer until he was close enough to Darlana.

"Darlana…" he whispered. "Darlana."

She turned to face him. Her mouth was bound. She saw him and donned a look of desperation. It was clear to him she had no desire to be there and he was determined to get her back to the tower of Alzar safely. He crept up to her and kept a close eye on Dartan and the two others that were sleeping near her.

"Are you all right?" he whispered as he took her gag off.

"You came for me," she said.

"Of course I did. After all I have done. I could not leave you to these animals. Alzar gave me a teleportation stone. Lets get out of…" he was saying before Darlana looked behind him with a terrified look.

Meric turned to face Dartan who was standing behind him smiling the moment before clubbing Meric in the head and knocking him out cold. The teleportation stone landed behind Darlana. Dartan looked at Darlana.

"So, you can speak," said Dartan with sarcasm in his voice. He then dragged Meric to the others.

She scooted back to grab the stone and tucked it in her pants while Dartan and the others tied Meric up.

The next day they began to journey again. Meric had a look of defeat and regret on his face. He looked at Darlana.

"I am so sor…" he was interrupted by Dartan punching him in the face. Meric was dazed and his nose began to bleed.

"I think you broke my no…" he tried to say before Dartan punched him again. His nose was definitely broken.

"Tanimaran trash. You do not speak, you do not think. You do not do anything unless I tell you to. Nod if you understand," said Dartan.

"I understa…" Meric began before Dartan punched him in the face twice more. Meric was out for now. Darlana would keep her mouth shut. Meric's face was black, blue and swollen. Dried blood covered his lips and chin. His white hair was a tangled mess and covered in a mix of bloody dirt. Darlana felt pity.

They traveled for several days, and they could feel the temperature drop. Soon they came upon a structure built in between two mountains. It was tall and black. It had sharp jagged protrusions built into the wall to prevent anything from scaling them. This was the black gate.

Along the road leading to the actual gate itself were the impaled corpses of Lavanians. Thousands of them were lined up along the road as a clear warning to anyone who would challenge the Umbramari. Some had their faces peeled down. It was a horrifying sight to see someone's face hanging from their chin.

They passed through the gate and were both given blankets to keep them warm enough to not go into hypothermia. The Umbramari did not wear anything of the sort. In fact, they did not wear much of anything.

The road ahead was long. Darlana's bound feet and hands were beginning to hurt. The ropes the Umbramari used were too constricting but she did not want to say anything. She was depressed and it seemed like everything she loved was being taken from her and killed.

Dartan noticed the marks caused by the ropes on Darlana's hands.

"Loosen the ropes around her hands. We want her pretty when we sell her. Any marks decrease her value," he ordered one of the warparty. One of them approached and loosened Darlana's ropes just enough to ease the pain, but not enough for escape. Meric's hands, feet and face were also in bad shape.

"My hands hurt too," he said. Dartan snarled and punched him in the face. "Now your face hurts too. You do not speak unless spoken to!"

Meric was wheezing and groaning. His face was severely swollen, black and blue. Dartan had hit him so much that his eyes were swollen shut. His nose was crooked in several places. He had several knots on his cheeks and forehead. His upper lip and chin were covered in both dried and fresh blood.

Darlana looked over at him with pity. She knew he was not a warrior and did not have much skill with a blade let alone his hands. Darlana was confident that she could take the whole warband if she could get her hands free but it was in vain.

The warparty came to an Umbramari trading hub. There were banners hanging all over the place that had the symbol of a hand holding a bloody elven crown. Darlana did not recognize the symbol and would not dare ask. She looked over at Meric who could not see anything anyway.

Soon, they came to a stop. The talonasaurs were tied to a post. The warparty grabbed Meric and Darlana. They were hauled through the city to a crowded area. There was a small forge and several brands. They moved to a line and Dartan was holding onto both of them tightly.

When the time came for him to step up onto the stage, he took them with him just like everyone else did. An elf, with a quite jovial accent considering the dark, cold, and desolate place, began taking bids for Darlana. Every male was desperately trying to outbid the other.

A fight in the crowd broke out before bidding closed on Darlana. Several Umbramari were killed or severely wounded. The force policing the hub showed up and dispersed the crowd to make way for what appeared to be some sort of important person.

The dark elf walked up to the auctioneer wearing clothes that clearly symbolized his status. He had long wavy black hair, eyes of purple and skin so light in complexion that was almost transparent. All of the elves here did. None were pink like the Tanimarans or Nagrimarans.

The auctioneer motioned for Dartan to come over.

"He wants to buy all the slaves in the market. How many do you have?" asked the auctioneer.

"I have these two but this one is very pretty. I expect she is worth quite a bit more than he is," said Dartan while motioning to Meric.

"Ten for the male mari and twenty five for the female mari," said the auctioneer.

"One hundred for the female and the male is still healthy. I want twenty five for him," said Dartan.

Before the auctioneer spoke, the dark elf that wanted to purchase them all motioned him over and they began to talk amongst themselves. Meric was terrified and could not see anything. Darlana tried to keep her head down and not make eye contact with anyone. The auctioneer came back to Dartan. "One hundred for the female and five for the male. That umbral one is taking them back to the emperor in Unarith."

Dartan looked angry but after thinking it over for a moment, he agreed and handed them over. They were quickly taken to the little forge where an elf grabbed a branding iron with the symbol of the hand holding a bloody crown.

He put it in the coals. Meric could not see what was going on but knew something was coming. He was getting nervous. Darlana was brought over first. She was about to get branded with the emperor's symbol but the Umbramari that purchased her stopped him.

"Do not mark her. I think the emperor will be pleased with this one."

The brander nodded and then immediately shoved the brand into Meric's buttocks. He tried to howl in pain but what came out was a muffled whistle. The brander was delighted to pain Meric. It was clear that the Umbramari hated other elves. Human slaves were treated with more respect than Meric was.

Chapter 15
Doubt

Magris began contemplating leaving the city. He knew it was only a matter of time before the Tanimarans would find out that Madir was taken with only five hundred Nagrimarans. Imra knew that if the Magistrate found out that Madir was taken by so small a force that it would be her neck in the garrote.

Over the last few months that they have been there, Imra came to like Magris. He treated her with respect and was kind to her even though she was technically his prisoner. His order to put her under house arrest rather than be placed in the dungeon meant a lot to her.

"I have not heard from Darlana in some time. Last I heard, she was at the tower of Alzar. I am not sure what to do. I am thinking of abandoning the city," admitted Magris to Imra.

She began to panic but kept herself under control.

"If you leave the city, the Tanimarans will surely take it back and that may discourage other regions from rebelling against Tarvana and the Magistrate," replied Imra.

"I only have five hundred soldiers that I can trust fully. That is not enough to keep the city if the Tanimarans find out and attack."

"You have ten dragons and the Madiran guard as well. The guard alone swells the troop count to fifty thousand. That is more than sufficient to at least defend the city," said Imra.

"If all I can do is defend it from the Tanimarans then it is only a matter of time until we run out of food. The dragons are doing their best to feed everyone but three million people is too difficult. Ten whales a day is not enough to feed that many. They also need their rest and we need them here in the event the Tanimarans attack. It has become increasingly more dangerous every time they leave. It runs the risk that the Tanimarans will pick up a pattern. We cannot destroy every scrying orb they send our way," said Magris.

"The people of Madir look to you for liberation. You would abandon them?" Imra was trying everything she could to keep the Nagrimarans and Magris there. Her survival depended on it and she knew it. She genuinely cared for the people of Madir as well and thought that their best hope was liberation from the dictatorship of Tarvana."

"I do not know what to do, Imra."

Imra thought about several options. She was good at coming up with solid solutions on the fly but her options were limited. She was getting scared and it became increasingly difficult for her to think. "I will go to Atlan and Caphry. I know their Magistrates will join us. They need assurance that you will not abandon Madir and they will muster their guard and we can do this," she said. It sounded better in her head.

Magris looked at her. "You think I am foolish. I have made many mistakes but to assume that I had not learned from them," he said smiling at her while tapping his forehead.

"Take my daughter as a hostage then. I will come back for her," she said.

Magris was unaware she even had a daughter. "You never mentioned you had a child. Where is she," demanded Magris.

"At my personal residence. I let her live there while I serve in the Magistrate."

"How come this is the first I am hearing of her."

"I meant to keep her safe. Know that I would not put her in danger if I did not believe that you could liberate us with the help of the other city guards, or I would not have told you of her existence. Send me to Atlan and Caphry. If all three of these regions unite and go against Tarvana, it divides the continent. Perhaps other regions are tired of Raftens regime and will join us. Even if they do not, we would still equal them in number plus you have ten dragons!"

Magris thought about it some more. After thinking about every reason why he should not let her go, he decided he had nothing to lose. If she betrayed him, at least he had her daughter a powerful bargaining wager. "Very well. I release you from my custody. You are free to go to Atlan and Caphry to try and persuade them to join us but there is a catch."

"What is the catch?" she inquired curiously.

"Vysol will accompany you. She will carry you to Atlan and Caphry. If they do not join, you cannot allow their garrisons to remain. Vysol will destroy them," said Magris as he moved closer and locked his eye with hers."

Imra looked at him with concern. "If they do not join us then they die?"

"Just the soldiers. Leave the denizens unharmed. We are at war Imra and you are a rebellious Magister. The Tanimarans do not yet know that but I imagine they will when you attempt to persuade their members to join the so-called rebellion."

"Fair enough," said Imra.

Magris called for Vysol who was in her Visage form. She had long blonde hair that was heavily braided. Her horns were visible like Ismi's were and she had human features. It would be strange seeing a human in Tanimara nowadays.

Magris informed Vysol of the plan. They went out to the balcony and Vysol morphed into her natural dragon form. Imra had never ridden a dragon and it was obvious. She kept stumbling and cursing. It was beginning to annoy Vysol. Finally, Imra was able to successfully mount Vysol and she strapped herself into a seat. They took to the sky and made their way to Atlan first.

Magris had retreated to the magister's chambers to begin planning the possible withdrawal in case of failure. The chamber doors flung open. Two guards rushed in with haste.

"General, hundreds of ships were spotted off the coast," said one of the guards.

Magris jumped up and rushed over to the balcony in the adjacent tower overlooking the bay and docks. There were indeed hundreds of ships. Human ships but they were not manned by humans. Those were Nagrimarans and to the delight of Magris, Nythint was soaring high above them providing excellent protection. Not a Tanimaran ship in sight.

Magris ordered the town criers to make ready the docks to receive the Nagrimaran soldiers as smoothly as possible. Madir had a massive dock, and it was big enough for rapid disembarking. Just what he needed. He then made his way down there to receive them himself.

Nythint landed and morphed into his visage form. Magris approached him and much to Nythint's surprise, Magris also hugged him.

"Nythint, my boy, it is so good to see you," he said while his face was buried in Nythint's hair.

"General, the pleasure is mine," said Nythint in a confused tone. "One hundred thousand reinforcements as you requested, General."

"One hundred thousand… why that is…" he began before Nythint finished his sentence for him.

"Her entire army with the exception of a defensive garrison and the centaur, General. She has put her faith in you."

"I have one hell of a responsibility then," he said as he tried to smile. Any time Magris tried to smile, it caused mild pain. The damage done to his face and the imperfect reconstruction left permanent nerve damage but this did not stop him. He was genuinely happy to see Nythint and the army.

The Nagrimarans disembarked and began filing in columns just like the Tanimarans. Their armor was the same color of blue as Magris and had the same ornaments. The soldiers all carried the same crossed bow weapons, shields and spears as the Shades did only they did not have invisibility cloaks. The Tanimarans held their children close to them while standing in their doorways. Many shut the shutters and windows as they marched by. The sound of rhythmic armor clanking and boots marching began to fill the entire city of Madir.

The supplies and soldiers were all disembarked and the human ships were sailing back to Maphis within only a few hours. Madirans began to open up to the Nagrimarans despite their frightening armor and weapons once they realized they meant no harm. It would seem that the people were still somewhat weary of Magris but he was determined to prove to them that his queen is a liberator.

It was time for Nythint to return to Darlana now that he did his duty. He said his farewell to Magris and took to the sky making his way toward Nemis. Magris was overjoyed.

***

Imra was fascinated by Vysol. She looked around her back and thought, *"How did the Nagrimarans manage to do all of this?"* It would take a few days to get to Atlan but she would do the best she could to enjoy the peace of flying.

Atlan could be seen in the distance. Vysol knew exactly what to do. She came in low and the wall mounted bolt throwers did not fire upon her. She flew through the city and saw the people of Atlan begin to panic but most stood there and watched. She came to land in the courtyard in front of the palace.

"I am Magister Imra of Madir and I have come to speak with Magister Kaelina," she said to the guards.

They looked at each other in disbelief for a moment before granting her access. Imra dismounted Vysol who chose to remain in her dragon form. This made the guards uneasy but Imra did not care and made her way past them into the Magisters chambers.

"Magister Imra, you are alive, this is wonderful," said Kaelina before giving her a hug. "Word has reached us about the disaster in Madir. Velnir was publicly executed in Tarvana. Elves have not done such unspeakable things for ages, especially against their own."

This was the first time Imra had heard about Velnir's fate. She expected nothing less but to be publicly executed was in bad taste. Her dislike for Raften only grew and she saw this knowledge as an opportunity for leverage. "Yes, it was an abhorrent abuse of authority. Raften has illegally declared himself emperor of Tanimara and its colonies. I am here on behalf of General Magris of Nagrimar."

Kaelina stepped back and had a look of confusion. She took her time thinking about what to say next. "Many of the noble Atlantans have openly spoken of rebellion and of course I have not brought this information to Tarvana. These people have been through enough and when they heard that Velnir was executed, riots broke out and quashing them was difficult. I am sure you noticed the guards I had to post outside my chambers. These have been some trying times, Imra."

"Then understand what I am about to ask. On behalf of General Magris, I am asking you to join the rebellion and depose Raften to restore the republic, Kaelina."

"Rebellion? I thought Madir was occupied."

"It is complicated. The Nagrimarans did take the city however, Magris assures me that he intends to restore the republic. They have agreed to be our allies. The resentment for Raften's regime was already rife before the Nagrimarans came. It is time to take back our nation and restore the republic."

Kaelina looked as though she was about to cry. She began to nod. "I want nothing more than to put an end to the evil dictatorship in Tarvana. I want nothing more than to have our republic back. I will do everything I can to support the rebellion. We cannot commit our guard to Madir without Caphrian support. We will need time to recruit but we will. Vengeance for Velnir and victory for the Republic of Tanimara."

Imra was pleased. She was good friends with Kaelina and glad for her support.

They worked out an arrangement before Imra took to the sky again with Vysol. It was as if the people of Atlan knew why she was there. Many were cheering as she was leaving for Caphry.

Vysol flew high above the clouds in an effort to evade Tanimaran detection. So far things were going well and she had not been detected. It seemed too good to be true and when things felt like this, it usually meant they were so she kept her guard up and so did Vysol.

From above the clouds, she could see the majestic Caphrian gates, the marvelous spires throughout the flat land and the several motes throughout the city. It looked as though this city was floating on water when in fact the land had been arranged to perfectly align with the buildings built on top of it. The canal system was intricate throughout the city which led to a harbor. The water came from the sea and the design allowed for it to flow in a certain direction. It made the primary mode of transportation throughout the city a lot easier since they used boats.

Several griffins took up formation and began to approach Vysol and Imra.

"I do not like the looks of this," said Imra.

"Griffins? Hah! Mere animals," retorted Vysol. Griffins were not just mere animals though.

Imra brought with her one of those nifty repeater crossbows as a gift from Magris and for her protection. She got it ready and when eight fireballs came their way, Vysol unleashed a hellish breath attack and incinerated two of the griffins instantly.

Imra shot one of the pyromancers off their griffin but expended her magazine and forgot how to reload it. As she was struggling to reload, Vysol was moving every which way she could to dodge the remaining griffins and their pyromancers.

Dragon riding was very difficult. By the time she was loaded and ready to go, the griffins took off and several bolts from wall mounted bolt throwers whizzed past Vysol, startling Imra.

Vysol had gone through this before, and it did not phase her now. She rolled downward dodging bolts left and right. She maneuvered to the right and descended along the wall. The Tanimarans were desperately trying to turn the bolt throwers to aim at her but she was moving too quickly.

When she was close enough, she brought her wings out and leveled off. She then unleashed her fire breath at every bolt thrower with such precision, it terrified Imra. Vysol was able to destroy every bolt thrower and tower in one single pass on the north side of the city. One dragon could do all that damage, surprising not only Imra but the people of Caphry as well. They began to panic and retreat.

"That will teach them not to mess with an ancient dragon… hrmph," said Vysol.

They made their way to the palace which in Caphry did not have a courtyard or really anywhere for Vysol to land. She was forced to land on the dome of the hall and Imra had to dismount up there. It was scary because the dome was not designed to hold the weight of a dragon or be an offloading platform for obvious reasons. Imra struggled to keep her balance while she made her way down to a balcony. Vysol had assumed her visage form to avoid being an easy target from pyromancer mounted griffins.

They both entered the Magistrates chambers from the roof dome and made it safely inside. Soldiers could be heard mustering outside.

"Quickly, this way," said Imra. The two ran out of the room and down the hall toward where the Magister would be. Upon entrance, they were met by two pyromancers poised for the attack and the Magister who Imra did not recognize.

Imra looked around and knew they had let their guard down by bursting in there the way they did. They could have both been easily killed if the Tanimarans wanted to, but to capture them would bring glory to the Magister and boost their political intrigue.

"I am Magister Imra of Madir, I demand an audience with the Magister of Caphry."

The elf in purple robes standing behind the two pyromancers stepped past them. He was a scrawny elf with long black hair, a pointy nose and ridiculously long and pointy ears. They were disproportionate to the rest of his body. His eyebrows extended out past his face and were incredibly bushy. By elven standards, this elf was very ugly.

"I, Geblyn Arnan, am the Magister of Caphry, appointed by the High Magistrate of Tarvana. Word moved quickly these days, Imra. You will stand down and surrender or you will die here and now," said Geblyn.

Imra's heart began to race. Vysol looked ready to fight. "You know why I am here. Let's not act too hastily. Madir and Atlan are in open rebellion against Tarvana. Everyone is unhappy with the dictatorship. We will fight to restore the republic to its former glory and make Tanimara great again," said Imra, trying to avoid a fight. Vysol was ready, she could still breath fire even in her visage form and poised to do so, only it could kill them all.

"Nonsense, what you ask is treason and it will not be tolerated. Shame on you and Kaelina for even considering committing such a travesty," he said. He then turned and walked behind the pyromancers.

"Kill them," he ordered.

The pyromancers did not move. They looked at each other for a moment and turned on Geblyn.

"No, for far too long our republic has been tainted by Raften's regime. Long live the republic," said one of the pyromancers.

"Outrageous. Treason, unspeakable treason! How dare you, you, you ignoramus, you fools…" Vysol had enough. She walked past the pyromancers and laid Geblyn out. He was detained and taken to the dungeon. There was no Magister of Caphry however there was a lord who was under house arrest. The pyromancers that were in the Magisters chambers released him and escorted him to Imra.

"Greetings and salutations, Imra of Madir," he said gleefully. "I am Beric, and regent lord of Caphry and I hear you put Geblyn down for a nap. Bravo," he said before beginning to clap excitedly. "I could not stand him."

"Will you join the rebellion?" said Imra, refusing to beat around the bush.

"Remind me of who is involved again?" asked Beric.

"Madir of course, Kaelina of Atlan, ten dragons and the Nagrimaran queen, Darlana."

"The apostate hmm, intriguing. Ten dragons and two houses. It would seem that dissent is gaining momentum throughout the empire." He moved to the Magister's chair, sat back and threw his feet up. If I do this and we lose. I will lose my head or worse. I may be paraded through Tarvana like Prince Velnir was and garroted in front of a mob. Such a public display is most displeasing to ponder. What do I gain from joining this rebellion?"

"For starters, you can keep your life," said Imra.

"And you claim to be a liberator," said Beric.

Imra sighed. "I will not kill you but you need to understand, Beric, if you do not join us, it will be assumed that you would join Raften. If you do not join him, he will kill you. If you join him, Magris will kill you. I do apologize for putting you into this position. I have no choice, the die is cast.

"I understand, Imra. I am not afraid to lose my life. I wish to bring peace to our island as a republic or empire, either is good with me however, I do expect to gain something for my loyalty. For the sake of my people who will have to stand against Tarvana in the coming weeks either way," he said before popping a delicious Caphryian grape into his mouth.

"I cannot make guarantees that will only benefit you. I can state that we will restore the republic and you will retain your right of lordship over Caphry," said Imra.

"Regent-lordship. My brother, Meric is still the Lord of Caphry and they labeled him a traitor for supporting our cousin. If you can guarantee that his title and rights will be restored to him, I will commit Caphry to the cause."

"Very well," said Imra. Now she had documents declaring war against Tarvana from Atlan and Caphry. She was very pleased with herself and Vysol took to the sky again with Imra on her back.

Chapter 16
Unthinkable

They were packed and bound within a slavers cart with other slaves that Darlana assumed were also for the emperor. One caught her attention, and she could not help but wonder what the emperor would want with this one.

Darlana was unable to discern the gender of the slave. She thought it to be human but the hair was wild and skin was saggy. They resembled an elderly human and they could very well be. She felt pity for this person.

The slave cart rumbled toward Unarith's towering gates. The city was massive like those in Tanimara. It was recently renovated with the tastes of the new emperor, but the city itself was actually quite old. The walls were tall and black. They had tall spires that held the city's defenses.

As they entered, Darlana was amazed by the architecture. The Umbramari built their homes with an emphasis on the artistic aspect. All their buildings were black and brimmed with gold and purple tapestries.

Unarith was so large that it took almost an hour to get to the city center. Most of the other slaves were offloaded until just a few remained including Darlana, Meric and that elderly human. It would take equally as long to reach the palace which looked more like a citadel. Several outer walls protected it should an army be able to break through Unarith's defenses.

The cart stopped and the driver got off. He went to inform the palace guards that the shipment had arrived. They came out to secure the load.

One by one, each slave was taken off the cart and had their ropes removed and replaced with shackles and chains. They were much heavier but were not as painful. Meric was pulled off first and shackled, but Darlana was saved for last. She would be taken off the cart and not shackled. She was brought to a rather elegant looking room inside of the palace where several Umbramari females were waiting.

In their own way, they were very beautiful. They were obviously elves and Darlana actually resembled them to a degree, only her skin was not as pale. They gazed upon her with delight.

"You are a gorgeous one," said one of the Umbramari.

They sat Darlana down and began to clean her up. They were then adorned with what Darlana assumed to be an elegant Umbramarian gown. It did not suit her taste. The dress was a dress, but it had sharp metal ornaments all over it. It was a very dark red and black. They put her in front of a mirror seemingly proud of their work. Darlana looked at herself and was quite surprised. She pulled off the dark Umbramari fashion quite well.

The guards were invited back in, and they took her. The palace was enormous. Thrice the size of her own. It was a long walk up the stairs and through many halls and corridors and through several false rooms before she finally got to the tower where he was.

Ralnor's eyes burned with a unholy hunger as he stalked towards her, his gaze raking over her form with an unbridled lust that made her skin crawl. His hot breath danced across her skin as he leaned in, his nostrils flaring as he inhaled the scent of her hair. His fingers slid through her locks like a snake slithering through grass, sending shivers down her spine.

As he sniffed her hair, his eyes seemed to gleam with a feral light, his pupils dilating like a predator sizing up its prey. His tongue slid out, leaving a wet trail on her cheek as he licked her slowly, deliberately. The sensation sent a wave of revulsion through her, but she was frozen in place, unable to move.

Ralnor pulled back, his eyes locking onto hers with an unnerving intensity. He licked his lips, his tongue darting out to taste the air.

"Welcome to Unarith, my domain of ice and shadow," he growled, his voice low and menacing. "I am Ralnor, emperor of this frozen realm and lord of the Umbramari tribes. You will kneel before me, and you will serve." His eyes seemed to bore into her soul, his words dripping with a dark, foreboding power.

Darlana hesitated. One of the guards gently pressed his boot against the back of her leg and forced her down without bruising her.

"You are most beautiful. How was I so fortunate to have you brought for me. Celestials damn you." He cackled. "Tomorrow, we will have you examined."

She said nothing. Fear began to flow through her. *"What did he mean by examined? Will he hurt me?"* she thought.

A moment later the guard took her from his chambers and brought her back down to a different room full of females of several races. Mostly human and elven. They all looked miserable. Several of them were pregnant but seemed to be in good spirits.

"Welcome, I am Leta and this is the harem. We are all his concubines, and it appears you are the latest edition. Let's have a look at you," said Leta. "You are a gem my dear. I think he will be seeing a lot less of us and more of you in the next few weeks."

Darlana looked at her strangely.

"Not that we are ungrateful. Believe me, any other Umbramari would beat the piss out of you. Be glad you are beautiful enough to be his. Anyway, you will bunk over there," she said pointing to an elegant bed next to another Umbramari woman. "What is your name?"

"Darlana."

"And where are you from, Darlana," asked Leta with a smile.

"I came from Tarvana, Tanimara but for the last four hundred years, I have been in Nagrimar."

"Darlana, Queen of Nagrimar? I know of you," mocked Leta. "The apostate of Tanimara." She looked around the harem at all the other women then back to Darlana. "You poor soul. You have no idea what you have gotten yourself into, do you?" asked Leta.

Darlana was surprised to hear she knew of her as the apostate. She shook her head.

"Let me get you caught up then. Umbramari are tribal people that have adapted to live here for thousands of years. Tanimaran and I imagine Nagrimaran culture values moderation while ours values excess in all forms of pleasure. Tanimarans and Nagrimarans worship the Celestials of the Phatra. We worship the Celestials of the Shadow realms, the gods of violence, darkness, excess and lust."

Darlana tilted her head slightly agreeing though she too valued excess to a degree.

"Everything we do is for the emperor. Our lives depend on it. Please do not forget that when you are with him, if you mess up, we also get punished and we do not mess up. Do whatever he wants and then some. If you can do that, you will have no enemies here, Princess," said Leta in a condescending tone.

Darlana felt terrible. She agreed with Leta and took her place in her new bed. She lay there turned away from the rest as they gossip among themselves.

Darlana felt alone and isolated. She thought of all those who died in Nagrimar. All those people who escaped and then were slaughtered by the Tanimarans outside of the Forlorn Forest.

She thought of Magris in Madir and wondered if he was still there. She thought of Rizim and Dravon and hoped they were safe with Alzar. She thought of Nythint and missed him standing outside her door. If only he could be here now.

She thought of Meric too. She was livid with him but too exhausted to do anything about it and for the moment she was glad. She did not believe he was responsible for the Tanimaran attack on Nagrimar. She knew that it was only a matter of time before they would and that in reality, the taking of Madir probably stalled the attack and led to a smaller force being sent to deal with the Nagrimarans.

Ultimately, she took solace in knowing that Meric destroyed the Tanimaran expeditionary force and their fleet with the dragons. For that, she was grateful.

She lay there thinking about how she was going to get herself and Meric out of this predicament.

Darlana woke up to the other Umbramari women getting ready to do their daily business. The elf who purchased her was announced to be waiting outside the harem for Darlana. Today would be her first time with the emperor. She was brought to his chambers and there sat several other mari who seemed to be wearing the clothing of a religious order.

The emperor lifted Darlana's dress up and gently bent her over. She did not resist and did as expected. Her primary focus was figuring out how to get away from Unarith and back to the Tower of Alzar.

Nothing was happening. Darlana subtly looked behind her and saw the other Umbramari examining her. They were whispering something and the emperor looked displeased.

"This slave has had children. She is able to produce an heir for you. We can calculate her ovulation after her first menstrual cycle. Then, you may consummate," said the one wearing what Darlana thought might be religious robes.

"Very well then. Until it is consummated, she will not stay in the harem. The harem is reserved for my concubines only," said Ralnor.

"Of course, Emperor." The elf that escorted her to the emperor pulled her dress back down and told her to stand up. He paid his respects to all those present and then took Darlana out. She was brought below the palace into an area clearly reserved for slaves. The floor was cobblestone, the chamber pots were full and there were six bunks to a room. Her escort left her at the entrance and to his leave. Darlana stood there and closed her eyes.

"Darlana," said a familiar voice.

She turned around to see Meric. She immediately hugged him and held on. He held onto her as well. His eyes were not too swollen, and the wheezing had stopped.

"I thought you left," said Darlana.

"I was going to and decided I could not. I tried to save you Darlana," said Meric.

"I know, the effort is appreciated. We have to find a way out of here."

Several other slaves were eavesdropping, and it was obvious.

"Come, I know a place where we can be alone," said Meric.

He led her through the pens and to a pillar that had several grain bags stacked up against it. They were arranged in such a way to look like it was a full stack. He looked around and made sure no one was watching before he crawled under them.

Darlana followed and it revealed that Meric had stacked sacks of grain on top of several crates and made himself a hiding area.

"When they threw me in here, I immediately got to work. This is inconspicuous and relatively safe. I had done something similar when I was hiding in Atlan after Arlen killed Baefric and took over."

Darlana looked around and nodded. "No one will find us here?" she asked.

Meric shook his head no. "Not likely. It would take considerable effort to locate the entrance through all the grain," said Meric.

"We have to get out of here. He wants me to be one of his concubines and to produce an heir for him," said Darlana with disgust and fear in her voice.

"I see no way out, Darlana. If we did get out, where would we go? It seems to me like you might have it pretty good if all you need to do is produce an heir. Why not consider an Umbramari? You did it with a human."

Darlana slapped him. "I loved Prince Sampsin of Araba and wanted a future with him," she said with disdain.

Meric grabbed his already bruised cheek and remained quiet.

"We will escape and go to the Tower of Alzar," she said before noticing his knapsack in the corner. "You still have your stuff," she asked. She then pulled out his teleportation stone.

Meric's eyes widened in excitement. "By the celestials. We can escape," cheered Meric quietly.

Just then, two guards entered the pens and were scouring for contraband. Darlana heard them coming their way.

Meric motioned for Darlana to use the teleportation stone, but it was not charged. Meric realized this and moved over to his sack to grab an arcane stone.

The guards began throwing the sacks of grain to the side. It became clear that one of the other slaves had followed

Meric and observed him building his hideout.

Meric was desperately trying to find the stone but one of the guards climbed onto the sacks of grain and leapt onto Meric. Darlana was leaning up against the crates. When another guard jumped in, dislodging several sacks, and fell upon Darlana.

The guards detained Meric and Darlana with haste. They were taken to the dungeon and thrown in the same rat-infested, cold dark and damp cell.

Meric was furious, he got up and ran over to the cell door and began banging on it calling the guards out. Darlana sat on the cot and watched him trying to wrap her head around what had happened. She became worried that soon they would be executed and with a good reason.

The guards came to their cell and opened the gate. They beat Meric mercilessly. They grabbed him and hung him upside down against the wall before leaving. Darlana sat there and kept quiet. She no longer had the daggers and could not do much anyway.

After things had calmed down, Darlana looked to Meric.

"I thought you said no one knew about your hiding spot! Why would you get yourself in this predicament," she scolded, somewhat amused because she had seen him like this before.

"I thought that if I got their attention, you could use your martial skills to break us out," he said.

"And where would we go, you fool?"

They were interrupted by the individual in the cell across from them. It was a woman and the same woman that was in the cart with them when they first arrived.

"You wish to escape," she asked before moving her hair to the size revealing a clouded eye. Her face was very saggy and old. Her nose was long and had warts. She was skinny and smelled horrible.

"We do, yes," said Meric eagerly.

"Your time will come," she said followed by a maniacal laugh and smile.

A few hours later, the elf who purchased them came down to speak with the guards. It was decided that Ralnor did not want to wait for Darlana. He wanted her now, so she was pulled out of the cell and brought to his chambers.

When she returned, she was beaten and bruised. She was thrown in the cell.

"By the Celestials, what did they do to you," inquired Meric over her condition.

Darlana ignored him and went to lay down on the cot.

"It is so cold in here," he yelled to get the guards attention. "I have to urinate!"

He was not doing too well upside down. His cries went ignored.

"I cannot hold it, oh no," he said as he began to urinate. Gravity would of course take effect. "Bleh, it is getting in my mouth," he complained while trying to move his head as far as he could out of the way.

Darlana did not care anymore. What she had just experienced broke her. Never in her life had she been treated so lowly and objectified as she just was. Her body was violated many times by the emperor, and she ached all over. Her fear of this place was growing. She closed her eyes and clenched her fists before drifting off into sleep.

While dreaming, she was in her palace in Nagrimar. Velnir was next to her playing with Paeris. She began to sob and Velnir looked at her and inquired why she was crying. Paeris brought her the plushy of Ismi that Alzar gave her when she was first born. Darlana held them tightly and kissed both of them.

Day after day, she would be taken to Ralnor. She became increasingly paranoid and afraid. Every time the guards would come into their cell, she would melt down and beg them not to take her.

All Meric could do was sit there for if he budged at all, they would beat and torture him. She would come back all the same. Raped, beaten, bruised and in tears until one day she did not fight. Hopelessness had set in.

Upon her return, she was less beaten and bruised. She would simply go to sleep and try to dream of Velnir and Paeris as it was all she felt she had left.

Suddenly a ruckus woke her up. She turned over and saw that Meric was still upside down but sleeping. She looked over her shoulder across the dungeon into the other cell.

The guards were harassing the old woman. They beat her until she stopped resisting and pulled her halfway through the gate. They were amused and released the gate down upon her. The spikes that were normally meant to go into the ground upon closing to keep the gate in place were now driven through the inmate who cried out. They brought the gate up and did it again and again until the inmate was dead.

By this time, Darlana had turned back over and closed her eyes. As far as she was concerned, they would be next and she could hardly care at the moment.

The guards left the body there. A black tendril began to creep out of the body and slowly slithered its way into Darlana and Meric's cell. It moved toward the cot Darlana was on. She was unable to sleep. Her mind was racing of what was to come next. She dreaded the idea of going back to Ralnor.

Suddenly, something cold began to creep up her leg. She turned over to see a shadow black as night over her. Terrified, she could not even breathe. She could hardly think. The shadowy figure gently placed its hand on her cheek, instantly calming her down. Darlana was surprised as she knew nothing with such power.

"Who are you?"

"Who? … Or what," it said with a sinister whisper.

Darlana was no longer alarmed. She thought she should be scared of this thing that was on top of her naked body in a dungeon cell, but the thought faded. She was calm and relaxed.

"Your circumstances are unfavorable. You will end up like her" it said while pointing at the dead woman killed by the gate.

"I know," said Darlana.

"Would you like to escape?"

Darlana hesitated to answer at first. Just because she was now calm did not mean she would trust whatever this was. "I would."

A piece of parchment would manifest out of thin air along with an already dipped quill. The shadow moved them toward her.

"What will happen?"

"Your body will be a host for me as I can no longer be in that one," it said pointing at the corpse once more. "I will not only help us escape, I will give you strength and power beyond your own. You need only to consent."

Darlana was feeling too calm and too relaxed. Logic began to escape her. "Very well," she said as she grabbed the parchment and quill.

The moment she signed the document, it vanished and the shadow dove into her chest. Darlana could feel the shock of it entering her body. It was cold and evil but it did not hurt. Once it entered her entirely, she felt a jolt.

"Darlana... Darlana," said Meric.

She didn't even realize he had been brought down. All of a sudden, everything that just happened felt only like a dream and the reality of the circumstance came back. Hopelessness returned. The woman in the cell across the way was gone but the gate was still broken.

"Forgive me, Darlana. I thought you were ill," said Meric with concern and seemingly unaware of what happened. She did not say anything. The more she thought about it, the more she convinced herself it was just a dream.

"I will be all right. Thank you," she said as she lay down and turned over. Meric made his way to his corner where he had been sleeping. She was unsure of what happened but now that she was completely awake, there was no doubt that tomorrow would be more of the same. She fell asleep.

The next day, they were awakened by a commotion. The guards came into their cell and grabbed Meric. They then dragged him off and Darlana was powerless to do anything. They took him outside to the courtyard.

Darlana stood on her cot and peered through a hole in the wall which rats used to get in and out of the cell. She could see Meric outside and was mortified at what she saw around where they had him. Her heart began to pound.

The guards strapped Meric to a chair and held his head steady. They took a knife and began cutting around his face and ears.

Darlana put her hand over her mouth and began to cry. The horror of it. They peeled his face off and allowed it to hang from his chin. He was desperately pleading with them to stop. They unbound him from the chair and brought him over to an "X" plank. They then drove stakes through his hands and feet to secure him to it.

Another guard grabbed a pole that was sharp at the end while another grabbed a mallet. They inserted the pole into Meric's anus and began to pound it through him.

Each strike caused him to groan and howl in pain. Once the pole pierced his shoulder, Meric got quieter.

The guards hoisted Meric up and put the pole in the ground next to every other prisoner who had been impaled that day.

"The emperor's will," they shouted before taking their leave.

Darlana could not believe what she had just witnessed. It happened so fast and never in her life had she seen anything so cruel.

Several hours went by and she could still hear the emperor's victims groaning in agony albeit a lot less as many of them have died by now.

At first, she could not bring herself to look to see if Meric was still alive. When she mustered the courage, she got up and saw that he was still breathing. His breath was visible in the cold air.

The next morning, outside, the wet rip of tearing flesh and guttural growls sent chills through her. She got up and saw that talonasaurs were let loose on the courtyard. They were pulling the dead off the planks and eating them. They surrounded Meric and began jumping up trying to get a bite at him. He was impaled quite high off the ground however, one of the talonasaurs managed to grab his foot and pulled him farther down the pole.

Meric was still alive, and Darlana could not believe it. Her heart sank and she watched the talonasaurs rip his feet off. Meric groaned and moaned. They grabbed his hands next, then his legs and he kept getting pulled farther down the pole.

By the time a Talonasaur grabbed the skin from his face hanging from his chin, Darlana believed Meric was dead. She began to sob as she sank back down to her cot.

She heard a cry of pain and quickly got up and realized that Meric was still alive. The talonasaurs began disemboweling him and were throwing his innards up into the air to get a better grip for swallowing.

Her breath hitched as she began to sob. She turned to sit on her cot when she heard Meric scream yet again. The crunching of bone in the teeth of the talonasaur sent chills through her body. She began to tremble as she heard Meric was still screaming.

Darlana could not help herself. She climbed back up and still weeping, observed Meric, still impaled, missing his face, his innards, hands and feet while still crying. She watched in horror as a talonasaur casually went up to Meric, turned its head to the side and grabbed Meric's head.

It bit down and the crunching of skull indicated that he was finally dead. It had to be confirmed when the talonasaur took Meric's head and swallowed it.

Darlana was sobbing. She slumped down in her bed, clenching her trembling hands into fists. She had never bore witness to such horror in the six hundred years she had been alive. She began to break mentally. Groans could be heard again.

"There was absolutely no way, just end his suffering," she thought.

She got up and looked. Outside the hole was the talonasaur that grabbed Meric's face. It was standing there right in front of her cell dangling his face from its mouth. This was the material of nightmares. She could see through the mouth and eye openings. It was as if the last expression he would ever make was one of agony. The animal finally tossed it up and swallowed it.

Not long after, she heard another commotion. It was the guards cleaning up after the talonasaurs. One of them had stepped on a stake used to pin the victim to an "X" plank. Meric was dead and his suffering was over. Darlana felt relief for him but began to believe that it would be her on that plank next.

Unnatural hate began to manifest in her heart. Hate for the Umbramari, hate for the Emperor. Something inside her was triggering her traumatic memories.

Instead of fear or anxiety, she became angry. Time had allowed her to let go of hate. Even after she was exiled, she still reached out to Tanimara for diplomatic relations. She first began to loathe her father for what he did to her family.

She remembered that all this happened because of her hatred for her father and Tanimara. The war was her fault. Everything happened because she talked Velnir into a political marriage and tried to use him to get back to Tanimara from which she knew she was never allowed to return to because she had loved a human prince.

Guilt began to overcome her but once again, something inside her replaced her guilt with anger. Darlana struggled to understand what was happening to her.

She remembered what happened the night before. The shadow, the dream. Whatever was inside her was surely manifesting these emotions.

"Why do you tempt me?" cried Darlana.

Nothing or no one responded. It was as if she was talking to herself. She began to feel like she was losing her mind.

She awoke to footsteps coming down the hall. For several weeks, she had been brought to Ralnor's chambers where he beat and had his way with her. She learned if she complied and took the lead, he would not be so rough so long as she was.

It seemed he was a sadomasochist.

She kept coming up with more clever ways to please him, hoping he would not get bored and return to beating her. She never got a break from him as he favored her for her unique beauty, and it was wearing on her.

For one to be told how beautiful they are one moment and then to be beaten the next created insurmountable fear in her.

She sat up and put her feet on the ground. Her right foot landed on a cold metal object. She looked down and noticed it was one of the spikes from the gate that was dropped on that prisoner. She wondered how it could have remained there so long without her or anyone else noticing.

The footsteps were getting closer, and she knew it was almost time to go but she had had enough.

"The spike, Darlana, grab the spike and hide it," suggested someone but who.

"I have a cot and no clothes. Where could I possibly..." Just then, she had an idea and picked up the metal spike.

Ralnor's servant came to retrieve her. He brought her to Ralnor's chambers where he was eagerly awaiting her. It was obvious that he never had a slave or concubine act the way she did. She pretended to like it and served his every desire.

He was already in the bed and without clothes. He was stroking himself getting ready for her. She smiled and walked up to him as she had done many times, but she was nervous. There had been on several occasions that he desired to sodomize her however this time, that would prove fatal. She had to take control, so she had help from the shadow.

Darlana allowed the shadow to work with her by allowing her to take control of certain aspects of her body, but she could not completely focus on what the shadow was doing. This trust exercise would determine how their future as one would go.

Darlana threw her leg over his body and inserted him into herself. She straddled him with exceptional strength and he noticed.

When he became alarmed, she relaxed but she held her head high and looked down upon him like she had not done before. Ralnor was curious but she was pleasing him greatly. She got rough and began to move wildly. He grabbed on to the bedpost and seemed to be enjoying it.

Darlana knew what was to come.

"Wait for it," said that voice.

Darlana was focused on Ralnor. Her hate manifested and grew. She could feel him throb and knew he was about to climax.

The moment he began to, she put her hand under her backside and pushed the spike out of her anus. She lifted it up into the air and took pleasure seeing the look of surprise and horror on his face but before he could react, she plunged the spike into his chest and forced it as deep as she could get it.

Overjoyed with his misery, she got distracted and missed his heart. He grabbed her throat. It was then that Darlana's eyes and veins turned black and her skin turned pale. Fear gripped Ralnor and rightfully so. She smiled as she grabbed his arms and held them down. She lunged forward and sank her teeth into his throat. With one bite, she ripped his flesh and witnessed his consciousness slipping.

Darlana was surprised. She felt an overwhelming sense of euphoria and strength coursing through her body. All of her senses were heightened. He was dumbfounded and began choking. Then it was over.

The emperor was dead.

Murder had been something she always dreaded even if it was her enemies. She felt as if she was loving it. Guilt swept over her even if for a moment.

Again, whatever was inside of her replaced the guilt with anger. It was at this moment that Darlana knew the night the shadow came to her was no dream. She had made a deal with it and it was inside of her. It was making her stronger and manipulating her emotions. She did not like this and wanted her emotions to be hers.

The guards outside heard the commotion and normally would not rush in but when they heard Ralnor plea, they came in and saw her on top of him. They drew swords.

Darlana knew that this would likely be the end but she felt it was worth it to see him die by her hand. She jumped off of him and retrieved two swords hanging from the wall of his chambers and faced the two guards. She was sweaty, dripping and naked.

"Pour your malice into the blades and steal their souls," said the shadow.

Its voice was now indistinguishable from everything else. She had no time to question it. The two guards charged at her and engaged. She was of course wearing nothing and they were clad from head to toe in armor.

This would work to their disadvantage as they were slower. She dealt blow after blow to each of them knowing that if one were to succeed against her, it would be the end.

Darlana dispatched one of the guards by removing his head from his shoulders leaving the other one clearly nervous.

The blade in her right hand began to glow. The soul of the dead guard became visible. It was leaving the body but the blade was devouring it. The face of the ghost's and his deafening scream as he clawed at nothing in a vain attempt to get away pleased Darlana. The sword glowed purple once it had completely devoured the soul of the dead guard intriguing Darlana.

"Kill him, kill him!" demanded the shadow.

She threw the sword in her left hand toward him. It pierced and embedded itself into his neck. He fell to the ground choking on his own blood. His soul also began to leave his body but it seemed prematurely. The blade did not seem to care. It pulled the guards soul into itself also giving it a purple hue.

"Scatter, flee," said the shadow.

Darlana could not leave naked. She looked fairly similar to the Umbramari elves and decided she would take the armor from the smaller of the two male guards. The commotion was loud and she could expect the reinforcing guards any moment. She opened the door and looked slightly out and to her surprise, no one was stirred.

The thought that all the screaming and clashing of furniture would stir suspicion had given her such great anxiety only to see there was one guard outside the door completely oblivious to everything that just happened. She did not need the shadow to tell her what to do next.

Slowly, she opened the door just enough to get herself behind the guard. Quickly, she grabbed onto him and pulled him back before placing the blade against his neck and cutting his throat. He reached up to attempt to stop the bleeding in vain.

Darlana pulled him into the emperor's chambers and allowed him to bleed out. Now was the time to make her escape. She checked both ways to make sure it was clear before carefully and quietly making her way down the familiar path she had taken so many times before. She knew there was an outlet.

Darlana turned the corner when she noticed two guards making their way toward her direction. She was thankful to the celestials that they did not notice her. She grabbed her blades and made ready to strike when they stopped.

"You see the one that talonasaur grabbed and pulled down," said one guard.

"Aye, the one that kept screaming. Could never get that one to shut up. It pleased me greatly when it was time to execute him… Tanimari, sons of ogres," said the other guard.

Darlana knew that they were speaking of Meric. It pained her to remember that fateful night.

"When they got him down the pole, they began tearing into his belly. They grabbed all his innards and began yanking them out, swallowing them whole. That elf lived through getting his limbs torn off and his guts ripped out. You could still hear him scream."

The other guard cackled maniacally. "Indeed, the agonizing screams as they dug around his chest cavity for more of his innards. Wish he had lived long enough to watch that Talonasaur tear his whole face off and swallow it."

Darlana was sick to her stomach. The images of that were forever imprinted in her mind. Rage began to fill her heart.

"Yes, yes, do it," said the shadow.

Darlana leapt from around the corner and bolted toward the unsuspecting guards. By the time they noticed her, her blade had introduced itself to neck of the closest guard and nearly severed his head from his shoulders.

Before the other guard could even unsheathe his weapon, she drove her blade into his eye socket and pinned him against the wooden beam. She was not finished. She would make an example out of these two.

No one was coming so she took her time. She decorated the walls of the hall with their blood and arranged their intestines in such a way on the floor that if noticed would definitely gather attention. This was her intention.

Alarms began to ring. Someone had discovered the emperor's chambers. She had to escape now. The exit was not too far, and she found it with ease. It was nighttime and so it was easier to slip into the shadows.

The guards who discovered the dead emperor and his guards were making their way down the hall when they discovered the dismembered remains of two more guards. One guard slipped on the bits of entrails and fell to the floor alerting the others. As they helped him to his feat, they noticed that the entrails spelled something. Stepping away to get a clearer look, one read it aloud. "Terror comes."

By now, Unarith was in lock down. Guards were everywhere making sure that the denizens were in their homes.

Darlana was down an alley that had access into a building which she took advantage of. She went in and recognized the area. It was where her and Meric were when he got caught. She frantically started looking for his belongings when she heard dogs barking.

Alarmed, she abandoned the area in favor of a much safer one. Once she felt she was in a safe place, she lay down and began to weep quietly. She thought for certain that she was going to die. She felt disgusted with herself for going so lowly as to place the metal spike in her rectum if for no other reason other than she had not been able to wash her hands. They were smelly as was the rest of her. She did not feel like a queen anymore.

The shadow within her began to change her emotions once again. She leaned over and closed her eyes.

Despite the frigid air, sweat began to bead down her forehead. Try as she might, it was very difficult to stop it. Her body became calm again and her breathing slowed.

After a moment, she opened her eyes. Though she was calm, she was frustrated by the shadows' ability to change her emotional state. None of what she did was in her nature. It was easy for her to justify it as a means to escape but she couldn't help it. She enjoyed it.

This created conflict within her heart. Right now, she could only remember how Nythint would stand outside her door as she slept while her husband was recovering. He made her feel safe and now there was no one there for her. She was on her own and the more she thought about how these people killed Yzat and Meric, how the Emperor raped and beat her, the more rage began to build.

Never had Darlana felt so low in her life. Her tears stopped streaming down her cheeks. Her body began to heat up and the sad look on her face began to transform into a menacing one. She would allow herself to give in to the rage. She would unleash cruelty and malice upon the Umbramari.

These people would pay with their lives but that was not enough. They must suffer first! Darlana figured that if she were going to die there, she would make damn sure that as many Umbramari would suffer and die with her as she could.

Her thoughts returned to Nythint. The last dragon alive that was loyal to her. If only he were here now.

***

Something did not feel right. His heart ached and he did not know why. Nythint could wait no longer. Without telling anyone, he left in search of Darlana and Yzat. He knew they were going to the Twilight Wood so he studied a map and made his way there.

He was traveling as fast as he could but a dragon of his size and shape could not go more than sixty or so kilometers per hour. It would take him at least a full day to get to their first destination, the crossroads.

There wasn't a cloud in the sky. The moons were both dark and Nythint could see all the stars as bright as they could be. This was a truly magnificent sight for him. He wished he could share this moment with his brother.

As he climbed higher and higher to get over the massive peaks of Dhar' Modir, he noticed what looked like a winding blue stream weaving through the cosmos. It was beautiful and he made a mental note to ask what it was when he returned to the Tower of Alzar.

He was getting tired and losing momentum. For now, he was as high as he could be but was forced to glide around the peaks.

This set him back quite a bit of time and caused him to be frustrated. He knew his body well and understood that it would do no one good if he lost his strength and fell from the sky.

For a moment he thought about removing his heavy armor and dropping his sword for only a moment before the memory of his brother reminded him that they were gifts from him for which Nythint was extremely grateful.

***

Darlana had awakened to barking dogs once more. This time, they were too close for comfort. She was forced to make a hasty retreat toward the gorb pens.

Soon they would catch her scent and discover her if she did not act. The gorbs were filthy animals native to the waste lands. They had long snouts and tiny tusks. They were gray in color and had a horrible squeal. Gorbs were easy to keep for they ate anything and everything, even each other if they were hungry enough.

The Umbramari kept them for food and Darlana knew the dogs would eat them too. She trudged her way through the mud and around the docile feeding or sleeping gorbs over to a large one laying on a pile of tall grass. She quickly buried herself in the grass and leaned up next to the gorb who did not seem to mind the warmth of her body resting near its back.

It was then that she realized she was laying in a pile of gorb dung. The most foul smelling substance would linger far beyond the pens. This is why the Umbramari kept the slaves near the animals. It was better that the slaves lived near the smell insead of any denizen.

The dogs made their way to the gorb pens and began barking in the direction of Darlana.

"Mangy hound, now is not the time to eat," said the irritated handler.

The gorb opened one eye and looked at the much smaller dog. That was about all it cared to do and would expend no more energy on it. Darlana knew this would throw the dogs off. Eager to leave the stinky gorb pens, the handler yanked the dog which yelped before making a hasty retreat.

Thunder began to roll and rain began to fall. The rain was freezing and Darlana knew she could not remain out for long. Once she determined the way was clear, she got up and made her way through the roads traversed by few. She was not comfortable with so much of her face being visible so she walked through a market that was closing and stole a hood and cloak from one of the vendors.

She had nothing left to lose. She wanted to make those responsible for her pain suffer. Only then would she be content to die and be with her family.

Chapter 17
Respite or so It Would Seem

Magris had sent Imra out on a mission with low expectations. Truly he thought if she were to defect at this point, it would be of no consequence to him.

What was really getting to him was the fact that neither Darlana or Meric had contacted him since the arrival of the reinforcements and Commander Folwin was also not heard from again after he left and went back to Nagrimar to ask for assistance.

At the time, Magris did not expect the Madirans to join the Nagrimarans against Tarvana, and since they did, Magris now had reinforcements to not only keep the city but sally out if they wanted to fight the Tanimaran armies currently besieging Madir. He had heard rumors that Nagrimar had been burnt to the ground and hundreds of thousands of people died. The thought of this made him shudder. Where in the nether was Darlana?

Magris now had almost two hundred thousand soldiers under his command including the original five hundred Shades and nine full sized and armored dragons. He had gone out once, mounted on a dragon and harassed the Tanimarans to push their line out of reach of Madir.

They were once again becoming bold enough to get closer and had begun hurling fireballs and large stones into the city outskirts with some going over the walls.

Once again, the scrying orbs were hovering above the city and were being destroyed as often as they could. Magris knew the Tanimarans were aware of their dwindling food supply.

Soon, they would be forced to fight, surrender, or abandon Madir all together. He was sitting in a chair drinking tea and overlooking the city. Abrion's moons Canis and Majoris were full tonight and illuminated the countryside. The Tanimaran campfires were visible even from this far away. It looked like several straight orange lines on the horizon.

Many long nights had passed in solitude. Thoughts swirled, grief weighing heavy on his heart. Guilt tightened around him. "What have I gotten myself into?" he muttered.

He lost Velnir. He had no children and had no wife. He was tired of sleeping with a different woman every night. Depression did not come to an elf as easily as it would a human but he traced the rim of his glass absentmindedly.

The beverage had gone cold, much like the warmth of company he once had. The nights stretched long, and even the stars offered no comfort.

He would have to look at himself in the mirror and see a scarred elf with one eye and a peg leg. To others, he looked terrifying. A warrior willing to sacrifice. One who would stop at nothing to achieve victory and in truth, that is why many Madirans felt safe under his command. They believed he would not ask them to do anything he would not do himself, and after the first battle in the Sundered lands against the orcs, he never did.

This did not make him happy however and he had to deal with this often. Truly, he felt safe under Velnir's leadership and missed him terribly. The fear of the unknown. The uncertainty of Darlana coming to Madir and the certainty that if she did not bring the rest of the Nagrimaran army, Madir would fall, and he would be executed gripped him.

He needed a plan. If the walls were breached and they made it to the palace, he would enchant several jars of explosive goo to detonate on impact and would place them all around his body before jumping from the Magistrates chambers and into a crowd of Tanimaran soldiers trying to break into it.

One way or another, he was committed to fight until the very end if not for his queen, then for Velnir.

He sat there lost in thought when out of the corner of his eye, he saw something fluttering against the moon. He looked up and could make out a black streak, but it was moving. As it got closer to Madir, he realized it was Vysol, and his heart had skipped a beat. He was excited. He got up and made his way over to the rail to peer through his monocular. He could see the Tanimarans beginning to panic.

They tried launching bolts at her, but she was easily able to evade them and not allow the Tanimarans to fire on her without punishment.

Even from this far, her firebreath was extraordinary. The length of her fire breath easily tripled the length of her body. It was like a show of fireworks from this far. He felt foolish for despairing. The dragons would play a vital role in the defeat of Tanimara. He would have to act soon with or without Velnir or Darlana.

Madirans began to notice and started cheering. Soon, Vysol had enough fun harassing the Tanimarans and made her way to the balcony of the palace. The other dragons were pleased to see her and gave her a warm welcome back.

By the time Magris got up there, he did not see Imra at first. Vysol made eye contact with him and pointed into the palace.

"She is in the lavatory washing up," said Vysol.

Magris nodded and made his way into the palace. He stood outside of the lavatory and was about to knock when he thought it better to let her come to him. He turned around and began to make his way back to the Magister's chambers when the lavatory door opened up and Imra stepped out.

"General," she shouted.

Magris stopped. He let out a sigh and turned around. Truly he had hoped to make it to the magister's chambers, so he did not look desperate for information, but he was caught. He turned and walked to her.

"I am pleased you made it back to Madir safely, Imra. I will be honest, I did not entirely expect you to return," said Magris.

"That would be a reasonable assumption, General, given the circumstances. I harbor no ill will. I come with good news which will surely please you."

He turned and gave her his complete attention.

"Kealina and Beric have agreed to aid us. They want to see the republic restored," said Imra. Magris escorted her back to the Magister's chambers. He was incredibly relieved. Somehow, things were looking good for the Nagrimarans, and he began to believe that he had the blessing of the celestials.

"When can we expect reinforcements," asked Magris.

"Atlan and Caphry are still suffering from the loss sustained to their regions when Tarvana banished Velnir and all those who supported him. They will need time to recruit, but in the meantime, ships sailing from Thalnor will be arriving here delivering much needed supplies. Lossed are expected and whatever we sustain will be covered by Caphry as well. Tarvana will never know unless they can spot one of the ships leaving our harbor. Once Caphry is ready to defend against a Tarvanan invasion, Atlan will deploy its guard behind the Tanimaran lines. We will have to ride out and attack if we are to have any hope of defeating the two Armies."

"How long can we expect this to take," asked Magris.

"Several months but we have bought ourselves much needed time."

Magris looked pleased and was formulating new plans as they spoke.

"Magris, I also bring grim news regarding Velnir," said Imra in a somber tone.

Once again he gave her his full attention. His heart began to pound.

"Raften paraded Velnir and the head of the dragon that fell with him through the streets of Tarvana. There was no trial. They tied him to a post and strangled him to death before removing his head and delivering it to Darlana at the tower of Alzar."

Time and time again over hundreds of years, elves have experienced loss and one may think that by now, an elf would become numb to it.

This was not the case for Magris.

Pain gripped his chest like a vice. His knees buckled, and the world blurred. A laugh—Velnir's laugh—echoed in his memory. The firelight flickering on their faces as they played Dragons & Wizards. He clenched his fists.

Gone. All of it, gone.

He had loved Velnir as a brother. The shock of the news surprised him for he had thought this would likely happen. He had prepared for it or so he thought. He began to quietly sob and Imra felt for him.

Without a word, she lowered herself and hugged him. He wrapped his arms around her and placed his head on her shoulder. She gently held his head in her hand and let him mourn the loss of his king, his friend, his brother.

After a few moments, he pulled himself together and they both stood back up.

"Now, I wish to go see my daughter. I miss her," said Imra as if asking for permission.

Magris nodded, and off she went. She did Nagrimar a great service. Vysol validated her and Magris was pleased. Now if only he could find a way to tell his queen of the good news. Surely she needed it after receiving such a grotesque parcel.

Several weeks have passed with no change. Magris would get up every day and check the line of Tanimarans with scrying orbs. He would go down to the garrison and be greeted by eager and happy Madiran and Nagrimarin soldiers. Everyone was getting along and the dragons were enjoying themselves too but today was different.

When Magris got up to observe the Tanimaran line, he noticed that one of the armies had gone and only one remained. He was alarmed and immediately went to find Imra. He banged on her door.

"One moment please, I am coming," she shouted. She opened the door and Magris looked somewhere in between excited and worried.

"The Tanimaran army that was besieging the southern wall of the city has abandoned their siege. The Tanimaran army that besieges the western half is what remains. The odds have evened in numbers but we have superior weapons and Dragons. We can break the Siege, Imra," said Magris.

Imra looked at him wide eyed and confused, "That is wonderful news but where did the other army go?"

Magris had not thought of that and now wondered the same thing. Imra's demeanor changed from confused to dread.

"Atlantin," she said.

Magris' heart sank. "They are not ready."

"Their defense will hold and they will surely meet Raften's forces if they come within range but Caphry attacked us when we went to speak with them. Vysol destroyed all their defenses on the northern side where if a Tanimaran army were to attack, could easily take the city," said Imra.

"We must act then and do so with haste. Come," said Magris.

"General, I'd rather not discuss war strategies half-dressed. Give me five minutes."

Magris looked at her and had not realized that she was almost completely naked when he spoke to her. His cheeks blushed. "Of course, Imra, my apologies. I'll call a meeting in the Magistrates chambers. Kindly meet us there," he said before taking his leave.

The criers bellowed loudly for the dragons and commanding officers to meet in the Magister's chambers. Magris was waiting at the huge table for them when they started trickling in. The dragons in their visage form sat together on the right side of the table. The Madirans sat in the middle and the Shades on the left. Imra entered and was invited by Magris to sit next to him.

"The Tanimarans have lifted the siege on the southern half of the city but have not on the western half. We believe they are going to attack Atlantin and Caphry. Vysol, please take five dragons and find them. The other five and our army will march out and strike the Tanimarans on the western side. When you find the Tanimarans, do not attack them right away. Go and inform the Atlantins and escort their army to attack the Tanimaran army."

Vysol understood what Magris meant. She and her dragons being there would be a valuable weapon against the Tanimarans but it would also ensure they would not turn around and attack Madir. Magris wanted to keep five of her dragons with him in case the Madirans were playing a ruse. Magris could not risk a ruse.

Vysol and her five dragons left Madir under the cover of the night. The Nagrimarans had been manufacturing repeater crossbows and training the Madiran troops on how to use them. The army was strong and ready to move.

A garrison large enough to protect Madir would be left behind in case the Tanimarans would attack from the west once the army left to conquer the countryside. Madir, Atlan and Caphry were the only houses that sent a substantial amount of troops with Velnir.

Every other house sent nothing and had the full extent of their garrisoned forces at the disposal of Raften or so it was believed. Magris had to be careful. He knew that even now, the Tanimaran armies outnumbered his. Tarvana alone had eighty thousand full time troops. This was going to be long and bloody but he hoped to make it happen quickly.

Magris was now acting outside of Darlana's orders. Last time he did that, he received several lashes after nearly losing the battle. He spent hundreds of hours studying tactics and strategy and hoped he had improved since then. He was arguably the most powerful pyromancer in Tanimara as well and planned his strategy around using his magic and the dragons. He felt that now was the time. It had been too long since he had heard from the queen so he would take the initiative.

Now the rebels were manning the walls quietly and quickly. The five remaining dragons took to the sky with two hundred and fifty Shades with the intention of deploying them behind the enemy line. They had succeeded and the Tanimarans were none the wiser. The dragons came back and deployed the remaining Shades.

All the pieces were in play and it did not take long for Magris to execute his plan. For months, he had worked out how to best attack them if it came to that and he felt that he was more prepared now than ever.

Dawn was approaching and Magris decided to mount Bovir. He was a fast and agile dragon with a long neck gray in color with black accents. This proved useful when aiming fire in all directions and he did deliver a powerful fire breath.

Moving thousands of soldiers through a city without being detected was no easy task. He had to make sure every person moved inconspicuously and under the cover of night with the street lamps out. He also had to make sure that there were no scrying orbs observing.

Magris and Bovir took to the sky followed by the four other dragons and went east to where the sun would rise.

The signal for the Shades to attack was when the dragons attacked. The sun was beginning to rise over the horizon illuminating the land. The dragons had the sun to their backs as they approached the Tanimaran line from its flanks. The dragons descended in a diamond pattern.

The Tanimarans did not notice them before they unleashed their firebreaths. They first targeted the bolt throwers and in one stroke of luck and skill, managed to destroy them all. Now they had air superiority. Magris had begun to cast fire storms left and right but there were not that many as he was the only pyromancer available.

The Tanimarans began to quickly open ranks and attempt to shield themselves. The Shades snuck up upon them in their invisibility cloaks and began firing at them with their repeater crossbows.

The Tanimarans had no idea how many were out there. Five hundred would surely have been easy to defeat but there was only confusion in the Tanimaran ranks. They could not see them and their attack was fierce. The dragons came in for another pass and killed many more.

All around the Tanimarans, their brothers were screaming in agonizing pain as they tried desperately to put themselves out. Dragon fire was very difficult to put out. The Tanimarans began to break. With their bolt throwers destroyed, the Tanimarans were easy prey. They began to panic and started to flee.

This had taken an unexpected turn. Magris had calculated the exact right time to attack and it was so well executed, he did not have to call in the army. He and the dragons routed the entire Tanimaran army by themselves. He smiled as he watched them scatter and flee for their lives.

"Allow the ones going southeast to go, kill the ones going west. We cannot allow them to bolster the forces of Linia in Starland in case they do not join us," ordered Magris to the Shades.

They moved and dispatched as many as they could but some were able to escape.

Magris ordered the gates to open and the army to march. They would march southeast to Atlan, join forces with them if they could not defeat the Tanimaran army themselves.

After a few days of marching, Vysol came back and said she saw the Tanimaran army making their way toward Caphry. The Atlantins were ready to attack if he wished for them too.

He asked her to tell them to wait for him. Every now and then, the rebels would catch a Tanimaran escapee and detain them. They were to be liberators now, not conquerors.

Village by village, the rebels would liberate, Few soldiers garrisoned there would be killed, most would be given a choice to join or simply surrender their weapons and assimilate back into society if they did not wish to face Tarvanan justice should the rebels fail.

Such kindness was not expected and gained Magris more loyalty than he had anticipated. Any force that stood against the rebels was immediately destroyed by the dragons and Magris. Surprisingly, none of the rebel forces were killed. Magris' knowledge of the terrain certainly helped. The Shades kept watch for ambushes and notified Magris of any suspicious activity.

Soon word was getting around Tanimara of Magris, the one eyed pyromancer and his dragons were laying waste to the Tanimaran countryside and gaining the loyalty of the people. From Madir to Atlan, every town and village was liberated or surrendered to the rebels.

By the time Magris finally made it to Atlan, they welcomed him with open arms. It was a true sight to behold. Foreign and domestic Soldiers all in armor that looked so different from their own and holding strange looking weapons accompanied by ten majestic and very large dragons. Magris landed and dismounted Bovir.

Kaelina, wearing her armor, approached him. "The famous or infamous General Magris. We have all heard of Velnir's success in the Sundered lands and against Necrosith. May he be at peace," said Kaelina. Her new assistant or squire was fumbling through her things trying to keep up with her.

"Velnir was brave and victorious. He brought glory to Tanimara only to be declared an enemy by the Tyrant and self proclaimed emperor, Raften. The time has come to remove him and restore the republic. I am glad I can count on your support," said Magris.

"We are ready to deploy immediately," said Kaelina. She turned and blew the horn of Atlan. The gates opened and the Atlantin army began marching out. Magris was captivated by them. Their pointed helmets, long spears, shields, bows and quivers with their beautiful ornate silvered armor were as exquisite as he remembered. He felt proud to see his people marching as his allies once more but missed his old armor. Times have surely changed.

The Atlantin army and rebel army of Madir along with the Nagrimaran Shades and dragons merged into one army and now moved to Caphry. It would be several days before they got there.

Caphry was besieged on both its southern and northern section. When the Tanimarans heard that the rebels were coming, they moved around to the southern section and bolstered the forces there.

The Tanimarans were terrified and did not want to stick around outside the walls of a city. Some of them began to run and it started a domino effect. The Tanimarans were in full retreat.

Magris and the dragons pursued them. The dragons were devastating to the Tanimaran forces leaving scores and scores of dead before they were able to get to a mountain pass the dragons could not fly through.. This was one of the many natural defensive outposts the Tarvanans had.

Tarvana was built on a very tall cliff. The walls were built at the edge of the cliff and were thick enough inward that no conventional artillery could bring them down. Not even the sappers that were able to bring Atlan's giant walls down could scratch these. There were only two ways into Tarvana and Magris would approach from the east.

Sieging Tarvana would be difficult. The cliff on both sides of the city was cracked all the way down to the inlet which was several hundred meters below.

The inlet was wide enough to get ships through to the back side of Tarvana. Magris would have to position a few dragons on both sides to prevent supplies from being brought in or people being smuggled out and this was not an option. His only option was to secure the gate and drawbridge.

First he had to overcome the challenges he faced on the journey there. The pass was built with defenses carved into the mountain sides. The dragons could not fly through and had to go over the mountain which would force Magris to march his troops through without their support.

For now, Caphry was as far as he would go. Over the past few weeks, he had marched several hundred kilometers and liberated the entire eastern half of the island of Tanimara. He did not think he could achieve this without the help of Darlana or Velnir.

The dragons were the best allies he could have ever asked for and he was grateful to them. He rewarded the dragons as best he could. The people were pleased with them as well and willingly gave them their farm animals to eat. A well fed dragon was a happy dragon.

Magris would have a defensive position built near the pass and deploy his army there.. If the Tarvanans attacked, they would be bottlenecked and the dragons could destroy them. The pieces were beginning to be placed under Magris' watchful eye.

Everything had to be perfect. No stone left unturned, every i dotted and t crossed. Now they had the major port city of Thalnor under their control and hundreds of ships to deploy.

Magris set up his command center in Atlan as it was the center of the rebellion and built against a mountain. From there he commanded. He worked tirelessly to make sure that both fronts were heavily defended. The help of the people was invaluable.

Daily skirmishes began but were nothing of consequence. The rebels were far enough away that the Tarvanans could not reach them and there was no way the entirety of the Tarvanan army to form ranks before the rebels would descend and crush them.

If they attacked from Linia, it would not take long for the dragons to get there from Atlan and destroy them.

Beric was left in Caphry to supply the front with anything and everything they needed. Kaelina was left in Thalnor to facilitate shipping lanes. Imra was in Madir keeping things in order and bolstering their defenses. The dragons were out over the water destroying any Tanimaran ships they could see and turned it into a friendly competition. Magris was unsure of how Darlana would receive his success. He was determined to hold onto the eastern half of Tanimara until she could take command.

Magris was patrolling the coast and inland with several griffins, scrying orbs and dragons. The Shades were left in Atlan and ready to deploy anywhere at a moment's notice.

A griffin was secured for each of them and trained to pick up their rider when they blew a whistle and retreat with the others in the event of a death or capture of their rider. This rebel controlled area was under lock down and food was rationed out between all four cities based on population size.

None of these niceties would have been afforded to the Nagrimarans if the roles were reversed and many of the Tanimarans began to feel shame for what the High Magister had done to them in the Forlorn Forest. They would show their support any way they could and the fire in their hearts was burning hot. They also wanted their republic back.

Chapter 18
Search and Found

Nythint had reached the Crossroads. He did not bother morphing into his visage form but stood tall there unlike any dragon before him, wearing armor and wielding Razorheart. The whole town stopped and all was quiet.

"Do not be alarmed, I come in peace. I am looking for two elves and a dragon that may have passed through here," he said as he held out a sack containing gold coins. "Information of their whereabouts will be rewarded." The sound of his booming voice reverberated through the area and echoed off the sides of the mountains and cliffs.

Once the noise subsided, there was no sound at all. Everyone simply stood there and looked at him in awe and terror. Finally, three tiny bipedal rats wearing robes and spectacles approached Nythint. He did not notice them at first until the crowd began calling out to him that someone had approached. He was forced to transmorph into his visage form.

"Those of which you speak were spotted flying northeast," said one of the rats.

"Yes, yes. Northeast and from th-there, it-it is said th-that they met with th-the King of the Tw-Twilight wood, yes-yes…" said the other. The third rat simply nodded in agreement. Nythint remembered Darlana's plan to go to the twilight wood.

As they were speaking, several carts full of animals from the land of Northgarde bound for Protania had arrived. Nythint tossed the sack of coins toward the rats. The sack landed on one and pinned him to the ground. The other two quickly rendered aid. Other people in the area began to come to help and some even tried to steal their coins. This angered Nythint. He roared at them and the sound once again echoed through the valley and against the mountains and cliffs. He would not have any thievery.

"If any harm comes to these rat men, understand that I will rain fire down upon them and reduce them to ashes!" he said.

The would-be thieves scattered, including those who possibly had good intentions. The sack of gold was very large compared to the small rat men. The three of them could hardly muster the strength to drag it and Nythint felt bad.

He walked up to them in his visage form and grabbed the bag. "I apologize. Allow me to help you take this to your destination." The rats began to lead him to where they were staying.

Nythint had never set foot here before. The diversity of races surprised him. The rats led him to a building with a hole at the base. They told him they were staying in the crawl space which was about one meter high. Nythint was not willing to make himself smaller and tossed the bag of gold in there for them. They scurried over to it and that was that. He wipes his hands and made his way over to the carts of farm animals. His belly was growling.

He approached the man bringing the caravan of carts.

"What are those things," asked Nythint pointing to the carts directly behind the man.

"They are steer. These animals are spoken for and are to be butchered for their meat.

Meat was just what Nythint was looking for. He could fly down to the base of the mountains and catch himself some wild game but that would strip him of valuable time.

"How much for two steers?" asked Nythint.

"They are already paid for," said the man. Nythint pulled out another sack of gold roughly the same size as the one he had given to the rat men.

The man's eyes widened with excitement. "I am certain that two steer died of disease and that uh…" he said as he counted the coins. He pulled out two coins and pocketed the rest. "This ought to be enough to compensate for the loss," he said as he smiled. Nythint was confused.

He transmorphed into his natural form. "Give me two steers," he demanded.

Terrified, the man quickly ordered the cages containing the steers be opened. Nythint wasted no time sheathing his sword and grabbing both of them, one in each talon. He took to the sky and flew in the direction the rats had given him. He brought a steer up to his mouth and bit it in half.

The blood of the steer fell from the sky and rained over the area he took off from causing people to panic. He had not thought that through very well.

He was well fed and had been flying for several hours, no longer certain that he was going in the right direction, then something caught his eye. He could see a dragon on the ground below and became very excited. It could only be Yzat. He brought his wings in and dove straight for his brother as fast as he could.

As he got closer, something did not seem right. He was not moving and seemed to be wounded. Nythint landed and was met with the smell of decay. He could see that this dragon was dead, shot with a massive bolt and had begun to decompose. Nythint made his way around to see the face only to reveal that this dragon was in fact Yzat.

Grief filled his heart, but a dragon was unable to cry in his natural form. Nythint roared in sadness and began to mourn. He pulled the bolt out of Yzat's body but did not recognize it. He tossed it to the side and took a deep breath. He bellowed his flame against Yzat's body cremating his brother. This was his way of mourning him. He had seen the elves do this in Nagrimar and on the battlefield.

A patrol of Umbramari saw billowing smoke in the distance. They became excited and made their way to it. By now, Nythint had transmorphed to his visage form and sat down next to the ashes of his brother. The Umbramari approached quietly and noticed there appeared to be only one person. They casually approached.

"You Tanimari are quite foolish," said their would-be leader. They began to surround Nythint, their spears pointed at him. Nythint said nothing and observed that they were lightly armored and had no other means of bringing him down in his natural form and so he transmorphed and unsheathed Razorheart.

"I am Nythint, dragonborn and companion of Queen Darlana of Nagrimar."

The Umbramari fell on their backs. They dropped their spears and shields.

"You will tell me who is responsible for the murder of my brother and then you will tell me where my queen and her companion went!"

The Umbramari looked at each other unsure of what he was speaking of until one of them spoke up.

"Great and terrible dragon, do you speak of a beautiful Tanimari with purple and blackened hair along with a mouthy weak elven companion? They are the only ones I can think of that may match your description as they were with this dragon when he was killed."

"They do match the description and now you will tell me who killed my brother."

"First, you must give me your word you will not kill me then and only then, I will take you to their location and give the names of those responsible for…" he began before Nythint grabbed and pulled him away from the others. He unleashed a fire breath immediately incinerating the rest of the Umbramari.

"Take me to those responsible first!" He gently squeezed the Umbramari who nodded and said, the black gate. Go to the black gate. There you will find those responsible. Please, put me down."

Nythint ignored his request and took to the sky in the direction of the black gate.

***

A week had passed since the death of the emperor. Martial law had been in effect, and no one dared challenge the guard. Things were calming down and now it was time for her to strike again.

Darlana made her way back to the dungeon that her and Meric were held in. There she waited on the roof near the courtyard for those Umbramari who impaled Meric to return. She wanted revenge. The time came when they brought two more prisoners to be executed. She was unsure if they were the ones responsible. She slipped through the shadows and down the side of the building onto several crates draped with feed sacks just outside the fence of the courtyard. As the guards began driving the stake through one of the prisoners, she recognized the sinister smile to belong to the one that impaled Meric.

Without a moment more, she leapt over the fence and dashed toward guard. She unsheathed her weapons and leapt into the air just in time for him to turn and notice her but it was too late. His throat was cut wide open, and he fell to the ground choking on his own blood. To her surprise, her blades glowed a dark purple.

"More souls for the blade," said the ominous voice of the shadow within her.

The other guard ran over to the Talonasaur pens and pulled a lever to open the gates containing them. They came out and made their way toward Darlana. She had no choice but to climb up the wall to safety.

The Talonasaurs used their forked tongues to find what they were looking for. One found the bound prisoner who was not impaled yet. It bit his shoulder and began to violently jerk its head side to side tearing off the prisoner's skin. He screamed in pain alerting the other Talonasaurs.

Soon another came upon him and bit into the side of his abdomen and did the same as the other, tearing flesh from the prisoner. His entrails were now exposed and a third Talonasaur came and grabbed those. It pulled his innards out and swallowed them all up.

They began to eat all the succulent parts of the prisoner's body until his body was in pieces. The animals did the same thing to the dead guard. The prisoner who had a stake driven through him was surprisingly not dead yet. He had borne witness to the Talonasaurs eating the other elves and became terrified. He was unable to stand and was forced to crawl in vain. Darlana watched with amusement as he was almost to the fence before one of the animals grabbed his leg.

A blood curdling scream bellowed from the prisoner's lungs. He knew what was to come and Darlana reveled in it.

Alarms began to ring again. She has been distracted by the beasts feasting and momentarily forgot about the guard that got away. Once again, she got up over the roof and slipped into the shadows. His time would come.

***

Nythint and his captive Umbramari were approaching the black gate. Nythint knew to approach it with the sun at his back. The dark elf was unable to give him the name of the one in particular who killed his brother so Nythint decided he would punish them all.

He descended upon them with fury and rage. Stone was not so easily ignited but everything else was. He landed and threw his captive out of the way. He unsheathed his sword and began smashing the buildings and any who attempted to challenge him.

Once the Umbramari realized they could not defeat him, they began to withdraw to the other side of the gate. Nythint followed them, killing as many as he could. When he was finished, he stopped to rest. He looked around and noticed that there was nothing but snow and mountains. The road was made of ice and led northwest. It was bitterly cold, but Nythint did not care. Climate did not affect him that much.

He took to the sky and followed the road until he saw something moving on it. He approached them with caution. When they noticed him, they began to flee but the land was flat and frozen. There was nowhere for them to go that he could not be in a few moments. One of them stood his ground and drew his sword. Nythint approached him.

"I am Nythint, and I am searching for my queen and her companion. I am certain they came through here so tell me where they would have gone, and I will spare you and the others."

"It is likely they were enslaved and taken to Unarith," said the brave Umbramarian.

"Where is Unarith?"

"Northwest of here," he said carefully.

Nythint wasted no time. He kept his word and allowed them to live. He took to the sky and flew northwest.

***

Darlana had killed several patrols and was sparking panic among the people of Unarith. Soldiers were out night and day looking for her. They had hounds and were now on her trail. She was running out of places to hide and carefully found an area where she would make her last stand.

Finally, they had found her. The guards called in backup and surrounded the tower Darlana was hiding in.

"We know who you are, Ralnor's concubine. I will enjoy peeling the skin from you alive," said their leader. Darlana stepped out on the balcony. She looked upon all of them below and smiled. After a moment.

"It was indeed I who killed your emperor. I stabbed him in the chest while I was on top of him. He was the first that I ever took pleasure in killing. Throughout the night and day, I killed scores more of you Umbramari scum. None of you are safe so long as I draw breath," she said calmly.

"Indeed, it is the breath you draw which we wish to take, Nagrimari scum." Darlana's smile left at the mention of Nagrimar.

"So, you know who I am then. Darlana, Queen of Nagrimar." The people who gathered to observe the confrontation began to talk amongst themselves. It became clear that they did not realize who she actually was.

"It matters not, you murdered our emperor, and you must answer for it," said the now visibly uncomfortable Umbramari leader.

Darlana began to speak again when all of a sudden, fire burst from the sky igniting everything in its path. Scores of Umbramari were instantly incinerated, startling everyone in the area. Darlana looked up and saw Nythint enraged. He had found her and came to her rescue.

"Darlana," he yelled. "Tell me where she is, or I will reduce this wretched place into rubble."

"Nythint," she gleefully screamed from the balcony of the tower she was in. "Nythint, I am over here," she said as loud as she could. This caught his attention, and he made his way over to her. She looked down at the Umbramari soldiers and smiled. "It looks as though it is I who will enjoy peeling the skin off you alive," she yelled before calmly retreating back into the tower as she made her way down and outside.

Nythint had landed down the way a bit. He unsheathed Razorheart and with each swing, killed scores of soldiers and knocked even more over. They had never seen a full-sized dragon fight like this and they began to panic. The people ran for their lives and Nythint backed the soldiers into a corner.

Darlana came up to Nythint. "You came for me," she said happily.

Nythint nodded but did not take his eyes off the Umbramarian soldiers.

"You, come to me," she said, pointing to the dark elf that had threatened her. Realizing it was no use to fight, he obeyed.

"Queen Darlana of Nagrimar. We are no match to your power or the power of your dragon companion. I surrender, Unarith to you."

"I accept your surrender. I am, however, an elf of my word." She looked at the other Umbramari that he appeared to command. "Kill him but peel the skin from his body first," she ordered. They seemed to hesitate at first, but Nythint roared, spurring them to act. The elf to be skinned protested and begged for his life. His own soldiers showed no mercy and did as they were commanded much to the delight of Darlana and surprisingly Nythint.

Darlana began to casually walk toward the palace with Nythint not far behind. Word got out that she was going there, and people began to gather around albeit cowering in fear.

Nythint stood outside while she made her way through the palace and out to the balcony where she would address those who came to hear her speak.

"I am Queen Darlana of Nagrimar. Your city is now my city. Your emperor is dead and now I am your Queen. You will unquestionably follow my every command, or you will die in an unimaginable way. My word is law and my commands are final."

Everyone began to talk amongst themselves before Nythint roared prompting them to begin chanting "Long live Queen Darlana! Long live Queen Darlana."

She looked around the square and saw soldiers marching. At first, they thought they might challenge her but instead, they began policing the crowd.

"You were reduced to nothing and had lost everything. Now it appears that you once again have a people to rule over. It is amusing is it not?" asked the shadow menacingly.

Darlana could hardly believe it. She would not squander this opportunity but first, she would have Dartan detained and executed which she did by having him defaced and impaled.

Unarith did not have scrying orbs. They did not have griffins or teleportation runes. The Umbramari were fighters and few were sorcerers. She had to find a way to get a message to Alzar and Magris as soon as possible so she sent the most Nagrimaran-looking dark elf with two missives. She ordered her to ask Alzar for a griffin and fly to Madir to deliver a message to Magris as well. Darlana had a lot of work to do and not a lot of time to get things done. She called together the viceroys of all the areas that he had conquered. They came to Unarith under extreme duress. She sat on her throne and waited for the first one to arrive.

"Unarith is now under my rule! I will accept nothing less than your total allegiance." said Darlana.

"I have not come here to pledge allegiance to a Nagramarin. Hah, foolish queen of nothing. I have come to take your throne for myself. GUARDS." Darlana smiled as the guards came in. She stepped off her throne and approached them.

"Belay his order and swear allegiance to me," demanded Darlana. None of them took heed. Without a word, Nythint incinerated the defiant viceroy. The others with him began to flee. Nythint wasted no time incinerating them as well. Darlana appreciated that Nythint did not hesitate. She looked over at him and smiled. He morphed back into his visage form and returned the smile before returning to his position. Servants began to clean up the charred corpses before Darlana interrupted them.

"Leave them as an example to any else who would defy me." Her servants cowered, obeyed and backed off. Seeing this, Darlana became uncomfortable. Perhaps she was allowing herself to enjoy the brutality too much. She stopped and donned a look of concern. Her mind was flooded with the thought of all the people she helped who had suffered for centuries. She looked at the charred remains once more only this time, she had mixed feelings.

As she returned to her new throne, the next viceroy entered the room and saw the still smoking charred remains of the last one and his guards. His demeanor completely changed. It was clear that he understood she meant what she said in the missive she had sent to him. Having no desire to earn the same fate as the other viceroy, he would be significantly more careful but he came prepared for such an outcome.

"My queen, or Queen of Nagrimar. I come bearing gifts of fruit and good tidings. My tribe is…" he began before Darlana interrupted him. She was annoyed with herself and wanted to get away.

"Keep your treasures, all that I require is your allegiance."

"Of course, your magnificence. Of course, you have my allegiance and all that of my tribe. My people… I mean your people and the resources we control are at your disposal.

Sure enough, he was grateful to be able to leave alive and immediately ran out of there and told everyone else. The other viceroys were reluctant to speak with her out of fear. All of them offered her their allegiance and of the ones who asked for assistance, she granted it whereas the previous emperor had no interest. This marked a new era for the Umbramari.

The viceroys left to go to all corners of the frozen empire. The people of Unarith were adjusting to how things were going to be going forward. Several weeks had gone by and Darlana realized she could not rule here like she ruled in Nagrimar. These people, the Umbramari, were warlike and demanded a campaign.

They were getting restless and talked about overthrowing Darlana but none were brave enough to take her and her dragon companion on just yet and this was a problem.

Darlana needed a council. She ordered the military leaders to come together in the palace. She had a room set up like she did in Nagrimar. They all sat on the sides of the table while she sat at the end. None of them seemed very comfortable. Darlana immediately noticed they were dressed for the weather but lacked anything that would distinguish them as leaders.

"I am Queen Darlana of Nagrimar. This is Nythint. Tell me your names."

The first to speak was a female. She had short white hair but did not look aged. She had scars across her cheek, her armor was dented and worn though it seemed to have served its purpose.

"I am Ivi, I was the supreme overlord of the army we used to conquer most of the frozen wastes. These are all my lieutenants, Nogis, Vodu and Duci. We served Ralnor during his conquest and we maintained the peace between the conquered tribes." Ivi looked between all of her lieutenants who nodded at her and then turned their attention to Darlana. "You come here as a captured slave. You murdered our emperor and stalked the streets of Unarith killing all who wronged you and your dead companion,' she said with a smile.

Darlana suspected a scheme. She began to feel angry but would not allow it to manifest into violence. She had grown tired of doing that.

Detecting that Darlana was getting upset, Ivi continued, "When cornered, you remained defiant and threatened the guard. Out of nowhere, your dragon companion begins to lay waste to the city and now here we are with you in the emperor's throne at the head of the table," Ivi said gleefully.

Darlana felt as if Ivi would get hostile and kept her guard up. She reached for her daggers under the table as she gave Ivi a nod.

Ivi continued, "It is not uncommon for a leader of any Umbramari tribe to be assassinated by his own soldiers if they are not satisfied but to be assassinated by a concubine or whatever you were… that is impressive, and I can come to respect that. If you wish to be Queen, you must understand that you are also closer to death."

Darlana perceived her words as a threat but would remain slow to react. "I am unaware of Umbramari customs, and it is clear that you are unaware of what I will do if I feel my life or the life of Nythint is threatened. I will not hesitate to kill every last one of you starting with you. Then I will have Unarith turned into a ruin like Nagrimar was."

Ivi looked at Darlana, surprised. "Please do not misunderstand me. I only mean to tell you what to expect should you let the Umbramari people get out of control. You seem to me to be the kind of elf that would prefer to use the art of diplomacy given what you did for the viceroys who asked for assistance unlike your predecessor."

Darlana's interest was piqued now, however, she did not let her guard down. "Go on."

The Umbramari are tribal and warlike. It is customary for every new tribal leader to raid and plunder. When Ralnor united all the tribes, it disrupted many traditions and was beginning to lead to unrest. Now that you are here, an opportunity to mend it rests with you."

"I have no interest in mending tribal differences. I have no interest in upholding traditions," said Darlana before stopping and thinking.

Ivi and her lieutenants were looking nervous.

"No, no more tribes. We will remain united with a common goal. If it is war the Umbramari desire… well then, I know just where to lead them," Darlana said before donning a smile and meeting the eyes of everyone in the room. "United, the Umbramari could be incredibly strong and pose an actual threat to Tanimara."

Ivy turned her attention to Darlana and smiled while setting her hands on the table and lacing her fingers together. "Tanimara… we have only raided the coast of the island. No one has ever ventured inland and lived to tell of it." She looked at the lieutenants. "The glory, boys. Can you imagine," she asked them.

"I have led many raids against the Tanimari and human kingdoms. To plunder a city would bring about great wealth for our people," said Druci. The others agreed.

"Plunder Tanimara?" questioned Darlana. "No, we will not plunder Tanimaran cities."

As she gazed out the window, the bleak landscape of Unarith stretched before her like an endless canvas of ice and stone. The city's twisted spires and dark, imposing architecture seemed to cling to the edge of the frozen wasteland, as if defying the unforgiving environment. Her thoughts, however, were far away, in the lush heart of Tanimara.

"I for one, find this place opressive. I am used to the temperate climate of the Forlorn Forest. Tanimara is a massive Island with a flat coast and mountains in the center spanning from the south of the island to the north. All of its cities are close enough to the coast to never receive snow like this. It does not freeze like this. We can grow all year and the vast amount of resources within the land and mountains would bring about wealth. No. We will not plunder Tanimara. We will take it for ourselves."

The others began pounding with excitement. It initially startled Darlana but her heart swelled. "We will serve you, as our Queen. You need not to worry about our loyalty. We have no doubt of your capabilities," said Ivi. Her lieutenants agreed and continued pounding the table.

Something about Ivi intrigued Darlana.

"Very well then, you are dismissed," said Darlana.

The lieutenants were quick to leave, but Ivi stayed. She waited for the others to shut the door. Darlana would normally order her to leave but once again, she was intrigued by her actions. Ivi looked at Darlana, then looked toward the table and smiled. "Never in my life have I witnessed such a spectacular take over let alone by a female. I will not lie to you, it is inspiring."

"Inspiring you to challenge me?" asked Darlana while donning an amused expression.

"Not at all. Watching you order… oh what was his name? The uh… commander of the guard. Watching you order his own men to skin him alive," she began while grinning from ear to ear. "That was spectacular. I wouldn't have thought to do that myself. I truly admire you." She got up and began walking toward the door. "Oh, right. Forgive my manners." Ivi gave a crude salute and had the look of embarrassment. She tried to laugh it off. "Apologies, I do not know how to do it right but I will learn… for you," she said while looking at Darlana with the grin of someone who overly admired another. "My queen," whispered Ivi when she was about to leave.

"Wait, sit back down," ordered Darlana.

Ivi was quick to comply. Darlana was not sure how to feel about everything. It was surreal. Ivi was right and her words really struck Darlana.

She explained in the simplest of terms how the people of Unarith viewed her. "Tell me more of the Umbramari. I am aware that they do not worship the same gods."

Ivi was happy to comply. She cleared her throat and looked at Darlana. "Umbramari are savages and lack the culture of the other elves of this world. They value excess, lust, violence, and it always leads to tribal disputes. It doesn't matter what gods we worship. All of this is in our nature!" It became clear that Ivi was not the religious type.

"This is good, if I intend to go to war with Tanimara," said Darlana.

"I fear the Umbramari will not stay united long enough to conquer Tanimara. The Tanimari are way too organized and have substantially larger armies than we could ever muster. Ralnor was able to conquer most of the tribes within the frozen wastes, but the tribal culture still remains. You would have to demonstrate your strength to the other tribes as Ralnor did and even then we may not be able to muster enough able bodied fighters to take on Tanimara."

"I have several dragon allies, an army already in Tanimara and technology that your people could make excellent use of. The Tanimarans have their armies all over the world. If they recall them, they lose their resources and colonies."

Ivi rubbed her chin in thought. "I had not thought of that. We could strike the smaller armies within their colonies and slowly diminish their numbers to more manageable levels."

Darlana was impressed.

"All you must do… and I say that as if it will be easy," said Ivi smiling. "It will not," she also said while smiling, "convince the other tribes to follow you."

"Do not worry, Overlord. I plan to have my dragon companion, Nythint, convince the tribes outside the empire into joining us and we will attack the garrisons of their colonies before we invade Tanimara. That is the kind of strategy I look for in my advisors," said Darlana.

Ivi looked pleased. "I did not know that you had more than one dragon ally. You are just full of surprises, aren't you?"

"Conquering Tanimara is personal to me." Ivi was even more intrigued. "We will win or we will die trying. One way or another, Tanimara will suffer! For now, we need to organize what we have. I will not rule from the frozen wastes. I will rule from Tanimara instead. After all, it is my father that I plan to kill. Now that he is Emperor, by right of succession, Tanimara would legally be mine exactly as it was in the days of old."

"But if you wish to convince Umbramarians to invade a land like Tanimara, there must be a reward, my queen."

"I noticed that this place lacks many of the finer things that Tanimara offers. We must convince the Umbramari of all the wonders of Tanimara. How the people there have enormous, majestic cities, a beautiful temperate climate, aqueducts, running water, public showers and baths, things of value that the Umbramarians do not have access to here."

"With respect, my queen. It will not be that simple. I do believe in order for you to effectively convince the Umbramarians to go to Tanimara, you must abandon Unarith. Force them to take all their valuables and make them pay for a better home in blood."

Darlana thought for a moment before speaking. "The Tanimarans would make sure not to allow their beloved land to fall into the hands of elves such as the Umbramari. It has never been conquered by anyone but the elves themselves. I have no issue if we abandon Unarith and take everything of value with us. I will have Nythint fly around the frozen wastes and encourage not only the tribes Ralnor conquered but also those who resisted the emperor to come with us. They will serve either willingly or as slaves. He will see to that."

Darlana pulled out a map and finished it with a detailed drawing of the southern continent. "We will make our way through the black gate as a massive horde through Lavania."

"Hoooo, yeah, this is going to be marvelous. We can raid every human settlement and city we come across on the way," said Ivi with excitement.

Darlana was about to contest but she paused. No human nation came to her aid against the Tanimarans but the Maphisians and Nemisians. For hundreds of years, physicians from all of the human kingdoms were trained in Nagrimar. They had abandoned her in her time of greatest need and let her city fall to her enemies. None of them even attempted to stop Vulas and his army. She chose not to say anything regarding raiding the humans.

"Let us begin planning," said Darlana.

The heralds of Unarith began publicly talking about taking Tanimara. They also announced several of Darlana's decrees. The people were at first upset by some of the decrees however the words of the queen moved many to desire a more civilized Umbramarian culture and step away from tribalism that resulted in constant conflict.

Darlana had changed significantly during her stay in Unarith. No longer was she the forgiving and merciful leader she once was but fair she did remain. Any who were caught causing dissent or spreading lies were quickly weeded out and executed or enslaved.

The time had come to leave Unarith. It was cold and cloudy as it always was. The frigid wind was howling but the people were used to it. They had gathered everything they could carry and left everything else behind. It had been reported that several outlaws had taken advantage of the chaos and broken some of the queen's decrees. Those who were caught were executed on the spot as a reminder of

Darlana's power. They would be respected or there would be consequences. Darlana would not fool around with this. Managing this many people was a monumental task.

The people of Unarith walked out of the gates for the last time leaving the city to the elements. They made their way to the black gate while Nythint flew around to the free tribes off the coast and borders.

Nythint first encountered the Tibli tribe of Umbramarians. He had paid attention in the council meetings during his stay in Nagrimar and thought ahead to approach them in his visage form to not stir alarm. They stood outside of their village and waited for him to come out like any would if being challenged to single combat or face annihilation.

A young strapping Umbramarian elf covered in fur and leather armor approached Nythint. He had shaved the sides of his head and painted his eyes and lips black. His braid went all the way down his back and was as black as the night.

"I am Lagarn, Umbramari warlord of the Tiblimari free people. You come to my village uninvited and stand before me." He withdrew his massive sword. "I can only assume that you challenge me to single combat. The winner takes all!" said Lagarn. He then stood in a ready stance to fight.

"I am Nythint, dragon born. I come on behalf of Queen Darlana of Unarith, Queen of Nagrimar and Princess of Tanimara. I would like to…" he started before he arrogantly interrupted him.

"Ooo, a mighty dragon born in the service of a princess." He turned to face the people gathering behind him who began laughing. "You do not look like a dragon. I will take my chances," said Lagarn as he unsheathed his sword.

Nythint transmorphed into his natural form and towered over all who gathered. He unsheathed Razorheart and entered into a fighting stance. "You will join us and conquer Tanimara, or you will become slaves or die. The choice is yours, Tiblimari!"

Lagarn was terrified at first, but his eyes widened in excitement at the mention of conquering Tanimara.

"You could easily best me, Nythint dragonborn. I submit to you and will serve until my dying day. I sincerely hope it is in Tanimara, heh," said Lagarn.

Nythint sheathed Razorheart and transmorphed back into his visage form and extended a hand to him. He shook Nythint's hand and ordered his tribe to do as the Unarithians did.

Lagarn invited Nythint to his hut while the Tibili were gathering their things for the assimilation.

"Tibili warriors are strong and ferocious, dragon. The queen will not be disappointed."

He was proud and seemed eager to prove himself.

Nythint turned toward Lagarn. "Those ships in the harbor, you are raiders?"

"We are indeed. As you can see, we cannot grow food and have no resources. Therefore, we must take what we need."

***

Rumors began to spread that Darlana had taken over Unarith and that there was a mighty dragon gathering all the tribes together. They began to zealously follow her every whim. Darlana was not used to this kind of loyal behavior but did not care much. To her, the Umbramari were the savages that killed Yzat and Meric. The emperor paid and Darlana was awarded a fortunate circumstance for her part, but the Umbramari would never be welcome in Tanimara.

Darlana would try to use them to take Tanimara. If they survived then fine, they could live there under her authority. If they did not, it was of no consequence to her. She would never have what she held most dear again and those who took it from her would pay and now it would seem by any means.

It had been weeks of walking through the frozen waste, but the Umbramari were well adapted to it. Thousands of Umbramari have decided to go with Darlana to Tanimara and now they approached the black gate. They walked through the carnage of charred corpses that Nythint left there. Darlana stood on the side and watched. Some were completely unphased and others were sickened. This was interesting to her.

Darlana was distracted by Ivi and Druci trying to break up a brawl. Many others had gathered around. Two belligerent Umbramari from apparent past warring tribes were fighting. Soon the tribes members of both tribes began to form sides and ranks. They drew their shields and spears prompting Ivi and Druci to stand in between the two opposing forces. There were only twenty or so Umbramari, but Darlana could not have them kill each other. She needed them. She drew her daggers and joined Ivi and Druci.

"Save your fury, savages! Save it for the humans! Save it for the Tanimari! Do not waste it on each other. You all serve me! The Umbramari tribes are now united and together, we will lay waste to our enemies but we will not make enemies of ourselves anymore," said Darlana.

The two tribes stopped hurling insults. They began to talk amongst themselves prompting Ivi and Druci to sigh in relief. Darlana was frustrated. She knew they would start fighting again if she did not do something about it. "Form raiding parties, plunder the countryside and take what you please, leave none alive. We raid Lavanina then we conquer Tanimara!"

Thousands of Umbramari began to roar with excitement. Ivi furrowed her brow. "When I suggested this, you seemed apprehensive."

"I was at first. When I first came to this continent, I trained the human physicians of all human kingdoms. They had only crude knowledge of remedies. They began to send them to Nagrimar where we would teach generations. I personally saved several human kings, emperors and their children from illnesses and infections that would have otherwise killed them. When I asked for aid, not only did they ignore my plea, they allowed the Tanimaran commander to march his army through their lands and slaughter my people. While not exactly a betrayal, this will serve to punish the cowardice that led to the extermination of my people."

Ivi was pleased to hear it. Long have the Lavanians been an enemy of the Umbramari. She and her lieutenants organized raiding parties and began raiding the humans while more and more Umbramari tribes joined her over the next few days.

Several days later, Nythint had returned to Darlana with the last of the tribes of the frozen waste.

"Nythint," said Darlana as she approached him with her arms out to welcome him with a hug. "You have done well.

Thousands upon thousands more have arrived thanks to your efforts.

"It was rather easy to convince them. Of those I came into contact with that had ships, I ordered them to begin raiding Tanimaran colonies. They were very eager to have the backing of a dragon."

Darlana remembered Velnir telling her about Umbramarian raids. For a brief moment, she wondered if they ever crossed paths and for the first time, she wondered how he would feel about enlisting Umbramari in the first place.

They were interrupted by several scouts reporting that a Lavanian army was approaching. Darlana quickly ordered all of them to be ready but wait for her orders to attack. The rag tag group of Umbramari grabbed their spears and shields and formed a horde. It was messy and extremely disorganized. Darlana was not impressed and neither was Nythint. Ivi could tell.

"If we survive, I will personally see to it that they are as professional as the Tanimarans or better, my queen," assured Ivi.

Darlana nodded and set out to parlay with the King of Lavania.

"Steel yourselves men. Should you fall today, give yourselves to the Lavanian barrows and become part of the earth once more. Today will not be the last day of Lavainia," said King Cercival.

"King Cercival of Lavania," said Darlana as she approached him seemingly un-deterred by the large army standing behind him.

"Darlana, Queen of Nagrimar." He was clearly surprised. "I heard what happened to Nagrimar and was told you were with the wizard in Nemis. I am confused, why are you with the Umbramari raiding my lands?"

"It is a terribly long story. All you need to know is you are now looking at the Queen of the Umbramari. You and the Bronhelmians allowed the Tanimaran army to pass through your lands which led to the massacre of my people. I will have my vengeance against Tanimara! I sought out other allies since you and many other human kings ignored my request. I found myself in the frozen wastes where I had the opportunity to kill the emperor and take his title for myself."

The king looked confused. "I never allowed the Tanimarans to march through my land. I also never even received a request for aid from you. We were caught up fighting the orcish incursion spurred on by you and that Tanimaran Prince."

"We defeated the Orcs in the Sundered lands," she retorted.

"You defeated one horde of a few united clans in the Sundered lands. There are hundreds of clans more to contend with. How can you be so ignorant?"

She had understandably forgotten about the orcs. Her kingdom was destroyed and they became irrelevant to her. "Orcs? You lie, King Cercival. You did receive my request and you denied it. I hardly believe that was because you were busy fighting Orcs. I know Orcs rarely come this far north. No, you denied my request because you are a coward. If I had to guess, you were hoping other kings would answer the call so that you could take advantage and take their kingdoms for yourself."

King Cercival's face reddened. "Cowardice? This is madness!"

"Madness? All right. We will sack Savil and if we do not find any Tanimaran gold, we will cease all raiding. If we do, we will exterminate everyone in Lavania."

The king's face turned white. "Is there no other way, Darlana?"

She remained silent and observed his mannerisms. He was lying and she could easily tell.

"You face a mighty host. My family has ruled here for over a thousand years and today will not be the day…" he began to say as the massive horde of Umbramari began to come over the hill. The king's demeanor went from angry and confident to a realization of just how outnumbered he was. Never in his life has he seen such a large army of Umbramari.

"You really united them," he said with pain in his voice. "They will be the death of all the northern kingdoms. What have you done?" he asked bitterly.

"They are not soldiers, King Cercival. They are your people, once captured and made slaves by the Umbramari emperor Ralnor. As Queen of the Umbramari I vowed to return them to you in exchange for passage through your land. Now my intentions have changed. You will hand over all the Tanimaran gold you received, or we will slaughter all of them right here right now. Then we will destroy your army and lay waste to your nation as you allowed the Tanimarans to do to mine.

The king knew he could not deceive her, so he gave up. "I will negotiate then. If you cease all raiding, I will meet you at the border with the carts of Tanimaran gold."

Darlana was quite surprised. "Did you say carts?"

"I did. Leave Lavania and I will bring it to you, Queen Darlana. You may not think Orcs are a problem anymore, but they are for us, and I can hardly afford a war on two fronts."

Darlana walked over to Nythint and began speaking to him outside of the king's hearing range. They returned to the king together. "There will be no battle today, King Cercival. Nythint will go with you to Savil and see to it you do not try to deceive me again."

"That really will not be necessary as we uh…" he began before Nythint transmorphed into his natural form. "Right then. We will bring it to you as soon as possible," said the king. He turned on his horse and rode back to his line clearly frustrated. Nythint followed them.

Darlana and the Umbramari set out to the Twilight wood. When they were ready to go to Nemis. Ivi was looking down and seemed to be lost in thought.

"What are your thoughts, Overlord?" asked Darlana.

"The Umbramari will be upset that you made an agreement to cease raiding Lavainian cities in exchange for gold. Gold does not fill the bellies of elves. The food we take and the slaves we capture bring about immense wealth. The fight brings glory."

"There will be a great many things you will bear witness to while I am Queen. Perhaps you will learn faster than the others and can help to educate them on the new way of things."

"Tradition means a lot to them. Fighting is in their spirit. They have learned to enjoy the spoils and the fleeting glory keeps them going for more and more," said Ivi concerned.

"They must adapt then," said Darlana without even making eye contact with Ivi.

Ivi looked at Darlana with concern. "And if they do not?" she asked. Darlana ignored her and simply looked back at the Umbramari behind her. She thought about whether they were redeemable or not. Perhaps there was hope as they were elves or perhaps not. She did not put much thought into it. Her mind was focused on vengeance and she needed gold.

They would approach the Twilight Wood but knew better than to enter it. The forest was enchanted and they would be taken into the earth to suffocate by the trees if they entered. Only Darlana went forth and called out to Eldar.

Eventually he appeared with several of his followers and came out of the forest to greet her. He was pleased to see her return. Ivi was permitted to come up at this time and meet him.

"Darlana, what a pleasant surprise to see you again. I thought you would have been to Madir by now, harassing Tanimarans." He noticed Ivi approaching. "What is this elven abomination doing in your company?" he asked.

"This is Ivi, she was the overlord of Emperor Ralnor's warbands and is now the overlord of mine. I was captured by them and when the opportunity presented itself, I killed Ralnor and declared myself Queen. Nythint certainly helped to persuade them to accept me," said Darlana.

Eldar looked at her in bewilderment. "I see, who are they," he asked as he was pointing to the people approaching.

"They are your people that the Umbramari have captured and enslaved. I am returning them to you."

Eldar was stunned. He could hardly believe he would see them again and as they came into view, he was able to recognize a few faces and ran to them. They were all elated to see each other and were crying tears of joy. Eldar noticed the Umbramari horde in the distance. They were halted and standing far away but this raised an alarm.

"What are they doing here, Darlana?" he demanded.

"We are on our way to Nemis so that we may go to Tanimara," said Darlana.

Eldar was beginning to sense a change in Darlana. She seemed cold and uncaring and not the way he knew her.

"Tanimara hmm. With them?" he asked.

He took a deep breath and looked at Darlana. "I think you know how well that will go. Whether it be Tanimari or Umbramari, one side will be annihilated because you know that they would never be able to live together."

Darlana looked at him with steeled resolve. "I do not intend to coexist with Tanimarans. Take your people before I have a change of heart."

Eldar looked heartbroken. He was in complete disbelief. "If you need me, you know where to find me, Darlana."

"I needed you and you turned me away like the human kings, Eldar. Now I no longer need you. I have the Umbramari. Darlana simply turned and walked away. When she returned to the horde, she released the elven slaves to Eldar and the Umbramari began to make their way to Nemis. King Cercival and Nythint were on the road with a contingent of soldiers guarding ten full carts of gold.

"I have brought you the gold as promised yet your dragon destroyed half of Savil. He then forced us here with the gold anyway. What do you have to say for yourself, Queen of the Umbramari," he said distraught.

"Consider the gold as payment for sparing your people further suffering."

"What of the people the Umbramari kidnapped and made slaves. Will you not return them?"

She looked at him with disdain. "I will not. Humans make excellent laborers. The vast amount of resources in Tanimara wont mine or harvest themselves," she said with a smirk.

***

After several more days of marching, they were finally in Nemis and moved past where the Nagrimarans were slaughtered. Their bodies were left there and had begun to decompose. The smell of death was horrific.

"Ah, the smell of glorious battle. Looks like these ones were on the losing side," said Ivi.

Darlana seethed. "These were once my people. The vast majority of them were unarmed civilians. Slavery was not an option for them. Only death as you can see. It was not a battle that was fought here. It was a slaughter of my people."

Ivi looked over at Darlana with a worried expression. Darlana would not grace her with so much as a glance.

"I have much to learn about you, Queen. My apologies."

Darlana understood she did not know. Umbramari could not understand what Darlana felt or what she had been through. She did not intend to tell Ivi.

They were now camping far enough away from the stench of death and were a day away from the Tower of Alzar. Ivi began to pester her about trivial things and Darlana was not interested. She excused her and laid in her cot. She wanted to be alone with her thoughts.

"Your thoughts betray you, Darlana," said the shadow.

Darlana ignored it as she had for several weeks now.

"Your hatred grows. It is right to use the Umbramari for your gain. Revenge is sweet. Punishment is equally as sweet. The power of the blades will grow the more souls it consumes. I will be here anytime you need me. I am just playing with a fortix cube. Still have not solved this damned thing, blast it," said the shadow.

For a moment, Darlana wondered what a fortix cube was. This piqued the shadow's interest. Darlana could tell that the shadow was doing this with purpose but she did not have the energy to indulge her. Instead, she wanted to sleep.

The next day they all walked to the Tower of Alzar. Darlana waited by the gate to be allowed in.

"What, what is it? Who goes there," asked the door keeper. The gate had a face carved into it and it seemed to be alive. Darlana did not remember this being here before.

"I said who goes there? I am the keeper and if you wish to be allowed in, you must state your name and intentions."

"I am Darlana. Ask Alzar to let me in."

"Alzar will be out in a moment," said the keeper. Darlana looked displeased. "Why will he not allow me entry?" she thought.

Darlana waited patiently for Alzar to come. In the meantime, the Umbramari began to express interest in the tower. They had never seen anything like it. Ivi came up to

Darlana and had a visible expression of awe.

"We could see this for kilometers. How interesting that I have never heard of such a wonder." She turned to Darlana. "Did he build this himself?"

"From what I understand, he did build it himself and it is over an arcane line."

"What is an arcane line?" she asked with a genuine sense of intrigue.

"It is an area of Abrion where magic is at its strongest. People built magical towers and cities on top of them to maximize the potency of enchantments. I am not a wizard or mage so I do not know much more than that. The things here… are not like anything else on Abrion. If you think the outside is amazing, you should see the inside," Darlana said.

As the two elven women were talking, Alzar creaked the door open to take a peek. He wanted to make sure it was Darlana and not anyone looking for retribution.

"Did you in fact bring an Umbramari army to my doorstep, Darlana?" Asked Alzar. Dravon appeared to be with him and was visibly uncomfortable.

"They are not an army yet, Alzar. Do not worry. We are going to Tanimara." She looked at Dravon and Rizim. "Are your people ready, General?" she asked.

"Where is Yzat?" asked Rizim.

Darlana's heart had hardened but being reminded of the massacre and the death of Yzat tugged on her heart. "He fell," she said somberly.

Rizim's facial expression did not change but he began to breathe heavily. The more Darlana got to know the dragons, the easier it became to read their emotional responses. She knew he was grieving. He said nothing and could not look at anyone but Nythint who was also looking somber.

Dravon immediately noticed something was off with Darlana. He hesitated to ask but Alzar spoke first.

"How did you manage to achieve this," he said with genuine surprise in his voice. "This is very interesting. I do not recall ever seeing so many Umbramari in one place that were not viciously murdering each other or others."

She ignored Alzar and kept her eyes on Dravon. "General?"

Dravon missed her terribly. He had expected to at the very least hug her on her long awaited return. He could tell by her demeanor that something was not right and chose to hold the affection back.

"Yes, Darlana," he said.

"Queen. She is the queen," said Ivi.

Dravon looked at her with disgust. He was not impressed with Umbramari. He simply turned around and walked back into the inner area where the maze used to be around the tower of Alzar. The centaurs had waited there for her return. Magris was still in Tanimara however and time was of the essence. Whatever this was would have to wait and as far as he understood, Darlana understood as well.

Very soon afterward, the centaur and dragons joined with Darlana and the Umbramari. Alzar was generous and gave her several griffins and scrying orbs but would do no more. Darlana almost forgot she had Meric's knapsack which contained the orb of falling stars. She decided she would keep it for now. It may prove useful.

Of the few Nagrimaran elves that survived, there were none that Magris would recognize but still, she had to send one of them to him with the news. No one expected an army of Umbramari to help them.

She dug around through Meric's knapsack and found a quill, ink, and a piece of parchment. She began to scribble several of the events that had happened but left out the details. Once she was finished, she went to find the Nagrimaran survivors. She called them all up to her and the fact there were so few left made her heart sink again.

"I need one of you to take a griffin to Madir. For obvious reasons, I cannot send an Umbramari. I also cannot afford to send a dragon. General Magris will not recognize any of you but at least he will know what you bring is from me."

A young elven woman stepped up. "I will gladly do this, my queen."

"Take this to General Magris in Madir, that is if he is still in Madir. I have not been able to speak to him. Be careful when you are flying and try to know exactly where you are going. Take these scrying orbs with you. You simply toss it in the air, and it will go in the direction you wish. Use this crystal to see what it can see. I do apologize for asking you to take such a huge risk. We must build ships to cross the great sea."

The messenger took the furled-up letter and tucked it in her satchel. "It is my pleasure, my queen. I will deliver this message to General Magris."

Darlana realized she did not know the young elf's name. Her chances of survival were very slim if Magris was unable to hold Madir. The Tanimarans would not show her mercy and for that, Darlana hugged her but chose not to ask her name. The messenger took to the sky on her griffin and made her way to Tanimara.

Ivi saw the encounter and noticed how Darlana showed the Nagrimaran affection. She also noticed how she showed Nythint affection. She knew that Darlana was a slave to the Umbramari and that they would likely never receive such affection.

This bothered her greatly and she did not know why. Ivi had begun to notice a change in herself and she was not sure how she was feeling about it.

Chapter 19
Hatred Bound

Darlana led the Umbramari, dragons, and centaurs through Nemis without consulting the ruling council Alzar had appointed. Once they got to the Nemisian coast, they began to deforest the region to build the ships they needed to cross the great sea while they waited for Warlord Lagarn and his tribe. The Nemisian council was furious and they sent Darlana a message.

"My queen, a messenger from the council of Nemis, brings word from Archwizard Thoran," said Dravon.

She unfurled it and read it to herself. Dravon was curious so she indulged him. "Archwizard Throan plans to speak with me," she said, rather annoyed.

"Their capital was razed and their king murdered by the Tanimarans. I do not think they will be hostile." Darlana waited for the wizard to arrive. She had heard he was one of Alzar's most gifted students. It surprised her that a human was able to achieve such a high honor.

He approached by himself upon a majestic white horse that had a horn in the middle of its forehead and wings on its side. She had never seen an animal like this. It radiated the light off its body like she had never seen before and assumed it was a magical beast. The man atop it was a skinny old human with a very long white beard and bald head. He had a white pointed crooked hat and a white robe. His staff was sheathed on his back, and he held a long pipe in his hand. He intrigued her.

"I am Queen Darlana of Unarith, Queen of Nagrimar and Princess of Tanimara. I understand that Alzar appointed a council of wizards to rule Nemis after the Tanimarans destroyed it. Perhaps you will then appreciate my intentions of invading and overthrowing Raften."

The Archwizard smiled. "He did indeed appoint a council of wizards, and they elected me as Archwizard. We could have never started this magocracy without him. I would in fact appreciate vengeance against the Tanimarans but we do not wish to receive any retribution as a result. You can see what happened the last time," he said before placing the pipe in his mouth.

"I understand but we need ships to cross the great sea. I have some coming but it will not be enough to get them all across. We also need to camp here while we build them. I do apologize for the deforestation and for what the foragers have done to the land and local animal population," said Darlana with sincerity.

The Archwizard looked amused. He crossed his left arm over his saddle and rested his elbow on it while holding his pipe. He knew better than to create an issue with her. He knew the size of her army and what they were capable of. Still this was risky. Tanimarans were the dominant superpower of Abrion. No one dared cross them, especially these days and yet, he did not have a choice.

"You are most welcome to the wood and all that you can forage. We both have lost so much to these Tanimarans. I wish I could offer you more but we are in the midst of rebuilding our great new capital of Alzarlaran," he said gleefully.

"Alzarlaran," Darlana scoffed.

"Indeed. His help was invaluable. Anyway, you are welcome to whatever you need. Good luck," he said as he turned his mount around and trotted away smoking his pipe.

"What an odd man," said Nythint.

Dravon and Ivi agreed.

The number of ships being produced and completed at the end of each day was not meeting the expectations of Darlana. So far, they only had one hundred and twelve completed ships. She did not think this was going to be enough and she had not heard from Lagarn. She figured she would need at least six hundred ships of this size to get them across. This was an enormous undertaking, and Darlana began to feel the weight of it. Every day that passed was one more day that the Tanimarans had to discover her plans and attack.

She made her way into her tent and sat on her cot. She intended to consult the shadow, but footsteps outside caught her attention.

"My quee…Queen, may I come in?" asked Nythint.

For the first time in what felt like an eternity for her, her heart swelled with emotions. Nythint, her beloved young dragon companion who she had seemed to have forgotten about, did not forget her. He patiently waited for her, and she felt terrible.

"Of course, Nythint. Please come in."

He stepped in and stood before her. He had a somber expression on his face.

"I am terribly sorry about Yzat," said Darlana as sweetly as she could. She motioned for him to sit next to her, and he did. She placed her arm around him, and he rested his head on her shoulder.

"I mimic elven emotion to convey how I am feeling in an effort to be understood and to be understanding to others. Rizim does not understand why I do this. He says dragons are killed all of the time in the orc lands. The young and the old. He said that I am too influenced by you and the other elves because I was raised by all of you. He would like to take me to the dragon isles to observe dragon culture."

Darlana's heart skipped a beat. She needed the dragons now more than ever. They would be vital in her success to take Tanimara but she could not help but feel for the young dragon. She would understand exactly what he is going through. They both grieved over the loss of Velnir and now they grieve over the loss of a brother.

"If you feel that is what you need to do, Nythint, I will always support you. Losing a loved one is the hardest…" She paused, remembering Paeris and Velnir, Sampsin and her son Alnas and the one responsible for taking all of them from her. Her father, Raften. "My father killed my first love and son. He killed them because he did not want Alnas to inherit any elven titles, lands, or wealth. He could not allow a hybrid into his family let alone a human. It was not enough to allow Alnas to go back to Araba with Sampsin. They had to be made an example of as if they had committed such a terrible sin. He was a baby, Nythint," she told him. A tear left her eye and rolled down her cheek.

Nythint's gaze pierced the depths of Darlana's eyes, and he beheld a soul tormented by sorrow, anguish, and emptiness. The pain that ravaged her inner world was a palpable force, and it shattered his heart. Darlana's eyes, however, held a sincerity that was both haunting and mesmerizing.

"I avenged Yzat and Meric," she whispered, her voice trembling with the weight of her emotions. "I killed the elves responsible for their deaths. It was a hollow victory, but it was justice, nonetheless."

Nythint's nod was a gentle acknowledgment of her words, and his smile was a poignant blend of sadness and admiration.

"Your strength is awe-inspiring, Darlana," he said, his voice barely above a whisper. "You've lost everything, only to rise from the ashes and build a kingdom anew. And when that was taken from you, you found the resilience to carry on, to rescue others and forge a new path. What drives you, Darlana? What fuels the fire that burns within you?"

Darlana's gaze faltered, and she stared at the ground, as if the answer lay hidden in the shadows. It was a question she had never been asked before, and one she had never dared to confront. But here, in this moment, with Nythint's compassionate eyes upon her, she knew she had to confront the truth. She took a deep breath, and her voice was barely audible.

"Revenge."

Chapter 20
Reunion

"Sound the alarms!" said a sentry on the Madiran wall. The alarms began to sound and Imra began to panic.

"They are coming! We must prepare our defenses. Raften's forces are coming." She already had her armor on; she barely took it off anymore, wary of assassination or a surprise siege. She had hardly taken it off anymore out of fear of assassination or a surprise siege.

She made her way out of the Magister's chambers and noticed that several elven denizens were pointing up. She looked and saw a single griffin with a single rider holding on for dear life.

"*This was no invasion*," she thought.

"Stop the alarms, they are trying to bring a message." She ordered the captain of the guard.

Soon the alarms stopped and she began to call out to the griffin rider.

"It is safe for you to land, please do so in the courtyard of the palace."

The griffin rider complied and brought the griffin down to land. She was holding on for dear life. Imra made her way to them with haste.

"State your name," she demanded.

"Faelyn, messenger from Queen Darlana," said the messenger.

Imra became excited. "Magris will love this," she thought. "Faelyn, you are in allied territory. Welcome to Madir. I assume you are looking for Magris."

The young elfs face was flushed. Her long blonde hair was all over the place and she was breathing heavily. "Yeah, I am looking for Magris," she said in an exasperated tone. "Is he here? I have an urgent message," she said while holding the furled up message. Imra reached down and took it from her which put Faelyn off a bit.

"No, he is in Atlan. Your queen does not know what has been going on here?" asked Imra while she was reading the message. Faelyn looked at Imra and shrugged. "I am not sure. She was gone for a long time and only recently returned."

"Magris and his dragon allies along with many Madirans marched southeast and took Atlan and Caphry. Your forces have control of the northern and eastern part of Tanimara."

I need to get to him as soon as I can," said Faelyn as she took the message back with a bit of force and made her way toward the griffin which she was about to mount when Imra stopped her.

"Please stay and rest. I will take the message to him for you," said Imra.

Faelyn looked at Imra and furrowed her brow. She did not know the intentions of this Tanimaran elf and was not sure if she could trust her. She looked around the city and saw many elven denizens staring at her. Most with sympathy in their expressions. Faelyn was very tired and really could use some rest. She looked at Imra again and saw what she wanted to believe was genuine concern.

"All right, to Magris and only Magris. It is a message from the queen herself," said Faelyn.

"Of course. You have done so well. I am very proud of you for making it across the great sea to me. I will make sure this message goes to only General Magris." Imra then stood at attention, saluted Faelyn and smiled.

Faelyn thought it was strange that a Tanimaran Magister was allied with the Nagrimarans but was too tired to put any more thought into it.

Imra prepared to leave at once and when Faelyn was out of sight, her demeanor changed. She quickly made her way to a guard. Stable that griffin and do so with haste. She then pulled her hood up and over her head and made her way into her chambers. Her daughter was present and saw her mother acting strangely.

"Mother, what is wrong," she asked.

"Never mind, Keryth, the less you know, the better," said Imra.

Keryth looked puzzled but kept her mouth shut, Imra would look at the letter once again. She read it over and over, every detail and the more she read it the more bothered she was. Keryth noticed.

"Mother," she began.

"Have you ever heard of Darlana?" asked Imra.

"Of course, she is the apostate that had a child with a human and was exiled."

"She was a princess of Tanimara who fell in love with a human prince. They had a child and her father, High Magister Raften had her child, and the human prince killed which started a war that ultimately destroyed the Araban Empire. Then she built a kingdom of her own which the Tanimarans destroyed. Raften sent an assassin to kill her, but the assassin killed her husband and daughter instead. Now we have war with them. Supreme Commander Volas murdered two million of her people and burned Nagrimar to the ground."

"I did not know much of what happened after that. By the Celestials, that is awful," said Keryth.

"Awful indeed." Imra began to copy the message onto several other parchments.

Keryth's curiosity peaked. "Mother, what are you doing?"

"No matter what seems to happen to that poor princess, she always seems to overcome it. Everyone has a snapping point though. I imagine Darlana's was when she killed an Umbramarian Emperor for killing her companion among some other unmentionable things and somehow convinced five million Umbramari to join her in conquering and occupying Tanimara.

Keryth gasped, "Our republic."

Imra moved over to Keryth who was sitting in a chair. She got on one knee and held her daughter's hand. "Our republic indeed. Everything we have been fighting for, all the espionage, all the sabotage. Everything we are doing to restore our republic will be undone by her. We cannot allow her to come to Tanimara."

"What about Magris?" she asked.

"He has a level head. I believe he will want to see the republic restored. He was once Tanimaran and not that long ago. I believe I can convince him that he does not need her to restore the republic." She then got up and took her leave. She made her way to the stables and retrieved the griffin.

***

Magris stepped out onto his balcony and took a deep breath. He looked up at the sky and saw the stars he once gazed upon from here. Nighttime was magnificently beautiful in Atlan. He could see the streams of water glisten as they flow through the many aqueducts within the enormous elven city. The mountain behind the city provided the most mineral rich and best tasting water he ever had and he also missed that very much.

Magris made his way to a private bath house. The pool or bath was heated from the natural head provided by the lava flow under the land which came from the mountain behind Atlan. This city was in the most perfect of places and he used to take it for granted. But not anymore. He took his clothes off and removed his peg leg. He got in and leaned up against the stone edge and began to think.

He was glad to be back in Atlan though not under such circumstances. His army was stretched too thin to take it any further. He had sent messages to Linia and Starland asking for them to join and had not heard back. Istar had sided with Tarvana and politely declined to assist, which Magris thought was strange. The bulk of his army was at the base of the mountain separating Caphry and Tarvanan regions. The dragons were eager to be on patrol duty as they loved flying around at super high speeds. It provided air security and caused anyone who would challenge him to second guess their decision.

A commotion could be heard. Two elven ladies were conversing with each other and got undressed, seemingly unaware that Magris was there. Magris was annoyed as he thought this bath was private. The two elven women finally noticed him and began looking at each other worryingly. They had quickly come to agree on something and started smiling at Magris.

"Greetings," said one of the elven women.

"I thought this bath was reserved for the members of the Magistrate and nobility," said Magris.

"It has hardly been used since the rebellion started. My friend and I like to come here and relax," replied the elven woman.

Magris felt bad. It was arguably his fault they were stressed as with most of the city. "You are most welcome here, ladies."

They smiled at him and entered the water. Magris closed his eyes and continued to relax. The women were giggling and splashing. It was hard for Magris to concentrate on his thoughts when there were two beautiful naked elves having a mild water fight.

To make matters worse for his thoughts, they began to kiss and touch each other intimately. Magris could not help but watch. One of them decided to go underwater and by the look on the other one's face, she was getting a mouth full. She looked like she was enjoying it and when the one under came back up, the other one went under and returned the pleasure.

Magris was losing his mind. He could not concentrate at all whatsoever and was beginning to get excited. He too was naked and could not get out of the bath now.

"Nether damn this," he said quietly to himself. The woman must have heard him because they looked his way and were smiling. They both went under the water and began swimming over to Magris. He had placed his hands over his nithers in an effort to not offend. They got closer and closer. Then they both came up out of the water.

"We were going to entertain each other but felt it would be rude not to include you. If you liked what you saw, you are welcome to join us."

Magris smiled and that was all the confirmation they needed. The one on the left went under the water and removed his hands. She began to help herself and it had been a long time since he had felt this. The other one began to kiss him and from here it was on.

***

For the majority of the day, Imra had been flying and now she had finally reached Atlan. She took no time to take in the splendor of the city and immediately landed in the courtyard of the Magister's chambers. She made her way in and did not see anyone, not even Kaelina. More importantly, she could not find Magris. She searched high and low and then decided to go to the lord's palace. She knocked on the door of the

Lord's chambers where she expected Magris to be staying and there was no answer.

"Where in the nether is he," she thought. Then it dawned on her. The city was known for its public baths and it was that time of night where people would be off work and trying to relax. She made her way to the private bath reserved for the nobility on the other side of the palace.

As she walked in, she made her way to the bath.

"Magris," she said.

He had just put his peg leg back on but was still uncovered. "Imra," he said in a startled tone. "Do you mind?" Her face turned red, and she went around the corner to give him privacy.

"My apologies, you have a message from your Queen, Darlana."

Magris wrapped his towel around himself and wasted no time going up to Imra who was clad in armor and very tired looking. He took the message.

Magris, Nagramar has been destroyed and the denizens of my kingdom eradicated by the Tanimarans. We lost our forces on the border between Nemis and Helmgarde. I had intended to make my way to the Twilight Woods to recruit the elves there in our fight to take Tanimara. I left with nothing and on my way back to the Tower of Alzar, Yzat was shot by a bolt thrower and killed. We crashed and I was captured by an Umbramari warband. Meric tried to rescue me, but he was also captured. We were taken beyond the black gate to Unarith and enslaved. Meric was to labor, and I was to please the emperor. Meric was violently executed by defacing and impaling. I had to watch a Talonasaur eat his body. It is a long story, but I killed the emperor and by the traditions of the

Umbramari, I was made queen. I marched five million Umbramari from the frozen wastes. I only plan to send five hundred thousand to Tanimara at a time. We are building ships in Nemis now to cross the great sea. Soon we'll be reunited and together we can conquer Tanimara. I encourage you to keep doing what you are doing and if an opportunity presents itself, take it.

Yours sincerely, Queen Darlana.

Magris read the letter a few times. It was nice to hear from her until she got to the part about Meric. Magris was having a hard time controlling his emotions. He had grown to really like Meric and they were good friends.

"Are you all right, Magris?" asked Imra.

"Meric was a good friend. To find out he died like that… It was uneasy on the eyes simply to read. I cannot imagine having to watch."

Imra did not seem interested. "I thought we had discussed the restoration of the republic. This is alarming!"

"Do not worry, Imra. I know Darlana. She is not interested in disrupting the lives of everyday Tanimrans. I am positive she means Tarvana and more specifically, Raften."

Imra was visibly skeptical and Magris began to wonder if what he thought was even true at this point. The murder of her people and the fact she was able to conquer Unarith was mind blowing. He was unsure of her intentions now, but he was proud of her. Something he would keep to himself.

"Thank you, Imra. You look tired. You are welcome to stay in the Palace tonight before you return to Madir."

"Thank you, Magris. I look forward to meeting her." She left and took a room in the palace. She could not sleep though. The thought of Darlana ruling Tanimara troubled her deeply. She never felt right about what happened to her but knew she would not come here to rule, she would come here for revenge, and they would all pay, especially if she is bringing an army of Umbramari. On the off chance she did come here to rule, the republic would no longer exist and everything they were fighting for was for naught.

Magris retired to his chambers to grieve alone. Not long after that, he heard a faint knock at his door.

The next morning, Imra got ready to leave back to Madir. She was feeling troubled about the message and wanted to say goodbye to Magris. She viewed him as a dear friend and really valued his role in the rebellion but only wanted the republic restored. She felt bad for using him. She made her way to his chambers and before she could knock, she heard the muffled sound of his voice.

Worried, she threw open the door and to her surprise, Magris was lying sprawled over his bed completely naked. He looked like he was out so Imra tried to shut the door without disturbing him but he heard her and turned over.

"Imra, wait."

He grabbed his walking stick and made his way over to Imra wearing absolutely nothing. She still cannot imagine how he could have survived all he had been through. The scars all over his body, missing limbs and yet here he is. She looked embarrassed. He did not look like he got much sleep.

"I thought I would tell you I was on my way back to Madir. I also wanted to talk to you a bit more about Darlana. Magris, I am afraid. A united Umbramari army? Umbramari in Tanimara? Did you ever think you would live to see the day or even think about the repercussions of this?" asked Imra.

"I just found out that one of my good friends and one of the dragons who was very dear to Velnir was murdered by the Umbramari. The knowledge of my queen... I mean the queen is now somehow leading them, leaving me suspicious. I must investigate these claims further. Does this missive not seem far-fetched to you?"

Imra began to think about it. She was terrified of Darlana and the idea of an organized Umbramarian army. "Perhaps it is too soon to worry and you are probably right. You know her better than I do." She composed herself and tried to not look bothered. "It is of no consequence. I will return to Madir at once. I wanted to ask before I went, did you ever hear from Starland, Linia or Istar?"

Magris' demeanor changed. "I am afraid we are alone in this fight, Magister. We might be forced into negotiations if we do not receive a Miracle."

Imra nodded. "We will come up with something, I am sure." She left and hurried to her griffin.

In truth, she had copied Darlana's missive and intended to give it to the other Magisters. She had hoped Magris would help them. She thought for sure that Linia and Starland would join them. She spoke with both of the Magisters who would absolutely love to see Raften overthrown so it did not make sense why they would not respond.

Istar siding with Tarvana was not a surprise. Raften had the lord of Istar and its Magister executed for conspiracy to rebel long before the actual rebellion happened and had taken it upon himself to replace both of them.

***

He began to dwell on the letter. Many things bothered him about it. He wrote his own message and brought it to a trusted messenger.

"Take this missive to Queen Darlana. She should be near the coast of Nemis. If you cannot find her then take this to the tower of Alzar," said Magris to the messenger.

The messenger nodded and the next day, he left early in the morning and began his trans great sea flight toward Nemis. Several days later he spotted a massive camp off the coast of Nemis. "This had to be Darlana's camp," he thought. He made his way down to get a better look. The people down there didn't seem to mind and actually cleared a place for him to land his griffin and so he did.

When he dismounted, he noticed right away that they were not Tanimaran. He knew that they were Umbramari. They looked at him confused as if not expecting him but did not attack him. They began to approach him but not before Darlana made an appearance.

"State your business," she demanded.

"Aymon of Atlan here on behalf of General Magris of Nagrimar" said the messenger.

Darlana was surprised. "Did you say you were from Atlan?"

"Yes, Your Grace," he then handed her the message. She read it and smiled.

"Will you return straight to him?" she asked.

"I will and do so with haste, Your Grace," said Aymon.

Darlana began to scribble another message and quickly gave it to him. She sent the griffin rider off with a smile and friendly wave. Once he returned to Atlan, he gave Magris the message. Relief and disappointment overwhelmed him. He immediately left the palace and went to find Vysol. He found her with the other dragons sitting on the edge of a balcony in their visage forms overlooking the city.

"Vysol, would you please give me a flight to Thalnor? It is urgent," he asked.

"Absolutely, Magris." She morphed into her dragon form, and he climbed onto her back. They took to the sky and made their way to Thalnor.

"What troubles you, General?" asked Vysol.

Magris was surprised that she could detect something was wrong with him. "Someone I consider a dear friend shared some troubling thoughts she had and now, I think I share those thoughts," said Magris.

Once they got to Thalnor, Magris ordered that all ships be sent to Nemis and gave the admiral of the fleet the coordinates of where they needed to be and who they were expected to pick up. He was reluctant and was immediately fired and detained. The next in line was eager to do as he was told and so the fleet set sail to Nemis.

Roughly nine hundred ships had left Thalnor and were making their way across the great sea to pick up Darlana and the Umbramari. The Tanimaran fleet was destroyed and by now, everyone knew that. The ships used in this fleet were primarily used to transport trade goods and had a large amount of space in their hulls for troops. It would have to do.

Chapter 21
It Begins

Far off in the distance, Darlana could see hundreds of ships approaching. Archwizard Thoran had sympathized with her plight and brought her his spare ships. They were wide, flat and had several masts. They were fitted with what the humans called onagers which launch hooks to latch onto other ships. They would then drop a series of bridges so that they could board the vessels they captured. The bow of the ships also had a heavy metal spike which Darlana assumed was to ram a ship. Hundreds of oars drove the ship forward, turning it with calculated precision. It took a vast crew to command such a vessel.

"Why did humans persist in crafting such outdated and cumbersome vessels of war?" she thought but it did not matter.

Darlana needed ships and she would use whatever she could get her hands on now that she knew the coast of Tanimara was clear and patrolled by Vysol and the other dragons.

Two more weeks had passed, and Darlana had close to four hundred ships now. She had ordered Ivi and her lieutenants to begin training the Umbramari in Nagrimaran warfare. Only some of the repeater crossbows remained after the battle at the river but fortunately it was enough. They had been getting better and better training day in and day out. Things were still behind schedule and Darlana was becoming upset.

"My queen, ships are on the horizon. They appear to be Tanimaran!"

"Magris," Darlana smiled.

Nine hundred ships made it across the great sea and to the shores of Nemis. She had one thousand three hundred ships to take the Umbramari and all their supplies across the great sea into Tanimara. Everyone stopped production of the ships that were currently being built and began to pack up their camp.

The logistics of packing a camp of so many soldiers was complex. Darlana stood atop the command deck, watching as thousands of warriors packed their stuff. The rhythmic clang of armor, the hum of disciplined movement, it was a symphony of war, a testament to the army she had forged.

The Umbramari were experts at moving as for the longest time, they were a nomadic people. She had instructed the remaining Umbramari to wait for warlord Lagarn. She assured them that she would send the ships back once the army had disembarked.

***

"Blasted telescope. Why must I be cursed with the limitations of mortal men?" whined Alzar as he was trying to get it to work. He sat down to take a break and picked up a piece of parchment on his desk. It detailed the accounts of an astromancer only hours earlier detecting something massive heading toward Abrion. Alzar was determined to recalculate its trajectory to be sure but for now, it was no use.

He got up and left his study to go to the platform where the dragons would take off from. He was pleased to see that Rizim had just returned.

"Greetings, Alzar. I was not expecting to meet you here."

"Ah, yes. I was in my study trying to figure out the trajectory of a celestial body. Memories of Ismi and I working together on such things flooded my mind. I came out here to remember her for a moment."

Rizim sighed. "Ah yes, she was fascinated with the stars. Long ago, we would transmorph into our visage forms and lay down on the top of a cliff on clear nights to watch them. She always wanted to fly beyond the firmament." Alzar looked at Rizim with a furrowed brow. It was unlike him to be so sentimental.

"Indeed. I appreciate that you and your brood have come to the tower, Rizim." He took a deep breath. "The company of dragons always lessens the burden of my calling. You all can do so much that I simply cannot."

"If you could not do it alone, Ata would not have charged you, Alzar. I can't help but think this feeling stems from the human side of you… doubt."

"Perhaps you are correct. I curse these human emotions all the time but… they have their purpose, I suppose."

They both looked up at the stars in the beautifully clear night sky. The life stream's blue flowing color was very prominent.

"How many souls do you think move through the life stream and into the Phatra daily?" asked Alzar.

"I could not say for certain. I understand that the life stream collects all souls in the cosmos and carries them to the Phatra so I can imagine that what we see at any given time is but a small portion of how many are actually getting carried through it."

"That makes sense." Alzar turned his attention down and waited a moment before speaking again. "I feel something strange, Rizim. I cannot grasp what it is but it feels ominous. I do not exactly possess the gift of foresight but I feel like my end may come soon."

Rizim continued gazing at the stars. "Then live every day as though it may be your last."

"The Nemisians handled the Tanimaran attack quite well, you think?"

"I would expect nothing less from a magocracy whose governing members are former students of yours."

"Indeed they are. That is why I will begin transferring all my work to the rebuilt and appropriately renamed capital of Alzarlaran."

Rizim gave Alzar a sly look. "You have always wanted the elves to create a wizard kingdom. Now you would allow humans to inherit your wisdom?"

"The elves are broken and divided. In case you could not

tell, Tanimara is about to get ravaged. Whether they win the war matters not. I cannot entrust someone like Raften with this knowledge. I cannot trust Darlana either. It is strange that humans have been pursuing knowledge and have been at war with each other a lot less of late."

"They have not been at war with each other; however the orcs have been constantly raiding the border kingdoms. It was difficult, Alzar. I lost so many of my brood to the orcs. They are not like any of the other races on Abrion."

"Nemis is nowhere near the border Kingdoms. Archwizard, Thoran and his apprentices are more than capable of carrying on my work. Rubus and Lemmi have agreed to help move the Academy of Higher arts to Alzarlaran and recruit those gifted in the arcane arts." He looked over to Rizim. "I have entrusted you with the tower, my friend."

"The tower? If you are moving the academy to Alzarlaran in Nemis, why would I need to remain here?"

"Its secrets are remaining here and can never be allowed to leave. The trinkets I have created have been moved deep underground to be locked away forever. Should something happen to me, you must guard the vaults in the caverns below until you can find a way to destroy them. Of course, I made them too powerful to be destroyed even by me."

"If you cannot, then how will I? Besides, what all do you have down there?"

Alzar tapped his chin in thought. "You know… I made so many trinkets over the millennia that I lost track. The most dangerous ones, the most forbidden ones are down there and must be kept from the mortals at all costs."

Rizim sighed. "All right, Alzar. If something happens to

you then I will guard the tower. I just hope that the cavern is large enough to house me in my natural form, but I remain optimistic. You have survived events I thought not possible many times."

"It is massive, Rizim. You will be able to even fly down there. Well, my friend, I must return to my study. There is more work to be done."

"I will see you in the morning, old friend."

***

"Finally," said Darlana as she looked back and observed the shores of Nemis moving below the horizon. Dusk was approaching and the ships were making steady speed to Thalnor, Atlantin in Tanimara.

"Tens of thousands of Umbramarians and surviving Nagrimarans, and a dragon. Not bad," said Ivi as Nythint approached. She decided to wander around and leave them alone.

Nythint was in his visage form.

"The invasion of Tanimara at last," he said.

Darlana wrapped her arms around him and smiled. She rested her head on his shoulder. "Indeed. I could not have ever even come close to this far if it were not for you, your brother, your father and everyone else who brought us here to this point."

Nythint turned around and looked at her. Darlana looked up at him.

"We will avenge Paeris, Velnir and Nagrimar. We will wash

our anguish away with their blood," said Darlana.

Nythint rested his forehead against hers. "Finally, retribution has come. I do believe that Yzat would have loved this."

She placed her hand on his cheek and looked at him with assurance. "Loss is never an easy burden to bear."

Nythint's orange eyes reflected the fire within him.

She looked down at his blade. "Razorheart is beautiful, Nythint. I have never seen a blade like it, nor have I ever known a dragon to forge one."

"I will cherish this gift so long as I live. It bears the memory of my brother as does my armor."

"My queen," interrupted one of the surviving Nagrimarans who happened to be one of Velnir's original expedition members. "There is a kraken in these waters that helped Velnir sail across. It helped protect against beastmen, pirates, and orcs."

"We do not require the assistance of a kraken, friend or foe and we would welcome a fight against the Tanimaran fleet if they even have one left. The orcs were driven deep within the Sundered lands. If the beastmen come, then so be it. We have a dragon," said Darlana.

Nythint smiled. He walked out on the deck and morphed into his natural dragon form and took to the sky to join the other dragons circling and patrolling the sky above the ships.

Darlana was getting anxious and excited. She retreated to her cabin and began to think about many things. Thoughts of Velnir, Paeris or Nagrimar were not among them. Instead she had revenge on her mind and how she would execute it. As she lay down to sleep, thoughts of the horrors her father committed upon her flooded her mind. The images of Alnas and Sampson, Velnir and Paeris, both of her families torn from her. She closed her eyes tightly in a vain attempt to clear her thoughts. She was exhausted and needed her sleep, however vengeance was keeping her awake, vengeance was fueling her!

Nythint was flying in a circle over the fleet scanning the horizon. It was night time now and the ships were illuminated with candlelight. Abrion's moons Canis and Majoris were full this evening and brightened up the sky more than usual. He noticed a large fleet on the horizon.

Nythint flew down to Darlana's ship and morphed into his visage form, He approached her door and gently knocked, awakening her. She opened the door and looked up to meet Nythint's eyes.

"Good evening, Nythint," she said smiling.

"My queen, I have spotted a fleet on the horizon. What are your orders?"

"Notify all the ships to extinguish their light immediately. We cannot risk being spotted."

"Very well," said Nythint. He made his way to the helm and ordered the lookout to signal all the ships to put out their lights. One by one they snuffed them out. Darlana came up to the helm.

"If they spot us, kill them all," she said. She then went back into her cabin.

Nythint morphed back into his natural dragon form and took to the sky.

He quietly observed the ships on the horizon. They began to turn and move in the direction of the Umbramarian fleet.

They got closer and closer. Nythint was becoming agitated. He knew there were twelve hundred Umbramari ships here. He did not know much about sailing but he knew simply turning toward them did not mean they noticed the Umbramari.

After all, he could barely see the ships from all the way up there. He kept watching. The ships kept coming and he was anxious for it to go one way or another. The Umbramarian fleet was moving quietly in the dark. They were naturally going slow to not create a massive wake in case the other ships passed behind them.

Slowly they got closer and closer and then they began to gradually change course northeast. Nythint let out a sigh of relief. It was a lot for one dragon to handle and he wasn't sure he was ready. Not a moment sooner, their fleet abruptly turned around and began sailing as fast as it could away from the Umbramari.

"We have been spotted," he said loud enough for Umbramari ships to hear. Suddenly and with great speed, he raced toward the approaching ships now moving away. It did not take long for him to catch up. He came in from behind them and began letting out massive bellowing roars and screeches making sure that whoever they were, knew he was a dragon. Nythint was about to unleash his firebreath on the closest ship to him before he noticed a Maphisian flag.

He stopped and halted to regain his balance before going to find their flagship to meet with their commander.

He flew down within earshot and halted once more. "I am Nythint, I represent Queen Darlana of Nagrimar and the Umbramari, will the flagship flash their light?" he asked.

A ship far to the left of him flashed its light and he made

his way to it and landed on its deck. The Maphisian ships were not at all like the Nemisian ships. They were very tall and elegant as if inspired by elven design. They had many tall masts, broad hulls and were absolutely colossal. Maphisian ships were akin to floating fortresses. They were plated with metal and had hundreds of ballistae. This made him uncomfortable as he had halted in place many times. If they were his enemies, he would have ended up like his brother.

He morphed into his visage form in front of the Maphisians on the ship. They were terrified and bewildered. It was clear they were unaware of dragon magic.

"I am Admiral Ra'het of Maphis. We heard that Nagrimar was destroyed, and we also heard that the Nagrimarans were successfully conquering the east side of Tanimara. We observed both the ruins of Nagrimar and sent envoys to General Magris who confirmed that he was in Atlan. Queen Sabreen has honored her agreement with Queen Darlana and sent her army to assist with the Tanimarans."

Nythint looked around and saw many thick burly humans wearing scaled bronze armor, domed chain helmets with the most beautifully kept black wavy beards he had ever seen. They had with them scimitars among many other blades.

"She sent fifty thousand of her finest warriors, great dragon," said Ra'het.

"Queen Darlana will be pleased. I will inform her at once. Please rendezvous with the Umbramaran fleet."

Ra'het placed his fisted hand over his chest and stood at attention. Nythint understood this to be a salute in their culture. He simply bowed his head and morphed back into his dragon form and took to the sky and flew back to the

Umbramaran fleet.

"This fleet belongs to Darlana's allies, the Maphisians. They were the only people who Darlana reached out to who agreed to provide military support. They will rendezvous with our fleet as soon as possible. Let's get back there."

Nythint made his way back to their ships. He flew down to Darlana who was still awake.

"They are Maphisian, my queen. They have come to honor their pledge to you against Tanimara."

Darlana looked genuinely surprised. She expected Dwarves to be more trustworthy than humans by their nature and always desiring to beguile her. When they found out Nagrimar was destroyed, they never came to her aid when the Tanimarans landed on the shores of the eastern continent and, like the humans, betrayed her. She thought for sure the humans, especially Arabans would abandon her. Truth be told, she forgot about them entirely.

"Queen Sabreen of Maphis. Praise her. How many did the queen send?"

"Fifty thousand of her finest," said Nythint.

The two fleets rendezvoused and merged.

Chapter 22
Tanimara

For the first time in four hundred years, the coast of Tanimara became visible to Darlana. Memories began to flood her mind of times long since passed. Thalnor was visible and had no ships in the harbor. They began disembarking.

The centaurs were excited. The forest was not dense and there was plenty of space for them to run. Dravon ordered them to forage but not disturb the people. He began to quietly observe Darlana.

Darlana disembarked and was reminded of all the elegant splendor she had left behind. The Umbramari were undoubtedly the most awestruck. It became evident that none of them have ever dreamed of being in such a place. Many stood there and looked around Thalnor in complete bewilderment.

Darlana, Ivi, Nythint and Dravon moved to the city center. Many of the Tanimarans were visibly uncomfortable even though they rebelled against their government. The demeanor on their faces would suggest they were second guessing their decision now. The contrast between Umbramari and Tanimara was night and day. One could tell that they were both types of elves but it was obvious that they were not of the same stock.

Magris was there along with elves that Darlana did not recognize. She did not seem to care. She was happy to see him and they embraced each other. Nythint witnessed this and felt a sense of jealousy for the first time in his life.

"When I heard that you led a small army to capture Madir, I was upset even though you were successful. Meric spent some time in the dungeon for it. Now, I could not be more pleased with you, General. Not only have you captured Madir and repelled several Tanimaran attempts to retake the city, you somehow convinced the Magister… What was her name?"

"Imra," said Magris.

"Yes, Imra, to rebel and convince two other houses to follow. Truly an accomplishment. Velnir would be so proud of you."

"Thank you, my queen. I know he would be."

"Have you not heard, General? I am Queen of the Umbramari now!"

Magris looked around seeing so many Umbramari. He was visibly uncomfortable. "Ah yes, Queen of the Umbramari. You never cease to amaze me, Queen Darlana."

She was eager for the details of his success. "Give me your report, General."

Magris took a deep breath. "The rebels have control of half the northern and all of the eastern side of Tanimara. The army was spread thin but received Nagramaran training. We had begun manufacturing the repeater crossbows in Atlan.

In fact, we have begun the production of many things in anticipation of your arrival. Scrying crystals and orbs, Dragon steel armor and many other essential goods. Production is very good at the moment, and I can assure you that there will be enough repeater crossbows and suits of armor for all the Centaur and... Umbramari in good time."

"This is excellent to hear, General. This far exceeds my expectations and for the first time in a while, things are starting to look favorable." She turned and looked at all of the Umbramari on the shore making their way off the ships and into the city of Thalnor. "They must begin training at once. We gave them some training while we were building ships in Nemis. I wish to wait no longer for the war to end. We have a lot to catch up on, Magris."

"Nemis? I wanted to ask, what happened?"

"Supreme Commander Vulas razed Bali. Alzar and his students are helping them rebuild the city. They are the reason we were able to bring this many troops on this many ships right now."

"This would explain why shipments were halted," said Magris.

"Indeed, it was tragic to say the least, but we are here now. Let us be grateful for that and move forward with our plans."

"About the plans, Queen," began Magris before she interrupted him.

"We will discuss them later. For now, we need to make sure this goes without issues. Umbramari and Tanimari are not going to assimilate without violence."

Magris understood and could not agree more. This was very dangerous. He was not at all comfortable with the Umbramari on Tanimaran shores and he knew the rest of Tanimara would not be so keen on having them there either. He was now thinking how Imra and Kaelina would react when he told them. It was already hard enough convincing the people of Tanimara to accept the return of Darlana, that is if they really even have.

For all he knew, they would rebel against her the moment they get the chance. This was a very dangerous game and Darlana did not seem to be too worried. It had been such a long time since he had seen her and he had so much to say, so many concerns and issues that already needed to be addressed outside of the Umbramari being here.

He was beginning to think that this was not going to go well at all. His thoughts became even more dangerous when he began to think that Darlana had other plans now. Plans that perhaps did not include the assimilation but perhaps vengeance by annihilation. He aimed to discover the truth as soon as possible.

The Umbramari finished disembarking along with the Maphisians and Centaur. Thalnor was not built to sustain so many so they began to march to Atlan. They were under strict orders not to harm anyone that had rebelled against Tarvana. This was ignored to enough of a degree that Darlana had to make an example out of several disobedient Umbramari. She saw it fit to use their own method of execution so she had Ivi deface and impale them. They were lined up along the road as a warning to the others when they marched by hearing their whimpers and cries.

Soon Atlan was in view. Darlana did not remember the last time she was here nor did she remember the city having such tall walls and spires. It was a magnificent but dreadful reminder of how tall Tarvana's walls would be. The gate was open and they marched in. Such was the splendor of the city, the Umbramari were beside themselves. Elven towers covered the landscape.

Darlana ordered all of the Umbramari to begin training in the Tanimaran art of warfare as well as honing the Nagriman. She believed that knowledge in both styles would give them a superior advantage along with the superior technology they had. They used the Tanimaran shields, spears and the Nagrimaran repeater crossbows.

The Tanimarans in Atlan were reluctant to train the Umbramari in their art of warfare out of fear that it would be used against them. They were set straight by the commanding officers and the training was going quite well. The dragons began to help smelt electhril to fashion dragon steel armor. The unique blue hue ever visible was loved by the Umbramari. They have never seen magical armor. Atlan was built on an arcane line so the magic here was as strong as it could be. Weapons, armor and siege weapons were produced of the highest quality by the artisans of Atlan who were known for their smithing ability honed over hundreds of years.

It was discovered that many Umbramari were naturally gifted in the arcane. After a series of tests were administered, several were given the opportunity to study pyromancy at the academy of Atlan however, they did not value discipline and were ignorant to its potency. Many were self ignited and turned to ash as a result prompting reforms. The more gifted ones began experimenting in darker magic unique to their culture in secret.

Magris had sent out an invitation to the rebel Magistrates to come to Atlan. Meanwhile, Darlana and Magris met with Kaelina outside the Magistrate building.

"It is such a pleasure to meet you, Darlana. Welcome home!" said Kaelina. Darlana ignored the pleasantries. Since she had arrived, she was constantly reminded of how these people treated her. Her hate for them was stewed ever more by the insincere niceties of a people that she knew feared her.

Kaelina was not expecting Darlana to act as though she did not exist and keep walking past her. It was an embarrassment to a magister of Tanimara, especially the one to the greatest house that bore her husband's name. They all made their way to the lord's palace and into the council chambers. Darlana looked around and really appreciated the art of the room.

Massive pillars were carved to look like strong elves holding the globe of Abrion on their backs which were holding up the ceiling. The room was elegantly decorated with vines, flowers and gold ornaments. She thought of how Velnir wandered through these halls. What he must have thought about and did even as a child. She missed him so much. Darlana did not remember such splendor in Tarvana.

For so long, she lived in a rebuilt ancient ruin reminiscent of a time long since passed with overgrown vines and massive ancient trees.

"We cannot wait for Imra to begin plans. We can brief her when she arrives," said Darlana.

"We have Madir, Atlan and Caphry under our control. The dragons have been patrolling and we have seen no signs of action from Linia, Starland or Istar, the latter openly siding with Tarvana. We have reached out to Linia and Starland but received no response," said Magris.

Darlana had balled her hand into a fist and rested her lips against it. She was concerned. "An empire in civil war yet there are regions who have not chosen a side? Whether or not they are neutral is moot. If I remember my father well, Tarvana will see them as an enemy since they did not side with him. We must also view them as such. Do not think of this as a rebellion against Tarvana. It is a war against Tanimara," said Darlana.

The room was quiet. Kaelina looked offended but kept her mouth shut. Dravon was interested to know more. He had not spoken up since they were in Nemis. Now that he was rested and off those ships, it would seem a good time as ever.

"The nation is fractured and will experience a power struggle the moment we take Tarvana. We must crush all who stand against us before we take Tarvana," said Dravon.

"The combined forces of Madir, Atlan and some of Caphry are at the southern pass which is heavily fortified on both sides. No one is getting through either side. We must march around Tanimara and capture all of the regions before proceeding. The garrison of Tanimarans in the pass will have to retreat to Tarvana to defend it. Then we can march the army through and surround it on both sides," said Magris.

"We must be careful. Darlana, you especially cannot simply march into these regions and demand surrender. They know you. You will have to convince them like Magris and Imra convinced us," said Kaelina in an untrusting manner.

"The Tanimarans burnt the Forlorn Forest and razed my kingdom to the ground. They slaughtered thousands of my people. They had destroyed everything I held dear. Do not speak to me about being careful. No one thought of the woman or children that burned alive in Nagrimar. They sent an assassin to kill my daughter. From what I understand, none of you stood up to defend Velnir before he was executed despite hailing him as a hero. Tanimarans did not care about us. Why should we care about them?" asked Darlana.

"Because you will not be seen as liberators," said Kaelina. Darlana turned her attention to Magris who shrugged at her. She looked at Dravon, Ivi, Nythint, Rizim and back to Kaelina.

"We are not liberators, Magister. Allow me to make this very clear," said Darlana as she got up and made her way to Kaelina. She approached her while she was still sitting in her chair and stood over her. She brought her face close to hers. "We are conquerors! Blood and vengeance is what we seek and we will have it," she said. Her eyes were beginning to blacken along with her veins. Darlana's physical appearance changing was off putting to Kaelina who was visibly terrified of her.

Ra'het and Dravon nodded in agreement with Darlana as did Nythint. Ivi simply smiled but Magris and Vysol looked disappointed.

There was a knock at the chamber door. Magris got up to address it and it was a messenger for Darlana. He took the message and read it. Nythint noticed Magris' demeanor change.

"Imra will not be coming," was all he said. Darlana nodded as if expecting it. They concluded their meeting and everyone left except Magris and Darlana. Nythint waited outside.

"You came here knowing we did not intend to restore the republic. We came here to avenge Paeris," scolded Darlana.

"I understand but we could do a great deed here. You have an opportunity to show them who you really are. Compassionate, caring and loving. They will be receptive to that especially since they have seen what Raften has done," said Magris.

"I do not care what the elves of Tanimara think of me. I will not show them compassion for they do not deserve it. I took in the destitute of Tanimara into Nagrimar and showed them compassion because I saw myself in them. The elves here see me as a means to end the dictatorship of Raften. Who is to stop them from rebelling against me when I achieve my goal?

"They will not rebel if you restore the republic," said Magris.

"Tanimara was a republic when I was exiled. They were a republic when they oppressed the dwarves and humans. It seems to me that the magisters who represent the people never actually did serve their best interest. Only their own, Magris," she scolded.

"If you show them what you have shown me or Velnir and his people, they will come to welcome you."

"I do not want them to welcome me." Her voice was venomous. "I want them to fear me!" She began to pace back and forth. "I captured Velnir, and I married him all with one purpose: vengeance!" Her voice faltered.

She stopped and looked at Magris. Her gaze held a cold disdain. "Then I fell in love with him and became content living in Nagrimar with my husband and daughter."

Magris saw the ghost of a vulnerable soul. He had never witnessed such raw emotion from an elf.

"I believed I could be happy again and let go of my anger. Tanimara did not allow me." She regained her composure, her eyes flashing with icy contempt. "The magisters saw fit to try and kill Velnir and my daughter, dishonoring everything we hold sacred."

She stood there silent and looked at Magris. He began to feel the weight of her anguish.

She moved closer to him and they locked eyes. "Truly, Magris, I have wanted to do this for four hundred years. I will make them all suffer the same way I have," she said quietly.

The look Darlana gave Magris had the weight of hundreds of years of pain and agony and so much loss by the hands of his people. To his knowledge, Raften did not have the power to force the Magisters and Lords to issue an order like that. They had to support it. Pride and arrogance filled their hearts. He understood what Tanimara did to her, but this was not the Darlana he knew.

She was looking at him longing for a response. He began to second guess many things. "May I be excused," he asked. It was clear she was disappointed. Without looking up at him, she waved him off. Magris left the palace feeling conflicted and very frustrated. He was unsure what to do.

Darlana felt her anger brewing. The heightened sense of emotions were brought on by the shadow that possessed her and she began to dislike it however, she felt even stronger and faster. Her senses were sharper than ever. She found her way to the washroom and looked in a mirror. She began to look more and more like the Umbramari. Her corruption was complete. The shadow had been completely absorbed into her body and now she had control of its power. All that was left to do was harness it.

***

Kaelina hurried back to her chambers. She quickly started to write a message to Imra. When she was finished, she gave it to her messenger and ordered him to fly straight to Madir. She returned to her chambers and locked the door. She sat on her bed thinking to herself. She was an elected Magister of Tanimara. The people of Atlan chose her to represent them in the capital. None of that would matter very soon. It was overwhelming for her and she began to cry into her pillow. Regret swelled in her heart.

***

Darlana went to Velnir's chambers. She looked around and took in the smells and visuals of his room. She picked up some of the books he read from his shelf and saw his interests were mostly in sword fighting and warfare strategy. She began to cry as she sat on his bed and huffed his pillow. It still smelled like him even after all this time.

She got up and moved to the balcony overlooking the city as was common in all the chambers of the nobles. She saw what her late husband would have seen his whole life. She heard a knock at the door.

"You may enter," she said. It was Magris and he carefully approached her. She turned to face him.

"You must know what happened," she said in an authoritative tone.

Magris moved over to the balcony and took a seat next to her. "What happened, my queen?"

"Yzat was shot out of the sky by an Umbramari warband. They took Meric and I captive. Meric did try to rescue me but failed."

Magris looked at her in awe. "They took us to the frozen wastes where we were sold into slavery."

"Yet you returned. Where is Meric?"

"Meric was subjected to the same punishment. I had the Umbramari who raided the Tanimaran town outside of Thalnor executed. He was also fed alive to these beasts called talonasaurs. It was gruesome, Magris."

Magris put his hand over his mouth and sat down. She could tell this was becoming difficult for him to process. "I was selected for the Emperor's bed as his personal plaything. I resigned myself to fate thinking that submission would be enough but no. The beatings came regardless." Her words, devoid of emotion.

Magris sat there silent. His eye began to well with tears. He was in disbelief. Darlana shifted. As the memories began to resurface her composure began to fray. She leaned against the wall, her hand instinctively shielding her eyes for a moment before continuing. The words tumbled out hesitant and raw. "The cell adjacent to mine held an elderly woman. Her screams still echo in my mind—they crushed her with the cell gate. Shortly after, something unnatural emerged from her lifeless body. A dark presence reminiscent of a living shadow crept up to me. I felt its presence suffocating at first... then it calmed me. The shadow offered..." She stopped and thought for a moment before deciding she did not desire to tell him anymore.

He could sense that she did not want to go on about it so he changed the topic. "How did you come to command the Umbramari?"

"Hm? Oh," she said seemingly lost in thought. "After he killed Meric, I got a hold of a sharp object and the next time I saw the emperor, I killed him with it. This is how I got command of the Umbramari."

"You did what you had to do, Darlana. Words cannot express my regret for not being there to protect you."

"Regret nothing, Magris. You have achieved far more than what any of us thought possible. You deserve a proper congratulations," said Darlana.

"Not necessary. I did my duty and will continue to." Or so he thought. He assumed that the republic would be restored.

"I would like to sleep here tonight if that is all right," she asked.

Magris was somewhat confused. "You need not ask, my queen."

"I just thought... well I wanted... all right," she said. "Nythint likes to stand outside my door at night to protect me. Please let him know I will be here."

"Yes, my queen," said Magris. He quietly closed the door and made his way to where the dragons were staying. He began to think about what Darlana told him. It bothered him greatly that she bargained with an unknown shadow creature. The Umbramari that killed Yzat are the same that she brought to Tanimara? Why have the dragons not dispensed retribution, especially Nythint.

Magris walked in as Nythint was updating the other dragons that came with Magris to Tanimara on everything that had happened. Vysol and the others seemed to be angry and Magris thought rightfully so.

"Nythint, you are requested by the queen to her chambers in the lord's palace."

Nythint did not waste any time. He didn't even say farewell to the other dragons. He simply bolted straight to her chambers.

"The Umbramari killed Yzat," said Magris. "Did any of you know this?"

"Yes, we are aware. Darlana had the ones responsible defaced and impaled," said Vysol.

Magris understood that this was now the way of things. It disgusted him.

Chapter 23
Subterfuge

The messenger made it to Madir undetected. He gave Imra the letter from Kaelina and it confirmed Imra's fears. Darlana had no intention of restoring the republic. This confirmation was all she needed to move forward with her plan. She packed her things and told Keryth that she would be back but did not tell her where she was going.

Discreetly, she slipped into the griffin stables and found hers. Under the cover of night, she took to the sky, heading first to Linia. Magris' forces were still in the city. She did not know how loyal they were since she announced that the rebellion would side with Darlana. Still, she could not risk detection out of fear someone would tell Magris who she believed was now spying on her.

Once she made it above the clouds, she took it easy. Many things were flooding her mind. How terribly wrong everything went and now a third faction was being created at her behest to not only combat Tarvana but Darlana as well. Three factions vying for power.

She was genuinely hurt and felt somewhat responsible for the fall of the republic. She was in Tarvana when Raften declared himself Emperor of Tanimara. She could have stood up and said no but his mages were present and ready to incinerate anyone who defied him. She, like many other Magistrates, felt their lives were at risk if they did not vote in favor. Of those Magisters that did not really approve were Kaelina of Atlan, Deryth of Linia, Elad of Starland and herself. It was enough support.

***

Magris stayed up late wondering about the letter that Imra had sent him. He thought about bringing it to the attention of his queen but could not. Even if he did it now, he would face retribution for waiting too long. He began to suspect something was awry when she brought the letter to him in the first place. Now that she did not come at the behest of the queen, he knew something was up. He could not simply rely on a messenger to reach her. He must go himself and confront her.

The next morning, Magris moved around the city checking on the progress of the Umbramari and Tanimari training them. It was going surprisingly well. They have adapted well to the Tanimari shield wall phalanx and seemed to have improved upon it with their own tactics. Now the doctrine would require that every soldier have a repeater crossbow, shield and spear. No longer will there be standalone archers.

He made his way to the lord's council chambers within the palace of Atlan. Dravon, Nythint, and Ivi were there.

"Magris, we have not heard from Imra nor have we seen Kaelina. Where are they?" asked Darlana.

"I was wondering the same thing. With your permission, I will go and find out," said Magris.

Magris left the meeting and went to the Magister's chambers. He knocked on the door, but no one answered. He let himself in and had a look around. A lot of things were out of place and it looked as though someone was in a hurry to leave. Magris became worried. He noticed that several scrolls were missing from her shelves. The labels of the missing scrolls were for the city defenses and architectural plans.

"Why would Kaelina need to take those?" he thought.

He searched her desk and found nothing of interest. He went downstairs and into her bedroom only to find that her clothing was strewn all over the place and that her toiletries were gone. Magris had come to the conclusion that Kaelina had left Atlan, but why. He thought about it for a moment and began to put it together. He sent Imra to Kaelina and Beric. Imra and Kaelina are rebellious Magisters and conspire against Tarvana. Imra did not show when Darlana requested her presence and now Kaelina is gone. Perhaps, Kaelina is in Madir.

Magris returned to the palace and searched for Vysol. He came upon the dragons in their visage forms discussing things amongst themselves. Magris was surprised to see so many dragons in one place. He felt out of place and waited patiently. Vysol noticed him though and made her way over to him. Her visage was interesting. She chose a female elf with a tightly woven braided hairstyle like the ancient female warriors that helped to settle Tanimara thousands of years ago.

"Magris, we have made ourselves at home for the time being. I was in charge of the decorating. What do you think of our den?" asked Vysol.

From the outside, Magris thought the den was quite small for so many dragons but once he entered, he realized they were in their visage forms. Even now it was impressive to him that dragons could do this. He felt that he never really took the time to appreciate it.

There were beds, candles, chandeliers and a few chests but that was it. Vysol's attempts at decorating were futile but to humor he said he thought it was fitting. This clearly pleased her.

"None of the others care. I thought I would attempt to fit in with the Tanimarans. All the different kinds of Elves are very interesting creatures," said Vysol.

"I have a favor to ask. Between you and I, Kaelina has left Atlan. I suspect she might be in Madir. Could you take me there to investigate?"

Vysol looked at him with a furrowed brow. "You sound as if you are disturbed. Is everything all right, Magris?"

"I mean to get to the bottom of something. I do not wish to say anything as I do not want to rouse suspicions in anyone else or panic. The sooner we get there, the better," he said.

"Very well. I will meet you on the new balcony you had constructed for us at the top of the palace."

Magris left and went to his chambers to grab his things. He put his new armor on, grabbed his sword and mage staff.

He stood in front of the mirror and was rather fond of the new armor. He chose not to wear a helmet and let his long black hair hang over his armor. He replaced his eye patch with a black leather one and replaced his peg leg with a metal one that could be fitted to his new greaves. His intentions were to go to Madir not as a Tanimaran or as a Nagrimaran but as a representation of the unification of many elven peoples all in one and he planned to bring Vysol because she was an enormous and terrifying dragon with combat experience if anything went wrong.

He left his chambers and made his way up to the balcony where he agreed to meet Vysol. Darlana saw him going up the stairs.

"General, wait."

Magris turned around and saw his queen. He was quick to kneel.

"You are headed up to the dragon's balcony. Where are you going?"

"I intend to go to Madir. Imra is there and I want to know why she has not responded to our invitations."

Darlana looked at him then moved her eyes away from him.

"Something doesn't feel right. Be careful, General." She turned around and left without saying anything more.

Magris was confused but made his way to the balcony anyway. When he got there, he met Vysol. He gathered his things and mounted her. He asked her to let out a boisterous roar. She was happy to oblige. Vysol jumped off the balcony and once she gained momentum, she spread her wings, and they flew over the city of Atlan. She let out a roar that made everyone duck for cover except the Umbramari who kept training without even flinching. Magris thought it was funny and surprising that the Umbramari did not seem bothered.

Vysol gained altitude and soon they were above the clouds making their way to Madir. The sky was clear, and the sun was setting. Magris had asked Vysol to fly through the night. Dragons could sleep while flying so this would not be a problem for her though it could be an issue for any passenger. Magris did not care about the wind or the cold air. He was strapped in.

Magris noticed something different in the night sky. Canis and Majoris were very close to each other. The moonlight was the brightest he had ever seen. It was not like daytime, the moonlight illuminated everything. It was quite nice.

***

Madir was in sight. Vysol had begun her descent. She made her way over the city flying low until she got to the courtyard where she landed. Magris dismounted her and asked her to remain in her natural dragon form in case there was trouble. He then made his way through the palace of Madir to the Magisters chambers.

He did not knock but instead let himself in and of course found no one. It was empty though Imra's stuff was not like Kaelina's. Hers was still nice and neat. Magris decided to go to Imra's personal residence within the city. He went back outside the palace and asked Vysol to come with him. She morphed into her visage form and they began walking.

The Madirans were giving them strange looks. It was clear to Magris that they did not recognize his armor. He waved and greeted some of them but while some greeted him back, most ignored him and simply looked at them. This was strange, they did not recognize him?

Once they got to Imra's residence, he found it polite to knock in case Keryth was home. A few moments later, Keryth answered the door, surprised to see Magris.

"General, I was not expecting you."

"I came unannounced. My apologies. I need to speak with your mother and I did not find her at the palace."

Keryth looked nervous and hesitant. "Oh, that is because she is in Linia or Starland on a diplomatic mission."

Magris looked surprised. "The queen has not received any notice from Linia or Starland regarding their support. She has received notice that Istar has sided with Tarvana. Why is Imra in Linia or Starland without Darlana knowing?"

"I do not know. I have to go, General. Forgive me," she said before shutting the door.

Magris was conflicted. Something was up and he knew it. He wondered if he should go to Linia but given that they had not responded, he was unsure they would welcome him. Darlana was also not notified. He had no time to go all the way back to Atlan and tell her. He no longer trusted any Madiran to go tell her. He decided to go to Linia.

Vysol and Magris made their way back to the palace courtyard where she morphed into a dragon and he mounted her. They took to the sky and were off to Linia.

Chapter 24
Suprise

It was a crisp cool night at the encampment outside of the canyon leading into Tarvana. The trenches were dug deep and all of the elves were quite comfortable as they were receiving everything they needed. The war felt like a stalemate even though the only city they had taken by force was Madir. It did not seem like a war at all.

A sentry was high in the watchtower and turned his attention toward the canyon. Several shadows began to appear on the ground and when he looked up he couldn't really see much as the sun was blocking his view. He squinted and peered through his fingers to make out hundreds of griffins descending upon them.

"Sound the alarm! Tarvanan griffins incoming," he shouted.

The rebels were excited and began to form ranks. They aimed their repeater crossbows. The griffins were coming in hard and fast. The mages atop them began conjuring fireballs but before they could get them off, a hail of bolts pierced them and their griffins.

The griffins halted midair causing some of their riders to fall to their deaths. They panicked and allowed the rebels to fire more and more bolts. From above, the griffins saw the ground disappear beneath a sea of black. Below, the rebels saw the sky darken as the sun vanished behind a storm of arrows. The hail of bolts annihilated most of the griffins and they began to retreat.

The rebels began to cheer but then another alarm sounded. While the rebels were distracted with the griffins, the Tarvanans made their way through the canyon and began to form ranks. Three massive armies began marching toward the rebel ranks. The rebels could not believe how fast the Tarvanans were able to assemble.

They formed ranks and moved to meet them in battle. The front line of the rebels formed a shield wall as did the Tarvanans. The Tarvanans advanced and the rebels began firing their repeater crossbows into their ranks. Many pierced the shields and the elves behind them. This did not deter the Tarvanans and they kept advancing.

Soon they clashed and began surrounding the rebel army. Fear gripped the rebels and they began to retreat. Tarvanan mages on griffins came through the canyon and began casting firestorms and fire bolts in the ranks of the rebels. Many burned alive and were cooking in their armor.

The Tarvanans pushed and pushed. The rebels were in full retreat and could not move fast enough. Many were killed. By the time the rebels made it to Caphry, they had lost twenty thousand troops and were weary.

Beric began to panic as he saw the Tarvanan troops digging in around Caphry. Fortunately for him, his city was built on several artificial islands in a lake and able to withstand a siege for years but he did not have years. He felt it was necessary for him to stay in Caphry so he sent a messenger to Darlana.

When the messenger got to Atlan he came running through the palace up and around the halls until he came to a massive door guarded by two burly elves. He took a minute to compose himself and catch his breath. The guards each grabbed a handle on the door and pulled it open.

Waiting for him was Darlana and her council. He quickly brought the message to her.

"My queen, a missive sent from Lord Beric of Caphry."

Darlana grabbed the message and began to read it.

"Caphry is under siege, the Tarvanans broke through the canyon pass." She looked over to her council. "Ready the centaur, General Dravon. Ivi, I am promoting you to general. Ready the Umbramari. They seem eager to fight." She turned her attention to Nythint. "I do not think we will need all the dragons. The missive says three Tarvanan armies. I think the only dragons we will need are you both and three more of your strongest. I regret that Magris is away with Vysol. We could use her, but we will be all right. Let us mobilize and move at once," ordered Darlana.

Ivy rallied the Umbramari who were excited and ready for a fight. Dravon rallied the centaur and Atlan began bustling. Hundreds of thousands of troops began flooding the streets and marching all in brand new finely crafted elven armor, shields, spears and repeater crossbows.

Several hours went by and still they were marching. Not many Atlantians have seen such a sizable army. As the last of them left the city, one could witness several columns of thousands of elves, bolt throwers, griffins mounted by mages and the dragons could be heard screeching and roaring above them. Tanimara had never witnessed such a terrifying spectacle.

It is the worst nightmare come true for Tarvana and most Tanimarans. An army of Umbramarians, Tanimaran sworn enemies more so than even Orcs or Dwarves. None have left such a bitter mark on elven society like the Umbramari. The Atlantians would know that first hand as the last war before the war with the Orcs was with the Umbramari. Though they had won, it was at a terrible cost and one they barely fully recovered from by the time the Orcs invaded.

What made it even worse was the fact that the Umbramari were led by the apostate herself. The one whose children and husband were murdered by Tarvana. "What terrible retribution they must face," said one Atlantin to another as they witnessed the army passing through their village.

Tarvana had made their move again only this time, it is Darlana's turn.

Darlana began thinking about how she would react to them. Her thoughts riddled with plans of their demise and torture. They would pay. All this to the delight of the shadow inside her. It craved chaos and destruction and who better than by the hands of the one who hated the Tarvanans most. Its host.

***

Vysol had entered Linian airspace. Magris was cautious as well as Vysol. Soon, the city of Linia was in their sight. Most of the buildings here were tall spires. Linia did not have a palace like most of the cities in Tanimara. There was no real platform or ground open enough within the city itself for Vysol to land on. Her wings could not make it between the spires. They were forced to land outside the city gate.

"I am General Magris of Nagrimar. I understand that Magistrate Imra is here. I demand to speak with her at once," said Magris.

He stood there confidently, sword in one hand and staff in the other. He was ready to let them have it if they ignored his request. Several minutes passed and he heard nothing. He was not going to mess around. If he had to make an example of these people, he would.

"Show me Imra immediately. I must know that she is all right," he lied.

Vysol roared. Now they began to stir. He could hear some of the guards at the gate begin to panic. A moment later, the gate opened slightly and there stood Imra though not in armor or her Magister's garb. Just a dress with a leafy headdress. Her ears were decorated with silver and her long blonde hair was braided.

Magris had not ever seen her in such a way. He found her to be quite appealing but felt she was out of his league. Who could truly love one as ugly as he.

"Magris, I am all right. I came here on my own volition," said Imra from the gate. She was far enough away that she had to raise her voice for him to hear her.

"I need to speak with you," he said.

She looked back and started speaking with someone else. Magris was stunned. He recognized her to be Kaelina. "You as well Kaelina!"

The two Magisters came out of the Linian gate and made their way toward Magris and Vysol who was still in her dragon form. Archers began to post along the wall. This made Magris uncomfortable.

The two Magisters got within a few meters of Magris and Vysol before they stopped.

"What is the meaning of this? Why are you not with us in Atlan?" Magris glanced past them at the nervous Linian soldiers which were upsetting him.

Kaelina turned her attention to Imra who insisted that she tell him. "As of now, officially you must consider our alliance broken. Linia, Starland, Madir and Atlan have declared independence from Tarvana and from your queen. We do not recognize her as the ruler of Tanimara. We will aim to restore the republic," said Kaelina.

"Silence, Kaelina," said Magris. "Imra, we have Madir and Atlan under our control right now. I was just in Madir. I spoke with Keryth. She seemed nervous. Have you been planning this?"

"I thought that you and I had hoped that Darlana would be willing to restore the republic. Kaelina informed me that Darlana said she would not restore the republic. She would destroy everything we have built over thousands of years. Her anger is clouding her judgment. She will not take Tarvana and then rule Tanimara. She will take Tarvana and kill everyone. Her desire for revenge will destroy Tanimara, not preserve it. Do you really want to see your nation fall? Do you not see the hate she has for us," asked Imra.

Magris had been thinking a lot about the future of Tanimara. In truth, he did want the republic restored. He also wanted revenge for Velnir. "She deserves revenge and only desires to punish Raften."

"Do not be so naive, Magris. She brought thousands of Umbramari with her to do this. Umbramari have been our enemies for thousands of years. You and Velnir fought them time and time again. What purpose do they serve if not to slaughter Tanimarans and destroy our culture," said Imra.

"Tanimara eradicated Nagrimar. They killed her daughter and then her husband. You know the rest. Darlana has a way of bringing people together. I have faith that she will unite the Nagrimari, Umbramari and Tanimari people. You do not know her like I do. She will bring peace to the world if she wins," argued Magris.

"I understand your faith in her, Magris. We do not share the sentiment. The republic must stand after Raften is removed or the continent will be divided. If she stays in Tarvana and declares herself Queen of Tanimara, the war will continue. You must understand. We cannot replace one tyrant with another," said Imra.

Magris began to think about the Umbramari. He had been so focused on other things, the thought of them in the ranks occurred to him before but he paid it no heed. Now Imra had reminded him that he fought them, and he did know what they were like. It began to bother him.

He knew Darlana did have other plans. He was aware she did not want to restore the republic and knew she wanted revenge. He had hoped that she would see the error in her ways. As he thought more about it, they were probably right but he could not simply abandon her. Not now. He loved the Tanimaran republic, and he also loved his queen.

"I…" he said before looking at Vysol. He was not sure where Vysol's loyalty stood and did not want to say anything to upset a dragon. He was aware that Dragons outside of Nythint did not have an undying loyalty to mortals and only dwelled with them as long as they were interesting or in Rizim's circumstance, necessity. They only followed orders if they wanted to, hence why he asked her for a ride rather than ordered her. They have earned the respect of mortals but are not to be entirely trusted.

"I would invite you into Linia so that we may discuss this further… both of you," said Imra.

"Even if I were to go into Linia with you, I swore allegiance to Darlana. I was Atlantian and served under Lord Ruvyn and then Lord Velnir. She has inherited Velnir's estate despite what the Magistrate in Tarvana says."

"Magris, what about that thing inside of her. Who knows what it's tempting her to do. Who knows who is in control," said Kaelina.

Magris had momentarily forgotten about that. He had not seen it in her and thought it to be some sort of psychological disorder brought on by trauma. He did not believe it was an actual manifestation though she did admit to bargaining with a shadow creature.

"As far as I know, I have never seen anything like that in her and have been with her for some time now. I would say that is slander. Now that I know where both of you stand… I will take my leave."

Magris mounted Vysol. The two Magisters had a look of worry on their faces but did not say anything.

"If you understand what we are capable of, you will not attempt to kill Vysol or myself. If you do plan to, make sure not to miss," he said before taking to the sky.

He was angry that they had betrayed Darlana but deep down, he understood. They were the rebellion, Darlana and the Umbramari were invaders and conquerors. He kept telling himself that Darlana would do what was right and now he was second guessing his decision and beliefs. He decided to make his way back to Atlan and speak with Darlana.

Chapter 25
Eager for More

The Umbramarian army marched in their new armor, shields gleaming, and spears at the ready. Repeater crossbows hung at their sides. The Centaur, clad in fresh armor, wielded massive spears fit for their size. Among them, the Maphisian humans moved with quiet menace, their signature turbans and curved scimitars marking them as deadly warriors.

The people of Atlan remembered the war that destroyed the Araban Empire and more recently the wars against the Umbramari. The fact that Darlana was widely regarded as responsible for the war against the Araban Empire and was leading the Umbramari did not sit well with them. Many were not happy to see them as they marched by. Darlana took notice and rather than pity she gave them a look of scorn.

Four hundred years of malice and hatred had sculpted her face into contempt and scorn.

It had been bottled up and now, the bottle was spilling slowly releasing its contents until that resentment turned into more hatred. Hatred for the Tanimari burned within her for their cruelty, their rejection, and the slaughter of her kin.. The reminder had transformed her minor contempt into seething hatred and it was not helping that the shadow was whispering in her head all the delicious things she could do to them with its power. The thoughts began to fester.

Though she was marching them out to counter the Tanimarans, she did not wish to take the army to Tarvana just yet. Despite having more soldiers in Tanimara than Tanimara itself did, she knew she did not have enough to gain more than a pyrrhic victory. She reached into her satchel and grabbed the orb of falling stars. It was charged and ready for use should she feel compelled to use it. She understood the power of such a weapon. The fear it could bring.

It was midday and Caphry was now in their sights. The Umbramari became adept at using scrying orbs. They threw them in the sky and they moved toward the Tanimaran line. Dravon confirmed that there were roughly three hundred thousand Tarvanans besieging the city. Darlana knew it would take time to go around the city so she had asked Dravon to take his centaur around the westside of Caphry and attack their bolt throwers. Dravon complied and took his forces and moved with surprising stealth through the woods west of Caphry. Dravon noticed that the scrying orbs caught the attention of the Tanimarans who were now in ready stance.

Thousands of Centaur had formed up behind the Tarvanan line undetected, a testament to their stealth capability. He understood the plan and when everyone was in position, he spoke.

"My kin, we are not here just to conquer. We are here for revenge! These people burned our beloved forest to the ground and destroyed our Queen's lands. Your homes, your kin and your lives were destroyed by them. Now is not the time for mercy or pity. Now is the time for revenge and it is yours to take. Onward kin, to Victory!"

Dravon blew his horn signaling the attack. Thousands of centaur came out of the tree line at full gallop clad in heavy dragon steel armor. Their hooves shook the ground and the sound resonated. The look on their faces was of anger and vengeance.

The Tarvanans tried to turn the bolt throwers in the direction of the centaurs but the centaurs were charging their flank. The position of the bolt throwers was not suitable for firing all of them without risking hitting their own troops. Two or three of them fired their bolts toward Dravon's troops. Once in the middle of the air, blades sprung from their shafts and they began to spin very quickly. Many of the centaurs tried to get out of the way but they were too crowded. The bolts landed in the ranks, shredding scores of them. This failed to deter Dravon and only served to anger the rest. The general ordered them to press the attack.

The scrying orbs observed Dravon's charge. The dragons morphed into their dragon forms now that the bolt throwers were turned. They took to the sky and scattered in all directions. Darlana trusted that they knew what they were doing. She ordered the Umbramari to move with haste around the city's east side and get behind the Tarvanans and they did with excellent precision. They were as good as any fresh Tanimaran soldier.

The dragons descended upon the Tarvanans. Some came from the east and unleashed a hellfire of breath upon them. Some came from the west and did the same. More came from the city itself and landed in the ranks which sewed confusion.

The Tarvanans clearly did not expect this many dragons with Darlana. The commanders did not see an army outside of some centaurs, so they ordered the Tarvanans to break ranks and kill the dragons and centaurs. Once Dravon's forces were receiving heavy resistance, he sounded a retreat and would turn around and charge back in, killing scores of Tarvanans. Their armor was protecting them a lot better than they thought but they were beginning to overheat. It was only a matter of time before the tables would turn. They were vastly outnumbered but were successfully pulling the Tarvanans away from the siege. Meanwhile, Darlana was leading the Umbramari around the Tarvanans. She had the element of surprise.

The dragons would attack again and again. Now the Umbramari griffin riders entered the fray. The mages on their backs were conjuring firestorms and fire bolts but they were largely ineffective as they were novices. Still, they hurled them into the Tarvanan ranks with a modicum of skill. Fire did not affect the dragons. Everywhere you looked, the Tarvanans were being slaughtered.

By the time Darlana was behind the Tarvanans, several hundred centaurs were injured or killed. Though tired, Dravon kept regrouping and charging in. The Tarvanans sounded a tactical retreat but began to panic when the centaurs gave chase.

As the Tarvanans began to panic and run toward the canyon, they realized that Darlana had moved her force with incredible speed to get behind them completely undetected. A sense of dread was felt throughout the Tarvanan army of which roughly two thirds remained. They now stood against the mighty force of the Umbramari and Darlana. Thousands of soldiers, many of which were eager to begin the slaughter.

The Tarvanans noticed that the dragons and centaur did not pursue them. They stopped and formed ranks and began to march toward the Umbramari line. The commanders noticed they were severely outnumbered but felt that their training was superior and that the odds were still in their favor, after all, they were simply Umbramari, a foe they have defeated time and time again. Not this time, however. They were trained in the Tanimaran art of war unbeknownst to the Tarvanan commanders. When they did not lash out, battle cry and jump at them flailing their weapons but maintained their discipline and held their line, many Tarvanan's seemed confused and began to experience fear. This was amplified when the Umbramari ranks were dead silent and moving in synchronized motion, spears out.

The moment they got within range, The Umbramari fired their bolts into the ranks of the Tarvanans killing scores and scores of them. Their line still held and they kept advancing despite their mounting losses every time the Umbramari fired.

In truth, the Tarvanan's did not have a choice. If they could not break through the Umbramari line, they would perish. The Tarvanan commanders ordered a spear head formation to penetrate through the enemy line. Once it clashed with them, they pushed their way through Darlana's forces and were seemingly successful. The Umbramaris beat on their shields but did not kill as many as they had hoped which was frustrating, however, they remained undeterred.

Darlana siphoned the shadows powers using her own willpower. Her physical features changed and looked terrifyingly ominous befitting one who was possessed. Shadowy wings sprouted from her back and she took to the sky. Those of her soldiers who noticed were in awe. She aimed for the spearhead of the Tarvanan line breaking through her army. She dove on them unsheathing her daggers.

The Tarvanan soldier leading the spearhead did not even see it coming. He likely did not feel his head leave his shoulders nor did the several other soldiers in the spearhead. Her daggers began to flow a dark purple. Tendrils sprawled from her enemies and entered her blades much to the delight of the shadow within her.

Darlana was moving so fast, she looked like a black cloudy blur slaying only the Tarvanans. The Umbramari began to roar in excitement but held their ground. The spear head began to crumble and many began to try and retreat the other way. By now, the Umbramaris had surrounded the Tarvanans completely and had their shields and spears up at them. They packed together in a giant circle of elves with no hope of escape. The commanders were caught and pulled out their white flags.

Darlana stopped killing the Tarvanans for the moment and took to the sky. She approached the Tarvanan commanders but did not ask for their names. Instead, she grabbed both of them off their stags and carried them behind the Umbramari line on top of a hill, and in plain view of both armies. She wanted to send a message to Tarvana, to her father. She ordered the commanders to hastily have their hands and feet nailed to an X plank.

Then a sharpened stake was placed up their backsides and the executioner took a mallet and began pounding it through their bodies until it broke through their shoulders. Their strikes were so precise that the stake missed every vital organ that would cause instant death and kept their victims alive. A testament to the skill of an Umbramari executioner.

The two commanders were then placed upright for all to see. The Umbramari then took out their knives and began to deface them. The Tarvanans were visibly horrified. The executioners carved around the faces of the Tarvanans causing them to howl in agonizing pain. They peeled their skin down to their chin and allowed their face to hang.

After bearing witness to this, the Tarvanans began dropping their weapons and putting their hands up in surrender.

Darlana flew over them and came to a stop in mid air. Her hair was down and her blades were out. A black mist was dripping from her body and everyone cowered, including her own soldiers. She was terrifying to behold yet eerily beautiful. The shadow's influence has physically manifested however Darlana was in control.

"You ignored the pleas of my people as you slaughtered them. The unarmed women and children along with tens of thousands of Nagrimaran soldiers. You mercilessly burned our forest and my city. You killed so many Nagrimarans and now…" She paused and looked upon them, loathing all. "You think you can surrender?" she said with venomous disdain. You think that I would simply allow you to?" she began to cackle maniacally. The Umbramaris began to cheer and advanced on the now unarmed Tarvanans.

They had to save their bolts so spears it was. Every step they took, they would thrust their spears into the Tarvanans who were completely helpless. This method would take a while and Darlana would allow as much time as they needed to kill every last one.

The griffin riders approached but did not want the fire storms to enter the Umbramari ranks so they remained on standby however, the dragons were reluctant. Unbeknownst to Darlana, they had decided not to participate.

Darlana was observing the slaughter before her. They cried for mercy, the helpless whimpering and begging. The screams and gargling of blood, the doomed elves reflected in her wide eyes. She remembered seeing her kin burn and the helpless feeling that it gave her.

"Now they get but a small taste of what I felt, and my vengeance will be tenfold on Tarvana," she said to herself.

The Umbramari were taking so much delight in killing the doomed high elves. Watching them writhe in agony, lusting over the chaos and destruction. They were very pleased to be executing all of them for their queen.

***

Vysol landed on the balcony of the palace of Atlan. Magris dismounted and Vysol assumed her visage form. Together they walked though the palace and noticed that no one was in there. Their confusion was increased when they went outside the palace and saw no one in the streets.

"Interesting, there is no one here yet everything is in order. What is this all about," asked Magris. Just then, several hundred Atlantin soldiers surrounded Magris and Vysol with their spears drawn.

"General Magris. You are to be detained by the order of the new republic. Please place your sword and your staff on the ground and allow us to take you without incident. No blood needs to be shed," said the commanding officer.

"You understand that fire will consume all of you if you take another step," said Vysol before assuming her dragon form. "The first mistake you made was confronting us in the open courtyard where I could assume my dragon form," she said. The guards began to advance and Vysol began to take in air.

"Stop," demanded Magris. "You are right. No blood needs to be shed. I cannot allow my fellow Atlantians to die by my hand or yours, Vysol." He turned to the commander of the guard. "Please call your guard back and stand down!"

The commander did not comply. Vysol grabbed Magris and took to the sky. The bolt throwers in the towers aimed and fired at Vysol. She was getting angry.

"Please do not destroy them, I will get to the bottom of this," pleaded Magris.

"If they hit me with one of those damned bolts, I will incinerate them. It is only fair," she stated. Magris could not argue but fortunately she was very good at evading them. Magris could tell that they were not even trying. The elves operating the bolt throwers knew what they were doing and if they wanted to hit something as big as Vysol, they could. They were sympathetic but had to follow Kaelina's orders.

Magris climbed onto Vysol's back. "Thank you for holding back your fury, Vysol."

It was clear to him she was not happy with what just happened. "Where could Darlana and the Umbramari be," she asked.

Magris had to think about that for a moment. They were not spotted going to Madir and there was no way that the Atlantins could slaughter the Umbramari. Thalnor was not an option as it was the port of Atlantin, and he could not see a reason for her to be there anyway. Umbramari were still coming into Thalnor. "The only logical place she could have gone was Caphry and she must be completely unaware of the rebellion of Atlan and Madir." Then the thought occurred to him. "Atlantians had marched out with her…"

***

Several hours had gone by and there were still thousands of Tarvanans left to kill. The Umbramari were holding their ground but the smaller the circle of high elves got, the less dark ones needed to be there. They began to set up camp. The smell of burnt flesh and massive plumes of smoke were billowing in the air. They had been piling up the bodies of the dead Tarvanans and burning them.

The cries and pleas of the Tarvanans was music to Darlana's ears.

"Have you got your fill?" asked the shadow.

"I am pleased to behold their suffering," she replied. Darlana stood there and continued observing.

Nythint walked up behind her in his dragon form welding Razorheart. The battle was over. The field was littered with corpses and weapons. Smoke was thick, and the sky was dark.

"Our first major victory against your father's army," said Nythint as he looked around at the same carnage she was observing.

"Yes, it pales in comparison to what is to come." The mental images of Nagrimarans burning only fueled her desire to want more for the Tarvanans. She had successfully destroyed three Tarvanan armies. Soon, every elf in this one would be incinerated and left a burning husk of what once was a proud soldier of her fathers.

Her mind swirled with memories of the day she was cast into the Tarvana dungeons—Raften throwing Alnas out the window as a helpless baby. And Sampsin… was he thrown as well, or executed before the crowd? Her memories of that fateful day have been clouded for centuries. She had suppressed them in order to cope but had she truly forgotten how Sampsin was executed? A mixture of emotions began to stir.

The voice of the shadow returned. "Focus, Darlana, focus on slaughter and chaos…" The word chaos resonated with her mind.

"What am I…" she began to say out loud before Nythint arrived. He was truly the only one left who could calm her and bring a sense of joy.

"My queen, are you pleased with the punishment we have dispensed upon the Tarvanans?"

"I am my dear dragon. Their debt is paid with their lives."

"The Tarvanans in the canyon pass have retreated back to Tarvana. Would you like us to pursue?"

"The soldiers are weary despite the victory and will need time to rest, Nythint but in time, we will march on the city. I have a secret weapon."

"Your shadow, is it?" inquired Nythint with genuine curiosity.

"No." She smiled and looked over to her satchel. She got up to retrieve it and pulled out the orb of falling stars. Nythint moved closer and observed. "This is the enchanted item Alzar used at the battle for the Sundered lands." She looked up at him. "Do you remember that meteor falling from the sky and obliterating the orcs?"

"Such power, how did you obtain it," asked Nythint. He was grinning and loved the thought of her having this kind of power.

"I wonder when and where I should use this," she said while smiling at him.

"Use it in a city. I would enjoy seeing that."

The thought intrigued her. She gazed upon the orb of falling stars. "It always went against my nature to do such things… but, perhaps they truly deserve it," she said calmly without taking her eyes off the orb.

So many thoughts were rampaging through her head. The burden of the memories was heavy and she began to wear it. Her appearance of late was that of being tired and worn out.

"This will bring an end to the war and usher in a new age of Tanimara," she said as Nythint moved next to her.

They both gazed upon the orb and then turned their attention to each other. His presence calmed her. The shadow was very good at suppressing the memories of her traumatic past and distracting her. It has become very influential as her mental state began to descend into madness but Nythint always made her feel like she used to and she appreciated that. For the first time, she met his eyes with her own. The feelings between them were growing.

***

Thousands of Tarvanan high elves lay dead all over the field. The smell of death filled the air. Nythint and the other dragons were piling the dead elves up and incinerating the corpses. The smoke was rising high and had to be noticed by everyone nearby. The sound of dragons roaring and unleashing fire was not a sound the Tanimarans were too familiar with and terrified them while also making most of the Umbramari uncomfortable and this was not unintentional. Darlana had given the order to send a message to all those who might oppose her.

The dragons started tearing the armor off the dead elves and began to eat them. This did not sit well with the Umbramari as they were unaware that the dragons had a taste for elven flesh until now.

The dragons required respite. There were only a few thousand Tarvanan's left so the Umbramari took it upon themselves to gather up the living ones, deface and impale them. They would line them all up on either side of the road leading into the canyon pass. It was a forest of impaled elves and was sickening to look at. The moans and groans of the dying elves lasted through the night and even the next day.

Vysol had been spotted in the distance. Magris had found their camp outside of Caphry. Vysol landed and Magris dismounted. Dravon was fast approaching Magris as if anticipating his arrival. This spurred worry.

"What is wrong, General?"

"The Umbramari surrounded the Tarvanans and the slaughter began. She executed all of them, Magris," said Dravon, his voice raspy and broken.

He could hardly believe what he was hearing. This was not the actions of the queen he knew. "I could see the smoke from kilometers away. The smell did not hit me until I got closer. What a horrible sight of barbarity," said Magris as he observed the destruction. He placed a cloth over his mouth and began walking through the heaps of charred elven corpses still smoldering and smoking.

As he walked through the field of death which seemed endless, he came upon the sight that was most chilling of all. Thousands of impaled and defaced elves lining each side of the road leading into the canyon. His breath caught. His knees buckled as he stumbled forward, staring at the endless rows of impaled elves. His pulse pounded in his ears. This… this was not war. This was a slaughter! Guilt had infiltrated his heart.

"They deserved a soldier's death, not this," he said to Dravon.

He began to wonder how he would inform her of the new republic and betrayal of Madir and Atlan. How she might handle it considering what happened to the Tarvanans.

"I agree. This is not the way of things. Our Queen is not the same elf I met all those years ago. Tragedy has hardened her heart, and I fear it is only a matter of time before…" he was saying before Magris hushed him when he noticed Ivi approaching them.

"Gaze upon my work and despair," she said, laughing madly. "Be glad that is not you on that pike or in that field of charred corpses. They thought they had a chance, hah. I can hardly wait until we get to Tarvana."

Magris was not at all interested in hearing any of this. "Where is the queen?" he asked.

"She is in her command tent with that dragon pet of hers. They have been in there for several hours."

"Careful, Ivi. Dragons are not pets. It is not wise to think of them as such. You may offend," warned Dravon, his voice scornful.

Ivi ignored him and continued speaking to Magris. "I thought I would come out here and revel in the destructive power of my people and the dragons," she said in a sarcastic tone. Ivi laughed and went about her own business.

Magris was visibly disgusted as was Dravon.

The pair made their way over to the queen's tent and saw Nythint outside. "Greetings, Generals."

"I have returned," said Magris.

"Come in, General. We have much to discuss," said Darlana. Nythint stepped aside and let him in. "What news do you bring from Madir?"

He stood there unsure of the best way to inform her. He let out a sigh, "Atlan, Madir, Linia and Starland have reformed the republic and do not wish to see you as Queen of Tanimara."

"That was fast. We only left Atlan a little over a week ago," she said, clearly unconcerned.

"Yes, and when Vysol and I landed back in Atlan, the guard tried to detain us and shot bolts at Vysol when we were escaping."

Darlana's demeanor changed. She stood up. Magris was trying not to push her. He was worried about the Atlantin soldiers in her army now. "They shot at her? Is she all right?"

"She is a remarkable dragon," stated Magris with confidence.

Vysol smiled.

"Very well then," she said, relieved. "Execute all of the Atlantins and Madirans within our ranks. We cannot risk a mutiny."

Magris began to panic. "Wait, please reconsider. They likely do not even know about it. I did not know about it."

Darlana looked at him and scowled. "So naive, Magris. For four hundred years, I have mistrusted Tanimarans and with good reason! I am not going to risk it."

Nythint was eager to follow her orders. He left to find Ivi.

"Darlana, please, I am begging you, do not do this!" pleaded Magris. Several Umbramari guards stepped into the tent. This caught Magris, Dravon and Vysol by surprise.

"You are being detained for the time being until I get to the bottom of this."

Vysol would have none of it.

"I will incinerate…" she began before Magris placed his hand on her shoulder. "Always the voice of reason, Magris." Darlana scoffed and took her leave.

Nythint found Ivi and approached her gleefully. "Nythint, you draconic stud," she said, smiling, seemingly happy to see him.

"I come bearing good news, Ivi. The queen has ordered the execution of all Atlantin and Madiran elves within our ranks. Atlan, Madir, and a few other regions betrayed Darlana," Ivi could hardly believe what she was hearing. Excitement filled her dark heart.

"We must be discrete. Let us find my lieutenants and get the Umbramari army in position." The two went searching for her lieutenants but there was something off putting.

"I do not see any Atlantians or Madirans. I only see Umbramari." Nythint said nervously. Ivi looked around and noticed it too. They separated and searched around the camp for them and met on the other side. "No sign of them, we must inform our Queen!"

Darlana was looking for Nythint and Ivi herself and when she saw them running up to her, she sensed something was wrong.

"What is it," she demanded.

"The Atlantians and Madirans are gone, my queen." Ivi's voice was shaken. Darlana's eyes blackened. Rage began to manifest.

"They have returned to Atlan!" Her voice was calm though it was obvious by the look on her face that she was furious.

"I am sorry, my queen," said Nythint. She turned to him and furrowed her brow.

"I am sorry, my Nythint. I did not mean to make you feel like you failed. You did what I asked, and they betrayed me."

Nythint took a deep breath, pleased to hear her words. "What are we to do?" he asked.

She looked between both of them. "I have a secret weapon and a plan to bring them all to heel. Do not worry. I would like to make an example out of one of those celestial forsaken cities but which one will it be? Madir or Atlan?" she asked with a slight grin.

"Atlan is closer," said Ivi. Nythint agreed.

"Very well." She turned to Nythint. "My dear dragon, would you take me to Atlan so I can show them what happens when they betray me?" He was more than happy to oblige.

Magris, Vysol and Dravon were calmly waiting for her return. They could hear her approach and when she entered, they all stood.

"My queen, if I could make a suggestion," asked Magris. She perked her ears up. "They are afraid of you. They need more time to acclimate to you. If you win this war, I am sure they will be willing to negotiate."

She moved over to him scowling, "Negotiate? Magris, I will not negotiate. You know this. If they wish to be our enemies then fine. They have outlived their use to me now that the Umbramari and I are here. We will take Tarvana and then we will conquer all of Tanimara."

Magris was visibly upset.

"I will make an example out of Atlan since they not only attempted to capture and kill you, they betrayed me. When I capture Kaelina and Imra, you will execute them!"

Magris was caught off guard. He understood why she was demanding this but on the other hand, he had grown quite fond of Imra over his time with her in Madir. He wondered how he would be able to do it or if he even would at all. He became conflicted. Darlana was right to be upset and demand blood. "Allow me to go with you so that I may try and persuade them. This could be a great opportunity for you to show them the side of you that we all came to love," pleaded Magris. Dravon nodded in agreement.

"You are to remain here… detained! Nythint and I alone will make the journey."

Desperation overcame Magris. Fear gripped his heart. "They will not surrender to you my queen, I beg of you, please heed me."

"Surrender? I do not require surrender. They betrayed me. I only require death, General." Her tone was now very serious. Her eyes began to turn black. Magris was on his knees.

"My family is in Atlan," he said, his voice cracking.

She was visibly disappointed. "Very well, General. Nythint and I will pay a visit to Atlan and sort this out."

Magris was grateful. He understood that it was necessary to have control of Atlan for Thalnor. She put her armor on and grabbed her satchel. Nythint was outside and morphed into his dragon form.

She climbed onto his back and yelled to Ivi, "Do not march through the canyon and keep them detained until I get back."

Ivi nodded and off they went. Magris did not like the sound of it but he had faith she would heed his plea. He was hoping she would understand.

Chapter 26
Reprisal

Darlana and Nythint were flying high above the clouds. She was laying on him and smiling. The thoughts of the Tarvanans burning was to exhilarate her. She was happy that Nythint was there to enjoy it with her. She had allowed the shadow to cloud her judgment, unbeknownst to Darlana. She began to obsess over thoughts of malice and cruelty. Thoughts of Velnir and Paeris were no longer present at the forefront of her mind but buried deep.

"Atlan is on the horizon, my queen," said Nythint. Darlana sat up and looked at the city she had only recently revisited. Now that the time for retribution had come closer, the thought of collateral damage occurred to her. Atlan was home to thousands of elves and more importantly, at least to Magris, his family. It was also the home of her late husband. The sentimental value of this city to her was distracting. She began to have second thoughts.

"Do not pity them, Darlana," said the shadow. Darlana closed her eyes and tried to ignore it. "Bury your past here and forget it… forget them forever," said the shadow.

"Shut up, shadow," said Darlana out loud.

"What?" asked Nythint.

"I am having…" she began before Nythint interrupted her by stopping midair in front of the gates of Atlan.

"Queen Darlana of Nagrimar, Atlan has declared its allegiance to the republic of Tanimara and will seek to restore it across the continent. The new Magistrate has elected Elad of Starland as High Magister of the Republic. He has made it clear that he does not want war with you but if you refuse to join us, you may face retribution."

"I come in peace. I have not brought my army. I would speak with Kaelina and Imra in an effort to settle this matter," she said in a pleasant demeanor.

"Kaelina and Imra are not here. You must consider what I have told you for the good of your people and …" he continued as the sound of his voice began to fade while her thoughts were racing.

"They have all betrayed you! They would plot against you! Your past haunts you and holds you back, Darlana. Do it. Bury them, bury your past here and fulfill your destiny," said the shadow. Her heart throbbed and ached. She could no longer ignore it. Her desire was vengeance. Whatever mercy she had considered had vanished. A testament to the change she had experienced of late. She could hear nothing but her own thoughts. She could feel nothing but malice and hate. It stewed and cruelty manifested. Only a moment had passed but the herald at the gate was interrupted by the sound of horrific screams.

The people began to scatter throughout Atlan at the sight of the sky ripping open. From the tear, a fiery meteor appeared and roared through the sky. Darlana gazed upon the meteor, its descent reflected in her eye and burned into her mind. She desired to remember this. She was holding the orb of falling stars and nearly standing on Nythint's back while he was still in the air.

The impact was terrible. Immediately, the buildings under or close to the impact zone were pulverized and a massive shockwave leveled most of the city. The tall majestic spires that stood for thousands of years were reduced to rubble. The palace crumbled and the aqueducts collapsed. All that remained standing were Atlan's reinforced walls but they too were heavily damaged by debris.

She had not realized how much this instance would impact her. She felt despair and exhilaration. Nythint and Darlana remained stationary until the dust settled. Thousands were trapped under the rubble and needed help. The herald at the gate could not believe his eyes. He looked at Darlana with an expression of utter defeat. He climbed up to the edge of the wall and jumped to his death. The guards tried to stop him but failed and watched him meet his demise at the base of the wall. They were confused and not sure what to do.

Darlana's mind reeled, struggling to comprehend the cruel devastation she had unleashed upon them. A wave of emotions crashed down upon her, leaving her breathless and numb. The weight of her action settled heavily on her conscience—she had never harmed a civilian before, nor would she have ever condoned such brutality only a year ago.

As she gazed at the orb still clutched in her trembling hands, the true extent of her newfound power dawned on her. Before her lay the ravaged city, once the proud jewel of Tanimaran civilization. Its revered libraries were now reduced to rubble. Its ancient secrets and soon-to-be-forgotten lore. Memories of her beloved late husband flooded her thoughts and the realization pierced her soul—his city, his legacy now lay in ruins by her own hand. The anguish overwhelmed her and she collapsed onto Nythint's back.

In that fleeting moment of vulnerability, the shadow seized control, shifting her emotions beneath its dark veil. Darlana's turmoil subsided, replaced by unsettling numbness at first. Then the trembling stopped. She was calm and free of thought. The corruption was complete. Her blades glowed and from them appeared to be thousands of streams of purple tendrils entering them. It was beautiful, she thought.

Chapter 27
Betrayal

As Darlana and Nythint approached, the Umbramari eagerly rushed towards them like enthusiastic children, their faces alight with excitement. Darlana dismounted and Nythint morphed back into his visage form beside her. Within the command tent, Magris, Dravon, Vysol remained detained and Ivi awaited their arrival.

"For once, I had no need to summon all of you," Darlana said, her voice devoid of emotion as she took her seat.

"My queen," Magris said before Darlana's words cut him off.

"Atlan is no more." Her expression remained eerily calm but the weight of her statement hung heavily. Magris' eyes widened in stunned silence.

"You… did not speak with them or reconcile," Magris ventured.

Darlana's tone sent shivers down the spines of all present except for Nythint and Ivi. "Unfortunately, Kaelina and Imra were not there. The herald was making statements I did not care to hear. The Atlantians and Madirans all betrayed me, Magris so I reduced Atlan to rubble. Only its walls and a few buildings remain."

Magris' voice trembled. "You killed thousands of Tanimaran civilians?" Her response was chillingly serene.

"I made an example of Atlan. Soon, all Tanimarans will understand the price of betrayal."

Magris knew that Nythint could not have wrought such destruction on his own. "How... how did you do it?" he stammered, his voice trembling with shock, disgust and dread.

Darlana pulled out the orb of falling stars and rested her elbow on the table while holding it up and gazing upon it. "This is the trinket that Alzar used at the battle for the Sundered lands which saved us. Meric had it in his knapsack and after his execution, I retrieved it."

"*Never mind how she obtained it*," he thought.

Magris knew Alzar would not simply give anyone that kind of a weapon. He had forced Velnir to go with him and slay Necrosith for stealing Illuminar.

"Magris," said Darlana. Magris looked up at her with a distressed expression and watery eyes. "I know you are from Atlan, but they tried to kill you and Vysol. The moment they made an enemy out of you, they made an enemy out of me. They are no longer your kin."

Magris was stunned by how she could say all of this in such a calming yet charming voice. "My mother and father still lived there. My brothers and sisters were still there. All of my family and everyone I loved..." he began before she interrupted him. "They betrayed me," she snapped. Her features darkened and skin became pale. The black mist coming off her body was really off putting. Magris brought his head up in defiance.

"The shadow," Magris' eyes blazed with desperation and fury as he rose, staff and sword at the ready. "Begone, darkness," his thundering voice shaking with anguish. "Release our Queen and restore her to us!"

Darlana stood, her face pale, shocked by his ferocity. With lightning haste, Magris closed the distance, grasping her by the shoulders, his towering frame looming over her, his grip unyielding.

They looked upon each other—Magris' tormented eyes burning with sorrow, Darlana's black orbs reflecting the shadows' hold. The depth of his pain crushed her. Overwhelmed, her emotions shattered, her body trembling beneath his grasp.

Nythint grabbed Magris by the throat and lifted him off the ground. Vysol and Dravon stepped up.

"Put him down," demanded Vysol. The matriarch of his brood had an interesting effect on subordinate dragons. Nythint reluctantly put Magris down but the display of power and loyalty was clear. Nythint would stand by Darlana no matter what. Darlana was sitting up on the ground contemplating her actions and processing what just happened.

Magris loomed over her, his eyes blazing with despair "I will not serve shadows." His voice was heavy with grief. "My queen is lost!" As he turned to depart, Nythint blocked the exit, his gaze piercing with accusation. "Traitor," he yelled.

Darlana's voice trembled, "Let him go, dear Nythint." She turned to look at Magris. His glare piercing. Laden with contempt and sorrow, Magris' glare cut deep, and Darlana felt the crushing weight of guilt. Vysol and Dravon rose, their faces etched with resolve.

"We can no longer serve you Darlana," said Dravon, his tone firm. "The shadow has too much influence over you."

Vysol's words dripped with disdain. "We tolerated your inaction against Yzat's murderers but this brutality and your surrender to darkness is unforgivable." She looked at Nythint. "Remember what your father told you. Dragons and elves are not compatible species. She will die some day, and you will be alone."

As Magris, Dravon and Vysol took their leave, the shadow seemed to deepen, and Darlana's isolation grew.

"I will stand by you, my queen, to the ends of Abrion, I will be by your side," said Nythint.

Ivi nodded in agreement.

Nythint helped her up to her chair. She was in despair. They were right. The shadow did have a strong influence over her. She would never have done any of this outside of its influence but as she sat there and thought more about it, she loved all of it.

The shadow gave her the strength to not hold back or show mercy which had set her back many times before. The feeling was liberating and exhilarating. She was able to do whatever she wanted with the shadow.

"Give yourself to me, Darlana. I will take it all away and you will be stronger than ever." The voice was ominous, but she wanted so badly for it to be true. The guilt was destroying her, her emotions were overwhelming her, but Tanimara must pay. They must suffer!

"I will have my vengeance," she whispered. "I give myself to you."

Instantly, her heart was wiped clean of all pain and suffering. The shadow enveloped her as Nythint and Ivi watched. Her body radiated in a dark purple glow. Exhilaration came over her. She opened her eyes revealing black orbs, as dark as the abyss.

***

Magris was walking away from the camp wiping tears from his cheeks when Dravon and Vysol caught up.

"Magris…Magris… wait please," said Dravon.

Magris turned around as they approached.

"Where will you go," asked Vysol.

"To Atlan and I will, by the grace of the celestials, find my family and either rescue or bury them," he said as he sniffled and wiped more tears from his cheek. It was obvious just how hurt and betrayed Magris felt.

"I cannot ask my people to remain here and do this. As for the centaur, we got our vengeance. Now we must let bygones be bygones and return to the Forlorn and try to rebuild," said Dravon.

"There are plenty of ships in Thalnor, help yourself, General, and thank you for your service. It has been an honor serving next to you," said Magris before giving him his last crisp salute. Dravon returned the salute and set off to collect the centaur and march to Thalnor.

Magris looked at Vysol. "I could use some help with rescue efforts in Atlan."

"I would be glad to help you," said Vysol.

"Please start by going to inform the new republic of what happened and see if you can convince them to help. Start with Imra… oh and Vysol, if you could take me to Atlan, I would really appreciate it." His voice trembled as he asked.

As Vysol unfolded her majestic wings, Magris climbed onto her back, and they took to the skies, leaving the Umbramirans behind. Magris's eyes lingered on the camp, his heart heavy with resolve.

"She is my queen no longer," he declared, the words echoing through the wind. "Our alliance is at an end."

About the Author

Writing has been a passion for J.A. Peter since he was in third grade when he wrote his first short story about an apocalyptic event forcing people to live in massive submarines. Since then, he has written several short stories and even more backstories for characters he created.

J.A. Peter was introduced to fantasy at a young age by his father who showed him the 1978 animated lord of the rings, collected ceramic statues of wizards and dragons and brought home a game called Asheron's Call. In 2010, he began roleplaying in World of Warcraft and has loved high fantasy ever since.

If you enjoyed the read, considering leaving a review!

www.ingramcontent.com/pod-product-compliance
Ingram Content Group UK Ltd.
Pitfield, Milton Keynes, MK11 3LW, UK
UKHW042003230426
12048UKWH00009B/511